The War at Troy

LINDSAY CLARKE

HarperCollins*Publishers*

HarperCollins*Publishers*
77–85 Fulham Palace Road,
Hammersmith, London W6 8JB

www.harpercollins.co.uk

Published by HarperCollins*Publishers* 2004
1 3 5 7 9 8 6 4 2

Map © Hardlines Ltd.

A catalogue record for this book
is available from the British Library

ISBN 0 00 715026 1

Typeset in Bembo by
Palimpsest Book Production Limited,
Polmont, Stirlingshire

Printed and bound in Great Britain by
Clays Limited, St Ives plc

For
Sean, Steve, Allen and Charlie

Contents

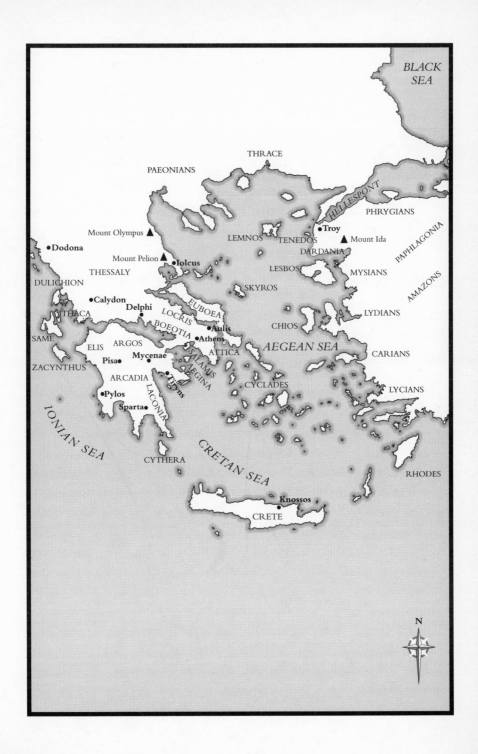

BLACK
SEA

THRACE

PAEONIANS

HELLESPONT

PHRYGIANS

Mount Olympus ▲

●Dodona

LEMNOS   TENEDOS   ●Troy   ▲ Mount Ida

Mount Pelion ▲   ●Iolcus   DARDANIA   PAPHLAGONIA

THESSALY   LESBOS   MYSIANS   AMAZONS

DULICHION   SKYROS

●Calydon   ●Delphi   CHIOS   LYDIANS

ITHACA   LOCRIS   EUBOEA

SAME   BOEOTIA   ●Aulis

ELIS   ARGOS   ●Athens   AEGEAN SEA   CARIANS

ZACYNTHUS   Pisa● ●Mycenae   ATTICA

                ARCADIA   SALAMIS   AEGINA

              ●Pylos   Tiryns●   CYCLADES   LYCIANS

        Sparta●   LACONIA

IONIAN
SEA   CYTHERA   RHODES

              CRETAN SEA

                        ●Knossos

                    CRETE

                                                            N

The Bard of Ithaca

In those days the realm of the gods lay closer to the world of men, and the gods were often seen to appear among us, sometimes manifesting as themselves, sometimes in human form, and sometimes in the form of animals. Also the people who lived at that time were closer to gods than we are and great deeds and marvels were much commoner then, which is why their stories are nobler and richer than our own. So that those stories should not pass from the earth, I have decided to set down all I have been told of the war at Troy — of the way it began, of the way it was fought, and of the way in which it was ended.

Today is a good day to begin. The sun stands at its zenith in the summer sky. When I lift my head I can hear the sound of lyres above the sea-swell, and voices singing in the town, and the beat of feet stamping in the dance. It is the feast day of Apollo. Forty years ago today, Odysseus returned to Ithaca, and I have good reason to recall that day for it was almost my last.

I was twenty years old, and all around me was blood and slaughter and the frenzy of a vengeful man. I can still see myself cowering beside the silver-studded throne. I remember the rank taste of fear in my mouth, the smell of blood in my nose, and when I close my eyes I see Odysseus standing over me, lifting his bloody sword.

Because Ares is not a god I serve, that feast of Apollo was the closest I have come — that I ever wish to come — to war. Yet the stories I have to tell are the tales of a war, and it was from Odysseus that I had them. How can that be? Because his son Telemachus saved me from the blind fury of Odysseus's sword by crying out that I was not among those who had sought to seize his wife and kingdom. So I was there, later, beside the hearth in the great hall of Ithaca, long after the frenzy had passed, when Odysseus told these stories to his son.

One day perhaps some other bard will do for Odysseus what I, Phemius of Ithaca, have failed to do and make a great song out of these stories, a song that men will sing for ever. Until that day, may a kind fate let what I set down stand as an honest man's memorial to the passions of both gods and men.

PART ONE

THE BOOK OF
Aphrodite

The Apple of Discord

The world is full of gods and no one can serve all of them. It is true, therefore, that a man's fate will hang upon the choices that he makes among the gods, and most accounts now say that the war at Troy began with such a choice when the Trojan hero Paris was summoned before the goddesses one hot afternoon on the high slopes of Mount Ida.

The Idaean Mountains stand some ten miles from the sea, across the River Scamander in that part of the kingdom of Troy which is known as Dardania. Odysseus assured me that an ancient cult of Phrygian Aphrodite existed among the Dardanian clan of Trojans at that time, and that as one of their chief herdsmen, Paris would have grown up in an atmosphere charged with the power of that seductive goddess. So it seems probable that he was gifted with a vision that brought him into her divine presence during the course of an initiatory ordeal on the summit of Mount Ida. But it is not permissible to speak directly of such secret rites, so we bards must employ imagination.

It began with a prickling sensation that he was being watched. Paris looked up from a pensive daydream and saw only his herd of grazing animals. They seemed, if anything, less alert than he was. Then, out of the corner of his eye, he caught a brief shimmering of light. When he turned his head, the trembling in the air shifted to the other side. Perplexed, Paris moved his gaze in that direction and heard a soft chuckle. Directly ahead of him in the dense shade of a pine, a male figure shivered into focus. Wearing a broad-brimmed travelling-hat and a light cloak draped across his slender form, he leaned against the trunk of the tree with the thumb of one hand tucked into his belt and holding a white-ribboned wand in the other. His head was tilted quizzically as though to appraise the herdsman's startled face.

Paris leapt to his feet, sensing that he was in the presence of a god.

A buzzard still glided through the sky's unsullied blue. The familiar view stretched below him to the rivers watering the plain of Troy. Yet it was as though he had stepped across a threshold of light into a more intense arena of awareness, for the feel of everything was altered. Even the air tasted thinner and sharper as though he had been lifted to a higher altitude. And it was the god Hermes who gestured with his staff.

'Zeus has commanded me to come. We need to talk, you and I.'

And with no sign of having moved at all, he was standing beside Paris, suggesting that they both recline on the grass while he explained his mission.

'Firstly,' Hermes said, 'you might care to examine this.' He took something shiny from the bag slung at his belt and handed it to Paris who looked down at the flash of sunlight from the golden apple that now lay in the palm of his hand. Turning it there, he ran his thumb over the words of an inscription and glanced back up at the god in bewilderment.

Hermes smiled. 'It says *To the Fairest*. Pretty, isn't it? But you wouldn't believe the trouble it's caused. That's what brings me here. We gods are in need of help, you see.' He took in the young man's puzzled frown. 'But none of this will make any sense to you unless I first tell you something of the story of Peleus.'

★   ★   ★

It's possible, I suppose, that it all started that way, though Odysseus always insisted that the war at Troy began where all wars begin – in the hearts and minds of mortal men. By then he had come to think of war as a dreadful patrimony passed on from one generation to the next, and he traced the seeds of the conflict back to the fathers of the men who fought those battles on the windy plain. Peleus was one of those fathers.

Odysseus himself was still a young man when he befriended Peleus, who had long been honoured as among the noblest souls in a generation of great Argive heroes. There had been a time too when Peleus had seemed, of all mortals, the one most favoured by the gods. Yet, much to his dismay, the young Ithacan adventurer found him to be a man of sorrows, prone to long fits of silent gloom over a life that had been shadowed by terrible losses. During the course of a single night Peleus told Odysseus as much of his story as he could bear to tell.

It began with a quarrel among three young men on the island of Aegina, a quarrel which ended with two of them in exile, and the other dead. Only just out of boyhood, Peleus and Telamon were the elder sons of Aeacus, a king renowned throughout all Argos and beyond for his great piety and justice. If Aeacus had a weakness it was that he favoured the youngest of his sons, a youth named Phocus, who had been born not to his wife, but to a priestess of the seal-cult on the island.

Displaced in their ageing father's affections, Peleus and Telamon nursed a lively dislike for this good-looking half-brother who was as sleek and muscular as the seal for which he was named, and excelled in all things, especially as an athlete. Their resentment turned to hatred when they began to suspect that Aeacus intended to name Phocus as his successor to the throne. Why else should he have been recalled to the island after he had voluntarily gone abroad to keep the peace? Certainly, the king's wife thought so, and she urged her own sons to look to their interests.

What happened next remains uncertain. We know that Telamon

and Peleus challenged their half-brother to a fivefold contest of athletics. We know that they emerged alive from that contest and that Phocus did not. We know too that the elder brothers claimed that his death was an accident – a stroke of ill luck when the stone discus thrown by Telamon went astray and struck him in the head. But there were also reports that there was more than one wound on the body, which was, in any case, found hidden in a wood.

Aeacus had no doubt of his sons' guilt, and both would have been killed if they had not realized their danger in time and fled the island. But the brothers then went separate ways, which leads me to believe that Peleus spoke the truth when he told his friend Odysseus that he had only reluctantly gone along with Telamon's plan to murder Phocus.

Whatever the case, when his father refused to listen to his claims of innocence, Telamon sought refuge on the island of Salamis, where he married the king's daughter and eventually succeeded to the throne. Peleus meanwhile fled northwards into Thessaly and found sanctuary there at the court of Actor, King of the Myrmidons.

Peleus was warmly welcomed by King Actor's son Eurytion. The two men quickly became friends, and when he learned what had happened on Aegina, Eurytion agreed to purify Peleus of the guilt of Phocus's death. Their friendship was sealed when Peleus was married to Eurytion's sister Polymela.

Not long after the wedding, reports came in of a great boar that was ravaging the cattle and crops of the neighbouring kingdom of Calydon. When Peleus heard that many of the greatest heroes of the age, including Theseus and Jason, were gathering to hunt down the boar, and that his brother Telamon would be numbered among them, he set out with Eurytion to join the chase.

Outside of warfare, there can rarely have been a more disastrous expedition than the hunt for the Calydonian boar. Because the king of that country had neglected to observe her rites, Divine Artemis had driven the boar mad, and it fought for its life with a fearful frenzy. By the time it was flushed into the open out of a densely thicketed stream, two men had already been killed, and a third hamstrung. An arrow was loosed by the virgin huntress Atalanta which struck the boar behind the ear. Telamon leapt forward with his boar-spear to finish the brute off, but he tripped on a tree-root and lost his footing. When Peleus rushed in to pull his brother to his feet, he looked up and saw the boar goring the guts out of another huntsman with its tusks. In too much haste, he hurled his javelin and saw it fly wide to lodge in the ribs of his friend Eurytion.

With two deaths on his conscience now, Peleus could not bear to face his bride Polymela or his friend's grieving father. So he retreated to the city of Iolcus with one of the other huntsmen, King Acastus, who offered to purify him of this new blood-guilt. But the shadows were still deepening around Peleus's life for while he was in Iolcus, Cretheis, the wife of Acastus, developed an unholy passion for him.

Embarrassed by her approaches, Peleus tried to fend her off, but when he rebuffed her more firmly, she sulked at first, and then her passion turned cruel. To avenge her humiliation, she sent word to Polymela that Peleus had forsaken her and intended to marry her own daughter. Two days later, having no idea what Cretheis had done, and assuming therefore that all the dreadful guilt of it was his, Peleus learned that his wife had hanged herself.

For a time he was out of his mind with grief. But his trials were not yet over. Alarmed by the consequences of her malice, Cretheis sought to cover her tracks by telling her husband that Peleus had tried to rape her. But having bound himself to Peleus in the rites of cleansing, Acastus had no wish to incur a sacrilegious blood-guilt of his own, so he took advice from his priests. Some time later he approached Peleus with a proposal.

'If you dwell on Polymela's death too long,' he said, 'you'll go mad from grief. Eurytion's death was an accident. In the confusion of the chase, it could have happened to anyone. And if your wife couldn't live with the thought of it, you are not to blame.

You must live your life, Peleus. You need air and light. How would it be if you and I took to the mountains again? If I challenged you to a hunting contest would you have the heart to rise to it?'

Thinking only that his friend meant well by him, Peleus seized the chance to get away from the pain of his blighted life. A hunting party was assembled. Taking spears and nets, and a belling pack of dogs, Peleus and Acastus set out at dawn for the high, forested crags of Mount Pelion. They hunted all day and at night they feasted under the stars. Relieved to be out there at altitude, in the uncomplicated world of male comradeship, Peleus drank too much of the heady wine they had brought, and fell into a stupor of bad dreams.

He woke in the damp chill of the early hours to find himself abandoned beside a burned-out fire, disarmed, and surrounded by a shaggy band of Centaur tribesmen who stank like their ponies and were arguing in their thick mountain speech over what to do with him. Some were for killing him there and then, but their leader – a young buck dressed in deerskins, with a bristling mane of chestnut hair – argued that there might be something to be learned from a man who had been cast out by the people of the city, and they decided to take him before their king. So Peleus was kicked to his feet and hustled upwards among steep falls of rock and scree, through gorse thickets and stands of oak and birch, across swiftly plunging cataracts, and on into a high gorge of the mountain that rang loud with falling water.

As the band approached with their prisoner, a group of women looked up from where they were beating skins against the flat stones of a stream and fell silent. The leader of the band climbed up a stairway of rocks and entered a cave half-way up a cliff-face. Kept waiting below, Peleus took in the stocky, untethered ponies that grazed a rough slope of grass. Goats stared at him from the rocks through black slotted eyes. He could see no sign of dwellings but patches of charred grass ringed with stones showed where fires were lit, and his nose was assailed by a pervasive smell of raw meat and rancid milk. Two children clad in goatskin smickets came to stand a few yards away. Their faces were stained with berry-juice. If he had moved suddenly, they would have shied like foals.

Eventually he was brought inside the cave where an old man with lank white hair, and shoulders gnarled and dark as olive wood, reclined on a pallet of leaves and deeply piled fresh grass. The air of the cave was made fragrant by the many bundles of medicinal herbs and simples hanging from its dry walls. The man gestured for Peleus to sit down beside him and silently offered him water from an earthenware jug. Then, wrinkling his eyes in a patient smile that seemed drawn from what felt like unfathomable depths of sadness, he spoke in the perfect, courtly accent of the Argive people. 'Tell me your story.'

Peleus later told Odysseus that he regained his sanity in his time among the Centaurs, but the truth is that he was lucky to fall into their hands at a moment when their king, Cheiron, was gravely concerned for the survival of his tribe.

The Centaurs had always been a reclusive, aboriginal people, living their own rough mountain life remote from the city dwellers and the farmers of the plain. Cheiron himself was renowned for his wisdom and healing powers and had, for many years, run a wilderness school in the mountains to which many kings used to send their sons for initiation at an early age. Pirithous, King of the Lapith people on the coast, had attended that school when he was a boy and always cherished fond memories of King Cheiron and his half-wild Centaurs. For that reason he invited them to come as guests to his wedding feast, but that day someone made the mistake of giving them wine to drink. The wine, to which their heads were quite unused, quickly maddened them. When they began to molest the women at the feast, a bloody fight broke out in which many people were killed and injured. Since that terrible day the tribe of Centaurs had been regarded by the uninitiated as less than human. Those who survived the battle at the feast fled to the mountains where men hunted them down like animals for sport.

By the time Peleus was brought before Cheiron in his cave there were very few of his people left. So during the long hours when they first talked, the two men came to recognize each other as noble souls who had suffered unjustly. At that moment Peleus had no desire to return to the world, so he accepted the offer gladly when Cheiron suggested that he might heal his wounded mind by living a simple life among the Centaurs for a time.

The days of that life proved strenuous, and in the nights Peleus was visited by vivid, disturbing dreams which Cheiron taught him how to read. He felt healed too by the music of the Centaurs, which seemed filled with the strains of wind and wild water yet had a haunting enchantment of its own. Through initiation into Cheiron's mysteries, Peleus rediscovered meaning in his world. And through his bond with Peleus, Cheiron began to hope that one day he might ensure the survival of his tribe by restoring good relations with the people of the cities below. So as well as friendship, the old man and the young man found hope in one another. That hope was strengthened one day when Peleus said that if he ever had a son, he would certainly send him to Cheiron for his education, and would encourage other princes to do the same.

'But first you must have a wife,' said Cheiron, and when he saw Pelion's face darken at the memory of Polymela, the old man stretched out a mottled hand. 'That dark time is past,' he said quietly, 'and a new life is opening for you. Several nights ago Sky-Father Zeus came to me in a dream and told me that it was time for my daughter to take a husband.'

Amazed to discover that Cheiron had a daughter, Peleus asked which one of the women of the tribe she might be. 'Thetis has not lived among us for a long time,' Cheiron answered. 'She followed her mother's ways and became a priestess of the cuttle-fish cult among the shore people, who honour her as an immortal goddess. She has given herself as daughter to the sea-god Nereus, but Zeus wants her and her cult must accept him. She is a woman of great beauty – though she has sworn never to marry unless she marries a god. In my dream, however, Zeus said that any son born to Thetis would prove to be even more powerful than his father, so she must be given to a mortal man.' Cheiron smiled. 'That man is you, my friend – though you must win her first. And to do that, you must undergo her rites and enter into her mystery.'

As with all mysteries, the true nature of the shore women's rites can be comprehended only by those who undergo them, so I can tell only what Odysseus told me of the account Peleus gave him of his first encounter with Thetis. It took place on a small island off the coast of Thessaly. Cheiron had advised him that his daughter was often carried across the strait on a dolphin's back. If Peleus concealed himself among the rocks, Thetis might be caught sleeping at mid-day in a sea-cave on the strand.

Following his mentor's instructions, Peleus crossed to the island, took cover behind a myrtle bush, and waited till the sun rose to its zenith. Then all his senses were ravished as he watched Thetis gliding towards the shore in the rainbow spume of spindrift blowing off the back of the dolphin she rode. Naked and glistening in the salt-light, she dismounted in the surf and waded ashore. He followed her at a distance, keeping out of sight, till she entered the narrow mouth of a sea-cave to shelter from the noonday sun.

Once sure she was asleep, he made his prayer to Zeus, lay down over her and clasped her body in a firm embrace. Thetis started awake at his touch, alarmed to find her limbs pinioned in the grip of a man. Immediately her body burst into flame. A torrent of fire licked round Peleus's arms, scorching his flesh and threatening to set his hair alight, but Cheiron had warned him that the nymph had acquired her sea-father's power of shape-shifting, and that he must not loosen his hold for a moment whatever dangerous form she took. So he grasped the figure of flame more tightly as Thetis writhed beneath him and took him on a fierce dance that wrestled him through all the elements.

When she saw that fire had failed to throw him, the nymph again changed shape. Peleus found himself floundering breathlessly as he clutched at the weight of water in a falling wave. His ears and lungs felt as though they were about to burst, but still he held on until the waters vanished and the hot maw of a ferocious lion was snarling up at him, only to be displaced in turn by a fanged serpent that hissed and twisted round him, viciously resisting his embrace. Then, under his exhausted gaze, the serpent took the shape of a giant cuttlefish, which sprayed a sticky gush of sepia ink over his face and body. Already burnt, half-drowned, mauled by fangs and talons, and almost blinded by the ink, Peleus was on the point of releasing his prize, when Thetis suddenly yielded to this resolute mortal who had withstood all her powers.

Gasping and breathless, Peleus looked down, saw the nymph resume her own beautiful form, and felt her body soften in his embrace. The embrace became more urgent and tender, and in the hour of passion that followed, the seed of their first son was sown.

The wedding-feast of Peleus and Thetis was celebrated at the full moon outside King Cheiron's cave in the high crags of Mount Pelion. It was the last occasion in the history of the world when all twelve immortal gods came down from Mount Olympus together to mingle happily with mortal men. A dozen golden thrones were set up for them on either side of the bride and groom. Sky-Father Zeus himself gave away the bride, and it was his wife Hera who lifted the bridal torch. The Three Fates attended the ceremony, and the Muses came to chant the nuptial hymns, while the fifty daughters of the sea-god Nereus twisted their line about the gorge in a spiral dance of celebration.

As their gift to Peleus, the Olympian gods presented him with a suit of armour made of shining gold, together with two immortal horses sired by the West Wind. King Cheiron gave the groom a matchless hunting spear, the head of which had been wrought by the lame god Hephaestus in his forge, while its ash-wood shaft had been cut and polished by the hands of Divine Athena. With the whole remaining tribe of Centaurs gathered in garlands for the occasion, and all the other revellers carousing on nectar served by Zeus's cup-bearer Ganymede, everyone agreed that there had been no more joyful marriage-feast since the Olympians had honoured the wedding of Cadmus and Harmony with their presence many years before.

Yet alone among the immortal gods, Eris had not been invited. Her name means *Strife* or *Discord,* and she is twin-sister to the war god Ares. Like him she delights in the fury and tumult of human conflict. It is Eris who stirs up trouble in the world by spreading rumours. She takes particular pleasure in the use of malicious gossip to create envy and jealousy, and for that reason none of the gods and goddesses other than her brother cares to have too much to do with her. For that same reason her name had been omitted from the list of guests at the wedding-feast of Peleus and Thetis. Yet all of the immortals have their place in the world and we ignore any of them at our peril.

Furious and slighted that she alone among the immortals had not been invited, Eris looked on at the festivities from the shadows of a nearby grove, waiting for the right moment to take her revenge. That moment came as Hera, Athene and Aphrodite were congratulating Peleus. The groom's eye was caught by a flash of light as something rolled towards him across the ground. All three of the goddesses exclaimed in wonder when he picked up a golden apple that lay glistening at his feet. With their curiosity excited by the goddesses' cries of delight, other guests quickly gathered round. Only Cheiron, to his dismay, saw the figure of Eris in her chequered robe slip away into the trees.

'Look', Peleus exclaimed, 'there's an inscription here.' Holding the apple to catch the light, he read aloud, '*To the Fairest.*' He turned to appraise the three goddesses standing beside him, and his smile instantly faded with the realization that he could not give the apple to any one of them without immediately offending the others.

'But I'm surrounded by beauty,' he prevaricated. 'This riddle is too hard.'

Aphrodite smiled at him. 'To the Fairest, you say? Then there's no difficulty. The apple must be meant for me.' The goddess was holding out her hand to take it when Hera said that as wife to Zeus, Lord of Olympus, there could hardly be any doubt that the apple should be hers.

'There is every possibility of doubt,' Athena put in. 'Any discriminating judge would agree that my claim to the apple is as strong as either of yours – if not a good deal stronger.'

Aphrodite laughed, dismissing Athena's claim as ridiculous. Who would look twice, she asked, at a goddess who insisted on wearing a helmet even to a wedding? Smiling in reparation, she conceded that Athena might be wiser than she was, and there was no doubting Hera's matronly virtue, but if beauty was the issue, then she had the advantage over both of them. Again, sidling closer to Peleus who stood in a consternation, wondering how he had got into this quandary and how to get out of it again, she held out her hand.

'Can't you see you're embarrassing our host, flaunting yourself like that with his bride looking on?' Athena protested. 'Perhaps one day you'll learn that true beauty is also modest.'

Sensing the imminence of an unseemly quarrel, Hera intervened, warning her divine sisters to restrain themselves. Then she smiled at Peleus and suggested that it would be best to settle the matter quickly by giving the apple to her. At which both the other goddesses turned on her, each clamouring to be heard over the other until all three were tangled in a rancorous exchange. The Muses faltered in their song, the Nereids ceased their dance, a nervous silence fell across the Centaurs, and the bride and groom looked on in dismay as the dispute became ever more acrimonious.

Hera spoke sharply above the others. 'If you two won't see reason, there's only one way to resolve the matter – Zeus must decide.' But neither of the others was about to accept that solution, nor did Almighty Zeus show any enthusiasm for it. Though he'd been drinking nectar all afternoon, he remained too astute to put himself in a position where his life would be made miserable by his wife if he was honest, or by two resentful goddesses if he was not. Hoping the row would peter out, he turned away. Only moments later, netted in a trance of rage, all three contenders began hurling insults at each other.

'Enough!' bellowed Zeus in a voice that briefly silenced everyone. 'If it's golden apples you want, all three of you can have a whole orchard of them any time you like.'

'It's not the apple!' Hera answered hotly. 'None of us cares about the apple!'

'Of course we don't,' Athena agreed.

'Then why are you embarrassing us all like this?' Zeus demanded. When no immediate answer came, he said it was time the goddesses remembered who they were and where they were. They should stop this bickering and sit down and enjoy them-selves, so that everyone else could do the same. Again he tried to turn away but Aphrodite widened her eyes, protesting that the dispute was a matter of simple justice. She wasn't about to let some pretender lay claim to a title that everyone knew was rightly hers.

Sensing that her husband might be wavering, Hera hissed, 'Don't you dare take any notice of that mindless bitch.'

'And you shouldn't let your wife push you around,' Athena put in, 'not if you expect anyone ever to respect your judgement again.'

At which point Zeus shouted that he was damned if he would choose between them. Looking around in embarrassment, he turned back to the goddesses and said more quietly that, in his opinion, they were all beautiful. All three of them. Each in her own inimitable way. They should forget the apple and let that be an end to it.

'Things have gone too far for that,' said Hera. 'We demand a decision.'

Zeus met his wife's eyes with gloomy displeasure. For all his might, he could see no way of resolving this argument without causing endless resentment on Olympus. Yet when he shifted his gaze, it was only to see the assembled mortals staring at him, aghast and bewildered. Part of him already begrudged having ceded a nymph as beautiful as Thetis to a mere human. Now he was thinking that this trouble had come from mixing up the affairs of mortals and immortals, and when he caught himself thinking that way, he realized that Eris must be at the back of this quarrel and, if that was the case, there could be no reasonable solution. But the harm was done and he couldn't yet see how to undo it. Neither could he allow this disgraceful performance to carry on in front of mortal eyes.

'My decision,' he said at last, 'is that we shall return to Olympus immediately, and leave these good people to their feast.'

Moments later the immortals were back among the clouds on high Olympus. But when it quickly became clear that Zeus was still not prepared to make a judgement, the goddesses resumed their argument with uninhibited vehemence and no sign of a solution.

Meanwhile, having begun so joyfully, the wedding feast faltered to a dismal end. Thunderheads had been building over Pelion for some time and the gods had vanished in a livid flap of lightning. Now came the rain, and people ran for shelter, slipping among the rocks and stumbling about as though the storm had wrecked all expectations of peace and order in the world. As soon as the downpour eased, they made their apologies and dispersed back down the mountainside to their comfortable lives in the cities of the plain.

Dismayed that Sky Father Zeus had not been able to contain the fractious energy of the goddesses, Cheiron withdrew gloomily to his cave. The last time his Centaurs had attended a wedding-feast they had been depraved by wine and then hunted down like wolves. That had been the fault of men; but now it seemed even the gods had lost their senses. With the world so out of joint he decided that his people would keep to themselves from now on. If Peleus and his friends wanted to send their sons to be educated in the mountains, he would care for them, instruct them in music and the healing arts, and do what he could to set them on the path of wisdom. But with the gods at loggerheads, and most men's hearts no longer content with a simple, wilderness life such as he and his people led, he saw only dark omens for the future.

The years passed and things did not go well with the marriage of Peleus and Thetis. However uneasily, the couple had tried to laugh off the dismal fiasco of their wedding day, but it wasn't long before Peleus woke up to the fact that he knew almost nothing about his wife.

For a time, out there on the mountain, he had come to believe he might be happy once again. Exhilarated by his passionate encounter with Thetis, he began to be sure of it. They would make a good life together, raising children in the clear air of the mountains, far away from the ambitions and duplicity of the courtly world. But Thetis was a creature of the shore. She loved the salt-wind off the sea, the surge of a dolphin's back beneath her, the moonlit rush of surf, the smell of sea-wrack, the way the shingle tugged between her toes, and the marble world of rock pools. Up there in the mountains, she felt stranded. She pined for the long strands of sand and the sound of the sea, or raged with disgust and frustration at the horsy smell of the Centaur people and their stubborn, earth-bound ways. Having quarrelled with her father, and offended his chief tribesmen, she made it clear to Peleus that though they had been consigned to each other by Zeus himself, if he kept her in that gloomy mountain gorge against her will she would, quite simply, die.

Peleus already had a dead brother and a dead bride on his conscience. The first had been named for a seal and had also loved the sea. The second had hanged herself because instead of staying at her side, he had gone chasing a wild boar in the

Calydonian hills and killed her brother. The thought of another such death was more than he could bear. So he had already made up his mind that they would have to leave the mountain by the end of the summer, when a rider came looking for him out of Thessaly.

He brought the news that King Actor, who had never recovered from the loss of his son and his daughter, was now dead. The Myrmidons – those implacable soldier-ants of Thessaly – were now leaderless, and the messenger had been sent to ask Peleus to return and take up his rightful heritage as Actor's heir. He could be sure of a warm welcome, for some of the Myrmidons had been on the Calydonian boar-hunt and knew that Eurytion's death was an accident. Moreover the wife of Acastus had gone mad and had been heard boasting crazily that she was responsible for Polymela's suicide. In these circumstances, Peleus's right to rule would go unquestioned.

Here was a god-given answer to his problems. Both duty to his people and concern for his wife required him to leave the mountain. He would move the royal court from Athena's sanctuary in the inland city of Itonus down to one of the coastal strongholds. His wife would soon have the sound of the sea in her ears again. Thetis would be happy there.

Immediately Peleus set about making preparations for his return. Solemnly he said his farewells to the friends he had made among the Centaur people, promising that he would not forget them and that they would be welcomed as guests in his house should they ever want to come. Then he spent a long time alone with Cheiron, up on a windy shelf of rock high above the gorge, from where they could look out across all the summits of Thessaly and Magnesia to the eastern sea beyond. An eagle scaled the blue spaces about their heads. Everything else felt still and ancient round them. They were almost outside time up there, and watching the wind blow among the white locks of the old king's hair, Peleus knew that Cheiron was looking deeper into the heart of things than words could reach. And his own heart too was lost for speech − not because there was nothing to say but because there was too much. Yet in the silence of the mountain it felt as though it went understood.

After a time, Cheiron turned to look at him. 'You will do what you can for my people when I am gone?'

'It goes without saying. But you Centaurs live long. I think you have many years in you yet.'

'Perhaps.' Cheiron turned his face back to the wind. 'But my daughter,' he sighed. 'When I first spoke of her, I did not understand that she has immortal longings. A man will find it hard to live with that.'

Peleus frowned at the thought, and then made light of it. 'I'm not easy to live with myself. And Thetis will be content when we are by the sea.'

Again the Centaur said, 'Perhaps.'

The eagle glided high above them now, its pinions bent like a bow against the wind. Cheiron stared up at the way that strong span gleamed in flawless sunlight. Quietly he said, 'Remember that your son will be greater than you. Try not to resent him for it.'

'I shan't − because it will be your blood that makes him so. When he is of age I will send him to you.'

Cheiron nodded his old head. 'Then I shall live for that.'

Yet Thetis fell pregnant six times in the following years and each time she came to term, but not one of the infants lived for more than a week or two.

At each small death, Peleus found the sadness harder to bear, and all the more so because it was his wife's custom to withdraw to a sanctuary of the shore people between the start of her labour and the day when she hoped to present a living child to the world. When Peleus asked the reason for this practice, she told him it was a woman's mystery and not to be questioned.

Yet she returned each time, pallid and drawn, as if hollowed out by failure.

But she would say nothing more, so Peleus harboured his grief and returned to giving judgement in the world of men, and they lived a life that became ever more fraught with the silence that was left between them.

After the loss of the third child, he argued more strongly that it would be wise for them to consult her father who was more renowned for his medical knowledge than almost any man alive. But Thetis would not hear of it. She was a woman, she said, not a sick mare, and she wanted no truck with his mountain magic. Her trust was in her own understanding of these things as a sea-priestess to the moon-mother. In any case, had it not been prophesied that her son would be a stronger man than his father? Any child of hers that was not strong enough to survive the trials of birth had no place on the earth. He should not mourn them so.

Her ferocity astounded him, but he put it down in part to an effort to mask her own sorrow, and in part to the influence of the Dolopian priestess who was his wife's constant companion. A small, intense woman with deep-set eyes and a strawberry-birth mark shaped like a sea-horse on her neck, her name was Harpale. Thetis honoured her as a kinswoman, one of her mother's people, and she had begged Harpale to stay with her at the court of Peleus rather than joining her clan's recent migration to the island of Skyros.

The Dolopians were a restless people who had travelled from the far west a generation or two ago and settled about the shores of Thessaly. Now, under their king Lycomedes, some of them had felt the urge to move out to the Scattered Islands in the eastern sea and they had established a stronghold of their own on the windy island of Skyros. The move happened not long after Peleus had established his kingship over the Myrmidons, and feeling the strong call of island life, Thetis had wanted to go with them.

For a time it had been a struggle between them. Born on an island himself, Peleus knew the nature of the call, but he was king over a mainland people now and it was his wife's duty to remain with him and provide him with an heir. Was it not enough that he had already shifted the court to the coast for her sake?

He had understood her need for the sea. He was content for her to hold to cult practices which he did not share, and which – though he did not say it – he did not greatly trust. But she must respect the constraints imposed by royal duty on their life. They would remain where they were in Thessaly.

Meanwhile Peleus had been kept busy enough. Once he was secure on his throne he had harnessed the power of the Myrmidons to settle his score with Acastus. A swift, brutal campaign took them through Magnesia into Iolcus. Acastus was killed in the fight and his mad wife was quickly put to death. Giving thanks to Zeus and Artemis, who had a powerful cult centre in Iolcus, Peleus was declared king there and made Iolcus his new coastal capital.

Having learned the laws and customs of the Myrmidons, he set now about harmonizing them with those of Magnesia, trying to run a peaceable kingdom, and giving judgement in the quarrels with which his warlike men filled the boredom of their peaceful days. Also there was always a pressing need to raise money. To feed and clothe the royal households, to pay his retainers, arm his warriors, carry out his building projects, repair his ships, and make expensive offerings to the gods, all of this took a lot of gold. What could not be raised as tribute must be found elsewhere, so in company with the ageing Theseus, he turned pirate in the summer months and took to raiding the merchant ships and rich estates of the eastern seaboard.

He made his reputation as a valiant warrior and a generous king on those voyages, though his exploits never ranged as widely as those of his brother. Telamon had already sailed on Jason's *Argo* in the quest for the Golden Fleece, and had become a close comrade to Heracles, who was renowned and feared from Epirus to Paphlagonia as the boldest, most vigorous and, at times, the maddest hero of the age. Having already made a further expedition round the coast of the Black Sea into the land of the Amazons, Telamon and Heracles were now mounting a campaign against the Phrygian city of Troy.

Telamon tried to talk his brother into joining forces with them, but Peleus lacked his restless appetite for battle and was reluctant to risk his kingdom's hard won wealth in what promised to be an unprofitable attack on a bankrupt city recently visited by plague and earthquake. But neither did he wish to look weak in Telamon's eyes. In the end the decision was made for him by a wound he took in a ship-fight that spring. A Sidonian sword cut his right hamstring as he leapt aboard the galley, putting him out of action for months.

That was also the year in which his sixth child died in early infancy, and the grief of it was more than he could bear. A marriage that had begun so inauspiciously was now eroded by mutual disappointment, and its passion had faded as its tensions increased. Peleus was often given cause to puzzle over what Cheiron had said about Thetis entertaining immortal longings, but it seemed to account for her restlessness and the way her spirit sometimes chafed against his own more practical concerns. These days she seemed to take comfort only in Harpale's company, and Peleus grew to resent the power that the little Dolopian exercised over his wife's imagination. Harpale soon learned to stay out of his way, though her name frequently cropped up in conversation with his wife, reproaching him like the sting of a sea-urchin for the island life she was denied.

Of Thetis's failure to provide him with an heir it became ever harder to speak, so when he finally decided to consult Cheiron about his injured leg, Peleus went against his wife's wishes and raised this other, graver matter with him too.

Cheiron listened carefully as he applied thick poultices to his son-in-law's leg. He asked questions about the practices of the cuttlefish cult, and took a particular interest in the part that Harpale had come to play in his daughter's life. Knowing something of the Dolopians, he asked Peleus whether there had been any unusual signs of the use of fire in his daughter's rites. Peleus was unable to answer, however, because he was now excluded from all that part of his wife's life. His own service was to Zeus, to Apollo, and to the goddess, whether worshipped as Athena in Itonus or as Artemis in Iolcus; but as to his wife's most secret mysteries, he was as ignorant as his horse.

Cheiron nodded. 'Remain here till these herbs have shared their virtue. Had you come sooner I could have done more, but now you will always walk with a limp. Still,' he smiled up into his friend's face, 'if you had been your horse I would have had to cut your windpipe!' He fastened the bandage and sat back to wash his hands. 'As to the other matter, I will reflect on it.'

When Peleus travelled back down the mountain he brought with him a Centaur woman called Euhippe, who wept such fat tears when they left the gorge that Peleus guessed that the old king's pallet of grass would be a lonelier place after the parting. She was a small, round woman with a shyly attentive manner, and large, surprisingly delicate hands. Overtly she was to be taken into the household as a nurse for the care of Peleus's wound, but he soon intended to make it known that Euhippe was a skilful midwife too.

By the time he returned to his palace at Iolcus, Thetis was already over two months pregnant. Moody, and still prey to sickness, she at once made it clear that she would have nothing to do with the little mountain woman, whom she dismissed first as her father's hairy brood-mare, and then, after the cruel pretence of a closer look, as his jaded nag. Peleus protested. There was an unholy row between them that night, and silence for two weeks after.

Then the sickness passed, they talked and made love again, only to resume the queasy truce their life had become. Thetis still refused to include Euhippe among the women of her bed-chamber, but the Centaur found an unobtrusive place for herself in the royal household and her medical skills soon won her grateful friends. After successfully treating one woman for a rash around her midriff, and another for a dangerous fever, she gained a reputation as a wise woman and became a great favourite among the Myrmidon barons and their wives. Only Thetis, as her belly grew rounder by the month, continued to ignore her existence.

If she feared that Euhippe had been placed to spy on her, then her fears were justified, for on the occasions when she came to examine his leg, Peleus questioned her closely about anything she had learned of his wife's activities. For several weeks she found nothing unusual to report, but in the eighth month of Thetis's pregnancy, Euhippe made friends with a young woman who was complaining of intense pain from her monthly bleeding. Euhippe gave her a potion made up of guelder rose, skullcap and black haw for immediate relief, and advised her to return soon for further treatment. When she came back, they began to chat, and it emerged that the girl served as a handmaid in the cuttlefish cult. Through cautiously worded questions, Euhippe learned that there had been nothing outwardly wrong with any of Thetis's babies – no fevers or defects, nothing that would account for their early death. It was a mystery, the girl said, unless the Goddess had called them back to her.

When Euhippe asked her casually about Harpale's role in the cult, the girl flushed a little, looked away, and said that her own degree was lowly and she was too young to be initiated into such matters. Nor was she prepared to speculate.

'But there was a smell of fear about her,' Euhippe decided. 'She may not know much, but she knows more than she was letting on, and it frightens her.'

With his own suspicions now confirmed, Peleus asked Euhippe to keep her ears open, and eventually more emerged through one of the baron's wives. It was this woman who first dared to speak of witchcraft, but she did so darkly, casting her suspicions only on the Dolopian, not on Thetis herself, and in a way that left Euhippe feeling the woman meant her to report what she said.

Knowing that Thetis had once offended this woman, Peleus suggested that she might be spreading rumours out of spite, but Euhippe merely shrugged.

'You truly believe that something terrible is happening?' he demanded.

'For you it would be terrible,' she said.

'Do you know what it is?'

'I may be wrong.'

'Tell me anyway.'

Euhippe thought for a moment, then shook her head.

'Then what am I to think,' he demanded, 'what am I to do?'

'You need do nothing. Not until the baby is born.'

'And then?'

'Let us wait in patience. When the time comes we will see what to do.'

The truth of what happened at that time was known only to Peleus himself and he would not speak of it – not, that is, until some six years later when Odysseus arrived at his court for the first time. By then the child – Peleus's seventh son, and the only one to survive – was already in the mountains with Cheiron, learning how to live. Peleus lived alone in his gloomy palace under the patient, mostly silent care of Euhippe, and for a time his melancholic condition had been the talk of Argos. Telamon and Theseus had both tried to shake him out of it and failed. Cheiron was too old to come down from the mountains, and Peleus lacked the heart to seek him out. So the King of the Myrmidons wasted in his loneliness, limping from hall to chamber, hardly speaking, and increasingly reliant on trusted ministers to handle the affairs of state. Old friends like Pirithous and Theseus died. Power shifted south to Mycenae. People began to forget about him.

Then Odysseus ran his ship ashore on the strand at Iolcus. King Nestor of Pylos had encouraged him to come. Everyone responded to the lively young prince of Ithaca, he'd said – perhaps old Peleus might. 'Why not see if you can't tempt him to join you in your raid along the Mysian coast. Peleus was a good pirate in his day. He might be so again.'

There was, Odysseus quickly saw, no chance of it. The man could barely lift a smile let alone a sword. Shrugging his shoulders, he had made up his mind to cut his losses and push off at dawn, when Peleus looked up from his wine-cup for the first time in nearly an hour and said, 'It was good of you to come. Everyone has forgotten how to smile around me. You seem to do little else.'

'It costs me nothing,' Odysseus smiled. 'Does it disturb you?'

Unsmiling, Peleus shook his head. After a time he began to talk and a god must have entered him, for once he began it became unstoppable. That night witnessed a huge unburdening because Odysseus was the only person to whom Peleus ever spoke about what happened between himself and his wife. Odysseus listened in spellbound horror to a tormented account of how, at the prompting of Euhippe, he had cleansed himself before Zeus, begged forgiveness of the Goddess, and broken in to the sacred precinct around the sea-cave where Thetis held her rites. It was the dark of the moon after the birth of the child. Pushing aside the drug-intoxicated women who tried to stop him, Peleus entered the cave and saw the dark figures of Thetis and Harpale standing under a primitive wooden idol to the Goddess beside an altar of burning coals. Harpale held a finely meshed net of mail. Thetis was unwrapping the swaddling bands from her howling baby, and Peleus saw at once what they intended to do. If he had he not come in time to prevent it, she and Harpale would have done what they must have done many times before – they would have seined the child with fire, passing its tiny body back and forth along the shimmer of hot air above the altar's glowing coals until it was immortalized.

With a howl of execration, Peleus drew his sword, cut Harpale down where she stood, and snatched the baby from its screaming mother. Had the child not been squalling in his grip like a small storm, he might have killed Thetis also, but by the time he could lift the sword again the frenzied moment had passed and he could not bring himself to do it. Thetis saw the conflict in his face. Astoundingly, she released a small, frustrated laugh.

With the baby tussling in his arm, he stared at her as at a mad woman. She held his gaze, and they stood unmoving in the heat and sea-smell of the cave, knowing that the infant might have been spared its flames, but the fire that Thetis had lit had instantly consumed all traces of their love for one another.

Heart-broken, and unwilling to command the death of Cheiron's daughter, Peleus had her kept under close confinement for a time. The child he gave to a wet-nurse, one of Euhippe's friends, a Centaur woman who had been brought back from a hunt, freed at Peleus's insistence, and now lived with one of the palace cooks. It was she who named her tiny charge Achilles, the lipless one, because his lips had never been warmed into life at his mother's breast. But Peleus found it hard even to look at his son because the child's cries always recalled the horror of that night. On one thing, however, he was resolved — that Thetis should never come close either to the child or to himself. So in the end, on the understanding that she would die if ever she returned to Thessaly, he gave her leave to do what she had always wished to do and Thetis joined her mother's people on the remote island of Skyros.

'But the boy lived,' Odysseus said at last, filled with sympathy for the man who sat across from him, staring at the dying embers of the fire. 'You have a son and heir.'

'Whom I hardly know,' Peleus answered, 'and who knows nothing of me.'

'That can be repaired. You can recall him from Cheiron's school at any time.'

'To live in this darkness with me?'

'The child might lighten it.'

Sighing, Peleus searched the young Ithacan's face. 'Fortunately, it was prophesied that the boy will be a greater man than his father.'

Odysseus said, 'Then he will be a great soul indeed.'

*   *   *

Warmed by the company of this new friend, Peleus asked Odysseus to stay with him in Iolcus for a time. The Ithacan gladly agreed and the two men talked often together, exchanging stories of former exploits and discussing the changes in the world now that Agamemnon, the son of Atreus, had reclaimed the throne in Mycenae and was expanding his power to such an extent that he must soon be acclaimed as High King of all Argos. They talked of lighter matters too and Odysseus had at last got his host laughing merrily one evening when the arrival of another visitor was announced.

As a bastard son of King Actor, Menoetius was loosely related to Peleus by marriage, and he had sailed around the straits from the Locrian city of Opus in search of help from him. Menoetius had a six year old son who was in trouble, having killed one of his friends when an argument over a game of knucklebones turned into a fight.

'There's no great harm in the boy,' he said, frowning, 'apart from his passionate temper. And it breaks my heart, but I can't keep him with me in Opus. There's blood guilt on him now, and the father of the boy he killed loved his son as much as I do mine.'

Peleus nodded. 'So what are you asking of me?'

Menoetius asked if he might bring his son into the hall, and when permission was given, Peleus and Odysseus found themselves confronted by a scrawny six-year-old with a thick shock of hair and a downcast gaze firmly fixed on his own freshly scrubbed feet. Remembering how his own early fate had been shaped by the death of another, Peleus said, 'What's your name, boy?'

Briefly the small face glowered up at him in sulky defiance, then immediately looked down again, saying nothing.

'His name's Patroclus,' Menoetius said, 'though, as you see, he hasn't brought much glory on his father so far.'

'There's still plenty of time,' Odysseus put in lightly.

Menoetius looked back at Peleus in appeal. 'I hear that you've sent your own son to the Centaur?' When Peleus nodded again, he added. 'I was wondering if you thought he might be able to sort this boy out.'

'He sorted me out,' Peleus said quietly.

'But that dreadful business at the wedding of Pirithous . . . when they got drunk . . .' Menoetius saw Peleus frown. He hesitated and began again. 'I mean, weren't you already a man when you went to Cheiron.'

'I was more of a man when I came away. As were Pirithous and Jason, though they were sent to him as boys. And I might have been a better man still if I'd stayed among the Centaurs.' Peleus shook his head. 'But that was not my fate. As it is, I was glad to send my son to Cheiron. And since then a number of my Myrmidons have done the same.' He turned back to where Patroclus shifted uneasily on his feet. 'Look at me, boy.' Grimly, Patroclus did as he was bidden. 'Would you like to hunt and learn how to talk to horses? Would you like to know the magic locked in herbs, and how to sing and finger the lyre so that the animals come out of the trees to listen?'

Uncertainly Patroclus nodded.

'I think I'd like to go to this school myself,' Odysseus smiled.

Astounded by himself, Peleus said suddenly, 'Then come up the mountain with me tomorrow.'

Odysseus looked up, surprised at the transformation in his friend. Some god must be at work here. He felt the hairs prickle at the nape of his neck. But he smiled and nodded. Why not? Yes, he would be glad to go.

Peleus turned back to Menoetius. 'It's time I went to see how my own son's doing. You've done the right thing. Leave your boy with me.'

Apart from a tree that had been struck by lightning and the number of scruffy children to be fed, Peleus found the gorge hardly changed since the last time he had been there. But Cheiron felt much older, his cheeks were hollower than Peleus remembered, and the wrinkles deeply pouched about his eyes. His movements were slower too, though he was still limber, and his hands trembled as he offered a libation of mare's milk in thanksgiving for the return of his son and friend. He welcomed Odysseus warmly among his people, and smiled kindly at Patroclus, questioning him a little, before packing him off to play with some of the other children by the stream. A boy was sent to search for Achilles in the woods and, as they walked to the cave, Peleus explained why Patroclus had been sent to him. But Cheiron merely nodded in reply, and then shook his head over the way Peleus was limping across the rocks. 'You should have come to me sooner,' he said, 'then as now.'

As they ate together, Odysseus expressed his admiration for Cheiron's way of life. 'We still like to keep things simple on Ithaca,' he said. 'Some people find us rude and barbarous, yet we're honest and we have all we need there. It's only a restless lust for adventure that draws me away, but I'm always glad to get home again.'

Peleus sighed. 'I should never have left this place.'

'A man must follow his fate,' Cheiron said, 'and yours has been a hard one. I should have seen it sooner, but there are things the heart sees and will not believe.' Peleus insisted that none of the blame for his fate had been Cheiron's, but the old king gravely shook his head. 'Though she followed her mother's ways, Thetis is of my blood, and I have failed as a father.'

When Odysseus protested that Cheiron had been a good father to many of the greatest heroes of the age, the old Centaur sighed that a man could care well for the children of others yet be a fumbler with his own. 'It is only boys who come to me here,' he said, 'and though the power in the world may have passed to Sky-Father Zeus, the Goddess still has her claims to make on us – though sometimes it is hard for men to understand her mysteries.' He gazed up into the troubled eyes of Peleus and drew in his breath. 'But you have a fine son. He's already a skilful huntsman and he runs like the wind. Also he has a singing voice that will break your heart. You will be proud of Achilles – as he is already proud of you.' Cheiron took in the dubious tilt of Peleus's head. 'Oh yes, he knows that his father is a great king in Thessaly and has already taken a knock or two for bragging of it.'

At that moment all three men heard the eager, rowdy sound of boy's voices shouting in the gorge. They tried to resume their conversation, but the noise went on until Cheiron got up and said, 'It's time I put a stop to it.'

His guests followed him to the mouth of the cave where they looked down at the sward of rough grass among the rocks and saw two boys scrapping like fighting dogs inside a shifting circle of young, tousle-headed spectators who were urging them on. When they struggled back to their feet from where they had been flinging punches at each other on the ground, blood was bubbling from both their noses.

Peleus recognized Patroclus by the dark red tunic he was wearing. 'His father warned me that he had a bad temper, but this is a poor start. I trust the other fellow is strong enough to stand up to him.'

'I should think so,' Cheiron turned to him and smiled. 'He is your son.'

An Oracle of Fire

After the wedding-day of Peleus and Thetis a whole generation passed in the world of mortals, but the quarrel among the goddesses raged on and Zeus was no nearer to finding a solution. At last, out of all patience with the bitter atmosphere around him, he called a council among the gods, and Hermes, the shrewdest and most eloquent of the immortals, conceived of a possible way through.

It was obvious, he said, that none of the three goddesses would be satisfied until a judgement was made. It was equally clear that none of the immortals were in a position to choose among them without giving everlasting offence. Therefore it was his opinion that the decision should be placed in the hands of an impartial mortal.

Not at all displeased by the idea of returning the dispute to the mortal realm, Zeus asked if he had anyone particular in mind.

'I think,' smiled Hermes, 'that this is a matter for Paris to decide.'

Ares looked up at the mention of the name. That handsome bully of a god, who had come swaggering back from Thrace where they make war their sport and take as much delight in the lopping off of heads as others do in the finer points of art, had no doubt about which of the goddesses should be given the apple. He had long since grown bored therefore by a conflict that lacked real violence. Now he declared impatiently that Paris was an excellent choice. He knew him to be a fair-minded fellow with a good eye for the best fighting bulls in the Idaean Mountains.

Though she was restless to get back into the wilds, Artemis pointed out that being a bull fancier might not be the ideal qualification for the matter in hand. But before Hermes could respond, Ares went on to tell how Paris had once offered a crown as prize for any bull that could beat the champion he had raised. Just for the sport of it, Ares had transformed himself into a bull and thoroughly trounced Paris's beast. Yet even though the odds had been stacked against him, Paris had cheerfully awarded him the crown. So yes, Ares was quite sure of it – Paris could be relied on to give a fair judgement.

'I should perhaps add,' said Hermes, smiling amiably at the goddesses, who had, at that moment, no passionate interest in fighting bulls, 'that Paris is also the most handsome of mortal men.'

Zeus grunted at that. Sternly he looked back at the goddesses. 'Will all three of you be content to submit to this handsome mortal's judgement?' And when they nodded their assent, the lord of Olympus sighed with relief.

'Very well, Paris it shall be.' And asking Hermes to conduct the goddesses to Mount Ida, Zeus gratefully turned his thoughts to other matters.

As he sat in the sunlight watching his herd graze the pastures of Mount Ida, Paris was, of course, quite unaware that the gods had elected him to solve a problem that they could not solve themselves. But at that time he was ignorant of many other matters too, not least of the mystery of his own birth, for the youth entrusted with this awesome responsibility was rather more than the humble herdsman he believed himself to be.

Many years earlier, in the hours before he was born, his pregnant mother had woken in terror from a prophetic dream, and that dream was now beginning to cast a lurid light across the world. Yet as parents beget children, so one story begets another, and one cannot understand who Paris was without also knowing something about his parents, and something of his father's father too.

There were many Troys before the last Troy fell. One of them was ruled by a king called Laomedon, and the lore of the city tells how, as a humiliating punishment for displeasing Zeus, the gods Apollo and Poseidon were once forced to work for a year as day-labourers in that king's service. In return for a stipulated fee, Apollo played the lyre and tended Laomedon's flocks on Mount Ida while Poseidon toiled to build the walls around the city. Knowing that the walls would never fall unless some mortal was also involved in their construction, Poseidon delegated part of the work to Aeacus, who was the father of Peleus and Telamon. But Laomedon had a perfidious streak in his nature, and when the work was done he refused to make the agreed payment of all the cattle born in the kingdom during the course of that year.

It was not he but Zeus, he argued, who had put the gods to their tasks, and in any case what needs did the immortals have that they could not supply for themselves? So he turned them away from the city empty-handed.

The gods were not slow to take their revenge. In his aspect of a mouse-god, Apollo visited a plague upon Troy, while Earth-shaker Poseidon unleashed a huge sea-monster to terrorize its coastline. When a people already sickening from pestilence found their land made infertile by the huge breakers of salt-water that the monster set crashing across their fields, they demanded that Laomedon seek counsel from the oracle of Zeus as to how the gods might be appeased. The answer came that nothing less than the sacrifice of his beloved daughter Hesione would suffice.

Laomedon did all he could to resist the judgement, trying to force others in the city to offer their own daughters to the monster in Hesione's place. But the members of the Trojan assembly were fully aware that the king's perfidy was the cause of their grief, and would consent to no more than a casting of lots. In accordance with the will of the gods, the lot fell on Hesione. So Laomedon had to look on helplessly as his daughter was stripped of everything but her jewels, chained to a rock by the shore, and left alone to die.

The sea was rising and breaking round Hesione's naked body when she was found by Heracles as he returned with his friend Telamon from their expedition to the land of the Amazons. Using his prodigious strength, Heracles broke the chains and set Hesione free. But the sea-monster was still at large, so the hero struck a bargain with Laomedon, offering to put an end to the beast in return for two immortal white mares which were the pride of the king's herd.

The king accepted the offer and, after a fight that lasted for three terrible days, Heracles managed to kill the monster.

Once again Laomedon proved faithless. Ignoring the counsel of his son Podarces, he substituted mortal horses for the immortal mares that had been promised, and when Heracles discovered the deceit he declared war on Troy.

It was a war that left the city ravaged. As the son of Aeacus, Telamon was able to discover which part of Troy's walls had been built by his father and were, therefore, the weakest. He breached the city's defences at that place, Heracles joined him in the assault, and the palace was sacked. Driven by vengeful rage, Heracles killed Laomedon together with most of his family. Though Hesione's life was spared, she was given against her will to Telamon, and carried off by him to his stronghold on Salamis. But before she left Troy, Hesione was allowed to ransom the life of one other captive. The life she chose to save was that of her sole surviving brother, Podarces. It was he whom Heracles appointed as the king of a city reduced to smoking rubble. The new king was known ever afterwards as Priam, the ransomed one.

That anyway is how the story is told among the Trojan bards, and there were aspects of the tale that Telamon and Heracles were pleased to propagate among the Argives. But Odysseus was given a rather different version of the story by Telamon's brother Peleus. This is how he told it to me.

When they were boys, Telamon and Peleus had known for years of the longstanding feud between their father and King Laomedon of Troy. As a man widely known for his wisdom and skill, Aeacus had indeed been commissioned to rebuild and strengthen the ring wall around Troy. Because the city stood on a site prone to earthquakes, Aeacus entreated the divine help of Poseidon and those who understood his mysteries. He also brought with him a bard consecrated to Apollo. It was he who led the music which eased the men in the hard labour of carving, moving and lifting the great blocks of stone. The work went well. Lofty new gates guarded by bastions were built. The limestone blocks were skilfully laid to give a steeply angled batter to the lower part of the wall. Above it rose a gleaming crenellated parapet. So the new walls of Troy, rising from the windy hill above the plain, were both robust and beautiful.

Before the work was complete, however, it became clear that Laomedon was running short of money. When Aeacus saw that the king was unlikely to pay for the remainder of the work, he downed tools and returned to Salamis, leaving a stretch of the western wall unimproved and vulnerable. Eventually, infuriated by Laomedon's failure to come up with the money he was still owed, he called down the curses of Poseidon and Apollo on the city.

Many years later the Trojans were woken one morning by a dreadful sound. The waters of the bay between their two head-lands were being sucked back towards the Hellespont, leaving the sea-bed exposed as a stinking marsh, strewn with rocks and slime and the carcasses of ancient ships. The ground under the city began to move. Buildings cracked, sagged and collapsed. People fled their houses as the sea came crashing back in a huge tumbling wall, higher than a house, that did not stop at the shore but rushed on to flood the fertile plain, destroying the harvest and salting the land.

Though the walls of Aeacus withstood the shock, the western defences and many houses inside the walls did not. Hundreds of lives were lost that day, trapped under fallen masonry or drowned by the wave. Soon a stench of decay polluted the city's air. Within a few days pestilence came.

Telamon and Heracles were caught in the turbulent waters as they sailed through the Black Sea into the Hellespont in the single ship that remained to them after their violent expedition to the land of the Amazons. By the time they sailed along the coast of Troy, the dirty weather had cleared and the waters calmed a little. But as they followed the shoreline, they were amazed to see a naked young woman bound to the rocks with the breakers surging round her.

The girl was half-dead from cold and fear, but Heracles cut her down, took her aboard ship and brought her round. She was not Princess Hesione, of course, for Laomedon had taken precautions to withhold his daughter's name from the lottery that had been held in the city. It was from the young woman on whom the lot had fallen that they learned of the city's desperate condition. Reduced to a primitive state of terror by their misfortunes, the Trojan people had resorted to human sacrifice to propitiate the gods.

Seeing an opportunity, Telamon sailed to Aegina and told his father that his curse had finally born fruit. If Aeacus would finance ten ships, he would return to Troy and take as plunder what had been withheld as payment. Aeacus agreed to put up only part of the money, so Telamon approached Peleus for the rest, but without success. In the end he and Heracles advanced against Troy with only six ships, but they carried enough men to breach the weakest part of the wall and sack the already devastated city.

In terms of hard coin and plunder, the expedition failed to make much profit, but Laomedon was killed and Telamon took his beautiful daughter Hesione as part of his share in the spoils. Priam's most prudent son, Podarces, only survived the slaughter when he ransomed his life by revealing where Laomedon had hidden what was left of his treasure. Before sailing away, Telamon placed a battered crown on the young Trojan's head and hailed him as King Priam.

Terrified, humiliated, but alive, Podarces swore to himself that he would wear the new name with pride, that he would do whatever was needed to redeem the fortunes of Troy, and that one day he would have his revenge on the barbarians from across the sea.

Before that time the Trojan people had tended to look westwards across the sea to Argos from where their ancestors had come in previous generations. The young King Priam now turned eastwards, opening up negotiations with the great bureaucratic regime of the Hittite empire, looking for loans to help him rebuild, and for trade to repay them. He met with a favourable response. Merchants of the Asian seaboard were also quick to see the advantages of a well-ruled city on a site commanding access to the Black Sea trade. Soon ships were putting in from Egypt too. New buildings began to rise inside the walls of Troy, not just new palaces and houses but also great weaving halls where the people were put to work manufacturing textiles from the raw materials that came into the city from the east as well as from their own mountain flocks. The Trojans' capacity for work became proverbial and the quality of that work was high, so trade profited. Beyond the city walls, Priam encouraged his people's traditional skills as horse-breakers until discriminating buyers began to look to Troy for their horses. And the king also took a particular delight in the powerful strain of bulls raised by his Dardanian kinsmen on the pastures of the Idaean Mountains.

Priam was not slow to thank the gods for the favour they had shown him. Soon after coming to the throne, he endowed an ancient mountain shrine to Apollo Smintheus, the bringer and healer of pestilence. Next he gave a new temple to the god inside the city, and then dedicated another on the sacred site at Thymbra. As his wealth increased, he built a spacious market square, surrounded by workshops and warehouses, and overlooked by a new temple which housed the Palladium, an ancient wooden image of the goddess standing only three cubits high that had been made by Pallas Athena herself, and on which the preservation of the city was said to depend.

Meanwhile the king had married. His wife Hecuba was the daughter of a Thracian king and their wedding sealed an important military and trading alliance. But there was also love between them, and Priam's happiness seemed complete when his queen gave birth to a strong son whom they named Hector because he was destined to be the mainstay of the city. Not long afterwards, Hecuba fell pregnant again and everything seemed set fair until a night shortly before the new child was due, when Hecuba woke in terror from an ominous dream.

In the dream she had given birth to a burning brand from which a spawn of fiery serpents swarmed until the entire city of Troy and all the forests of Mount Ida were ablaze. Disturbed by this dreadful oracle of fire, Priam summoned his soothsayer, who was the priest to Apollo at Thymbra and had the gift of interpreting dreams. The priest confirmed the king's fears – that if the child in Hecuba's womb was allowed to live, it would bring ruin on the city.

Two mornings later, the seer emerged from a prophetic trance to declare that a child would be born to a member of the royal house that day. Evil fortune would be averted only if both mother and child were put to death. To Priam's horror, Hecuba immediately went into labour.

Yet the queen was not the only pregnant woman in the royal household, and during the course of the morning, Priam received news that his sister Cilla had given birth to an infant son. Sick at heart, yet relieved to be spared the loss of his own wife and child, he commanded the immediate death of both his sister and her baby. Having seen the bodies buried in the sacred precinct of the city, Priam returned to his wife's chamber hopeful that the gods were now satisfied and the safety of his city assured.

But night had not yet fallen when Hecuba also gave birth to a son.

Priam looked up from the peaceful face of the child to see the priest and priestess of Apollo entering the bedchamber. He knew at once what was required of him, yet he could not bring himself to order these further and still closer deaths. 'Isn't it enough that one royal mother and her child have died today?' he demanded. 'Let the gods be content.'

Gravely the priest reminded him of the terrible fate that had fallen on Troy when his father Laomedon had tried to cheat the gods, and the priestess remained implacable in her conviction that the child at least must die. Had not Hecuba's own dream warned her that she carried the ruin of the city in her womb? Could it be wise to let it live at such dreadful cost?

'You have brought this evil into the world,' she said. 'Have the strength and wisdom to let it die by your own hand.'

When Hecuba could only wail out her refusal, the priest turned his gaze on the king. 'Will you risk all you have built for the sake of an ill-omened child?'

'I have served Apollo well,' Priam protested. 'How have I wronged him that he should persecute me so?'

The priest opened his hands. 'Apollo looks deep into the well of time. His concern is for the protection of this city.'

'If your kingdom is to live,' the priestess insisted, 'the child must die.'

'My sister and her newborn child are already dead at my command,' Priam cried. 'Would you have all the Furies roost in my mind? How much blood guilt do you think I can bear?'

The priest looked away. 'It's not we who demand this sacrifice. The king must choose between his city and the child.'

Looking for mercy where none was to be found, Priam lifted his eyes. 'Then let it be the child. But not at my wife's hand. And not at mine either.' He dragged the wailing infant from his wife's arms and gave it to the priestess. 'Do with it as you will,' he gasped, 'and leave us to our grief.'

With Hecuba screaming behind them, the priests left the chamber and handed over the baby to be killed by a palace guard. But the man could not bring himself to do the deed. When he consulted his friends, one of them said, 'Give the job to Agelaus. He's used to butchery.'

And so, hours later, in the village where he lived in the Dardanian mountains beyond the plain of Troy, the king's chief herdsman was drawn from sleep by a horseman hammering at his door. Told what was required of him, Agelaus looked down where the infant's swaddling bands were coming unwrapped.

'It seems a fine boy,' he said. 'Why does he have to die?'

'Because the king commands it,' the horseman replied.

Wondering why this unwanted task should have fallen to him, Agelaus shook his head. 'Did the king say by what means the child should die?'

'By any means you choose.' The man wheeled his mount to gallop away. 'This thing is the will of the gods,' he shouted over his shoulder. 'Be free of it.'

Though he had slaughtered countless animals in his time, Agelaus had no more stomach than the guard for cutting an infant's throat. Frowning down at the scrap of life in his arms, he muttered, 'If the gods think you should die, let the gods attend to it.' Then he took the child to a forest glade on the slopes of Mount Ida and left it there to perish or survive as fate decided.

Three days later, driven by his wife's insistence, the herdsman returned to the glade. When he saw the tracks of a bear headed that way, he expected to find nothing more than bloodied swaddling bands, but as he came closer a thin sound of crying drifted towards him on the breeze. Hurrying through the brakes, he found the baby still alive, bawling for food and almost blue with cold. Instantly his heart went out to it.

Holding the infant against his chest for warmth, he said, 'If the gods have sent a she-bear to suckle you, boy, they must mean you to live.' Tenderly, he placed the baby in the wallet slung at his side, and brought it home to his wife. It was she who spotted the birthmark like a kiss on the baby's neck and her heart was quickly lost to it. This child had been sent to them, she declared, and she would care for it. She named him Paris, which means 'wallet', because of the strange way in which he had come to her.

As the years went by, Paris soon distinguished himself both in courage and intelligence from the herdsmen round him. Even as a child he showed no fear among the bulls, and his greatest delight was to watch them fight one another and to see his own beast triumph. Under the patient tutelage of Agelaus, he soon proved himself a good huntsman and a skilful archer too. And he was still only ten years old on the day when he used his bow for a deadlier purpose than shooting wildfowl, though that had been his only intention when he took off into the woods.

The sun was thunderously hot that day and the air heavy. Paris had set out cheerfully enough but by early afternoon he was feeling drowsy and irritable. Casting about in the bracken for the arrows he had loosed and lost, he felt as though the thunder had got inside his head, so with only an old buck-rabbit and a partridge hanging at his belt, the boy was coming listlessly back down the hillside through the trees when he heard a restive sound of lowing from the cattle penned below.

Dismayed that his father had decided to move the herd without telling him, Paris was about to run down to join the drive when he heard men shouting – unfamiliar voices, strangely accented, barking out commands. He came to a halt while still under the cover of the trees and saw a gang of cattle-lifters breaking down a fence that Agelaus had built that spring.

He had counted nine of them, all armed with spears or swords, when more shouts drew his eyes to the right where Agelaus was running across the hillside from the settlement, followed by two of his herdsmen. They had no more than staves and a single hunting-spear between them. A burly man wearing a helmet and a studded leather jerkin advanced to meet them, drawing his sword and shouting to the others for support.

Paris's grip tightened on his bow. He saw that there were seven arrows left in his quiver. Swallowing, dry-mouthed, he took one of them between his fingers and nocked it to his bowstring.

By now six of the rustlers confronted Agelaus and his followers on the open meadow, and the other three were coming up quickly. As Agelaus grabbed the spear from the older man at his side, the helmeted leader brandished his sword and ordered one of his spearmen to throw. The man lifted his spear and was about to loose it when an arrow whistled out of the trees and pierced his neck. Herdsmen and rustlers alike watched in amazement as a gush of blood spluttered from his mouth, the spear fell from his hand and he crumpled to the ground. Seconds later, with a sparking of metal against metal, another arrow glanced off the leader's helmet. Taking advantage of the shock, Agelaus hurled his spear with such force that it drove through the jerkin and dragged the man down to the ground where he lay writhing and slobbering.

Again, for several moments, everyone stood transfixed.

A third arrow flew wide and stuck quivering in the grass. The rustlers had lost their leader but all three herdsmen were now weaponless with seven armed men standing only yards away. Paris loosed another shot at a scrawny rustler, who instantly dropped his spear to clutch at the shaft stuck in his thigh. The remaining cattle-lifters turned uncertainly, not knowing how many assailants were hidden in the trees. When a fourth man grunted and stared down to see an arrow trembling in his belly, three of the others started to run off down the hill. Moments later, unnerved as much by the unexpected alteration in their fortunes as by the groans of those dying around them, the others made off, stopping only to aid their injured comrade.

Agelaus and his companions were watching them hobble away down the hill when Paris came out from between the trees, carrying his bow. He heard his friends calling to him as if from a far distance. The air wobbled about his head. His throat was very dry. 'I had only two arrows left,' he mumbled as he fought free of Agelaus's embrace. Then he stood, looking down at where the dead leader lay with the spear-shaft through his lungs. Turning away in recoil, he saw the body of the man with the barb through his throat, and a third, who gazed up at him as if beseeching him to take back the arrow from his belly.

A nimbus of darkness circled behind the boy's eyes. He was watching the dying rustler choke on a gush of blood from his mouth when that dark circle widened and thickened so swiftly that it consumed all the light in the day.

He woke to the sound of water running over stones. He was beside a river in the shade of a thatched awning, lying on a litter, and the flash of white rapids came harsh against his eyes. The air about his head was aromatic with herbs. Savouring the mingled scents of balm, camomile and lavender, he moved his head and moaned a little at the dizziness. Then he saw the grey haired man sitting on a nearby rock, fingering the long curls of his beard.

A girl's voice said, 'I think he's awake.' Paris turned to look at her. 'Yes,' she cried, 'he is,' and her face broke into a bright, gap-toothed smile. Her hair also hung in curls, but so fair and fine they might have been spun from the light about her head. Wearing a white smock marked with grass stains, she was playing with a mouse that ran between her small hands. She was perhaps six years old. At her back, some distance away, were two grassy hummocks with stone portals, which looked like burial mounds.

'Bring him some water,' her father said, putting a gently restraining hand to the boy's shoulder. 'Lie still for a while,' he smiled. 'All will be well.'

Paris tilted his face to watch the girl as she stretched out to hold a drinking cup under a freshet of water bursting from a dark cleft in the rocks. The inside of his head felt burned out with pain. It was as though his violent dreams of fire and smoke and blazing buildings were still smouldering in there.

The girl came back and lifted the cup to his lips. 'You've been very sick, Alexander,' she said with the air of one endowed with privileged knowledge, 'but my father has the gift of healing. You'll soon be strong again.'

The water flowed across his tongue to break like light in his throat. He licked his parched lips, drank some more, then laid his head back. Struggling to retrieve the recent past, he remembered how the flies had gathered round the bloody wounds of the men he had slaughtered. His breath whimpered a little. Then he said, 'My name isn't Alexander.'

'No, it's Paris, I know. But you've been given another name since you drove off those cattle-lifters. They say you may only be a boy but you've become a defender of men, so that's what they call you now – Alexander. I like it better.'

'That's enough now,' her father said. 'Give him time to come to himself.' He smiled down at the boy again. 'I'm Apollo's priest at this shrine. My name's Cebren. Your father brought you here three days ago to be cured of the burning fever. He'll be glad to learn that the mouse-god has looked kindly on you. In two days he'll come to bring you home. All you need now is rest.'

'It's all right, Alexander,' the girl said. 'You needn't be afraid.'

'I'm not afraid.' Her arms were so thin they made him think of the stems of flowers. 'What's *your* name?' he asked.

'Oenone,' she answered. 'I'm the nymph of this fountain. One day I shall be a healer too.'

Paris smiled vaguely and, almost immediately, fell asleep again.

Agelaus came with a mule to carry his foster-son home bringing grateful offerings for the god and for the priest who served him. Received as a hero among his friends, Paris soon forgot how his mind had sickened at things he had done. In the years that followed, his boyish face developed the strong-lined, handsome features of a noble young man whose bodily strength had grown to match his courage. Renowned also for his good sense, he was often called upon for his counsel or to settle arguments among the herdsmen. So, as Agelaus aged and his muscles stiffened, Paris became the guardian of the herd, and out of love for the work he began to take an obsessive pride in breeding a formidable pedigree of fighting bulls.

Only once across the years was his chosen champion defeated in a fight. At that spring fair, a wild bull, blacker than a thunder-cloud, came down from the mountain, scattering the villagers and spreading alarm among the herd as it broke through the fence and began to storm and gore about the paddock. The bull fought with such ardour that Paris could only watch in astonish-ment while it bore down on his own favoured animal, trampled it under its hooves, and then twisted an immense horn through its breast to puncture the lungs. Though he was left aghast at the sight, the youth had no hesitation in honouring such ferocity with the victor's crown. Panting in its sweat, the bull quivered before him, tail swishing, black pelt splashed with blood. Paris gazed into the fierce roll of its eye. He heard someone mutter that the beast should be killed before it did more harm. Firmly he shook his head. 'No,' he entwined the crown of flowers about its horns, 'this bull goes free. Let him roam the mountains at his pleasure.'

Snorting in the dusty light, the bull dipped the blunt prow of its head as though in salute. Moments later, with the garland still gaily wreathed about its horns, it galloped back into the mountains.

When Agelaus remarked that never in all his long years as a herdsman had he seen a bull behave so strangely, Paris smiled and said, 'I think he was possessed by a god.'

At the spring fair two years later, Paris was garlanding the creamy-white curls of the bull he currently favoured, when he looked up and saw a young woman watching him from the edge of the trees across the paddock. Dappled sunlight shone off her hair. She was tall and lithe, and held a flower at her lips. All his senses instantly quickened to her presence. Then his heart jumped at the smile with which she studied him for a long moment. By the time she glanced modestly away he knew that never before had he seen anything so beautiful.

Unable to think of a sensible word to say, he crossed the few sunlit yards stretching between them and held out his hand to take the flower. Scarcely breathing, she watched him lift it to his lips. Then he strode back to where his bull panted in the afternoon light and twisted the stem into the garland already laid across its horns. Paris glanced back at the girl. 'Who are you? I don't recall having seen you before.'

Smiling she said, 'Perhaps if I had horns and a tail and snorted like a bull you would remember me.'

'I can't believe I would ever forget you.'

'But you clearly have,' she laughed. 'No doubt you will again.'

'Never. I swear it as I am a true man.'

She tilted her gaze away. 'Perhaps that is still to be proven – despite that leopard-skin you wear.'

He flushed at that. 'My name is Paris. No one doubts my courage. Or my faith.'

'I recall a boy whose bravery showed such promise,' she said. 'They called you Alexander then. You were a long sleeper in those days.'

Paris came closer, fixing her with a puzzled frown. The bright lilt of her voice brought the sound of water to his mind – white water, water over stones. 'You're the fountain nymph,' he said. 'From the shrine in the mountains. Your father healed me of the burning fever. You brought me water in a cup.'

'And you have never thought of me since!'

Again he flushed. 'You were only a child who played with a mouse.'

'While you were the great defender of men!' She laughed at his evident discomfiture, and then looked away into the trees, smiling still.

Not far from where they stood, the herdsmen and their wives were gathering under the awnings for the feast with children running noisily round them.

'Did you come down from the mountains to see the fair?' he asked. 'They say that King Anchises and his son will come to watch the games.'

'I came because the river told me to come.'

She glanced up at him. Their eyes might have been fixed on the same shaft of light. In a lower, less certain voice, she added, 'I have thought about you every day since then.'

Paris stood astonished as she turned away, back into the trees. Someone called out to him to join the feast. He raised a hand and answered that he would come soon. Then the girl's name came back to him. He whispered it to himself aloud: 'Oenone.'

But she was gone among the trees. Drawn by the thought that he could not let such beauty vanish from his life forever, he followed her into the green shades. She stopped when he called out her name. Timidly they talked for a time. Paris grew bolder. Laughing, Oenone turned away from him and ran deeper into the cover of the trees. He gave chase, following the sound of her laughter till he came out in a sunlit glade by the riverbank where the water sleeked its light through stones. It was there that she let herself be found.

Soon they were all but inseparable. Sometimes in the cool of the mornings they would hunt deer or wild boar together, traversing the mountain gorges where Paris carved Oenone's name into the bark of trees as loud torrents of melt-water cascaded down the rocks around them. And in the heat of the day they would often lie together in high alpine meadows that were bright with wild flowers as they watched the herds graze at their summer pasture.

Ignorant of his origins, free from all worldly cares, delighting in the strenuous country life which was all he had ever known, adored by his foster parents, admired by his friends, and deeply loved by Oenone, Paris might well have been considered as happy as a man can ever hope to be. Yet as the seasons passed a vague restlessness began to seize his soul. Not that he could have named it for himself, or that he was troubled by feelings of discontent;

but an obscure sense of horizons wider than that of the silent summits round him sometimes unsettled the reveries of the hours when he was alone. And it was on such an afternoon, while the heat was building over the high green pasture below the snow-line on Mount Ida, that fate ambushed him.

The Judgement of Paris

'So you see,' Hermes was saying, 'there'll be no peace till this argument is sorted out. We need an impartial judge to settle the issue and the general opinion was that you were the best man for the job.'

'Me?' Paris protested. 'How can a herdsman be expected to sort out a quarrel among the gods?'

Hermes tipped back the brim of his hat with his staff and cocked a wry eye at him. 'You have an eye for beauty, don't you? And Ares was impressed by your sense of justice. Anyway, the only thing the goddesses are agreed on is to abide by your decision. You should be flattered.'

But Paris was thinking quickly. 'How can I choose one of them without upsetting the others? Wouldn't it be simplest to divide the apple into three?'

'I'm afraid that none of the goddesses is prepared to compromise. It's gone too far for that. They want a decision.'

'Then I'm going to need your advice.'

Hermes held up his hands as though backing away. 'If I don't stay quite neutral my immortal life won't be worth living.'

'But I'm only human,' Paris protested, 'I'm bound to get it wrong.'

'Sooner or later every mortal has to make choices,' Hermes

said. 'This is your time. It's always a lonely moment but there's nothing to be done about that. If you're wise you'll assent to it. You never know, with three goddesses all eager for your good opinion, it might work out to your advantage.'

He tilted his head. 'Are you ready? Shall I summon them?'

As alarmed by the prospect ahead of him as he was strangely excited by it, Paris nodded. Hermes began to turn away, and then halted. 'One thing I will say. There's more at stake here than a golden apple.' Then he raised his staff and shook it so that the white ribbons flailed through the air.

Paris gasped as the three goddesses instantly appeared before him.

At the centre stood Hera, wearing her vine-wreathed crown from which dangled golden clusters of grapes. A shimmering, net-like robe embroidered with seeds and stars hung well on her shapely figure. She was, Paris saw at once, awesomely beautiful and entirely at ease in that relaxed kind of grace that knows its own power and has no need to make a show of it. With the poise of her regal authority, she acknowledged the wonder in his gaze.

To Hera's right, the more athletic Athena wore a light suit of finely crafted armour that was moulded to enhance her lissom form and the taut sinews of her slender limbs. In one hand she gripped a bronze-tipped spear, and in the other her aegis – the goatskin-covered shield on which a gorgon's head was depicted. It threw into contrast both the clear brilliance of her eyes and the grave, unclouded beauty of the face which studied Paris shrewdly now.

Aphrodite stood to Hera's left, leaning on one hip slightly to throw her form into relief beneath her simple, gauzy dress. She held her arms across her chest, with the palms of her hands pressed together and the tips of her fingers at her mouth. Violets were pinned in her hair and gilded flowers dangled from her ears. She tilted her head slightly to smile at Paris, then lowered her arms and watched the youth catch his breath as he took in the intricately-worked girdle that began as a necklace at her slender throat and curved down to separate and support the contours of her breasts.

Thinking she might have been too formal, Hera said, 'I see that Hermes didn't deceive us when he promised the most handsome mortal as our judge.'

Paris glanced away, gesturing towards his cattle. 'He's brought you a herdsman. One who's bound to make mistakes.' Still awestruck, he drew himself up to confront the goddesses. 'If I agree to make this judgement there have to be conditions.'

'Name them,' said Athena.

Paris took a deeper breath. 'All three of you have to forgive me in advance. Also I want an undertaking that none of you will harm me if the verdict goes against you.'

'That seems reasonable enough,' said Hera. Athena nodded. Aphrodite smiled and added, 'Very sensible too.'

'Then if you're all agreed to his terms,' said Hermes, 'we can proceed.' He looked back at Paris. 'Would you prefer to judge the contenders together or to examine each of them alone?'

Paris, who was having some difficulty keeping his eyes off Aphrodite's girdle, was about to reply, when Athena observed his air of distraction.

'I really must insist that Aphrodite takes off her *kestos,*' she said. 'We all know it makes men go weak at the knees.'

At once Aphrodite protested that her *kestos* was as much part of her own presentation as the heavenly crown was for Hera or Athena's armour was for her. When both the other goddesses dismissed her claim as preposterous, it seemed that the quarrel must break out again. Hermes was about to intervene but Paris, who had just begun to sense the power he might hold, lifted an imperious hand. 'I think its best if I see them one at a time,' he said. 'That way we should avoid arguments.'

'As you wish.'

'However, I don't see how we can avoid the suspicion of unfair advantage unless all the goddesses remove their jewellery and clothing.'

'You're the judge,' Hermes gravely replied. 'It's for you to set the rules.'

'Then let it be so.'

Hermes coughed. 'I believe you heard what Paris said. Would you kindly disrobe?' Turning discreetly away from the goddesses, he asked Paris in which order he would care to see the three contenders.

Paris thought for a moment. 'As Queen of Olympus, Divine Hera should take precedence. Then perhaps the Lady Athena, and lastly, Aphrodite.'

'Good luck then.' Hermes smiled.

And vanished.

Left in a state of agitation, Paris sat down. A moment later he was thinking, *Father Zeus forgive me*, as he found himself quite alone, staring at the Queen of Olympus who stood before him in all her naked majesty.

'You were quite wrong in what you said.' Hera turned so that the youth could admire the sweep of her back. 'You're rather more than a simple herdsman. Actually your birth is royal.' Turning again, she smiled down at his astonishment. 'King Priam is your true father. Go to his palace in Troy and announce yourself. Tell him the gods chose to spare your life. He'll rejoice to see you.'

Though the words astounded him, Paris experienced a jolt of recognition. Hadn't he always guessed at some such secret? Didn't it explain why he felt different from everybody round him? Didn't it account for his restlessness? With mounting excitement he listened as Hera told him the story of his birth.

'And there's more,' Hera smiled. 'You needn't be content with being a prince. Award me the prize today and you can be a king in your own right. I'll make you the mightiest sovereign in Asia. Wealth, empire and glory – all these can be yours. As Queen of Heaven and wife to Zeus, I can do this for you. You can be numbered among the wealthiest and most powerful of kings.'

Paris saw himself suddenly transported beyond the simple life of the hills into the teeming world of the cities – the world of princes and palaces, of ministers, ambassadors and slaves, of imperial command and luxury such as even his father, the High King of Troy, did not enjoy. How much might he achieve with such power? What pleasures might such riches buy? Ambition swelled inside him. He saw himself crowned and sceptred, sitting on a jewelled throne with lesser kings obeisant before him and Oenone as queen at his side. But the dissonance between such grandeur and her simplicity unsettled him. He came to himself. He stumbled out a reply. 'I shall always be grateful, Divine Hera – both for revealing your beauty to me and for disclosing the secret of my birth. If I find you the fairest of the three you shall certainly have the apple. But . . .' he looked up at the goddess and swallowed, 'my judgement is not for sale.'

The Queen of Olympus stared at his candid gaze for a long moment without speaking. Tight-lipped, she nodded her head, and disappeared.

Then Athena was standing before him, her vigorous body gleaming as she turned. Everything about her appealed to his hunter's senses, and when she faced him again, the serenity of her clear gaze fell like sunlight on his soul.

'I suppose Hera has just tried to bribe you with power and wealth,' she said. 'That's what matters to her. But there are more important things, you know. Things which last longer and give deeper satisfaction. If you want contentment then you'd better get wisdom, and wisdom only comes from deep self-knowledge. Without that everything else turns to dust.' The goddess moved again to display her lithe form. The air around her strummed like a lyre with kinetic energy. 'That's the deep law of things, and though you may know *what* you are now, you still don't know *who* you are.' Athena smiled down at him. 'So be wise today. Make the right choice, and for the rest of your life you'll have me beside you, both in war and peace, cultivating your wisdom, protecting you in battle, and strengthening your soul until you achieve perfect freedom and control. A mortal man can ask no more.'

Paris nodded in silence, frowning and thoughtful. Vast new horizons were sweeping open within him. He had begun to understand that the choice to be made was not just between three modes of female beauty but between the deep, undying principles which shaped the values by which a man might live his life. Filled with a vertiginous sense of how his entire future destiny would be determined by his choice, he was trembling a little as he thanked Athena for sharing her beauty and wisdom with him. Then she was gone.

In her place stood Aphrodite.

For a long time the third goddess said nothing. There was, she knew, no need for words. Where Hera's regal confidence had steadied the air around the youth, and Athena had left it vibrant with her poise, Aphrodite filled it with a fragrance that excited all his senses. If outward beauty was the issue – he made up his mind at once – there was no contest. Only a few minutes earlier he would have beseeched Aphrodite to take the apple and do with him as she pleased. But his life had been changed in the past hour. He was no longer just a bull-boy free to while away his life in sunlight. He was a great king's son with a heritage to claim. He might be a man of moral and spiritual consequence. He had important things to think about.

Yet this third goddess was so dizzyingly beautiful that he could scarcely think at all.

'I know,' Aphrodite whispered, and there was a melting sadness in the eyes she lifted towards him – eyes of a blue such as he had previously glimpsed only at a far distance in the changing light off the sea. 'But it's not just about beauty any more, is it?'

'I'm not sure,' he said.

'I can see what's happened.' She looked away. 'The others have been offering you things. Tremendous things. Things you don't have. Things you hadn't even dreamed of.'

'Yes.'

'And I can only offer you love, which you already have, don't you?'

'Yes,' said Paris hoarsely, 'I do.'

But he was still considering the possibility that he might faint.

Aphrodite gave a rueful smile. 'Well, at least we can talk for a while.' She sat down with her legs drawn together, her elbows resting on her knees, and her face cupped in her hands, as though conceding that any further display of her beautiful body was pointless. Her eyes, however, remained deeply troubling.

Overwhelmed by her closeness, by the unselfconscious, naked presence of such heart-shaking beauty, Paris heard her say. 'She's lovely, isn't she? The fountain nymph, I mean.'

'Oenone.' He spoke the name almost wistfully, as if the friend and lover of his youth was already beginning to vanish beyond recall.

'I can see why she's so dear to you.' Like sunlight off a fountain, her smile flashed across at him. 'You're very lucky.'

Paris nodded. And swallowed.

'After all, she's given you the first unforgettable taste of what it's like to love and to be loved.'

'Yes.'

'So she'll always be dear to you, whatever happens.'

There was a silence, in which he realized he was barely sipping at the air.

After a time the goddess stirred and said, 'The world's so strange, isn't it? I mean, look at you – a simple herdsman one minute, a king's son the next, with the whole world at your feet. And here's me – one of the immortals, knowing that the apple is rightfully mine yet quite unable to claim it.' Again she sighed. 'I wouldn't normally be this patient, but you've been so good-natured about all this . . . and so honest with us! And I know that it can't be easy for you so I don't want you to feel badly about it. Anyway,' she gave him another regretful smile, 'I just want to say that it's been a real pleasure meeting you.'

But as soon as she began to move, Paris said, 'No, wait . . . please.'

The goddess tilted her head.

'I mean . . . what you said about Oenone. It's true, but . . .'

'But?'

'Well, only this afternoon, before all this happened, I was wondering . . . is that all there is? To love, I mean.'

The eyes of the goddess narrowed in a puzzled frown. 'You don't think it's enough?'

Paris frowned. 'It's not that.'

'Then what? I don't understand.'

He tried to gather his thoughts. 'I know what you mean. In fact, I've never been happier than since Oenone and I found each other. It's just that sometimes I feel . . .'

'Yes?'

He glanced up at her – 'that there might be more?' – then away again.

'More?'

Amazed by his own presumption, Paris decided to hold the goddess's searching gaze as he said, very quietly, 'Yes.'

With a shrug of her smooth shoulders Aphrodite gave a little, understanding laugh. 'Well, yes, there is, of course. There's a great deal more. But you seemed so happy as you are. I didn't think you'd want to know about it.'

'Tell me anyway.'

She sat back as if in mild surprise, puckering her lips. 'Well, it's not really the kind of thing you can *tell* anyone. It has to happen to you. You have to give yourself to it – you have to let yourself be taken.' She thought for a moment. 'It's like trusting yourself to the strength of the sea . . . and sometimes it's like giving yourself to a fire even.'

'A fire?'

'Oh yes. A fire so clear and intense that it burns away everything except the pure delight of its own passion. And once that happens then everything else changes. It all begins to make sense . . .' The goddess smiled and shook her head at the inadequacy of mere words. 'I thought you'd know rather more about it than you appear to do.'

The words had been added gently enough but they left him ruffled. He was on the point of claiming more knowledge than he had so far revealed but when he looked up into her comprehending smile he saw that such bluster would be immediately transparent. So he glanced away.

She said, 'So tell me more about these feelings you've been having.'

Suddenly aware how small those feelings seemed by contrast with the scale on which the goddess felt and thought, he flushed. 'They're hard to explain.' But his imagination seized on what she had said a moment earlier, and his heart jumped with a simultaneous sense of admission and betrayal as he added, 'It's as though once an experience starts to be familiar, it wants to change . . . to become something larger and more powerful. Stranger even.'

He looked for understanding in her eyes and found it there. She said, 'That's the unlived life inside you wanting to come out. You should listen to it.'

'I have been listening. I suppose that's why I'm here. In fact, I'm beginning to wonder whether . . .'

'Yes?'

He hesitated. Oenone's loving smile flashed before his eyes and vanished in the bright aura of Aphrodite's presence. 'What you were just talking about – do you think it could ever happen to me?'

'I'd like to think so, although . . .' She hesitated, pushed back a stray ringlet of hair, smiled, shook her head, glanced away.

'Go on.'

Aphrodite turned her searching eyes back to him. 'Are you sure you want me to?'

'Yes.' Swallowing again, he held her gaze. 'I'm quite sure.'

The goddess appeared to give the matter further thought. 'These things are always mysterious, you know. It's the between-ness, you see. It can't just happen with anyone. There has to be a meeting of souls. Souls that recognize each other. And when they do, there's a sudden astonishing freedom of both the feelings and the senses there that . . . well, that they just can't find with anybody else. It's the most tremendous experience of all, and it doesn't happen for everyone.' She tilted another rueful smile at him. 'So I'm afraid it's not only up to you.'

Paris nodded, and looked away.

'Oh I'm sorry,' she said. 'I shouldn't have said anything.'

'Yes you should. I needed to know about it.'

Quietly she said, 'But it hasn't happened with Oenone, has it?' And sighed when, frowning, he shook his head.

'Perhaps . . .' he began.

His throat felt parched as a summer gulch. He tried again.

'Perhaps she's not the right person. For me, I mean.' Looking up, he added quickly, 'Or me for her, of course.'

'Well, only you can know that for yourself. But . . .' She turned her gentle gaze on him again. 'You don't have a great deal of experience, do you? It must be hard for you to tell.'

A little humiliated by her sympathy, Paris watched as she glanced away, turned back towards him, opened her mouth to speak, and then appeared to change her mind.

'What were you going to say?' he pressed.

'I was just wondering whether . . . No, I really shouldn't interfere.'

'It's not interfering. I'd really like to hear what you have to say.'

'It's just that one of the advantages of being a goddess—' she smiled up at him '—is that we can see deeper into time than mortals can, and sometimes we're painfully aware of possibilities that you just don't seem to see.'

'You're thinking of me?'

As if making a difficult decision, Aphrodite drew in her breath. 'The thing is, Oenone is quite the sweetest creature in these mountains, but there are women in the world beside whom she's as simple and brown as one of my sparrows, and . . . Well, I don't think you've quite woken up yet to just how attractive you are, and how much power you might have over women – if only you gave yourself the chance to meet more of them.'

After a moment he said, 'You think there might be someone else for me?'

'I'm sure of it.'

'Do you know who?'

Aphrodite nodded.

'Are you going to tell me?'

The thought appeared to make her uncomfortable. 'I shouldn't really.'

Paris's eyes strayed towards the golden apple on the grass beside him.

'Oh no,' she exclaimed, holding up her hands. 'I'm not trying to bribe you. It's not like that. Now you've made *me* feel bad. Look, her name's Helen. She lives in Sparta.'

'Is that near Troy?'

'It's a kingdom in Argos.'

He frowned. 'I haven't heard of Argos either.'

'Argos is a country three hundred miles away. Across the sea.'

His face fell in disappointment. 'Then she couldn't possibly know about me.'

'Not yet. No.'

'And she's a foreigner.'

Aphrodite smiled. 'In love there are no foreigners.'

'But three hundred miles! And I've never been to sea.'

'So you don't want to know any more about her?'

'I didn't say that.'

There was another silence.

'Helen,' he said. 'It's a beautiful name.'

'It suits her. She's the most beautiful woman in the world.'

His eyes widened at that. 'Tell me more.'

'Wouldn't you rather see her? Yes? Then come and look into my eyes.'

Scarcely breathing, Paris moved until he was only a few inches away from the naked body of the goddess. She lifted her hands and cupped his cheeks. He trembled at the delicate pressure of her fingertips. Every pore of his body seemed to be taking in her fragrance as he lifted his eyes to meet hers.

And he was gone, vanished to himself, softly drowning in a sea-green iris of light, deeper than he would have thought his heart could take him, until he felt he was gazing upwards through blue fathoms at the dazzling surface beyond. Except that now he was suddenly looking downwards into the human face of a woman who gazed back up at him through the same compelling light – a woman to whom he was making love with a tenderness and ardour such as he had never known. Hers was a face more luminous with passion and beauty than any he had ever seen before. It was as though, for those few timeless seconds, he was making love to the goddess herself, and even as the vision blurred he was feeling that, if it ever ended, his heart might die from yearning.

Then he was back on the mountain and the face smiling gently across at him was the face of Aphrodite.

'Helen,' she said simply.

Paris lowered his back against the grass and lay with his eyes closed, trying to hold on to the dream, savouring the exquisite pain of its loss. And yet, so intense was the memory, that he was filled with a fanatical conviction that, once having looked on that face, he could never forget it. Those eyes would be present to him each time he closed his own. There seemed no possibility that he would ever again dream any other dream than this.

Minutes passed. He was lost to the mountain, lost even to the presence of the goddess, and absolutely still – yet moving inwardly with a velocity that astonished him. Everything had changed. He could feel the blood pulsing through his veins. He could feel his heart blazing inside him. From this moment onwards, any instant of time less incandescent with life than this would not be life at all.

Without opening his eyes he said, 'I have to meet her. I have to make her mine.'

The goddess whispered, 'There's something else you should know.'

Eagerly he said, 'Yes?'

'Helen already has a husband.'

Paris sat up in shock.

Calmly she appraised his incredulous face. 'I know what you're thinking, and it's a problem, yes, but there are all kinds of things you don't understand yet.'

Outrage and betrayal darkened his eyes. Better never to have seen that face than to have looked on its beauty and have it snatched away like this.

'I understand well enough that she's already married, that she lives three hundred miles away in a place I've never heard of – and I suppose her husband's the King of Argos, right?'

'The King of Sparta actually.'

'So what chance have I got of winning her?'

'Without help,' she said quietly, 'probably none.'

But he was back inside the dream again. That face remained intimately alive inside him and indelibly present. It felt as inalienable as his soul. And the whole meaning of his life depended on it now. Surely it was unthinkable that a man should be gifted with such a vision unless it was possible to make it real?

Then he began to understand.

Clearing his throat, he said, 'What if you were to help me?'

Aphrodite pursed her lips in thought. 'It would be difficult.' She released a pensive sigh. 'And it might cause all kinds of trouble.'

'Suppose I gave you the apple in return?'

The goddess made a small offended grimace.

'It's rightly yours anyway,' he pressed.

'You're not just saying that because . . . ?'

'No, of course not. I wouldn't dream . . .'

She had glanced away. Now she looked back, unsmiling. 'Well, it could be done I suppose. But this is serious you understand? The matter of the heart is always serious – even when it looks like a game.' Her voice transfixed him.

'You would have to be sure that you really wanted her – whatever the cost.'

She allowed a moment for the thought to sink in. Then she said, 'Do you?'

He looked back into the solemn beauty of Aphrodite's face, and saw that the moment of choice had come. He glanced at the golden apple gleaming on the grass and saw that it was just as she had said – he had looked at Helen and everything had altered round him. Whatever else, he would never again be content to drive a dozy herd of cattle out to pasture and moon among the asphodels. He could no longer imagine what he would do with his life if he was denied the fulfilment of a desire that was now becoming an obsession.

Paris thought of everything he had been promised by the other goddesses. Hera would make him a great king, yes, but great kings had great troubles, and he was already a High King's son. Why should he want more wealth than that princely state would bring him? Athena had promised him wisdom and self-knowledge, but if he knew that the plain truth was that he wanted Helen, then wasn't that already self-knowledge enough? As for wisdom, surely that was as much a matter of the beating heart as of the intellect, and the vision of Helen had filled his heart with a fierce longing for the wilder reaches of love.

All the logic of the case pointed one way. Yet he looked up into the face of Aphrodite again and knew that none of that logic mattered to him in the least, for the truth lay far beyond logic in the hopeless, unrequited, irretrievable place from where, like a man passing sentence on himself, he said, 'I don't think I could live without her now.'

'Very well,' Aphrodite smiled. 'Give me the apple and I'll see what I can do.'

Priam's Son

Despite their earlier promise, Hera and Athena left the scene of
their joint humiliation united in hostility both to Paris and to
Troy. Happily, Paris was quite unaware of this, and Aphrodite was
too delighted by her triumph to be troubled by her divine sisters'
ill will. As a goddess never much concerned with moral consequence, she too had her powers. She would do what she could
for the city – though it was hard to see how to preserve Troy
from ruin while at the same time keeping her pledge to Paris.
But to the latter task she was now utterly committed, and if a
city had to burn as the price of passion, so be it.

Meanwhile, dazed with wonder and in the grip of obsession,
Paris cared only that the loveliest of goddesses had promised to
give him the most beautiful of women. He would not rest now
until this destiny was fulfilled.

Night had fallen by the time he came down from the mountain.

Knowing that Oenone was puzzled by his distant manner,
Paris retired without saying anything either to her or to his
foster-parents about what had happened on Mount Ida. For
much of the night he lay awake thinking about Helen and
wondering how best to assert his true identity. Yet the gloom of
his rough bothy was so far removed from the visionary presence

of the goddess on the high mountainside that there were times when he found it hard to believe that the events of the afternoon had been anything more than a marvellous dream. A dream from which he had woken into a world grown small around him.

The next day, as always happened at that season, servants of King Priam came out of Troy to select from the herd a bull to be offered as prize in the funeral games that were held each year in memory of the king's lost son. Paris had often resented losing some of his finest breeding stock this way. Now he began to understand how his own fate had always been deeply bound up with that of the chosen beast.

Standing beside Agelaus, he watched the men from the city conferring over the bulls where they panted in the noon glare of the paddock. He already knew which one they would choose.

As he expected the leader of the party, a wall-eyed man with a curled beard shaped like a sickle, eventually nodded at him and said, 'Hobble me that white brute over there.' He was pointing to the bull that Paris had once garlanded for Oenone.

In previous years Paris would simply have jumped the rail and done as he was bidden. This time he studied the man steadily and said, 'Would you not rather take the skewbald bull beneath the oak? The eating will be as good and he will give you a deal less trouble on the road back to the city.'

The man turned his squint on Agelaus. 'The King commands only the best. He will take the white.'

'Then let the king hobble it himself,' said Paris, and walked away, with the hobbling-rope slung across his bare shoulder. Behind him he heard his foster-father stammering out bewildered words of apology. Then he saw Oenone watching from a plane-tree's shade. Involuntarily his eyes flinched away from her bewildered glance. He heard the bearded man saying that he had not come here to endure a yokel's insolence. Nor did he have all day to waste. Then he was ordering Agelaus to bring the bull out himself. When the old man began to climb the fence, Paris turned quickly on his heel, shouting to his father that the bull was too fast for him and not to be trusted.

'I was hobbling bulls before you were born, boy,' Agelaus growled, and leapt down into the paddock. 'Give me your rope.' One of the younger bulls let out a low, disgruntled bellow. The herd shifted nervously in the packed arena. Dust rose from their hooves. Already heavy with the smell of dung, the heat seemed to shimmer where dust drifted between the old man and his son.

Paris used his free hand to vault the fence. 'You're no longer as quick on your feet as you were. He'll gore you where you stand.'

Agelaus glared at him. 'Do you mean to insult me also?'

'No, father, but the truth is the truth. The bull is mine. He knows me. Leave him to me.'

'Are you forgetting that this whole herd belongs to King Priam?' said the bearded man, haughty and impatient. Paris stared at him for a moment, yielding nothing in pride or dignity, but it was to his foster-father that he said, 'Does King Priam always take such care to hold on to his own?' Then without waiting for an answer, he took the rope from his shoulder and advanced across the paddock to where, blinking among flies, with a tonnage of muscle twitching under its pelt, the chosen bull scraped a fore-hoof at the dust.

An hour later, as they watched the king's servants cart the teth- ered beast away, Agelaus said to his foster-son, 'Are you going to explain yourself?'

Paris said quietly, 'I mean to follow the bull to the king this year.'

'Has some demon got into you today?' the old man demanded. 'Is there not enough to do here among the bulls that you must go chasing trouble in Troy? Take a dip in the river, boy. Cool your head.' He was about to walk away, when Paris said, 'Tell me again about the time of my birth.'

Agelaus stopped in his tracks. He turned, frowning, and was slow to reply. 'You know the story well enough.'

'Tell me again.'

'It is as I said. I found you lying in the woods. A she-bear had suckled you there. I brought you home in my wallet and raised you as my own.'

Amazed that he had never thought to ask the question before, Paris said, 'Yet who among the Dardanians would dream of leaving a child alone to die?' When Agelaus glanced away, he spoke more firmly. 'Do you swear to me that you know nothing else?'

The old herdsman studied Paris gravely now. This was the first time the youth had directly challenged him, but he had always known that the question must come, and he was too honest a man to lie to the foster-son he loved. Drawing in his breath, he told Paris of the night when the king's horseman had come to the house, ordering him to kill the child, and how his heart had refused to obey. 'So instead of becoming your murderer, I became your father. Have you not been happy with us?' he demanded gruffly. 'What better life could you have wished for?'

'None,' Paris answered, 'except the life to which I was born.'

'And what if that life was cursed?'

'Whatever the case, at least that life would be my own.'

Paris saw the hurt in the old man's eyes. Immediately he regretted his own curt manner. 'You have always been a good father to me,' he said more gently, 'and I love you for it with all my heart. But a god has told me who my true father is, and there is a fate that comes with such knowledge.'

Remembering all the years during which he had watched the boy grow, Agelaus looked up into the noble features of the young stranger who stood before him now. 'Then who am I to argue with a god?' Biting his lip, he began to walk away, leaving the youth standing alone. But he had gone only a few yards when he stopped and stared down at the ground, shaking his grizzled head. Then he turned to look back at his disconsolate son. 'If fate requires it, go to Troy,' he said. 'Present yourself before the king.

Tell him that Agelaus gave you to the gods on Mount Ida and that the gods gave you back to me. Tell him that if there is fault in this, it is none of mine.' Then he turned again and walked away.

As Paris watched him go, he saw Oenone waiting for him in the plane tree's shade. The nymph had listened to the exchange with the same anxious foreboding that had kept her awake throughout the night, and she already knew that nothing she could say would deter Paris from his purpose. Feeling grief gather inside her now, she watched him approach across the glade.

Oenone listened in silence as he told her how a vision of Hera had come to him on Mount Ida and informed him of his true estate. Clenching her breath, she nodded when Paris asked if she understood why he must seek out the fate to which he was born. But when he promised that he would never forget the love that was between them, it was as though a louder noise was roaring inside her head. And when Paris lowered his mouth to kiss her, Oenone pulled back a little to fix his eyes with her own.

'I have the gift of prophecy from my father,' she whispered. 'I know that if I begged you to stay, you would still go out into the world, and I know that the world will do you harm. But my father gave me the gift of healing too.' She gazed up at him. 'One day you will take a wound that only I can heal. Come back to me then.' She reached up to kiss him swiftly on the mouth, then pulled free of his embrace and – as she had done once before, on the day that first made them lovers – Oenone ran from him into the shelter of the trees.

The drums were beating as he approached the city. The sound carried on the wind that swept over the plain of Troy, across the sheen of the rivers and through the swaying fields of wheat. From the distance he could see a large crowd gathered around the walls, shouting and cheering as they urged on the chariots racing there. He had often looked down from the mountains on the walls of Troy, but he had never seen them shine like this. Nor, he saw as he came closer, had he ever dreamed how massive those stones were, or how dauntingly high they stood. And he had never seen so many people before either – charioteers checking their axles and harness, athletes oiling their limbs, horse-breakers and farriers debating the merits of their mounts, acrobats and fire-eaters, snake-charmers, musicians and dancing girls, mountebanks and merchants, all looking to lighten the purses of the crowd, while among them beggars made a show of their sores and drunkards lolled among the women or snored beneath the makeshift stalls. The air smelled of spiced wine and charring meat, and the skin of his cheeks smarted at the sharp sting of dust blowing everywhere on the wind.

No one took much notice of a farm-boy come down from the hills to mingle with the crowd and the youth was wondering how he would ever make his presence felt among this multitude when he heard a voice calling for more contenders in a bare-knuckle boxing championship. Approaching the ring of people, Paris recognized the young man at its centre as someone he had seen once before at the festival in Lyrnessus near the mountains. It was Aeneas, son of Anchises the King of the Dardanians, and though Paris had never spoken to the prince, he felt strengthened by the sight of a familiar face.

For a time he stood by the ring of sand, watching as one fighter after another got knocked down by a muscular, sandy-haired youth in a scarlet kilt who, for all the weight of brawn he carried, danced nimbly on his feet and dealt out blackened eyes and bloody noses with contemptuous skill. Paris had no such talent with his fists, but he had learned to dodge and weave among the bulls, and to trust his own lithe sinews. Also he reckoned he had a longer reach than the burly fellow who now calmly oiled his knuckles while his last opponent spat out a broken tooth. A party of girls were chanting out the winner's name. Deiphobus favoured them with a haughty smile as the umpire shouted, 'The King's son wins again. Does anyone else want to chance his arm?'

The tallest of the young women was already calling, 'Give him the crown, Aeneas,' when Paris stepped out of the crowd as if pushed by the unseen hand of a god. Somewhere he could hear the doleful bellow of his bull.

Aeneas grinned at him. 'Excellent, another challenger! And a Dardanian by the look of him. One of my own. But I shall strive to remain impartial.'

Paris had his eyes fixed on the muscular figure of Deiphobus where he stood laughing with the young women as he towelled himself. 'That is King Priam's son?' he asked, looking for something familiar in the youth's face and bearing.

'Deiphobus, yes.' Aeneas smiled. 'Is this your first time down from the hills?'

When Paris nodded one of the girls called out, 'Be gentle with the bull-boy, Deiphobus. It would be a shame to break that pretty nose.' A smaller, darker girl stood beside her, frowning at Paris with an air of puzzled hostility that he found slightly unnerving. But Deiphobus was ready to fight again. He stepped into the ring to loud applause from the crowd, measuring this fresh opponent with confident eyes. Then Paris was stripped to his breech-clout and standing across from him at the scratch-mark in the sand.

For a time Deiphobus sparred around him, flashing his fists in such swift jabs and feints that only Paris's agile movements prevented him from taking more than glancing blows. Growing impatient with the way this novice ducked and swerved, Deiphobus engaged him with concentrated aggression. More by luck than skill, Paris contrived to stay on his feet, and though his own blows hit only air, he was fresher than the other man and kept his wits about him. He had observed in the earlier fights how Deiphobus had a trick of pretending to drop his guard, then feinting to the left as he drove his right fist to the midriff, only to cut upwards with a rapid left to the head. He was waiting for that moment when it came. Deiphobus found his right thrust to the body parried by such a firm block that his own weight unbalanced him. Then his ears were ringing as Paris threw a stiff jab at his head. Paris closed quickly, pummelling at his opponent's body, and when he broke free of the clinch, he used his longer reach to crash a fist into his nose. Blood splashed. Deiphobus reeled, blinking for a few seconds. When Paris slammed him with another body-blow, his legs sagged under him and he was on his knees in the sand.

Amid the startled silence of the crowd, Paris leaned forward, offering a hand to pull him up. 'You fight well, brother,' he panted.

Scowling at what he took for a presumptuous insult, Deiphobus wiped the blood from his face, then brushed the proffered hand aside and staggered into the crowd. All the young women followed him except for the dark-eyed girl who stood for a moment, frowning at Paris as though she had seen him elsewhere and was still trying to place his face. But when he smiled at her she turned on her heel, darkening her frown, and hurried after the others.

'You fought well yourself,' said Aeneas. 'My cousin won't thank you for robbing him of this wreath.' Then he studied Paris more carefully. 'Weren't you at the fair in Lyrnessus last year? Didn't a bull of yours take first prize?' And when Paris nodded, his smile broadened. 'I thought so. It must have been the bulls who taught you to move as nimbly as that.'

'Deiphobus has more skill with his hands,' Paris said.

Aeneas warmed to the kind of openness that was commoner among the Dardanians than here in Troy. 'But you were a lot faster on your feet. Why not enter the footraces, friend? You might win yourself another crown.'

Three hours later Paris was summoned before the king where he sat among his courtiers in his gorgeously painted throne-room.

The rest of that afternoon had been a bright blur of heat and pace and building excitement. During the course of it, he had fallen foul of two more of Priam's sons by beating Antiphus in the dash and outstripping the people's favourite, Hector, in the cross-country race around the city walls. Now, with his blood running fast and high, he stood holding his three wreaths, tired and proud, and looking for the first time at the man who was his father.

'My nephew Aeneas tells me that you keep watch over my bulls in our Dardanian lands.' Priam stroked his perfumed beard as he gave Paris the distracted smile of a man who had carried the burdens of kingship for more than twenty years. Though he was in his middle-forties, Priam looked older. His thinning hair glistened towards silver and his gaunt face was creased with many lines. Yet he sat on his gilded throne with the air of one long familiar with its power as well as its cares, and when his eyes settled on Paris they left him more in awe at the king than eager to know more about his father. Only minutes earlier Priam had been given the news that a coastal town belonging to one of his allies had been pillaged and burned by yet another Argive raid. So as he fondled the ears of the boar-hound lying at his feet, the mind of the High King of Troy was still preoccupied with other things than a bull-boy come down from the hills to take the prizes at the games.

'It's not often a man wins a triple crown.' He gave a faint smile. 'Perhaps my sons would do well to pass more time in the mountain air?'

Holding his gaze, Paris answered, 'Perhaps they were lucky to have a father who did not expose them to the mountain air when they were born.'

'Was that your fate, boy?' Priam arched his brows. 'Well, I pity you for it. But it doesn't seem to have done you much harm. The gods must favour you. They have spared your life, given you a handsome enough face and the strength to make you winner of the games.' Priam glanced away, smiling at his counsellor Antenor. 'What more can a child of the mountain ask?'

'Nothing more,' Paris answered quietly, 'except his rightful heritage.'

Surprised how firm the voice, Priam looked sharply back at him. 'Which is?'

'To be acknowledged as your son.'

The King, his sons and the assembled courtiers were too aston-ished by the demand even to gasp. Before anyone could move or speak, Paris pressed on. 'I understand that these games are held in honour of the child you lost. Well, the child you lost has just won them. Those I have beaten are my brothers. I have come here to stake my life on the truth of this claim.'

At that moment the dark-haired girl who had been among the young women watching the boxing-match pushed her way forward between Hector and Antiphus. She had been staring at Paris ever since he had come into the hall and as soon as he had spoken, a familiar, tense pressure that was building inside her head broke like the release of lightning in a storm. 'Now I see you,' she said. 'You are the sacrifice that was not accepted.' She stood swaying on the balls of her feet. 'You are the brand that burns while my mother sleeps. There is the smell of smoke about you. I cannot breathe for it.' She turned to look at her father, white-faced. 'He will bring destruction on this city.'

'Be silent, Cassandra.' Impatiently, Priam signalled for some of the women of the palace to take the girl away, but Cassandra sought to resist them. 'He belongs to death,' she cried. 'He must be given back.'

Making the sign against the evil eye, Paris watched in dismay as the girl was hurried away out of the hall, but when he looked back at the people round him, they seemed less alarmed than embarrassed. Hector quickly stepped forward to cover that embar-rassment. 'It looks as though the winner's wreath has gone to this bull-boy's head,' he laughed. 'He seems to have mistaken it for a royal crown.'

Some of the courtiers joined in the laughter, but Deiphobus, whose nose had been broken in the fight, was not amused. 'He has the air of a troublemaker. No one comes before the king and speaks as he has done. Who knows who he is, or what he has in mind?'

Antiphus said, 'Perhaps Cassandra is right for once? It might be as well to kill him anyway.'

Paris stiffened as a hostile murmur of assent gathered around him, but Aeneas stepped forward at his side. 'I think your sons are still nursing their bruises, Lord,' he suggested calmly. 'This youth beat them fairly in the games. I will attest to that. As to his other claims, only an honest man or a fool would stand before the High King and speak as he did. Might it not be as well to hear what he has to say?'

Priam considered a moment. Then he leaned forward to look more closely at the young man who stood before him, wary-eyed but unflinching. 'It's common knowledge that the gods once demanded a son of me. But that child was not given to the mountain.'

'Nevertheless your herdsman Agelaus left me there.'

'Yet you stand before me now.'

'A she-bear might have killed me but she suckled me instead.' Paris heard the sound of scoffing from where the king's sons stood, but his eyes were fixed on his father's eyes, where he discerned a glint of conflict between doubt and hope. He pressed on. 'When Agelaus found me unharmed, he lacked the heart to kill me – as did the horseman who had brought me from this city.'

Priam narrowed his eyes, unwilling to believe what he heard yet troubled by the pride and dignity with which this bull-boy withstood his gaze. He looked uncertainly to his counsellor, Antenor.

'Anyone might come before the king with such a story,' Antenor said. 'What proof do you have?' But before Paris could answer, a woman's voice rang from the open door of the throne-room. 'Let me see this youth.' Worn from much childbearing, and older than her years, Queen Hecuba walked through the parted crowd of courtiers with her hands clasped at her chest. She stopped a yard away from Paris and studied the young man with a gaze of such penetrating gravity that it would have shaken his soul had he not been given the goddesses' warranty for the truth of his claim. 'You have the long bones and the tilted eyes of a royal

Trojan, but so do many of my husband's by-blows. What proof do you have that you are the child of my loins?'

'Surely a mother should know her own son,' Paris answered quietly.

'Twenty years have passed since that child was torn from my arms. But its image is branded on my mind. There was a mark from the birth. It lay across my baby's neck. I remember thinking that it was as though he had been bitten by passion there.' The Queen's eyes gazed fiercely up at Paris. 'Do you have such a mark? Be sure you will die if you do not.' She beckoned Paris closer and reached up to lift the locks of wheat-coloured hair that fell across his left ear to his jaw-line. Paris tilted his head at his mother's touch. He heard the sharp catch of breath as she saw the mark's faint blush still blemishing his skin. Quickly she caught a hand to her mouth. A moment later her soft brow was pressed to his chest and he could feel her body shaking.

Priam rose from his throne. His queen glanced towards him, tears streaming down her cheeks. 'He carries the mark,' she said. 'This is our son.'

Over the long years of his reign, King Priam had coped with many shocks and surprises but none had shaken him like this. He stood, staring the impossible in the face, wanting to believe, yet not trusting that the same fate that had robbed him of a son could now so capriciously return him. 'You are sure?' he demanded hoarsely. 'It is not just your wish that speaks?'

'He has the mark, I tell you,' Hecuba cried. 'Come, embrace your son.'

But it was hard for Priam to look at the child whose life he had condemned. He closed his eyes and reached out a hand to support his weight against the throne. Then he was whispering to himself, 'The ways of the gods are not the ways of men, and what comes to pass is not always what was expected.'

With the dazed air of a man waking from a dream, King Priam opened his eyes and looked at the young champion holding his wreaths across from him. Then he raised himself to his full height, and opened his hands as though to catch invisible blessings falling from the sky. 'Let the ways of the gods be praised,' he said, and advanced to fold Paris in his arms.

With the astonished court looking on, King Priam held his lost son for a long time before he turned and said, 'My sons and daughters, come and embrace your lost brother. You must learn to love him as your mother and I already do.' Hector and the others stared uncertainly. The hall was loud with murmuring around them as, one by one, in obedience to their father's urging, the many brothers and sisters of Paris came to greet him.

Confident of his father's love, Hector, the oldest and noblest, stepped forward first to welcome his new-found brother warmly enough, but the feelings of the others were mixed and not always well concealed. Deiphobus replied with no more than a curt nod when Paris asked forgiveness for breaking his nose. Antiphus merely stared at him in scornful disbelief, and when Cassandra was brought back into the hall, she recoiled from Paris's anxious embrace as though her skin was scorching under his touch.

Only with his open-hearted cousin Aeneas did Paris feel completely at ease. It was he who guided the awe-struck youth through the labyrinth of painted apartments to a spacious bath-house, where slaves were summoned to bathe and massage him with perfumed oils, and dress his unruly hair. King Priam had commanded that the whole city should feast that night and Aeneas had undertaken to make sure that Paris would appear at the banquet garbed like a prince of Troy. But Paris had been troubled by the ungracious way in which most of his brothers and sisters had received him, and as he soaked in the bath, he shared his anxieties with Aeneas.

'It must be hard for them,' Aeneas answered. 'After all, only Hector is senior to you in birth, and it's obvious that you have a special place in the hearts of your parents. How could it be otherwise? It's bound to take time for the others to come round. But they have no real choice. Sooner or later they will.'

'You think that's true of Cassandra?'

'Ah! Cassandra is different. Cassandra is . . .' Aeneas hesitated.

'There's something wrong with her?'

'It's a strange story. She says that Apollo came to her one night while she slept in his temple at Thymbra. She says that he promised to give her the gift of prophecy if she would let him make love to her, and that when she withheld herself, the god grabbed her by the head and spat into her mouth so that no one would believe her prophecies.' Aeneas looked at his friend and shrugged.

'Do you believe her?' Paris asked.

'Do you believe what she said about you?'

'Of course not.'

Aeneas smiled. 'Neither does anyone else. It's all very sad. Cassandra is the most beautiful of your parents' daughters and she drives them to despair. But you mustn't let her gloomy nonsense bother you. Now come on. You're smelling more like a prince than a bull-boy now. It's time we found you some clothes to match.'

Aeneas helped Paris to choose among the selection of finely woven tunics and mantles that the butlers brought for his approval, and he advised him on a discreet choice from the jewellery casket, so that it was a true figure of a prince whose arrival was applauded when he joined the banquet that night. Paris was brought to a seat of honour between his parents. His father poured a grateful libation to the gods, and then asked the whole company to join him in drinking to the long life and good fortune of his handsome son.

Flattered, worried by his lack of social graces, and frankly bewildered by this abrupt alteration in his circumstances, Paris was soon aware that, wherever his own eyes turned, he was the object of curious attention. His heart was already dizzy with wave after wave of unfamiliar emotion. Soon his head was swimming like the dolphins and sea-horses painted on the walls around him.

During a pause in the feasting, Hector raised a drinking cup to toast him and called across the table, 'Andromache tells me you're already causing such a stir among the palace maidens that there's some risk they may come to blows if we don't quickly find a wife for you.'

Smiling with embarrassment, Paris acknowledged the jest. 'I thank your good lady, but tell her that I mean to sacrifice at the altar of Aphrodite every morning until the goddess brings me the one for whom my heart is fated.'

He did not miss the amused exchange of glances round him, and they left him discomfited. He saw that he would have to learn to be less open among these clever, cultivated men and the painted women in their costly garments who left him feeling boyish and awkward. With a pang of regret, he thought about Oenone and the simple mountain life they had lived together. His heart quailed for a moment. But then his mother Hecuba was leaning towards him. 'My son considers himself a servant of Aphrodite?'

'I do, madam.'

Priam looked up from where he had been lost in thought and smiled across at Paris. 'It seems that they made a Dardanian of you out there on the mountains. The Golden One is greatly revered by Anchises and his people.'

Hector said, 'Then it's small wonder that you and Aeneas should be friends. I understand that in Lyrnessus they say that Aphrodite is his mother.' He turned, smiling archly, to Aeneas. 'Isn't that so, son of Anchises?'

Well used to the jibe, Aeneas raised his cup to him, and smiled at the astonishment on his friend's face, for though Aphrodite had not been far from Paris's mind in the past few hours, he had never for a moment thought of her as a mother. 'I was sired in Aphrodite's temple,' Aeneas explained. 'My mother was her priestess.'

'But the story is more colourful,' said Priam. 'Have you not heard it, Paris – how my cousin Anchises was blinded by the goddess for bragging of her love for him? Where is my bard? Let us have the song.'

The bard, who had been chattering among the ladies of the

court, reached for his lyre and began to play. As the chords thrilled across the air of the hall, the feasters fell silent. The bard lifted his voice and began to sing of how Zeus had once decided to humble Aphrodite by making her fall in love with a mere mortal. He made the heart of the goddess burn with such ardour for the young Anchises that she appeared before him in a stable disguised as a Phrygian princess and wearing a robe more brilliant than flames of fire. Aphrodite gave herself to him in a night of tremendous passion, but Anchises shook with terror when he woke in the dawn light to find that it wasn't a naked woman he held in his arms but an immortal goddess. Aphrodite told him that he need fear nothing so long as he preserved the secret of their love, but his heart was so full with the knowledge that he was bursting to make it known. When he did so, he was blinded by a thunderbolt.

Paris had heard neither the song nor the story before. It was more courtly and sophisticated than the country songs he used to sing with his friends in the mountains, and there was a wry edge to the words that left him wondering whether both Aphrodite and Anchises were being mocked by the bard. But Aeneas seemed to take it all in good part, so Paris relaxed and joined in the applause when the lay was ended.

Hecuba placed a mottled hand across his own. 'Golden Aphrodite can be a gentle goddess,' she said, 'but she is also ruthless. Perhaps you are a child of passion after all, but take care that her service does not consume you.'

'Your mother speaks wisely,' Priam nodded. 'It's best that a man tries to honour all the gods – though there are times when it seems they have little care for us.'

Looking earnestly back at his parents, Paris saw how, even in this hour of celebration, difficult questions of state still troubled his father's mind. He felt suddenly glad that he had refused Hera's offer of a kingly throne. And when he studied his mother he could see the strength of Hera in her matronly grace, and he could hear something of Athena's wisdom in her words. But the memory of Aphrodite's fragrance assailed his senses in the heady scent of lilies from the banquet table, in the way a serving-girl casually brushed against him as she filled his goblet with wine, and in the vivid eyes that reached out to him across the room, brightened a moment, and swiftly darted away. For better or worse, he belonged entirely to the Golden One now.

'I thank you both for your care,' he answered, smiling, 'but my vow was made before I came and I trust to Aphrodite's divine protection.' He took a deep draught from the cup of spiced wine he had raised. 'Believe me, if it is my fate to be consumed by beauty, I shall go to meet it with an eager heart.'

A Horse for Poseidon

A man must make his choices but to a god almost all things are possible. Thus when amorous Zeus takes a fancy to a woman he has many means of ensuring his desire is gratified. Once, having set eyes on Europa while she sported on the shore, he took the form of a bull and behaved so tamely before her that she dared to mount his massive back. A moment later the girl was carried through the breakers, out across the open sea to Crete, where the god took pleasure in planting the seed of Minos in her loins. Again, when Zeus came across the moon-maiden Danae shut inside a brazen tower where she had been imprisoned by her father, the god dissolved into a shower of gold, and through his incandescent act of lust the hero Perseus was conceived.

But the most momentous of his changes happened one fateful day when the Sky-Father saw the wife of Tyndareus, King of Sparta, bathing naked and alone in the river Eurotas. Inflamed by passion, he plumed his mighty form into a swan and bore down on her with his strong neck and white wings. Lacking strength or time to resist the god's sudden swoop, Leda was taken, gasping, into his embrace. When he was done, and his need satisfied, Zeus flew away, leaving her pregnant with the deaths of thousands of men, for it was Helen who was sired by this rape.

So graceful and delicate was the blush of beauty on the child that men said she had truly been hatched from the egg of a divine swan. But Leda had lain with her husband earlier that night, so when Helen was born, Tyndareus chose to raise her as his own child at the Spartan court. Not long afterwards, drawn by the god who had taken possession both of her body and her soul, Leda left Sparta and travelled northwards to the oak forest of Dodona where she gave herself in an ascetic life of prophetic service to Zeus.

Meanwhile, as the child grew, so did the rumour of her beauty until men everywhere began dreaming that one day Helen might be theirs. But Tyndareus had another, older daughter, one who found it hard to endure the way that Helen's poise and grace, those sea-green eyes and the long black fall of hair, consumed all the attention in a room the moment she entered it. Her name was Clytaemnestra, and though she was considered pretty in her own way, she had to learn from an early age that she must live in the shadow cast by the radiance of her younger sister's face. And what came hardest was the knowledge that even her father was infatuated by Helen's beauty, so there was little sisterly affection between the two girls.

Helen's delight was to be out in the sunlight, swimming in the Eurotas, or testing her slender body as an athlete among the other young men and women of Sparta. Above all things she loved to venture into lonely stretches of wilderness, discovering hidden springs or hunting with her bow in the wooded mountains that ringed the Laconian plain. Perhaps to console herself for the early loss of her mother, she developed a strong affinity for animals, and on one occasion – she was only eight years old at the time – she caused a great consternation among the huntsmen when they found her on a craggy outcrop, fondling the cubs of a mountain lion while their mother licked her huge paws on a sunlit rock nearby. Soon afterwards she became a devotee of the Virgin Artemis and could often be found singing hymns to the goddess in some wild shrine or leading the maidens of Sparta in her dance.

By contrast, Clytaemnestra rarely left the grounds of the palace, and tried to win her father's attention by taking an interest in the politics of his kingdom and his negotiations with ambassadors from other lands. When Tyndareus made it clear that her opinions were unwelcome, she withdrew into a studious world of her own where she developed a sharp, disputatious intellect, arguing over the interpretation of oracles with the priests, evolving a sharp-eyed pragmatic philosophy of her own, and dreaming of a time when a man of her choice would look her way rather than nursing fantasies of Helen.

One young man had already shown such a preference, but he was a big, coarse-grained, moody fellow of no great intelligence and not to her taste. He was one of two brothers who had fled to Sparta after their father Atreus was killed in the struggle for control of Mycenae, and the cast of his mind had been darkened by the bloody events he had survived. As was usually the case, the younger brother, Menelaus, soon began to moon over Helen's beauty, but the elder brother, Agamemnon, was drawn to the sullen fire he sensed burning in Clytaemnestra. When he was not working with Tyndareus on their plans for a campaign to retake Mycenae, he would hang about watching her work at her loom, or stalk her at a distance when she walked alone in the palace gardens, thinking her own thoughts. His attentions were all the more infuriating in that he could never bring himself to say anything. He would only blush and look miserable when she dismissed him with some cruel remark or other and, as she said to him one day, she would rather be shut up for ever in some gloomy castle than have to endure his hangdog face following her about like a shade. So, despising her father, resentful of her sister, furious at her mother's defection, and disdainful of the company round her, Clytaemnestra wanted nothing more than to get away from Sparta and live life on her own terms.

And then, two years later, when Helen was still only twelve years old, something happened which altered the life of the girls for ever. In northern Thessaly, far across the Isthmus from Sparta, the wife of King Pirithous the Lapith had died. When his time of mourning was over, Pirithous took ship to visit his old friend Theseus of Athens, who had fallen in a bad way when his wife Phaedra hanged herself after owning the blame for the death of his son Hippolytos. Pirithous was looking to lift Theseus's spirits, for these two ageing heroes had fought side by side many times, both as kings and pirates, and always brought out the dare-devil in each other. It wasn't long before they fell to talking about Helen's fabled beauty. The wine did its work. Both men were restless for excitement. Pirithous set about persuading Theseus that they should mount an expedition to kidnap so desirable a prize. They knew that Tyndareus was away from Sparta, leading his army in a bloody campaign to restore his young ally Agamemnon to the Mycenaean throne. Sparta's defences would be weak with no more than a rearguard keeping watch. It was a perfect opportunity. If the snatch was successful, Pirithous suggested, they could draw lots afterwards to see which of them should keep the girl.

Nevertheless it was a risky enterprise, and one made riskier by a sacrilegious act. When they advanced their small band of adventurers through the passes into the Laconian plain, they came across Helen in a woodland shrine where she was offering a sacrifice to Artemis with her friends. The chance was too good to miss. Pirithous grabbed the screaming girl and threw her over his saddle-bow. The kidnappers rode out of the sacred precinct, leaving her friends shouting and wailing behind them.

Once they had shaken off their pursuers, they drew lots as agreed, and Helen fell to Theseus.

Theseus was then more than forty years older than his captive. There had been a time when he would no more have dreamed of harming such a girl than he would have dreamed of ravishing his own child, and it seems that not every trace of his noble soul had quite expired. Perhaps he recalled the hero he had once been when he lived with Hippolyta the Amazon and they fought side by side in defence of Athens against the invading Scythians. Perhaps his conscience was stung by the memory of some insult that Phaedra might have given him. Or perhaps the curse of Virgin Artemis was on him. Whatever the case, some glimmer of sense must have returned to the old man's mind, for as he gazed into the frightened eyes of the young girl lying naked beneath him, he found it impossible to take her.

After a time, miserable and ashamed, he pulled away.

Instantly Helen closed her slender arms across her breast, drew up her legs, and lay trembling like the terrified child she was. Theseus sat for a while shaking his head, appalled that he had sunk so low. 'It's all right,' he was muttering. 'I won't hurt you. It's all right. It's all right.' He could hear the small, panting sobs of her breath. He saw that she was shivering. When he leaned over to cover her body with his cloak, he almost swooned with shame at the sight of such innocent beauty petrified with fear. He tried to comfort the girl but she would not be comforted. So he looked down on her sadly, saying, 'To be gifted with such beauty must be less a blessing than a curse.' And though he had been speaking to himself the words were blazed forever on Helen's mind.

Unable to return her to Sparta, and knowing that he could no longer keep her with him, Theseus entrusted Helen to the charge of one of his more reliable barons at Aphidna in Attica, and sent his own mother Aethra to care for her. Then he took to wandering again until he fetched up at last at the court of King Lycomedes on the island of Skyros. It was there that he died shortly afterwards, having fallen – or leapt – from a windy cliff that overlooks the sea.

Shortly after Helen's abduction, and before news of it had reached him, Sparta was visited by Tantalus, the young King of Elis. Having recently come to his throne, he was looking for a wife and had heard of Helen's beauty. But on his arrival in Sparta he found the city in a state of chaos with the king away at war and his favourite daughter ravished into captivity. As befitted his royal status, Tantalus was lodged in an apartment of the palace and it was there, in one of the state rooms, that he came upon Clytaemnestra.

By now she was approaching marriageable age and had developed a dark, strong-boned glamour of her own. When Tantalus sought to console her for the loss of her sister, he was amazed to discover that this intense young woman was in a frenzy of guilt because she had been praying secretly that Helen would never return. He encouraged her to talk and felt his sympathies stirred. When he remembered that he too had come to Sparta in search of Helen without sparing so much as a thought for her sister, his feelings deepened. They talked of other matters. Again he was surprised by the range of this young woman's interests and the quality of her mind. And as she relaxed, he was entertained too by her witty comments on her own predicament and the weaknesses of those around her. Soon he was in love.

Tantalus talked to Clytaemnestra about his kingdom. It lay beyond Arcadia beside the western sea, two hundred miles to the north, far away from Sparta. Zeus was worshipped there as first among the gods, and a lively festival of games was held in the Sky-Father's honour on the plain at Olympia. His own city of Pisa lay close by that sanctuary, and though it was not so large as Sparta, it was cultured and prosperous, and lacked for nothing but a queen. If Clytaemnestra would give him her consent, he would send messengers to her father asking if his elder daughter might be allowed to grace the throne of Elis.

Clytaemnestra was thinking very quickly. She was under no illusions about Tantalus. He was neither the wealthiest nor the most handsome king in Argos. He had a homely face, with a somewhat pointy nose and ears that stood a little too eagerly to attention. But he was a man of feeling, and gifted with a generous disposition. He was royal and came of an ancient house, yet he had interesting thoughts on how a state might be ruled for the welfare of its subjects without recourse to despotic power. Also he had plans to renovate his city and furnish it with all that was best in modern culture. And he was intelligent. She felt that she might talk to him about absolutely anything and that he would approach each subject with an open mind. After only an hour or so of conversation she had been impressed by his fine discriminating intellect and a range of cultural reference that left her feeling less educated than she had thought – though not humiliatingly so. Tantalus was far too kind for that.

All of this was a great deal, but more important than any of those considerations was the simple fact that he wanted *her*. He wanted her and not her sister. Since he had first learned of her plight and expressed a sincere anxiety for her well-being, Helen's name had scarcely crossed his lips. He seemed as surprised by this fact as she was herself, but Clytaemnestra saw all the greater earnest of his honesty in that.

And with a little effort and imagination, his kingdom could be heavenly.

Was it possible that the gods had begun to smile on her blighted life at last? She could make a new life with this man, a good life, the kind of life that she had always wanted, a life where she could put her own fine mind to use and do rather more than raise babies and wait for her husband to come home from the wars with a sulky gaggle of concubines in tow.

Yet she also knew that if Tantalus spoke to her father now there could be only one reply.

At a time when Tyndareus had his hands full with the struggle for Mycenae, his favourite daughter had been stolen from him. Helen had vanished into thin air somewhere between Sparta and Athens, and her father would think of nothing else till he had found her, brought her back home, and finished the business that would leave Mycenae in grateful vassalage to Sparta.

At such a time, when there was, in fact, no certainty that Helen would ever return, Tyndareus would have no interest in marrying his elder daughter off to a minor monarch with comparatively little wealth and less power, who lived somewhere west of everywhere important. He would say no. He would say it very loudly, and not least, Clytaemnestra suspected, because her father secretly entertained hopes of sealing a new Mycenaean alliance by giving her in marriage to Agamemnon.

That was a thing she would never permit to happen.

For a moment, therefore, she contemplated elopement. But she saw at once that such a course would be disastrous. If Tyndareus came home to find that, with one daughter taken from him, the other had defected of her own free will, his anger would be terrible. Battle-hardened Spartan troops would soon come marching into Elis. Tantalus would not live long enough to argue his case. She would be dragged back home a widow. Clytaemnestra could see the pictures in her mind and could have wept at them.

She shared both her hopes and her fears with Tantalus. They discussed the difficulties, and though he declared himself ready to fight for her, she knew her father's temper and strength better than he did. She saw that haste on their part could put everything at risk, so it would be necessary for them to wait. She was not yet quite of marriageable age but would soon be so. If she swore on her maiden honour that she would never agree to wed any other man, would Tantalus wait for her? Once Tyndareus was back from the war and Helen was rescued, he would be in a more tractable mood. Clytaemnestra would make it plain to him that she would marry Tantalus or no one. And she was prepared to make her father's life a misery until he agreed to what she wanted. In two years, three at the most, she would have won his consent. And then they would be free to live as they wished with nothing to fear from anyone. Was this not the wise thing to do?

They agreed that it was. Tantalus returned to Elis. In a restless dream of longing, Clytaemnestra waited.

Over a year had passed before the spies despatched by Tyndareus across Argos learned where Helen was being held. He sent a force to rescue her and the stronghold at Aphidna fell before it. Theseus's mother Aethra was taken into slavery, and Helen was brought back to Sparta in triumph.

As the war for Mycenae approached its conclusion, Tyndareus was still away at the front, but Clytaemnestra was appalled by the change in her sister. A girl who had once been adventurous and bold had turned into a nervous creature who lived inside her beauty like a woman trapped inside a fearful dream. She had been kept locked away in the draughty citadel at Aphidna, beyond public gaze, with only Aethra and her serving-women for company. And though she had seen nothing more of Theseus and Pirithous, she was still haunted by memories of her abduction – the smell of horse-sweat and saddle-leather as the raiders galloped off with her, the numb terror of watching two old men throwing dice as she trembled between them, the weight of Theseus's body pressing her down.

And the words he had spoken still rang in her ears. Her beauty was a curse, his judgement on it was a curse, and it seemed to Helen now that her whole life was cursed. She was afraid of the world around her. Beyond the confines of the palace, even Sparta, her homeland woods and hills that she had once wandered freely as a deer, had turned into places filled with dark imaginings. She became afraid of the avid way men looked at her whenever she stepped outside the women's quarters, as though every passing glance seemed to threaten a wishful act of rape. Her eyes, which had always possessed the power to leave men standing breathless, took on a hunted look. She felt safe only in the company of Aethra, who had, strangely, become a kind of mother to her during her time of captivity. So Helen chose to remain secluded at her side, scarcely speaking, avoiding the light.

Only gradually did the extent of her sister's fears become clear to Clytaemnestra, and the more her understanding grew the more her anxiety increased. She tried to persuade Helen that her fears were groundless, affording her all the gentle attention she could give. Whatever resentment there might have been between them, they were sisters after all, and she had a duty of care as well as a horrified, sympathetic awareness of how helpless all women were when men took it into their heads to behave in a way that would shame the beasts. But when she tried to encourage Helen to venture out into the world with her again, Clytaemnestra met only with panic-stricken refusals that she took for a kind of self-defeating obstinacy, and she lost patience when all her efforts seemed to make no difference. Beginning to dread that when their father returned he would expect her to carry on caring for her sister until she was well again or until she could be suitably married off, Clytaemnestra told herself that she had a life of her own to live, away from Helen, away from Sparta. It was a life for which she was increasingly impatient.

Then word came that the war was won at Mycenae. The usurper Thyestes was dead. Agamemnon had ascended to his throne. Tyndareus would soon come home. He rejoiced at the thought of seeing his beloved Helen again, and he had news that would excite Clytaemnestra's heart.

The decision to flee Sparta before her father's return was hastily taken but never for a moment regretted, for the year and a half that Clytaemnestra spent as the wife of King Tantalus in Elis proved to be the only unquestionably happy time in her life.

They were fortunate to be allowed so long. Their life together would have been ended sooner but for a development of which Clytaemnestra was ignorant when she fled. When he had first heard the news of Helen's abduction, the shock knocked Tyndareus off his feet as though he had been struck down by a god. For a time after he came round, his behaviour was so vague and uncertain that his friends feared that he had lost his wits. He also complained of numbness in his leg when he walked, so he had been forced to take things easy for a time, entrusting the campaign to Agamemnon's leadership. Tyndareus steamed and fumed like a hot spring in the tent where he lay, until eventually, by sheer strength of will, he got back on his feet again and returned to the battle. But things had changed in his absence. Even his own

Spartan warriors looked to the vigorous young leadership of Agamemnon now. He was the future, and that old warhorse Tyndareus was the past. Once Mycenae was regained, men had no doubt where the ruling power in Argos would lie.

Tyndareus saw that he needed the marriage between Agamemnon and his daughter more than ever, and not merely as an act of patronage to a younger ally, but as the only sure means of maintaining the security of Sparta. He could only thank the gods that, for reasons best known to himself, the elder son of Atreus favoured Clytaemnestra over Helen, whose whereabouts were still unknown.

Then the gods smiled on him again. Helen was found and rescued. After Aphidna was taken, Menestheus, who had succeeded Theseus as king in Athens, hastened to dissociate himself from his predecessor's crime. And in the following weeks the power of Thyestes began to crumble at last. The gate into Mycenae was sold, Thyestes fled the city and was cut down. Regrettably, his son Aegisthus – the murderer of Atreus – contrived to escape, but no one doubted that a great victory had been won, and one that signalled an even more momentous change in the times.

Tyndareus was already on his way home when he was told that Clytaemnestra had eloped to the city of Pisa in Elis where she was to marry King Tantalus. He erupted into rage so violent that the god struck him down again, and he entered Sparta less as a conquering hero than as an ageing cripple with trembling hands and slurred speech.

He was certainly in no shape to lead an army into Elis. Nor could he count on Agamemnon for immediate help because the young Lion of Mycenae would have his hands full for some time, securing his power base in the city, taking charge of its finances and administration and asserting his authority over the outlying domains. So Clytaemnestra and her husband were left in peace for many months, though the temper of the messages reaching them from Sparta left Tantalus in no doubt that he had better prepare for war.

War came shortly after the birth of their first child. By that time Agamemnon was ready to expand his empire and there were urgent reasons why he was drawn first to Elis. When he marched into that country at the head of his troops, Tantalus decided to meet him in the field rather than allowing him to lay siege to Pisa. He chose his ground well, intercepting the invaders at a narrow pass through the mountains where he commanded the heights.

But Agamemnon had learned a great deal through the way Mycenae had finally fallen to treachery. Tantalus ordered his army to charge and drove his chariot down towards the Mycenaean line. Only when he was too far advanced to turn back did he realize how few of his warriors had followed. The rest, convinced that sooner or later Elis must fall to the overwhelming might of Mycenae, had been bought off and were now Agamemnon's men.

Clytaemnestra learned of her husband's defeat as the Mycenaeans marched into the palace at Pisa. Terrified and distraught, she was clutching her infant son to her breast when Agamemnon burst open the chamber door. He snatched the child from her, gave it to one of his men with orders to bash out its brains, and informed Clytaemnestra that she was now a widow and would shortly be remarried.

Only with difficulty was she restrained from killing herself. Then, for a time, she fought him off like a lynx. But this strange, grim man, who had been obsessed by her for many years, doggedly laid siege to her.

When Clytaemnestra demanded in outrage how he could imagine that she would ever give herself to the murderer of her child, he told her that if he had spared the child, it would only have grown up looking to avenge its father – such was the way of things in the bloody history of Mycenae. Nor, he pointed out, was she the first woman to have been seized as a prize in war, and unlike most of the rest she was not condemned to the life of a concubine or a slave.

On the contrary, she was about to be married to a man who

had loved her like a faithful hound for years, and would become the wealthiest wife in all Argos. For if the gods had gifted the house of Aeacus with power, and the house of Amythaon with wisdom, they had blessed the house of Atreus with wealth. And where there was wealth there was power, and that surely, Agamemnon declared, was wisdom enough for any woman in her right mind.

So he left her alone to think things over for a time. Then one night he came to her with wine and gifts. He was trying to make a suitor of himself, and with every awkward gesture she could feel her hatred for him coursing through her veins. But there was a moment when she saw among the bluff crags of his face the eyes of the frightened boy who, many years before, had fled with his brother out of the bloody butcher's cave that was Mycenae. In that moment she sensed the power she might wield through him and over him.

Later, much later, he mounted her like a bull, and she let him take what was neither of meaning nor of value to her now. But her spirit – she vowed it as she lay with her eyes open – would remain for ever, and inalienably, her own.

In the meantime, Helen had found new purpose in her life by caring for her father. Tyndareus had always been soft with his younger daughter and pliant to her will. Even though he had been party to her sister's terrible suffering, he knew that Helen would never enquire into his actions too closely, and was grateful now to consign his weakened body to her care. So with Aethra in constant attendance, and her lovelorn cousin Penelope for company, Helen would have been content to live this quiet life indefinitely. But the world still had demands to make on her.

As Agamemnon brought Elis under subjugation and kingdom after kingdom acknowledged the supremacy of Mycenae, a time of peace settled across Argos. Young men whose thoughts had largely been given over to war began to think of marriage, and Helen – who was reputed to be the most beautiful woman ever to grace the earth – was now of marriageable age. Whoever was lucky enough to marry her would also shortly succeed to the throne of Sparta. So Helen soon became the unrivalled object of desire for all the great princes of Argos.

One by one they presented themselves as suitors at the court of Tyndareus, each of them bearing rich gifts and strutting in their finery like courting birds, or making an impressive show, like bull-seals, of their strength and prowess.

Among those most infatuated by Helen's beauty was Diomedes, Lord of Tiryns, who was renowned as one of the bravest of men. Unaware of her nervous temperament, or perhaps insensitive to it, he sought to impress her with stories of his triumph in the long and terrible war at Thebes. Helen listened to him patiently and gave him small signs of her favour, but withheld any certain answer to his eager proposal of marriage.

Menestheus of Athens was less warmly received. Though he was at pains to distinguish himself from his predecessor Theseus, he brought back memories of her confinement in Attica and was too evidently self-seeking in his manner. He would have been sent away with a clear rejection had Tyndareus not advised his daughter to reject no one yet for fear of stirring hostility to Sparta. So Idomeneus, heir to the Cretan King Deucalion, sailed from Knossos to plead his suit, and out of Salamis came Ajax, the valiant son of Telamon, along with his step-brother Teucer, who had been fathered on Telamon's captive bride Hesione. The great archer Philoctetes came from Aeolia, bringing the massive bow that Heracles had bequeathed to him in return for his armour-bearer's willingness to light his funeral pyre on Mount Oeta, and many others made the journey by land across the Peloponnese.

All together, there were thirty-eight contenders for Helen's hand, most of them mature warriors, men of power and influence who had already made their reputations. But among them were two young men of much the same age as Helen herself. Not yet seventeen, Palamedes, the Prince of Euboea, proved far more intelligent than any of his rivals, whom he kept amused by teaching them a complicated new game he had invented. The movement of stones across a patterned board according to the throw of dice provided a volatile form of gambling, from which Palamedes seemed to profit with astonishing regularity. The other young man had much less to say for himself but he carried his diffident good looks with a proud reserve and a strong, noble bearing. It was generally agreed that he stood little chance, but this graduate of Cheiron's school impressed everyone by the courteous modesty of his demeanour. His name was Patroclus, son of Menoetius.

Helen sat at the centre of all this attention in a state of panic. She had seen what had happened to her sister, who had now provided Agamemnon with an heir yet seemed to have surrendered all hope of happiness in this life. She watched as her uncle Icarius refused to allow his daughter Penelope to marry the man with whom she was clearly in love. And she had long since begun to wonder whether her own life could ever be anything more than a trophy to be grabbed by the strongest contender. Yet she also saw that her father could not have much longer to live, and that the world would give her no peace until she belonged to some other man. Sooner or later a choice must be made among the gang of suitors clamouring for her attention.

Tyndareus would also have preferred to despatch the contenders and carry on living a quiet life at the centre of his daughter's world. With so many mighty princes vying for Helen's hand, and feelings running high, he was uncertain how to favour any one of them without incurring the enmity of the others. And the risk of such enmity was increased by the fact that, of all the candidates, one had stronger claims on him than all the rest, and could exert more pressure.

Menelaus, the younger son of Atreus, had loved Helen with a passion for many years, and Tyndareus could see that Helen found a familiar gentleness and consideration in Agamemnon's milder brother that was less threatening to her than the claims of strangers.

Since the days of his boyhood, she had always responded with loving friendship to the shy, slightly askance smile with which he faced the world, as though it had always come at him like a big wind. But Menelaus was no longer a boy. He was a seasoned warrior who bore the mark of the wars in a scar that ran down his right cheek and clipped the corner of his mouth, fixing it in a wry tuck of the skin. And if he lacked his brother's oppressive bluster, he remained nevertheless a son of Atreus. Should he become King of Sparta through marriage to Helen, the brothers would have effective control of the entire Peloponnesus. Some of the others contending for Helen's hand, and the power that went with it, might be sufficiently worried by such a prospect to take steps to prevent it.

So Tyndareus dithered, and Helen was content to let him do so.

Fortunately, among that rowdy gathering of gallants Tyndareus had one resourceful friend. Odysseus, Prince of Ithaca, had come to Sparta not in the hope of snatching Helen from under the noses of much richer men, but to pursue a different claim of his own. Tyndareus had a brother called Icarius and he too had a desirable daughter. If less astonishingly beautiful than her cousin, Penelope had a poise and dignity that enchanted the heart of the Ithacan, and a shrewd intelligence that delighted his agile mind. But her father Icarius — a stiff-necked man who liked to assert what little power he had — was looking for a more prosperous son-in-law than the relatively penurious prince of a small island in the Ionian sea, and he made it plain from the first that he neither liked nor trusted this adventurer out of Ithaca.

His daughter might pine as long as she liked, he insisted, but sooner or later she would see the good sense of his opposition. Why on earth would she want to wear herself out in a hand-to-mouth life with a man who was no better than a pirate on a barren rock somewhere to the west of civilization, when she could take her pick among any of the princes that her more obedient cousin refused?

Penelope had only a single reason – a reason which satisfied her as much as it exasperated Icarius: she loved Odysseus and was more than happy to spend the rest of her life with him, however hard that life might be. So to her father's angry frustration, she remained obstinate in her resolve to marry no one else. But her nature was also too modest and loyal to do what her lover urged and compromise her reputation by an impetuous elopement.

Caught between two stubborn, Spartan temperaments, Odysseus eventually came to Tyndareus with his problem.

'We both seem to find ourselves in difficulties,' he said. 'I wonder if we can't be of assistance to one another.'

Tyndareus sighed. Knowing Odysseus of old, he had guessed that this scrawny fellow with short legs, bristling hair and a knocked-askew nose was fishing for something from the moment he'd requested this private audience. But his guest's rascally smile made a welcome change from the laconic gravity of those around him, and he could at least relax in the knowledge that the Ithacan was not in contention for his daughter's hand.

'Explain,' he said, and signalled for his cup-bearer to pour more wine.

Odysseus took the measure of the man across from him – a man well past his prime, more than twice his own age, who had once been a formidable warrior and was now reduced to the condition of a pampered cripple. Deciding that a breezy impudence might serve his purpose best, he said, 'It seems clear to me which way the wind blows.'

Tyndareus tilted his head.

'I've been watching Agamemnon lean his weight on you. The Mycenean lion is pushing his brother's cause, of course, but he also wants this marriage to consolidate the alliance between Sparta and the house of Atreus.' Odysseus glanced sharply up at the old Spartan king. 'My guess is that he has ambitions abroad, and with Sparta safely in his brother's hands, his power would be secured at home.'

In the slurred speech that was all he could manage these days,

Tyndareus whispered, 'The throne of Sparta is already occupied.'

'And by the wisest of kings,' Odysseus smiled. 'But you won't live for ever, old friend. And whoever marries Helen warms his bed with a woman as close to a goddess as a man can hope to get and inherits your kingdom.'

Tyndareus reproved his manner with a weary sigh. 'Your point?'

'My point is, I think it's what you want too. Marry Helen to Menelaus, make him your heir, and Sparta becomes unshakeable.' Odysseus grinned across at the old king, whose trembling hand fidgeted with a serpent arm-ring twisted round his wrist. 'Add to this the convenient fact that Menelaus seems to be sincerely insane with love for your daughter, and Helen knows that he'll take good care of her, then the marriage makes sense in every way.'

'Do you think that none of this has occurred to me?'

'But it's not quite so simple, is it? Disappoint any of the other ambitious princes here and you could have a deal of trouble on your hands.'

Tyndareus glanced away.

Odysseus brought his hands together at his lips. 'I think I can see a solution.' He smiled. 'But it comes at a price.'

Tyndareus turned to look at him again, narrow-eyed. 'Save your breath,' he said. 'My brother's face is set against you.'

Odysseus opened his palms. 'The King sees through me. But there are things he might say to his brother which I cannot say myself. He might tell him, for instance, that Odysseus of Ithaca has recently pulled off a number of successful ventures and is far richer than when he was last in Sparta.'

'Piracy will not endear you to him!'

Again Odysseus smiled. 'But a glance into my coffers might. And could he name me a royal house that was not founded on brigandage or piracy?'

Tyndareus grunted. 'How much richer?'

'Enough to make a couple of Lycian towns and several Sidonian merchants considerably poorer. Icarius will have his bride-price, and he can rest assured that his daughter will want for nothing when she comes to Ithaca.'

Tyndareus shook his head. 'Icarius looks to have her as Queen in Crete.'

Odysseus shook his head. 'There is bad blood in the House of the Axe. Penelope will not give herself to Deucalion's son.'

'Temper your speech,' Tyndareus frowned. 'The Cretan is my houseguest.'

'As is the better part of Argive royalty – eating your food and emptying your wine-cellar while you and your brother dither over your daughters' futures.'

Odysseus sighed impatiently now. 'Penelope wants only me for her husband. She wants me as certainly as Helen wants Menelaus, and if you and Icarius wish to sleep easier in your beds at night you would both do well to let your daughters have their way.'

But Tyndareus merely scowled. 'This is all the solution you have? I had expected something more ingenious.'

'That is part of it,' said Odysseus, smiling again, 'but not the whole. The rest I keep to myself till you agree to plead my cause with Icarius.'

Tyndareus studied the irrepressible sea-rover across from him. He guessed that Odysseus had already been in conference with Menelaus and Agamemnon and that they knew what he was about right now. He guessed that he'd discussed this business with Helen too, and that all three had felt what he was feeling: that something about this guileful rogue inspired one's confidence, even if you weren't quite sure you could trust him.

'What do you want me to say,' he sighed.

'It's simple enough,' Odysseus answered. 'Tell him that you've been thinking things over and that you've decided that the only sensible thing for a father to do in such a pass is to leave his daughter free to choose for herself. Tell him that's what you will let Helen do, and that if he cares for his own daughter's happiness, he should do the same for Penelope. Tell him Odysseus has been at pains to mend his fortune for his daughter's sake, and that not only does he love Penelope with undying passion, he's also a far more resourceful and reliable fellow than the scoundrel that Icarius mistakes him for. Tell him what you know to be true – that Penelope loves me and will continue to make his life a misery until he consents to this marriage.'

'And if I agree,' said Tyndareus, hearing nothing there that would come hard to his lips, 'shall I tell him that the resourceful Odysseus has helped me find a way out of my difficulties?'

'You shall.'

'And that way is?'

'Do we have a bargain?' Odysseus held out his hand. When Tyndareus nodded and took it, the Ithacan smiled. 'Tomorrow is the day when the King Horse must be sacrificed to Poseidon, is it not?'

'What of it?'

'Here is what you must do. Assemble all the suitors in the sacred precinct and tell them that with so many proud princes to choose among, you have been unable to see any other way than to leave Helen free to make the decision for herself. Tell them that is how it will be. But also tell them that before her choice is announced you will require every man present to swear a vow that he will defend her chosen husband against anyone who challenges his right to have her.'

Tyndareus sat back in his chair, stroking his beard. After a moment he said, 'Men have been known to break their oaths.'

Again Odysseus grinned. 'I have an oath in mind so terrible,' he said, 'that not one of them will dare to break it.'

The King Horse was brought in from his pasture at dawn the next day. With his mane and tail braided and garlanded, and his hooves painted gold, the sleek white stallion was led into the sacred precinct where the bronze statue of Poseidon brandished his trident fish-spear. There the stallion was offered to the god before all the assembled suitors. But the great beast did not go easily to the sacrifice. It was as if his nostrils already smelled death coming to him. He snorted and whinnied with rolling eyes. His ears were laid back and hooves restive as Tyndareus invoked the blue-haired god who moves both earth and sea. It took four men straining with all their weight against his rawhide tethers to keep the powerful animal in place.

The old king lacked the strength to ensure a clean kill, so it was his son-in-law, Agamemnon, acting as his surrogate, who took the sacred cleaver in hand and smote the sinews of the horse's neck, severing the windpipe with a single blow. Wide-eyed, screaming his grief and rage, the King Horse reared back against the tethers, flailing bright hooves against the air. He seemed to hang there for a long time as though gathering the force to trample death beneath him, then he frothed out his last gasps of breath before collapsing in his death throes at Agamemnon's feet. Blood spurted from the torn white flesh into a silver salver. Steam rose in the morning heat, and as flies began to gather, the men who had restrained the horse took cleavers of their own and began to joint the carcass till the once majestic animal lay in raw and bloody pieces on the precinct's holy ground.

Only then did Tyndareus announce to the suitors the terms of the oath that Odysseus had devised for them. Before his daughter declared the name of he who was to be the happy recipient of her hand, each of these mighty princes was required to stand with one foot on a portion of the great white stallion that had been offered to Poseidon, and ask that the god should visit ruin and destruction on his lands if he failed to defend the right of the successful candidate to hold Helen alone and unchallenged for the rest of his days.

For a few moments while they took in the gravity of what was being asked of them, the assembled princes stood in silence. A stir and murmur passed through the throng as they recalled the terrible havoc that had been wrought in living memory by angry shrugs of the Earthshaker's shoulders in Knossos and in Troy. Tyndareus glanced uncertainly at Odysseus, who merely smiled and gave a reassuring nod. 'Come, gentlemen,' said

Agamemnon, 'is not so dreadful an oath warranted by so fair a prize?'

Young Palamedes spoke up first. 'I for one will gladly make this pledge – though I confess I would rather have played dice for Helen's hand!' An uneasy laugh rippled among the suitors. Then Palamedes said, 'But should not he who devised so dreadful an oath be the first to utter it?'

Unprepared for this, Odysseus took in the general murmur of agreement. 'All men know that I am not a contender here,' he prevaricated.

'No more am I,' said Agamemnon, eager to move things on, 'but I too will gladly swear. Come, Lord Odysseus, show us how the thing is done.'

So Odysseus found himself with no choice but to untie his sandal and stand with his bare foot pressed against a portion of the horse's thigh to put his honour and the fate of his island at the mercy of Earthshaker Poseidon.

Agamemnon was next to take the oath. Then Diomedes, eager to display his love for Helen, stepped forward. Menelaus, Palamedes and the handsome Prince of Crete were quick to join them. One by one, with fear of the god heavy on their tongues, the others followed. Only when all the princes had sworn did Helen step forth in her bridal gown, holding the wreath she had made for this sacred occasion, and place it over the flowing red hair of Menelaus, who stood, beaming with joy, among the rivals he had bested.

'The gods are just,' he cried, with tears starting at his eyes. 'My thanks go forth to Divine Athena for guiding the choice of my betrothed.' Then looking at the number and quality of the men around him, and the glower of envy and disappointment in their eyes, he turned to the statue of the god. 'Hear my praises, Great Poseidon, Ruler of Horses and Shaker of Cities, for granting your divine protection to this union.'

Helen told herself again that Menelaus had always been her friend. Now he would be her safe haven in the turmoil of the world, and if, as a girl, she had ever dreamed of passion, she was glad to let go of such dreams. She wanted to believe that when she gave her body to Menelaus that night, the act would allay the curse of her beauty for ever. She wanted to believe it with all her heart. But the heart is a prophetic organ and can, for a time, keep secrets even from the one inside whose breast it beats.

Meanwhile, Tyndareus opened his arms to give the younger son of Atreus his blessing. He watched Agamemnon and Clytaemnestra gather Menelaus and Helen into their embrace, brother to brother and sister to sister. And as he did so, the weary old king was reflecting on the day many years earlier when, in sacrificing to the gods, he had foolishly neglected to make an offering to Aphrodite, and the Golden One had sworn to take her revenge by making sure that both his daughters would one day prove to be faithless wives.

The Supplicant

Within the year Tyndareus was found dead in his chamber. Already ruler in all but name, Menelaus ascended to the Lacadaemonian throne of Sparta, and shortly afterwards his beloved wife gave birth to a daughter. Helen's labour was so long and hard that there was a time when Aethra feared that the struggle might kill her, yet the infant Hermione emerged from those birth-pangs with so much of her mother's exquisite beauty that Menelaus felt more than ever blessed in the marriage he had made.

Helen too was strengthened by the marriage. With the long ordeal of being the object of every man's desire now over, her confidence returned. She took a new purchase on life, responding well to the pleasures and challenges of being a wife, a mother and a queen. In dealing with the affairs of a kingdom whose customs she knew and understood far better than he did, Menelaus often sought her counsel. This was the first time that anyone had ever valued her judgement, and she thrived on it, discovering a larger interest in public life. They drew up new plans for their palace together, extending both the state rooms and their private apartments, and making skilful use at her suggestion of the finely mottled porphyry from local quarries. The results so impressed her sister that Clytaemnestra ordered large quantities of Spartan stone for the refurbishment of her own gloomy palace in Mycenae.

Helen also took delight in redesigning the gardens around their home so that the tranquil hours that she and her adoring husband spent together with their child might be filled with fragrance and colour and the sound of water.

At such times they could look down from their palace beneath the Bronze House of Athena across a broad fertile plain ringed by its steep defending hills, on to a future in which their contentment seemed assured. For if there was little passion in their life together there was a great deal of affection, and Sparta was prospering around them. Already plans were laid for the day when Hermione would marry her cousin Orestes, the first-born child of Agamemnon and Clytaemnestra, thus uniting the thrones of Sparta and Mycenae for ever. The gods, it seemed, were kind.

Almost four years after the birth of Hermione, Menelaus received an urgent message from his brother. Agamemnon required his presence at the court of King Telamon on Salamis, where their joint show of strength would offer support to the king in the latest round of a long-standing wrangle with Troy.

Dismayed by the prospect of this first separation from her husband, Helen demanded to know why such a mission should be necessary.

'It's an old quarrel,' Menelaus explained. 'Telamon and Heracles captured Troy about thirty years ago and as part of his share in the spoils Telamon was given the Trojan King's daughter Hesione. She's been kept on Salamis against her will ever since and wants nothing more than to go home. When Priam first succeeded to his father's throne he was too weak to help his sister. These days he's one of the most powerful kings in the east, and he's determined to release her, but Telamon has turned down every offer of ransom.'

Firmly Helen said, 'I was once held captive in a strange land and I know the pain of it. If Hesione is miserable on Salamis, Telamon should let her go.'

Menelaus grunted and looked away.

'Why won't he?' she demanded.

'Because he's a hot-headed old war-horse who thinks he's the last of the heroes since Heracles and Theseus died. Sometimes I think he'd watch Salamis burn sooner than give up his rightful prize.'

'But that's just foolishness,' Helen protested. 'And anyway, I don't see how any of this concerns Sparta.'

'Telamon has asked for Agamemnon's support. Agamemnon has asked for mine. He's my brother. I have to go.'

He spoke as if that should be the end of the matter but Helen refused to be deterred. 'Don't you agree that it would be for the best if Hesione was given her wish and returned to her home in Troy?'

'Of course I do.' Menelaus frowned. 'But we can't just let the Trojans take her or they'll begin to think that Argos is weak.'

She said, 'That sounds more like your brother than yourself.'

He gave her a reassuring smile that puckered the scar at his lip. 'But I'm not my brother, and that's why it's important that I go to Salamis. It should be possible to sort this quarrel out without violence, and I think I might be able to act as a moderating influence.'

Uncertainly Helen nodded, hoping that he was right.

Meanwhile in Troy, King Priam had become so exasperated by Telamon's rejection of his many generous offers to ransom Hesione that he was ready to threaten war over the issue. His counsellor Antenor, firm in his conviction that Troy's interests were best served by peace, was opposed to such a dangerous course and called for support in his caution from Priam's cousin Anchises, the blind King of the Dardanians. Anchises reminded Priam of the disaster that had ensued the last time Troy came into conflict with the Argives. And since Agamemnon had been declared High King, those warlike tribes were no longer fighting each other. If Priam invaded Salamis, all Argos might come down about his ears.

Though he listened impatiently, Priam could hear the sense of it and reluctantly agreed that it would be wise not to resort to arms until all hope of a diplomatic solution was exhausted. So Anchises and Antenor were sent as his ambassadors to Salamis with a fresh, and final, demand for Hesione's return.

Menelaus arrived on the island two days after the Trojan legation and found his brother Agamemnon already there. Fortified by the presence of allies, Telamon, who was now well into his fifties and had put on a great deal of weight, called a council at which he invited Anchises and Antenor to state their case. Having heard them without interest, he turned to Agamemnon with a dismissive gesture. 'Every year I must listen to such wheedling and bluster. Since they got fat and rich the Trojans have turned into moaning old women – though I don't recall hearing Priam complain when – out of a generosity of spirit I've since come to regret – I allowed Hesione to ransom his life. Don't you agree it's time this nonsense was settled once and for all?'

Agamemnon nodded, 'Hesione was justly taken. Laomedon broke his word – as Troy has been prone to do. His perfidy cost him his city and all its spoils. There can be no question but that the woman is rightfully yours.'

Telamon's sons agreed. Menelaus said nothing until Agamemnon glanced towards him, when he too nodded, though with less vehement conviction.

Telamon turned to Antenor with a shrug. 'You see. The High King of Argos and his brother the King of Sparta are with me. Go home and tell Priam that both he and his sister would have been dead a long time ago if it wasn't for the merciful gallantry shown to them by myself and Heracles. They should both be thankful rather than testing our patience like this.'

'King Priam's patience also has limits,' said Anchises quietly.

'So a deaf king sends us a blind king as his ambassador!' Telamon glanced at Agamemnon with a mirthless chuckle, and then turned his smirk on the Trojan legation. 'If Priam wants his sister back so badly, he should come and fetch her for himself. Meanwhile I shall use her as I choose.'

'Is there not room for compromise here?' Menelaus put in quickly. 'Perhaps Hesione might be allowed to visit her brother for a time?'

Agamemnon glowered at his brother. Telamon firmly shook his head. 'Let her out of my sight and I'd never see her again. Her place is here with me.'

'And why should Salamis trust the word of Troy when history counsels otherwise?' Agamemnon put in. 'Telamon won Hesione by right of arms. Should he choose to keep her that way, he can rely on our support.'

Shortly afterwards, having suggested that Telamon would be wise to seek more measured counsel than that of the ambitious King of Mycenae, Antenor and Anchises returned gloomily to Troy.

Menelaus also came back from Salamis with a heavy heart, only to find that during his absence pestilence had struck Sparta. Helen had done everything she could to keep the people in good heart, entreating the gods on their behalf and offering help and advice from her wise woman Polydamna. But the first terrible death was followed by another, and soon the contagion began to spread throughout the poorer quarters of the city. Fearful both for his family and for the welfare of his kingdom, Menelaus imposed quarantine around the citadel and sent messengers to the oracle of Apollo at Delphi asking what remedy might be found for the plague that now threatened to ravage his country. After several days the answer came back that the king must seek out the tombs of a wolf and a goat that were brothers, and offer sacrifices there.

For some time the priests and counsellors of the kingdom puzzled over the answer. How could a wolf and a goat possibly be brothers, and why would either be buried in a tomb? At last, after many hours spent poring over the clay tablets in the temple archives, a young scholar-priest emerged with a story to tell. In ancient times, the priest declared, Prometheus, benefactor of men – he who had dared to steal fire from heaven and given to mankind a portion of the qualities possessed by all the other animals – had once fathered two sons on the Harpy Celaeno. The names she gave to them were Lycus and Chimaerus, the wolf and the he-goat. They had been servants of Apollo Smintheus – Apollo of the mice – the god who brought, and who might also cure, pestilence.

'Where are the tombs of these brothers to be found?' demanded Menelaus.

'Across the Aegean Sea,' he was told, 'at Sminthe, in the kingdom of Troy.'

Menelaus threw his hands in the air. 'Sometimes I wonder if the gods are toying with us. This is no good time to be going cap in hand to Troy.'

On the night after the oracle was interpreted, he turned in his bed for so long that Helen too was kept from sleep. 'Shall I ask Polydamna to prepare you a sleeping-draught?' she murmured at last.

'No,' he shook his head and turned again. 'Forgive me for disturbing you. I have much on my mind.'

Gathering a purple shawl about her shoulders, Helen sat up beside her husband and put a hand to his shoulder. 'Tell me,' she said.

'Try to sleep.' He withdrew into his own preoccupations, 'It's enough that one of us should go without rest.'

'Would you rather I nursed my fears in the dark as you do? If something is troubling you, you must share it with me.'

Sighing, Menelaus turned over onto his back. 'The riddle of the oracle was deciphered today. Its judgement is that Sparta can only be freed of pestilence if sacrifices are offered at some ancient tombs near Troy.'

'Then send there at once,' Helen exclaimed. 'Have the offerings made. What is the difficulty?'

Quietly he said, 'I must make the offerings myself.'

'You must voyage to Troy?'

'Yes.'

'Then I will come with you.'

He shook his head, 'No, I want you to stay here and watch over Hermione and the city for me.'

'And what of my wishes? Do they count for nothing? Hermione can come with us,' she added quickly. 'We have counsellors who will care for the city.'

Menelaus sat up to look at his wife. 'I've no more desire to leave you than you have to see me go, my love. But I can't take you with me.'

Sensing that there was more on his mind than he had so far shared, she pushed him further until at last he declared that he was unwilling to take her with him because the journey might well prove dangerous.

'Then we will share the dangers,' she countered. When he shook his head and turned away again, she said, 'What are you not telling me?'

He lay in troubled silence for a time, not wanting to alarm her. But his need to unburden his cares was also great, so when she pressed him again he said, 'I'm afraid that sooner or later war must come between Argos and Troy.'

'Why,' she demanded, 'why should it come to that?'

'Helen, there could be many reasons. Because Priam is an angry old man who has lost patience with Telamon. Because Troy would be the richest of prizes. Because men are fools who think there's more glory to be found in a bloody brawl over a burning city than in cultivating their fields in peace. Perhaps because the gods have grown bored and are spoiling for trouble.'

'Or because your brother is?'

Menelaus glanced away from the cold question. 'All I know is that the air smells of war every time Argives and Trojans jostle each other. It would take no more than a single reckless incident to provide a pretext and the whole eastern seaboard could go up in flames.'

Helen had listened to this with increasing dismay. She sat staring into the darkness now. 'Why have you said nothing of this before?'

'Because I wasn't certain. I didn't want to alarm you.'

'But you're certain now?'

'Not certain, no.' He looked back at her and saw the light from the oil-lamp gleaming in her eyes. 'But you're right of course,' he admitted. 'Since Agamemnon became High King of Argos, it seems as if his hunger for power is feeding on itself. I hadn't quite realized it till I saw him in Salamis but he's been at peace too long and he's looking eastwards now. He's been probing the Asian coast with pirate raids for years, but it's Troy that he wants.'

Helen gave vent to her anger. 'The man's a monster. Is all Argos not enough for him?'

'Apparently not. Fortunately, he can't take Troy on his own and he's not yet certain he can count on all the support he needs. Telamon and his sons would be quick to join him, of course, and there are others who are thinking about the plunder. Diomedes for one. But they wouldn't be enough on their own.'

Helen frowned into the gloom. 'And you?'

Menelaus turned to look at his wife. 'Like it or not, if it came to war I would have to commit the strength of Sparta.'

'Because Agamemnon is right? Or because he's your brother?'

There was a long silence between them.

Eventually Helen said, 'And the oracle demands that you go to Troy at such a time?'

Menelaus sighed. 'The only choice I have is not to take you with me.'

'Then you will go fully armed? You will take ships and fighting-men with you.'

'That would be Agamemnon's way – to go bustling in, demanding access to the tombs and cutting his way through if they so much as blinked at him. But it would start the war I'm trying to avoid. That's why I can't sleep.'

'Then what will you do?'

'I don't know. I just don't know.'

Helen put a hand tenderly to his cheek. 'Then perhaps you should try to sleep on it.' She pushed him gently back down onto the bed and laid her arm across his chest, but neither of them could sleep and they could almost hear each other thinking.

After a time, Helen said, 'What do you think Odysseus would advise if he was here?'

Menelaus thought about it. 'Antenor knows I'm trying to avoid conflict,' he said eventually. 'I'm sure he read it in my face on Salamis. And Anchises isn't looking for war. So I think Odysseus would tell me to go to Troy in a way which meant I could speak easily with them.'

'That sounds wise,' she said, 'but how could it be done?'

'Perhaps only honestly,' he realized quickly. 'Perhaps that's it. I think you've solved it for me. After all, I'm going to Troy as a supplicant so that's how I should present myself – unarmed, a pilgrim on a sacred errand to the god.'

He sat up in bed with sudden excitement. 'I'm sure that's it,' he exclaimed, and took her warmly into his embrace. 'What would I do without you?'

'What will I do without you?' she whispered. 'Are you sure about this?'

'Absolutely sure. And all the more so because the thought came to me through you. And I'll be back in Sparta just as soon as I can. Believe me, a man who shares his bed with the cleverest and most beautiful woman in the world won't stay away a night longer than he needs.'

'But the dangers,' she said.

'The best way of avoiding danger is not to provoke it. I should have seen it for myself. It's going to be all right, I promise you.'

Not long after that Menelaus fell asleep. But Helen lay awake for a long time that night, aware of the darkness behind everything, and fearful that for all her husband's protestations the world was changing round them in ways that neither of them could ever hope to control.

In Troy meanwhile, Priam had again summoned his council. Having listened while Anchises and Antenor reported on the failure of their mission, he said, 'I'm minded to accept Telamon's ungracious invitation. If he refuses our offers of gold then let him have bronze weaponry instead. How soon can we have a fleet ready to invade Salamis?'

'Within a few months,' his eldest son Hector replied, 'but we should think carefully about this. Troy's genius has always been for peace not war. If the High King of Argos should come to Telamon's aid, there may be more to lose here than there is to gain.'

'Hesione has suffered captivity for more than twenty years,' Priam snapped. 'How long would this council have me sit here doing nothing to aid her?'

'I don't doubt my brother's courage,' Deiphobus put in, 'but Hector is too cautious. We Trojans can fight as well as any, and our friends will stand with us. The Argive pirates have troubled our coastline long enough.'

'Mount such an expedition if you think it right,' said Antenor, 'but I greatly fear that war may be all that comes of it. I know the king cares for his sister. He should be aware that Telamon will see her dead sooner than give her up.'

Frowning, Priam looked to his blind cousin. 'Anchises, you were in Salamis. Do you believe that to be so?'

Anchises lifted his head. 'Telamon is a firebrand with an evil temper. Hesione's life means little to him. He's sacked this city once, remember. I could hear in his voice that he thinks he can do it again.'

'Then let him come and try,' said Deiphobus. 'He'll find it a different proposition this time.'

'He's eager to come,' said Antenor, 'and Agamemnon with him. And if Agamemnon comes, then his brother will come, and they will not come alone.'

Priam said heavily, 'When Agamemnon is ready for war he will find all the excuses he needs. The fate of my sister matters nothing to him. He knows that Troy is rich. He knows that we command the Asian seaboard and that we hold the gate to the trade roads of the east. Those are the reasons why he'll bring his ships against us sooner or later.'

'Then if war is coming,' Deiphobus declared, 'we should take it to him before he brings it to us. Let the time be now.'

Less impetuous than his brother, Hector sat at his father's side in the grave silence of the council chamber. After a moment he glanced up at Antenor. 'You said you thought that the younger son of Atreus might have doubts about looking for a war?'

Antenor smiled bleakly. 'The King of Sparta is comfortable enough staying at home in bed with Helen.'

Most of the men in the hall permitted themselves a smile, but Hector was not among them. 'Then might we reason with him?' he asked.

'More easily than with Agamemnon,' said blind Anchises.

'But we can't reason with Telamon,' Priam declared, 'and Menelaus will support his brother if it comes to war. The question is shall it be now or later?'

A new voice said, 'There may be another way.'

Everyone turned to see Paris leaning against a pillar with a half-smile on his lips. It was the first time he had ever spoken in council, but he had been listening eagerly and carefully for many months, while he was taught the rudiments of reading, writing and statecraft. Though the names of Argos and Sparta had been unknown to him when he first heard them at Aphrodite's lips, they were familiar enough to him now, and if, for everyone else, Argos was like the shadow of thunder looming across the prospects of the city, for Paris it was luminous with hope.

Deiphobus said, 'I'm sure our father values your opinion, but we're not discussing the finer points of bull-breeding today.'

'Peace, cousin,' said Aeneas. 'Let the king hear your brother.'

Paris cleared his throat. 'I think my father is wise to build a fleet ready for war. But while it is building, why not let me take ship westwards and see if I can't carry off some Argive princess to hold hostage in exchange for the release of Hesione? Telamon will not listen to us but he may take notice of his angry friends when they demand that he lets her go in return for the woman they have lost. That way we may save my father's sister and still be ready for Agamemnon if he comes against us. And – who knows? – with luck we might even avoid a costly war.'

'Paris is thinking more clearly than the rest of us,' Hector smiled. 'This strikes me as a cunning plan.'

'And one that is rather well-suited to his talents!' Aeneas laughed. 'Once the Argive women set eyes on him, they'll be fighting over which of them gets abducted first. I might even go along myself to watch it happen.'

'Then let it be so,' said Priam gravely and turned to Antenor. 'Have the ship-builder Phereclus summoned. I want a fleet of warships ready for an assault on Salamis before summer's end. My son Paris shall sail in the first of them.'

Two weeks later Paris was down at the shore clad only in a breech-clout as he worked among the shipwrights to help the timbers of his vessel take shape. Beside him Phereclus raised his craftsman's eyes from a further satisfied examination of the figure-head that a wood-carver had delivered earlier that day. 'She can never be as beautiful as the goddess herself,' he was saying, 'but this is as fine an Aphrodite as I've seen in a long time.'

When Paris did not immediately reply, the ship-builder glanced across at him and saw that the young man's attention had been taken elsewhere. A vessel had entered the mouth of the Hellespont and dropped sail while still some way out. Now she was coming in under oars with the sun behind her, leaving the boats of the fishing fleet bobbing in her wake.

Phereclus shielded his eyes to study the approaching vessel. 'She's Argive-built,' he muttered after a moment, 'but no warship. So who do we have here?'

The ship creaked closer inshore and ran aground about thirty yards down the strand. One of the crew leapt from the bow holding a painter to make her fast. With a jump of his heart Paris read the words painted above the eye on the scarlet prow. The name sprang in a whisper to his lips: *Helen of Sparta*.

Phereclus heard it and grunted, 'A good name for a pretty little craft!'

'She's more than pretty,' Paris said, 'she's beautiful!'

Almost without volition he fell to his knees, pressed a hand to his mouth, and then touched it to the lips of the figurehead where the goddess lay on an ox-cart, nestling the infant Eros at her breast. With his eyes briefly closed, and his mind on fire, Paris made a silent prayer of thanks.

Looking back at the ship again, he saw a tall man in a tunic of white linen standing at the bow, fanning himself with a sun hat as he stared ashore. His hair glowed like a beacon in the ruddy light of the late afternoon.

By now all the men working on the ship had downed their tools. Most of them were gazing in a mixture of admiration and apprehension at the foreign vessel, though one or two looked back at the city where a company of armed horsemen were already passing through the gates on their way to the shore.

'What business does an Argive have in Trojan waters?' Paris called.

'Peaceful business, and holy,' the red-haired man answered. 'I come here as a supplicant.'

Paris saw the long scar left by a sword across the man's cheek. He said, 'To beg forgiveness for the towns you've raided and burned?'

'Not I, friend,' the man smiled. 'I'm no pirate. My name is Menelaus, King of Sparta.' He glanced quickly askance at the approaching troop.

Again Paris felt his heart lurch. 'And husband to the lady for whom your ship is named?'

'I have that honour.'

'And with it every man's envy, I understand.'

Menelaus dipped his head in a courteous smile of acknowledgement. 'My wife will be flattered to learn that rumour of her beauty has travelled so far.'

'If you live to return to her.' Paris kept his voice light, covering the agitation of his heart. 'You still haven't told us what you want here.'

'I come at the bidding of the Delphic oracle. My country is afflicted with a plague that will lift only when I offer sacrifice at the tombs of Lycus and Chimaerus. I'm told they lie on Trojan land, near Apollo's shrine at Sminthe.'

A pang of guilt seared through Paris. He was thinking of Oenone and of the many times he and she had returned together to visit her father Cebren at Apollo's shrine.

But, 'I know the place,' he said. 'I used to raise bulls not far from there.'

'Then the gods are with me. Guide me there, herdsman, and I will pay you well, both for that service and for a hecatomb of your finest animals.'

Paris smiled at him. 'You'll need my father's permission first.'

'Is this your father?'

'No, this is Phereclus, son of Tecton, the most skilful shipwright in all Asia. My father is Priam, King of Troy, and this—' Paris smiled in the direction of the approaching horsemen '—is his palace guard coming to arrest you.'

Menelaus held up his hands. 'Forgive my mistake, Prince of Troy. It was an honest one – though I might have guessed as much from your noble bearing. Will you inform your men that I come in peace and am quite unarmed?'

'Do you swear to that?'

'I do.'

'On your wife's life?'

'That is a fearful oath – but yes, on my wife's life.'

'Then consider yourself under my protection, friend. My name is Paris, though some men call me Alexander. Be welcome here in Troy.'

With a prayer of thanks for a safe voyage, Menelaus leapt down from his ship and waded ashore through the surf. He was offering his hand to Paris as the troop of horsemen cantered up, led by

Antiphus who shouted a challenge at the stranger from under his high-plumed helmet.

Paris smiled up at him. 'We are honoured to entertain the King of Sparta in our city, brother. Before your men get too excited, tell them to lower their arms and lend a hand to haul this lovely ship inshore. I have taken Menelaus under my protection. His royal person is sacred, both as a holy supplicant here and as the guest of my house.'

True to his word, Paris took Menelaus into his own richly furnished apartment at the palace and placed himself as a buffer between his guest and the polite but suspicious way in which most of his brothers received the Spartan king within their walls. It was Paris too who conducted Menelaus into the presence of King Priam the next day, where he explained the urgent reason for this unannounced mission to Troy.

'Far-sighted Apollo is revered here in Troy,' Priam answered gravely. 'If his oracle sends you, son of Atreus, then be welcome among us. The holy place you seek lies on the Dardanian lands of my royal cousin Anchises, whom you have already met at Telamon's court. He speaks well of you and we value his wise counsel. No doubt his son Aeneas will conduct you to the tombs.'

'Gladly,' said Aeneas, 'and Paris will help us choose the bulls for sacrifice.'

'Then take the animals as our gift,' said Priam. 'Now come, Sparta. You and I must talk of other things. I have a sister who was carried away from us in an evil time and dearly wishes to return. Telamon listens neither to her pleas nor to my demands, but he does listen to your brother. Do you not think it would be well if Agamemnon and I were of the same mind on this matter?'

'My own wife, Helen, was abducted once,' Menelaus answered. 'We understand your sister's suffering, and your own concern.'

'Then you will help us in this matter?'

'Telamon is certain of the justice of his case,' said Menelaus quietly.

'And of the power of your brother's armies.'

'I am sure,' Menelaus smiled, 'that the High King of Troy also protects his friends and allies.'

'He does,' said Priam, 'should need arise. Do you anticipate such need?'

Menelaus considered for a moment before answering. 'Telamon's quarrels are not of immediate concern to me. At a time of pestilence, my thoughts lie only with the welfare of my family and country.'

'But if Agamemnon were to go to war,' Deiphobus taunted, 'would you let your wife keep you in her bed?'

'The King of Sparta is our guest,' Paris intervened. 'He deserves our courtesy. I am sure he would be as ready as I am to come to a brother's aid.'

'As I am to my sister's also,' said Priam. 'We will all fight for our own if need be.' He studied the Spartan king with narrowed eyes. 'Lord Menelaus, ours has long been a peaceful kingdom, but be in no doubt about our resolve. When you return to Argos, tell your brother that you have found Troy to be a strong and powerful city, one which prefers a reasoned solution to its conflicts. But tell him also that we will not hesitate to use her might should reason fail.'

Menelaus nodded. 'Then let us trust that with Apollo's guidance, reason will prevail. Such is my own earnest wish.'

The High King permitted himself a smile. 'I see that our son Paris has found good cause to make you his friend. It was brave to come here as you have, unarmed, but it was also wise. May Apollo the Healer take you under his protection and find your offerings acceptable.'

A banquet was thrown for the Spartan king that night, but he ate sparely and drank only water in order to remain cleansed for the forthcoming act of sacrifice. The most sober man at the feast, he replied with good humour to the occasional taunt and the many remarks about the enviable beauty of his wife.

'Can it be true what the minstrels say,' asked Aeneas, 'that she was hatched out of a swan's egg?'

'As true as what the minstrels say of your father,' Menelaus answered. 'That he was blinded by Aphrodite for boasting that he had lain with her!'

'Then you do not believe that I am Aphrodite's son?'

'As surely as I believe my wife to be Zeus's daughter.'

'Ah, but how sure is that?'

'As sure as I am that Helen's beauty – like your own manly form – has that about it which is certainly immortal.'

'Well answered, Sparta,' Hector put in, 'but as you see, I too have a desirable wife, and there are many beautiful women in this city. I dare wager that Asia has much to teach Argos in the arts of love. Can we not tempt you to try the skill of one of our Trojan beauties tonight?' He gestured to some of the young women sitting by the harper. They stood up, smiling, to make a show of themselves.

'An enticing offer, friend Hector,' Menelaus answered, 'but I trust you will understand that I mean no disrespect when I say that it is not only my condition as a supplicant that bids me decline.'

'And a man who lies nightly with Helen,' Paris supplied for his embarrassed friend, 'can want for no other in his bed.' He glanced at Menelaus, took a swig of spiced wine from his cup, and said, 'I would dearly love to look upon such beauty.'

'Then one day you must come to Sparta and I will entertain you there as royally as you have received me here. I know that my wife would wish to thank you in particular, Paris, for taking me so readily under your protection. Helen was fearful that I might find a colder welcome here in Troy.'

At that moment Cassandra rose from where she had been listening in rapt silence to the men's banter. She stood swaying for a moment with one hand held to her temple, then hissed across the table, 'Not cold, Atreides Menelaus – not cold but the heat of smoking flames awaits the Argive host in Troy. I have seen them writhe like serpents from a mouth that suckled on a bear. I have watched them lick and spread and burst untrammelled through the windows and the doors.' Andromache and her serving-women were already rising to escort Cassandra away, but the struggling girl was still shouting as they dragged her from the hall. 'Keep a close watch on your hearth, King of Sparta, or a serpent will steal fire from it that will set the world ablaze.'

When he saw Menelaus involuntarily making the sign to ward off the evil eye, Hector hastened to reassure him. 'You must forgive my sister. Since Apollo rejected her as his priestess she has been troubled in her mind. I beg you to think nothing of what she has said. It is only such craziness as she is often wont to utter.'

Menelaus had seen from the girl's upturned eyes and the harrowed darkness of her young features that all was not well with her. So though he had been startled by the outburst, he was ready to dismiss it. 'Please,' he said, 'my own family has known madness enough in its time. There is no need to apologize.'

But the conviviality of the evening had been dispelled and could not easily be recovered. After a time Menelaus yawned and got to his feet. 'You must forgive me, lords, but the hour grows late. Tomorrow I must perform my sacred duties, and right now I am much in need of sleep.'

'Come,' said Paris, 'I will accompany you from the hall. Tomorrow I will show you the beauty of our land.' He clapped a hand to his guest's back. 'And — who knows? — perhaps one day soon you will show me the beauty of yours.'

Yet Paris did not lie easily in his bed that night.

Ever since Aphrodite had promised to make Helen his wife, he had made a daily offering to the goddess. Each day, as the smoke rose and the doves flew about her statue, his offering had been accompanied by a fervent prayer that she remember her pledge and show him the way by which the path of his life might cross with that of the most beautiful woman in the world. At first sight, therefore, he had been certain that Menelaus must have come to Troy through the agency of Aphrodite. But the more he had come to know of the Spartan king the more he grew to like the man, and the less sure he became.

When Paris had first conceived the idea of carrying off Helen in a pirate raid, Menelaus had been no more than a name to him, and the name, moreover, of a likely enemy of Troy. The idea of stealing such a man's wife presented no difficulties. But he and Menelaus were no longer strangers, and Paris was finding it impossible not to respect and admire the noble-hearted man who had come so unexpectedly as a supplicant to Troy.

Already, on that first day, he and Aeneas had welcomed Menelaus more warmly and with less overt suspicion than had many others in Priam's court. By the end of the following day, after they had ridden out to the lands around Mount Ida with him, the three men were bonded in firm friendship.

Menelaus listened as Paris told him of the early years in which he had been raised as a herdsman in those parts, and warmly commended the courage with which, as a mere boy, he had fought off the gang of Argive cattle-lifters. In turn, the Spartan king spoke about the dark time of his own boyhood as a younger brother in the violent turmoil of the house of Atreus. So by the time Paris had escorted Menelaus to the mountain pastures of his youth and helped him to select the best bulls for the sacrifice, he was wondering how, in all conscience, he could ever permit himself to betray the trust of a man with such an open and generous nature? Yet without such betrayal he could never possess the woman whose face obsessed his heart.

There were many reasons, therefore, why he decided not to accompany Menelaus on the last stage of his journey to Apollo's shrine at Sminthe. Not the least of them were his qualms at the prospect of encountering Oenone. On many occasions since his arrival in Troy, Paris had intended to send her a message and each time he had failed to do so. With each failure it became more difficult even to think about her, and whenever he did so the memory of her face was instantly displaced by the image of

Helen. The truth was that Paris had shuffled off his previous life much as a snake sloughs its skin and the thought of the people he had wronged in this way left him uneasy with guilt. Above all this was true of Oenone. Suspecting that her love had proved more enduring than his own, he told himself it would be wiser to avoid her company rather than risk opening a wound that must surely by now have begun to heal. So with the excuse that he wished to spend some time with his foster-father Agelaus and the friends of his youth, he left Aeneas to act as guide to the shrine. Not long afterwards, having found himself no longer at ease among the herdsmen, he returned to wait for Menelaus and Aeneas in the palace of Anchises at Lyrnessus under Mount Ida.

Paris dined alone with the Dardanian king that night, but after the first exchange of courtesies, the silence between them was so prolonged that he began to wonder whether Anchises was disdainful of his company. After all, as this day had reminded him, he had once been no more than a herdsman on the blind king's land. Priam might have taken him warmly to his heart and required all Troy to do the same, but here in Dardania it seemed that Paris felt comfortable neither in the royal palace nor in the hovels of the herdsmen. Having trifled with his food, he was contemplating the various occasions he had given himself for shame, when Anchises turned abruptly from drying his hands after the meal and astonished him by saying, 'Come closer, boy. Let these hands have sight of your face.'

Apprehensively, Paris did as he was bidden. He sat staring into the dark sockets of a head that might have been carved from olive-wood as Anchises's fingers travelled across the contours of his face, pressing the eyelids, probing the lines of his mouth. Never in his life had he felt so intimately perceived. He had to fight the impulse to pull away, for it felt as if that powerful and sensitive touch must uncover every secret of his heart.

Eventually Anchises lowered his hands. 'I see it is true what they say. The gods have gifted you with great beauty, boy.' After a pensive moment he added, 'There is a fate that comes with such a gift.'

'Each man must meet the fate that he is given,' Paris answered, sensing that more was to come.

The older man nodded. 'They tell me that you devote yourself to Aphrodite over all the other gods.'

'A man must also choose.'

Again there was a long silence. Anchises fumbled with his right hand for the gold-mounted staff that he had left leaning against the wall at his back. Thinking that he meant to get up, Paris moved to help him but the old king gestured him away. Having found his staff, he sat with both hands over its pommel, and the jut of his chin resting on his hands. His face was turned towards the heat of the fire.

'In my youth,' he said quietly, 'I too abandoned myself to Aphrodite.'

Paris waited. For several moments Anchises seemed lost in thought, as though that distant past was more vivid to him than the darkness of this docile present. Then he turned his fierce blind gaze towards the place where Paris sat in tense anticipation. 'As you see,' he said, 'I found her a stern mistress.' He uttered a small, derisory sigh and turned that blighted face back towards the hearth before he added, almost as an afterthought, 'I would not wish to have you blinded by her too.'

Uncertain how to respond, Paris said, 'I believe she means well by me.'

'Perhaps.' Anchises scraped the bronze ferrule of his staff across the stones of the hearth. 'But there is more than one way to be blind.'

'Then I shall try to keep my eyes open.'

Paris had uttered the remark as lightly as he dared, but Anchises did not smile. Tapping his stick just once against the stone, he said, 'Are you listening to me, boy?'

Paris had jumped and nodded before he remembered that he could not be seen. 'I am,' he said softly.

'Then hear what I would not hear when I was young as you are, and just as sure of my own destiny.' Again Anchises tapped his stick once, sharply, on the stone hearth. 'Serve Aphrodite if it is your fate to do so. Serve her well. But remember she is not alone among the gods. *Nothing in extreme*, do you hear? That is the wisdom of Apollo. Nothing too much – not even in reverence for the goddess who has chosen you.'

The fire hissed on its stones. Somewhere outside the hall, the chamberlain was berating a slave in angry whispers. 'Do you hear me?' Anchises demanded again. And Paris, who had been reflecting that this old man must also have been arrogantly handsome once, said, 'I hear you, uncle.'

'Do you?' The blind king muttered without turning his head. 'Do you indeed?'

Nothing further was said. After a time, without explanation or apology, the old man got to his feet, called for his body-servant, and made his way to bed.

Paris sat up alone over his wine for a long time, brooding, drinking too much. His mood darkened. More gravely than at any time since he had come down from Mount Ida, he was troubled by doubts about the destiny which Aphrodite had promised him.

On the following night, Menelaus returned to Anchises's palace with Aeneas, having performed his acts of sacrifice at the tombs of Lycus and Chimaerus. He was exhausted but also glowing with exaltation, for he had been given clear signs that his offerings were found acceptable in the sight of the god. Aeneas insisted that they must banquet in celebration, and the three friends laughed often as they ate well and drank heavily together. Then Anchises, who had remained silent throughout most of the meal, tapped his staff and commanded his minstrel to sing the Lay of Troy.

With a quick, apologetic glance at his guest, Aeneas deferentially suggested that it had been a hard day and the lay might prove a little long and solemn for the occasion. But Anchises was insistent, and Menelaus politely averred that he would like to learn more of the land's ancestral history. Fortunately, the old minstrel's voice was still strong, and his touch on the harp proud and skilful.

The song told how the country south of the Hellespont had first been settled under the aegis of Apollo by Teucer, who had come to Phrygia from Athens. Then Dardanus had come there out of Arcadia and built a town on the lower slopes of Mount Ida. It was his grandson Tros who had given his name to the land, and *his* son, Ilus, who brought the Palladium – the ancient image of Pallas Athena – to the hill of Ate, where the citadel of Ilium was founded. Around that sacred precinct had grown the noble city of Troy itself. The song climaxed with an account of how Earth-shaker Poseidon had punished the impiety of Laomedon by destroying the city, which had then been sacked by Heracles and Telamon. The minstrel concluded his lay with a paean of praise for the way the High King Priam and his royal cousin Anchises, had restored the glory of the land and added to its riches.

'I tried to warn Laomedon of his folly,' Anchises sighed when the song had ended, 'but he would not listen. We Dardanians are a peaceful people. Though we will fight in a just cause, we prefer to hunt and breed good bulls and tend our herds.' He shook his head. 'I have smelled the dead in a burning city once. I have no wish to do so again.'

Menelaus raised his goblet. 'Then let us hope you never have to, my friend.'

'But that intransigent fool Telamon still lives,' Anchises said grimly, 'and he is no friend to Troy.' He turned his head in the direction from which Menelaus's voice had come. 'Nor, I think, is your brother.'

There was an uneasy moment of silence, which Paris was about to break when Anchises raised his hand and spoke again. 'Hear me, Menelaus. When Antenor and I were on Salamis, I listened carefully to you and your brother. Of the two sons of Atreus, I am convinced that the mind of Menelaus is more amenable to reason than that of Agamemnon. One might wish that it was you, not he, who sits on the high throne at Mycenae.'

'My brother knows that I am content in Sparta,' Menelaus warily replied.

Anchises nodded. 'But he would do well to listen to your sober counsel. And all the more so now that you know us and have seen our strength. Let us think about this together, friend. My cousin Priam has a great love for his sister. After all, he owes his very life to her. Also his heart is hasty, and where Hesione's fate is concerned, he is ready to let it overrule his head. Does it not seem to you, as it does to me, that if Priam and Agamemnon are left to their own devices, they will drag us into a war that neither you nor I, nor any reasonable man desires? Might it not be wise to temper their hot spirits with our own cooler reflections?'

Aware that the others were listening keenly for his response, Menelaus said quietly, 'What do you have in mind?'

Anchises sat in silence by the fire for a time before answering. 'My nephew Paris and my son Aeneas have proposed to make a voyage to Argos soon. Could they not build on the friendship that we have made here tonight? If you will speak privily to Agamemnon – as I will to Priam – then might he not be persuaded to receive them as ambassadors of peace and mutual prosperity rather than harbingers of war? Surely it would be in all our interests for him to blunt Telamon's horns rather than letting him rage far beyond his paddock?'

Now it was Menelaus who took time to consider his answer. He remembered how deeply Helen had dreaded the thought of war, and how sorely Sparta stood in need of a time of peace to recover from the ravages of plague. He reflected on how generously he had been received in the Trojan lands, and how fond he had grown, in so brief a time, of his new friends, Paris and Aeneas. He was filled with admiration for everything Priam had achieved in Troy, and with respect for the blind Dardanian king's appraisal of the situation. So when he searched his heart he could find no appetite for warfare – only the desire to rule over a peaceable kingdom with his beloved wife beside him.

'I think that you and I are of the same mind,' he said at last. 'I will speak with Agamemnon on my return and tell him what kindness and wisdom I have met with here. As for my two noble companions—' he smiled at Paris and Aeneas '—they have become dear friends and will receive the warmest of welcomes in Sparta at least. We shall see what transpires when I present them as ambassadors before the High King in Mycenae.'

Like a sudden alteration in the weather, the tension in the room dispersed.

'Then let it be a time for new beginnings,' said Anchises. 'Let us hope that youth and vigour can succeed where Antenor and I have failed.'

Aeneas lifted his cup to pledge the hope. After the others joined him, his father retired, and though the three of them were already drunk, Aeneas insisted that ten years was long enough for wine to stand and called for more. Soon they were drunker, and ready to swear undying friendship.

'Come to Argos,' Menelaus was already slurring his words, 'and I will show you . . . I will show you . . .' He blinked at Paris. 'Tell me, my handsome friend, what do you love most in all the world?'

'Bulls!' Aeneas said, and started chuckling. 'He loves bulls.'

'No, no,' Paris demurred woozily, 'that was all a long time ago.'

'But you're still a bull-fancier,' Aeneas insisted. 'You saw him fondling those monsters yesterday, Menelaus. He likes them meaty and big. The bigger the better. Be sure that if Argos has bulls to tame, our Paris is the man for it.'

'No,' Menelaus laughed. 'I think he's more interested in women! I think he's a heart-breaker as well as a bull-breaker.'

Aeneas wagged a tipsy finger at Paris. 'That reminds me. We came across a pretty little thing wandering by the Scamander yesterday. She asked after you rather tenderly. Can't recall her name, but she called you Alexander. Do you remember her? Or have there been too many others since then?'

Paris stared at his friend. Quite suddenly his heart had capsized and was tipping him out of drunkenness into misery.

'Oenone,' he said. 'Her name's Oenone.'

'So hers was the first heart you broke!' Aeneas shook his head in mock reproof. 'Ah well, she'll have more to remember you by than the others. She's big with child.' When he saw how Paris's face had blanched at the news, he added cheerfully, 'Don't worry, it won't be the first fatherless brat in Dardania. And I'm sure you'll leave lots of other by-blows in your wake, like your father before you. No doubt they'll all claim they're sons of a god!' Then Menelaus and Aeneas were chuckling together, the disproportionate laughter of tired and drunken men enjoying the spectacle of a friend on the run.

'Oh dear, we seem to have fingered a wound,' Aeneas said. 'I think she must have been his first love!'

'Is that right, Paris?' Menelaus asked more gently. 'Was she your first sweetheart – as Helen was mine?'

Paris glanced away. 'It was the herdsman who loved her, not the prince.'

'And for this prince,' Aeneas winked at Menelaus, 'there will be many others. What else should one expect from a devotee of the Golden One?'

Menelaus smiled benevolently at Paris. 'The Golden One, eh? Well, the Goddess Who Loves Laughter has beguiling powers, I grant you, but you can burn yourself at her altar. If you are wise you will follow my example. My service is to Athena and to Hera, and I've found great contentment there. Take a good wife, Paris. That's what you need to steady you. A good wife. Do it as soon as you can. A man can look for no surer foundation to his fortunes.'

'But in that respect,' Aeneas snorted, 'you're the envy of the world. Any man would be content if he knew that Helen lay waiting in his bed. Isn't that right, Paris?'

'If everything they say of her is true.'

'Oh, it's true all right!' Menelaus smiled. 'Had you the patience for it, friends, I could sing Helen's praises far into the night. But what is the point when words cannot match her beauty and you'll soon be in Sparta to judge for yourselves?' He stared deeply into his wine-cup, smiling fondly, as though seeing his wife's reflection there. 'In fact, I'm so sure you'll find her the loveliest creature you've ever set eyes on that I'd stake my life and happiness on it.'

'But wouldn't that be to lose Helen herself?' Aeneas laughed.

Menelaus opened his free hand. 'My point exactly,' and his bleary eyes beamed at Paris over the rim of his goblet with the serene satisfaction of one who knows himself privileged to be the most fortunate of men.

The Trojan Embassy

In the weeks before he sailed to Sparta, Paris endured a deeply unsettling time. It began on the morning of the day after Menelaus had made his sacrifices at the ancient burial mounds. Rather than returning at once to Troy, Aeneas had suggested that he and Paris take their guest hunting through the chasms of the Idaean mountains where boar were plentiful and bears and lion might still be found. They had chanced on one of the largest boars that any of them had ever seen, a bristling hunk of animal flesh, long-tusked and as nimble as it was muscular. By the time the men came up the blind ravine where the hounds had bayed it, the boar had torn the guts from two dogs, trampled another and unnerved the rest. It stood in dappled light, bleeding from one ear. Paris and Aeneas stood aside, inviting their guest to make the kill. But the boar was not yet ready to die. Even as Menelaus raised his spear, it swerved and lunged for the cover of a thicket to vanish in green shade.

A steep wall of rock rose beyond the undergrowth, preventing escape, so the hunters knew the animal must be lurking nearby. As Paris used his knife to cut the windpipe of a yelping dog, Aeneas whistled in the two remaining hounds, but they had heard the death gasp of their comrade, and had learned too much of this uncanny boar's ferocity and cunning to risk its frenzy in a confined space. Aeneas was impatiently urging them on when, from an entirely unexpected quarter, the boar made its break. It came crashing out of the thicket, driving its ferocious bulk directly at Aeneas, who lost his footing as he turned, and would have been gored in the belly if Menelaus had not loosed his spear in time to bring the beast down in a gush of blood across the legs of the Dardanian prince. The boar lay there, wheezing out its last breaths under the weight of the long shaft, blinking sullenly at death.

Aeneas came out of the scrape with no more than a gashed calf, and was already laughing as he thanked Menelaus for a timely throw. But Paris had seen everything from where he knelt above the dead dog with the knife in his hand and his spear lying useless on the ground beside him. He was watching still as Menelaus tore a strip from his own tunic to bind the wounded leg. He heard the jocular remarks they made without listening to them, for the day had fallen still around him, and he was struck by a numbing sense that everything of which he had once dreamed was now impossible. Already he had been troubled by the growing warmth of his affection for the Spartan king. Now he owed to that noble-hearted man the life of his dearest friend, and it had become unthinkable to contemplate betraying Menelaus by making off with the wife he so manifestly worshipped.

Paris saw that he had been living for too long with an illusion. His vision of the goddesses on Mount Ida could have been no more than an idle dream brought on by drowsiness and solitude. Now he was awake in the world again, and the world was suddenly a colder place.

The hunters returned to Troy that night, and the *Helen of Sparta* put out into the Hellespont two mornings later. But even before Menelaus had left to return to his beloved wife, Paris had begun to give over his own nights to a frenzy of love-making among the women of the city. Life had forbidden him to take what he had once dreamed that Aphrodite had offered him. Very well! If Helen was not to be his, he would renounce his foolish abstinence and take advantage of all the other women that the goddess placed at his disposal.

There were many of them.

The lovesick daughters of Troy found his passionate exploration of their young bodies more heartbreaking than his earlier vow of chastity had been, for his interest rarely lasted longer than a night or two. Their coyness lacked the wild innocence he had once loved in Oenone, and he soon tired of their claims and complaints and tears. After one bitter encounter with a young woman whose sultry demeanour was matched only by her temper, he seriously considered turning his back on the city and seeking out Oenone and the child she carried. But the thought of resuming a narrow life among the Dardanian cattle-herders held little appeal now that the whole world stood open to him, and he knew that Oenone would never be at ease among the painted and perfumed women of the Trojan court. So he turned to the courtesans of the city, and from them he swiftly learned the arts that turned him from an ardent animal into a skilful lover. Soon he was making assignations with those wives of worthy Trojan burghers who had made plain their amorous interest in him. The secrecy of these liaisons gave them an air of excitement for a time, particularly when he was juggling three women at once, none of whom knew that he was bedding the others, but it wasn't long before he was filled with self-loathing at his own duplicity. He was aware too that, as he grew more careless, he was making enemies among the men he cuckolded, and though his position as the High King's favoured son might stave off any open challenge, it would not protect him from a hired knife in the dark.

Dismayed by these unaccountable changes in his behaviour, Aeneas warned him of the risks he was running, yet Paris merely shrugged off his friend's concern. With no guiding vision left to direct his life, he had more or less resigned himself to a brief career of meaningless sensual pleasure when he was approached one evening by Hector's wife, Andromache. She reminded Paris that she had always been among his well-wishers, that she had rejoiced with Priam and Hecuba at the return of their lost son, and that she and Hector had entertained high hopes that he would bring fresh energy to the king's council and prove a stalwart defender of the city and its interests. Imagine their dismay, therefore, to watch him waste his youth and vigour in a dissolute life of reprehensible affairs. What had become of the native dignity he had brought with him from the mountains? It was natural enough that a young man had wild oats to sow, but Paris was in danger of offending all propriety and of throwing his life away. Did he imagine that such licentiousness was consonant with a proper devotion to love's service? Could she not prevail on him to ease the anxiety of his mother's heart by mending his ways?

Andromache left Paris overwhelmed by remorse. He vowed to himself that he would renew his interest in the political life of Troy and take a responsible role in the life of his family. He began to attend his father's court again, trying to understand the complex web of treaties and trade agreements that under-pinned the prosperity of the city. And he gave some of his leisure hours to sporting with his little brother Capys and his playmate Antheus, who was the son of Antenor, the king's chief counsellor. Finding in the boys some echo of his own lost innocence, Paris would lead them on expeditions to the rivers and the mountains, where he excited their young hearts with tales of the hunt or of fighting bulls, and of how, as a boy, he had driven off the Argive rustlers.

One day, near the end of the summer, they accompanied him to the shore for a last consultation with Phereclus about his ship, the *Aphrodite,* which stood complete now in everything but her final details. Paris had drunk too much wine the night before and his head was aching still, so he took little pleasure in visiting a ship that had now lost almost all purpose for him. As the boys clambered aboard and ran about the deck, playing at pirates with their wooden swords, Paris looked up into the eyes of the figure-head and felt a wave of yearning for the days when this was still a ship of dreams, not just the vessel which would shortly take him on a sober diplomatic journey to the Argive kingdoms. In the past hectic weeks, he'd tried to extinguish the vision of Helen from his mind, but the exquisitely carved face of Aphrodite smiled down from the prow with superior knowledge, and he knew the vision was inextinguishable. He would sail to Sparta and find Helen, yes. But the Helen he found would be the loyal wife of his friend, and would remain what she had always been – a forever unattainable fantasy of his restless heart.

The accident happened so abruptly that he was never quite sure afterwards how it had come about. He had been arguing with Phereclus over some minor detail in the way the after-awning was rigged. They were already shouting above the noise of saws and hammers from the other boats in the yard where Priam's fleet was under construction, when the boys came towards them, clattering their wooden swords together as they jumped from oar-bench to oar-bench, whooping out their battle-cries. Paris told them to make less noise, which they did for a moment, but Antheus poked Capys with his sword and soon their shrill voices were hooting out battlefield insults at each other. Then they were fighting their way back down the benches again, shouting as they came.

In a fit of anger, Paris shouted, 'Didn't I tell you to keep quiet?', and swung his arm to cuff the nearest boy across the ear. The blow landed harder than he intended, Antheus was knocked off the bench from which he had been about to leap and fell, twisting, to the deck below. His thin right arm hit the boards first, bending under the impact in such a way that the wooden sword turned in his grip and entered the socket of his eye. The force of the fall was strong enough to drive the point into his brain.

Paris looked down where the boy's skinny body lay crumpled in a widening pool of blood with his head propped at an improb-able angle on the sword. He looked up and saw Phereclus staring wide-eyed. Beside him, with the fingers of one hand pushed into his mouth, Capys gazed down in puzzled dismay at his dead friend.

★   ★   ★

No one doubted that the death of Antheus was an accident, and no one could doubt that Paris was responsible for it. Antheus had been the youngest, much spoiled son of Antenor, and neither the king's counsellor nor his wife, Theano, who was high-priestess to Athena in the city, could bring themselves even to look at Paris in the days after he carried their child's dead body back to them.

Nor could the grief-stricken parents find the forgiveness to cleanse him of his guilt, and no one else in the city had the power to do so. Unable to clear his mind of the dead child's ruined face, or to silence the sound of Theano's wailing in his ears, Paris lay awake at night, agonized by remorse, and with the Furies screeching through the darkness round him.

It seemed that his whole life amounted to no more than a vain tissue of futility and betrayal. He had neglected the foster-parents who had reared him, forsaken Oenone and the child she carried, toyed with the hearts of more women than he could recall, and cuckolded many good citizens of Troy. Worst of all, he had disavowed the vision that had once filled his life with meaning, and because of that he had now caused the death of a child – a deed terrible in itself, and one which added to the grievances that Athena held against him. Perhaps the priest and priestess of Apollo had been right all those years ago and his life was cursed from the start?

The one saving thought was that he and Aeneas would shortly set sail for Sparta. Somewhere out there on the blue ocean, far beyond the only horizon he had ever known, he must find a way either to redeem his afflicted life or to meet whatever end the gods intended for it.

On the night before he was due to sail, his father summoned him to his private chamber. King Priam sat in the chair he had rescued from the burning embers of his father's palace in Troy many years before – a flame-blackened throne that he kept as a reminder of Laomedon's folly and the justice of the gods. Around his shoulders he wore a richly embroidered cloak that was fastened

at his chest by a gold chain and clasp, figured with strange, mutu-
ally devouring beasts that some Thracian goldsmith had worked
for him. The flat of one bony hand supported his chin. The other,
gorgeously ringed, trembled where it lay against his thigh. He
looked, and felt, very old.

'It grieves my heart to think that you must put to sea unpu-
rified,' he sighed. 'Believe me, I know what it is like to lose a
son, but I was luckier than Antenor. His child can never be
restored to him. And the blow that killed Antheus has hardened
his father's heart. I greatly fear that your rash act has made my
old friend and counsellor your enemy for the remainder of his
days.'

Priam's eyes glanced away across the chamber. Paris merely
nodded his head in assent to the judgement. Then his father
added wearily, 'And Antenor may not be the only one. There
have been murmurings in the city. My spies tell me there are
husbands who say that it is one thing to be a devotee of Aphrodite,
but another to sacrifice the lives of children on her altar.'

Paris gasped and was about to protest when Priam silenced
him. 'The death of Antheus was an unhappy chance, I know. But
men will look for the hand of a god behind such things, and
you have taken many risks in service to the Golden One. It is
well that you are going from Troy right now. But we must take
thought for your return.'

'If this city tires of me I will remain abroad,' Paris answered
sullenly. 'There are even those among my brothers who will be
glad to see my back.'

'Then do not play the proud fool with the father who loves
you.' Priam shook his head. 'It is time your passions were bridled
by cool thought. Consider this: Antenor has always opposed my
plans for an assault on Salamis. He fears that to attack Telamon
would bring down the whole Argive host upon this city, and he
could be right. So you may do something to redeem yourself in
his eyes, if you can secure a treaty of peace with Agamemnon
through your friendship with the King of Sparta.' Priam drew

his breath in a deep sigh. 'I am not hopeful of it. The Mycenaean lion has been growing hungry and proud for some time now. I think he smells fat prey in Troy, and it will take more than subtle words to keep him from our gates. But see what can be done, my son. And if – as I predict – Agamemnon remains intransigent over the fate of my dear sister . . . well, remember that once you had another plan.'

The eyes of the two men met for a moment in the oil-lamp's unsteady light. The air of the chamber was very still. In its silence Priam licensed his son, if all else failed, to use the gifts the gods had given him, as lover and as warrior, to make off with some Argive princess that they might hold as hostage for the ransom of Hesione.

'I remember very well, father,' Paris answered. But what he remembered brought only a further pang of anguish to his troubled heart.

He knelt, dully, to receive his father's blessing. Priam laid both his hands across his bowed head and looked down at his son. 'One thing more occurs to me. Menelaus is a sacred king in Sparta. He has priestly powers, he is your friend and he stands in our debt. By permitting him to offer sacrifices in Dardania we enabled him to cleanse his own land of pestilence. As a true king he will not have forgotten this. So when he makes his offerings at the temple of Athena in Sparta, kneel before him as you kneel now before me, and ask him to cleanse you of the impurity that haunts your mind. Though Athena's priestess here in Ilium now carries only hatred in her heart for you, the goddess herself is merciful. Menelaus will not refuse you. May the gods go with you, and bring you safely home.'

The two ships put out at dawn, Paris in the *Aphrodite* and Aeneas in his own vessel, the *Gorgona*. At first the air was so still that the crews had to take to the oars, but as the day brightened, a breeze got up, and soon the two ships were cutting under sail through white-capped waves while dolphins plunged and shone about them. The pale blur of the coastline at their backs dropped below the horizon, and they were racing into open sea. Leaving his ship-master to watch the helm, Paris stood alone at the prow, taking the bright spray from the bow wave in his face and staring ahead into the blue-green glitter of the day. Hours passed without him uttering a word, and later, by night, he lay far from sleep on the afterdeck, gazing up into the steep black deeps where count-less stars tipped and swirled about the tinkling masthead. The voyage itself was quickly proving restorative. With each dip and surge of the ship he felt the shadows of Troy fall from him, as though he was quietly decanting the past from his soul in order to fill it with a future.

As he watched the surf break in spindrift at the bow, or fall shimmering off a dolphin's back, he was thinking of Aphrodite and how the goddess had taken her name from the white curdle of foam in which her naked beauty was born.

So he was following her now through her native element. She was both the vessel that bore him and the foam on which it floated, and her presence was manifest in the quick glances of the shining breeze and the sparkling light that lifted off the sea. With the force of returning memory it came clear to him again that in the same moment that he had chosen her, Aphrodite had chosen him, and he was held as securely in her embrace as was the infant Eros figured in her arms at the prow of the ship that bore her sacred name.

Yet that thought brought the picture of little Antheus back to his mind. His soul was not yet cleansed of that death, but he would submit himself in Sparta to the rites of purification, and once that was done he would be back inside his destiny again. If the blood of a child had been shed in his ship, then perhaps it had been a dreadful kind of sacrifice after all. For only through the death of innocence could his life be entirely consecrated to the service of that single-minded goddess, and he was utterly at her mercy now.

The realization came to him in almost the same moment that

a sailor at the yardarm of the *Gorgona* shouted that he had sighted land. Aeneas waved cheerily across the gap between the ships. Paris raised his own hand in reply.

They sailed among the islands off the coast of Attica, and across the uneventful waters of the Gulf of Argolis until they made landfall in a harbour on the Laconian coast. As the yardarm of the *Aphrodite* creaked down and the ship nudged her way towards the strand, Paris stood at the prow with both arms holding the painted figurehead of the goddess. He was looking north-eastwards to the rampart of mountains ringing the Spartan plain. Somewhere beyond those summits, not more than twenty miles away, lay the palace of Menelaus, and somewhere within its walls Helen would be going about her business, utterly unaware that an envoy sent by the goddess of love was thinking about her now, and with a heart that strummed as tautly as the full-bellied sail had done only moments before. The salt air quivered about his head. All his senses were alert. Each breath he took felt fresh with destiny. Yet strangely he felt more at peace with himself now than at any moment since Menelaus had sailed away from Troy. He had placed his life once more in the hands of the goddess. Aphrodite Pelagaia, She of the Fair Voyage, had brought him safely to Sparta. It was for her to decide his fate.

News of the arrival of the Trojan embassy reached the palace of Menelaus long before the visitors themselves came down through a high mountain pass to look upon the fertile plain of the Eurotas. To their amazement Paris and Aeneas saw how, beyond the rolling fields and groves, the city of Sparta stood unwalled. Though a gleaming acropolis crowned a low hill on the west bank of the river, the estates and houses of the city were scattered around it in small village communities across the valley floor with no apparent thought for their defence. Still further to the west, the late afternoon sun declined towards a range of mountains steeper than those through which their little cavalcade had just passed. Far beyond the tree-line, its summits reached for the burnished clouds, twice as high − Paris estimated in some awe − as his homeland mountain range of Ida.

With an ox-drawn wagon-load of gifts trundling behind them, the Trojans were following the river-road across the valley when a single chariot pulled by two black horses sped towards them from the city. The driver's red hair was blowing in the breeze, and long before the chariot skidded to a halt they had made out the burly, unarmed figure of Menelaus at the reins.

'I thought I should bid you welcome here in Sparta as informally as you once welcomed me to Troy, Paris,' he called. 'And you, friend Aeneas, do you recognize these horses? It's the pair your father gave me. Now they're the fastest team in all Argos. Even Agamemnon covets them. Come, leave your wagon to follow on − it'll be safe enough. Let's get you bathed and dined. My Lady Helen is impatient to meet my Trojan friends.' With a tug on the reins he wheeled his horses about, gesturing towards the citadel. 'Tell me, how do you like my land? Is it not beautiful?'

'Fairer even than I expected,' Paris answered, 'but Aeneas and I have been surprised to find that Sparta has no walls.'

'What need for walls,' Menelaus laughed, 'when the gods gave us this ring of mountains? Men think twice about invading Sparta when they know they will be cut down in the passes long before they set eyes on hollow Lacadaemon. My friends, you have entered the most contented kingdom in the world. What I have is yours to enjoy. I beg you to make free of it.'

In order that they might recover more easily from their journey, Menelaus had decided to spare his guests the demands of a public banquet that night, so they were to dine alone with the king and his wife in a private chamber. The Trojans soaked for a long time in hot baths and were massaged with aromatic oils by serving-women before being dressed in the fresh raiment put at their disposal. While they waited for the Queen of Sparta to appear, the two men strolled with their host through the nocturnal fragrance of a pleasure garden overlooking the city. They could see the river gleaming in the moonlight, and an expanse of olive-groves, orchards and wheat fields stretching away to the wooded foothills of the surrounding mountains.

When Aeneas turned to remark on the majestic pillared temple standing above the palace courtyard, Menelaus told him that he was looking at the Bronze House of Athena, the city's guardian deity.

Fearful that if he let this moment pass he might feel too compromised to ask it later, Paris made a sign of respect and self-protection. 'Then I stand near the sacred ground of the goddess in trepidation. Without intending it, I have given offence to Grey-eyed Athena.' He took in his host's frown of concern and opened his hands. 'I have come to Sparta, as you once came to Priam's city, with a boon to crave.'

Menelaus put a hand to Paris's shoulder. 'Haven't I already said that what is mine is yours? Speak freely. Anything I can do for you shall surely be done.'

Paris drew in his breath. 'My father has counselled me to abase myself before you as Athena's sacred priest in Sparta, for in the eyes of the goddess – as in my own – I am still polluted by a crime. I beseech you to cleanse me of it in Athena's holy house by whatever rite you think proper.'

'This is bitter news,' Menelaus answered gravely. 'Come inside, friend, take more wine, and tell me what ill fate has fallen to you since we last met.'

The three men sat down together in the shifting light of many oil-lamps and Paris recounted the events of the day on which Antheus had died. 'The boy was the much-loved child of my father's counsellor Antenor, who is well known to you,' he ended. 'And the pity of it is he was scarcely five years old.'

'I remember Antenor fondly,' said Menelaus quietly. 'A wise man, whose judgement I respect. I grieve for his loss. And all the more so in that I have no son of my own. But how is it that this ill fortune has offended Athena?'

'Antenor's wife, Theano, is priestess to the goddess in her most sacred shrine at Troy. I have sworn on my own wretched life that the child's death was an accident, but there's no denying that the fault of it was mine, and Theano has hardened her heart against me. Since that day the Furies have roosted in my mind and no one at Troy can cleanse me of the guilt. I must carry it for ever unless your rites here in Sparta can free me of it.'

Paris looked up into the solemn eyes of his friend. Menelaus was about to answer him when a woman's voice spoke softly from the open door. 'Is this King Priam's son, my lord – he who gave you his protection when you first set foot in Troy?'

'It is, my lady, and this is his cousin Aeneas, son to the Dardanian King. My friend Prince Paris was just telling me . . .'

'I heard,' said Helen, 'and like yourself I was so rapt in his sad story that I was aware of nothing else.' Smiling softly at her husband, she added, 'Does our city not stand greatly in this prince's debt – as I most certainly do myself?'

Paris had already jumped to his feet. Now it felt as though the room was afloat as he stared at the thrilling beauty of this woman where she stood in the lamplight, wearing a simple dress of Tyrian blue that hung in graceful folds from the lines of her body. The dark fall of her hair was bound up in a golden fillet that seemed to brighten the blue-green of her eyes. Paris had forgotten how to breathe. Everything had vanished from his mind except the living presence of the woman he had seen in his vision on Mount Ida. And it was as if that moment and this were continuous in time, and the long space between of no more significance than so much sleep. Surely she too must feel the power of that confluence?

But if she did, Helen gave no sign, and somewhere in what had become the far distance he could hear Menelaus speaking. 'It does indeed, and we are mindful of it. I think my queen and I are already of one heart in this matter.'

Helen smiled. 'Then surely we must do all we can for our friend in his hour of need.'

But every thought of guilt and shame and grief had gone from Paris's mind.

He was standing awestruck in the presence of Helen of Sparta and he could hear the whisper of his goddess in the jasmine fragrance from the night outside. 'Is it not as I promised you?' she was saying. 'Was ever a lovelier woman seen across the surface of the earth?'

In the same instant he became aware that countless men before him must have looked on Helen's face in exactly this way. He sensed too that she had never learned how to respond easily to the unintended impact of her beauty, for he could see the confusion already gathering behind the tender solicitude in her eyes as she glanced away, smiling, and brought her hands together just below the white hollow of her throat in a demure gesture of self-protection that made his heart swim. When he looked back to her face he saw that the smile had swiftly withdrawn behind a mask of proud reserve – a pride he might have taken for arrogance had he not observed that earlier chink of vulnerability – and in those brief moments Paris knew that the rest of his life would be worth nothing unless he did everything in his power to make this woman his own.

'I see that all the minstrels' reports are true,' Aeneas was saying. 'The Lady Helen is as gracious as she is beautiful.'

Helen smiled at him, shaking her head. 'If you take the minstrels too seriously, Lord Aeneas, they will have you believing I was born from the eggshell of a swan!'

'Because such beauty is so rare,' Paris said in a hoarse whisper, 'that they must reach for figures to encompass it. And still they fail. As all the rich gifts that Troy has tried to find for you will also fail to match such grace.'

'I'm sure that too is far from true,' Helen reached out a slender, white arm to take her husband's hand. 'And your friendship to my Lord Menelaus is already gift enough.'

'Then come,' Menelaus beamed, 'let us drink to friendship, and be joyful tonight, for tomorrow we will turn our minds to sober things.'

★   ★   ★

Paris slept hardly at all that night, and when he did so, it was only to start awake again minutes later. His body was filled with such appetite for life that it balked at every instant lost to consciousness. Such was the agitation of his heart and senses that he found it hard even to keep to his bed, so he wandered out to the balcony of his chamber where the air was heady with the scent of moon-flowers, and a star brighter than the rest – Aphrodite's star – dangled beneath the ripe moon like a jewel. He tried to recall every instant of this first encounter with Helen, every alteration of her face as he spoke to her, or as she became aware of his gaze observing her when the conversation moved elsewhere. He tried to remember every word she had spoken, sounding out each sentence for hidden signs or meanings, but though it exalted his heart simply to think of her at all, again and again he came up against the dispiriting truth that nothing she had said or done gave him a glimmer of hope that she regarded him as anything more than a welcome guest who deserved every courtesy because he was her husband's friend.

Still worse, if he was honest he was forced to admit that Menelaus's uxorious delight in Helen was met, on her side, by a devotion that seemed just as true. Divine Hera had brought this man and woman together in a marriage as unshakeable as Sparta herself, and its calm, ceremonious contentment was ruled by Athena's wisdom as the presiding deity of the city. There appeared to be no room left for Aphrodite's intervention.

Yet somehow Helen must be his. His life depended on it now. Helen *was* his life. Without her beside him, he would wander the world like some hungry shade tormented for ever by the thought of what might have been. The thought was not to be borne. Yet to yearn for the removal of the obstacles that stood between Helen and his desire felt like wishing for the death of a friend. A friend who had freely consented to cleanse his soul of guilt.

And so, as Aeneas slept on untroubled, Paris wandered the night, lurching from hope to despair and back again, finding rest neither inside nor outside himself. At one point, unable to lie on his bed any longer, he left the chamber altogether and walked back through the hall to the intimate room where they had dined that night. He sat where he had sat earlier and gazed across at Helen's chair as though she still reclined there, sipping from the chased silver of her drinking-cup or pushing back a stray lock of her hair. He remembered with what fond admiration she had smiled at Menelaus when Aeneas told the story of the manner in which the Spartan king had saved his life during the boar-hunt in Dardania – a story that she was evidently hearing for the first time. And he winced at the thought of her naked body now lying next to her husband only a few short yards away.

Aware how foolish and impotent the act, he crossed the room to kneel before the chair Helen had occupied at dinner as though some trace of fragrance from her musky perfume might still be discernible there. But there was nothing, only the carved wood and studded leather of the chair and the soft cushions embroidered with figures dancing the spiral dance. His chest felt huge with her absence.

Paris stood up, his mind hot with desperation, reminding himself that he had both a divine commission and the temporal authority of his father to steal the woman away by force if all else failed. This city seemed lax and complacent about its defences. Once out of the citadel there were no gates, no walls. A dash by night to the sea, and Helen was his. It could be done.

In a turmoil of conflicting feelings, he was about to return to his bed when he heard the sound of someone stirring in the hall. His heart leapt to the thought that Aphrodite had acted immediately on his prayer and drawn Helen from her sleep to come to his room. Furtively he moved to a place where he could look out into the hall. What he glimpsed there was not the woman of his dreams but the broad figure of a man in a loose night-robe moving from the chamber door that was just closing behind him to the stairway that led up to the royal apartment. The light of the small oil-lamp he was carrying glistened like bronze off the ruddy gleam of his hair.

The Madness of Aphrodite

For what seemed like hours he had endured the full sunlight of the courtyard in the sacred precinct as he waited to be admitted through the great bronze doors of Athena's temple. With Aeneas at his right and Eteoneus, the king's minister, to his left, Paris stood barehead and barefoot, wearing a simple white tunic over a loincloth. Earlier, under the curious gaze of the Spartan crowd, he had poured libations and offered sacrifices to the goddess at the stone altar at the foot of the steps before the porch. His forelock had been cut and burned. He had been ritually beaten with birch branches, then bathed for the third time that day and asperged with holy water and oils. Now, from inside the temple drifted the chanted strains of the hymn to the divine one who had sprung fully armed from the head of Zeus, and was about to pass judgement on whether or not this stranger in the land could be cleansed of the pollution he had brought there with him.

Alone of all the people assembled at the temple, Paris knew that there was more than one occasion on which he had given offence to Grey-eyed Athena, and that his rejection of her in favour of Aphrodite on the slopes of Mount Ida might weigh more heavily with her than did the hapless death of Antheus. The knowledge filled him with increasing dread.

At last a priest had appeared at the head of the stone steps to

summon him inside the temple. Accompanied by his two attendants, and with his head bowed low in respect and abjection,
Paris entered the cool shade of the Bronze House of Athena. The
priest signalled for Aeneas and Eteoneus to remain by the door
as Paris walked in silence between the lines of priests and priestesses, their ministers and choristers, to kneel before the impressive figure of Menelaus who was dressed in the ritual garments
of a priest and carried a golden staff. Behind the priest-king stood
a tall statue of the goddess, helmeted and wearing the aegis over
her snake-robe, with a gorgon-embossed shield over one arm and
her long, bronze-tipped spear leaning in the other. As Paris raised
his open palm to his brow in the gesture of adoration, the air
hung heavy with the swirl of incense about his head.

Menelaus addressed the goddess with solemn words of invo-
cation, then turned to Paris and demanded that he render a
truthful account of himself and of the guilt he had incurred
through the death of Antheus. When his confession ended with
heartfelt words of contrition and a ritual supplication of Athena's
mercy, the tunic was unlaced from his shoulders, his hands were
bound at his back, and a black hood was pulled down over his
head like the sudden thick fall of night. To the plangent sound
of music and chanting he was led around the temple until he
had lost all sense of direction. He heard a door scrape open, and
then he was passing down uneven stone steps where the air felt
cold and damp about him. He had not been prepared for any of
this. With a searing flash of panic, Paris wondered whether
Menelaus had divined his secret intention and meant to do away
with him in some dark declivity of this ancient place. His skin
was trembling in the chill air.

When the hood was removed he stood blinking in the torch-
lit gloom of a rocky cavern somewhere deep inside the hill. By
the unstable light, Paris made out flickering, stick-like pictures
painted on the stone and, directly ahead of him, the primitive
wooden figure of a goddess. She loomed above a charred altar
of rough stone with what appeared to be the head of an owl.

The air was acrid with smoke, and the hollow of the cave was suddenly loud with what his stunned heart took for the screaming of a frightened child. Then Menelaus appeared before him, red-haired in the torch-light, no longer dressed in priestly vestments, but wearing what might have been a butcher's leather apron over his naked form. A long blade glinted in his hand.

'Kneel,' he commanded, and when Paris hesitated, staring up at him wide-eyed, Menelaus spoke again above the terrible shrill of screaming. 'Kneel.'

With his hands still tied behind his back, and having no choice now but to pray for the mercy of a goddess whose very face had once been forbidden to the sight of men, Paris did as he was ordered. Words were exchanged in a dialect unknown to him. When he looked up he saw a priest holding a suckling pig by its hind legs in offering. The pale animal shrieked and twisted as it was passed into the grip of Menelaus, then the priest-king lifted its straining body, snout downwards, and drew his knife across its throat. The nerve-splitting squeals fell silent and the hot, bright gush of its life-blood spurted out over Paris's naked head and face and shoulders.

In the taut silence of the cave he could hear Menelaus chanting liturgical words he did not understand. The blood stuck in his hair, it splashed in thick gouts across his eyes and face, and dripped from his jaw to his chest. Tight-lipped, shuddering under the warm, sticky smell of its flow, appalled that so small an animal could hold so much blood, he thought he might choke in that hideous, scarlet shower.

Then it was over. He forced open the clotted lids of his eyes to look through a veil of blood at the ancient figure of the goddess. A priest and priestess at either side of him were pouring water from silver ewers to wash the vivid streaks from his flesh. As the cold streams sluiced about his shoulders, he thought he could feel the pollution of the little boy's death falling from him. But when he gazed up again into the piercing, owl-eyed face of the goddess, he felt like a shrew in her talons. With a certainty that struck to the bottom of his soul he knew there was one offence he had committed which remained so grave in the relentless eyes of Athena that, however long his life-thread might run, that insult to her divine pride would never be forgiven.

Yet he could not bring himself to regret it. He told himself that Aphrodite was there beside him, even in this deep fissure that had been hewn out of the rock at the dawn of time and made sacred to Athena. He stood to be dried, and as the tunic was laced again about his shoulders, Menelaus was smiling across at him, saying, 'The goddess has looked kindly on you, friend.' But there was only one thought pressing at his mind: that it could not be long now before he was back in the fragrance of daylight once again, and in Helen's presence.

A great banquet was held in the palace hall that night. To the applause of the assembled Spartan nobility, not all of whom had been glad to welcome Paris's unclean presence in their city, the Trojan princes presented the gifts they had brought for Menelaus and his queen. These were costly and plentiful, and many had travelled along the spice-roads from lands far to the east and south of the Black Sea. The sheer silks, rare perfumes and finely woven cashmere gowns occasioned much amazement and pleasure, as well as thoughtful remarks on the enviable wealth of Priam's kingdom, and everyone was delighted by a pair of chattering monkeys that were got up in Phrygian robes to look like Paris and Aeneas.

The last gift of all was greeted with wondering gasps of approval when Paris stood behind the queen's chair to fasten at her neck the clasp of a golden chain from which hung a gauzy, intricately worked cascade of jade, lapis and other precious stones. 'I am told that this necklace once adorned a great queen in the east,' he said, 'but were it Aphrodite's *kestos* itself, it would scarcely do justice to the beauty which graces it now.'

'No words of mine could do justice to King Priam's generosity,' Helen blushed with pleasure. 'I thank him for this gift with all my heart.'

Amid the loud exclamations of approval, Paris whispered in her ear, 'The gift is mine. I offer it in ransom for my heart.'

Before she could catch her breath to reply, he straightened, smiling at Menelaus, and returned to his chair. The King rose to express his own delight at the bounty of the gifts. Promising that his guests would not return empty-handed, he nodded to Eteoneus, who clapped his hands for the musicians to strike up. At a beating of drums and gongs a skimpily clad troop of Libyan tumblers sprang in somersaults and cartwheels across the floor of the hall.

Paris did not join the loud applause. Turbulent and emotional after the ordeal of his cleansing, he was still trembling from the intimacy of the brief contact with Helen's skin. Again and again he tried to catch her eye, eager to read some sign of response to his approach, but she was looking studiously elsewhere as she listened to Aeneas and her husband discussing plans for their forthcoming mission to Mycenae. Her hands did not finger the necklace at her breast. Even when a woman approached to admire its jewels more closely, remarking how finely the jade enhanced the green fire of her eyes, she gave no indication of anything more than momentary pleasure. It might have been some trinket she had bought at a fair.

Paris swigged heavily from his cup. The music clashed in his head. Fighting an urge to leap onto the table and shout at the noisy revellers that he was an emissary not just from Troy but from the goddess Aphrodite herself, he stared as a towering ziggurat of tumblers mounted upwards to loud applause. He was aware that the madness of love was making a base ingrate of him, yet he wanted to threaten these Spartan fools with the fury of the goddess if they did not immediately rise up and demand that their king surrender his queen to the arms of the man for whom fate had always destined her.

The tumblers were replaced by bangled dancing girls, and they in turn by an Arcadian minstrel who sang first of the hopeless passion of Echo for Narcissus, and then of Pygmalion's love for

Galatea. So the evening wore on with Paris sighing more than he spoke, and drinking more than he sighed, trying again and again to engage Helen's eyes. When he met only a polite, brief smile or a swiftly withdrawn glance as she turned away to whisper to her husband, Paris found such distant proximity increasingly hard to bear. The fury had long since burned itself out. Overwhelmed by sadness, he got up, making no excuses or apologies, and walked out of the hall to stand alone on a balcony.

He told himself that a kind of madness had possessed him, and there was nothing to be done about it. And though its claims were both too painful and too beautiful to be borne, bear them he must, for the goddess had offered him love and he had chosen to accept the gift. He had wished this fate on himself, and all the rites that went with it, and not for a single moment did he regret that choice – though it now seemed that it opened a need in his heart that could never be requited. But if that was the price of the exaltation he had felt on looking into Helen's eyes, then he was content to pay it. And if he was forbidden to savour the joys of love with her, then he would savour the pain.

After a time he heard a quiet cough at his back. When he turned, Eteoneus was standing there saying, 'My lord, the king is concerned lest our Spartan entertainment is not to your taste.'

'Not at all, not at all,' Paris answered dismally. 'The wine is strong. I needed to take the air. Tell the king that I will shortly return to his side.' But he had no heart for it. Minutes later, he was still staring across the river at the misty plain when he heard the soft notes of Helen's voice at his back. 'If you will not come of your own accord,' she said, 'my Lord Menelaus bids me come to fetch you.'

'Because no man in his right mind would refuse to do your bidding?' he said hoarsely, the blood beating in his throat.

Helen flushed a little and glanced away to collect herself. 'Because he misses your company, and fears that the ordeals of the day may have proved too much for you.'

Staring intently into her troubled eyes, he said, 'The ordeals of the day were as nothing compared to the ordeal of this night.'

Helen took a step back as though at a suddenly opened furnace door.

'Has someone displeased you?' she asked.

'You,' he accused her softly. 'You have displeased me.'

She stood before him, her chin tilted, her cheeks flushed as though he had struck her. Yet her voice was steady as she said, 'My lord?'

'I know you heard me when I clasped this bauble about your neck,' he hissed, 'yet you refuse me an answer.'

Angered by his abandonment of all discretion, she withstood his gaze. 'You are my husband's friend and I can refuse you nothing that honour permits. Sir, I thank you for this exquisite gift, which I cannot now accept.' But when she made to unfasten the clasp at her neck, he reached out to prevent her.

'Keep it, I beg you,' he said. 'Forgive me. I am not in my right mind.'

Her throat was dry, her alarmed heart knocking at her chest. Helen glanced quickly about to see if her turmoil was observed. Then she turned her slender body askance to him. 'I think you must be exhausted from the day,' she said. 'Shall I tell my husband that your need is to retire?'

'Tell him that you have looked on a man who is sickening with love for you. Tell him that the man may not have long to live unless that love is returned. Tell him that you have become a stranger to your former self and that his every glance now commands the entire attention of your soul. Tell him,' he added, urgently catching her wrist as she turned away, 'that when a god summons us it is madness to refuse.'

She stood, collecting her wits, her face flushed, eyes bright with the exaltation of her fear. 'Is Prince Paris so deluded that he thinks he is a god?'

'No. But I serve one, lady. And she is powerful.'

He heard her breath catch in her throat. He thought he saw a sudden hectic commotion of excitement in her eyes.

She said, 'If you do not release my hand, I will cry out that there is a traitor in my husband's house, one whose thankless heart is utterly unworthy of the kindness and friendship he has been shown.'

He found it intolerable that she should think of him so.

'And if I do?' he said.

Her eyes were turned away. 'We will forget this. We will think no more of it. We will try once more to be friends, you and I.'

Paris tightened his grip a moment longer before saying, 'I cannot promise so much. Say what you like to your husband. My life is in the hand I give back to you now – but it was already there, long before I came to Sparta. Crush it or set it free to love you. Either way, its desire for you will not be extinguished.'

Helen's lips were parted. She held the wrist he had gripped, tenderly, as though his touch had bruised it. Nothing in the world was quite behaving as it should. Even the lamp in the sconce by the door was smoking.

Then she shook her head and turned back into the hall.

Paris followed her scent through the din of revelry, watching the sway of her back, triumphing at least in the knowledge that she would sleep no better than he that night. They found Menelaus and Aeneas laughing together with a tawny-haired woman whose breasts hung loosely as she leaned over them to pour more wine. Raising his cup, the king beamed up at his wife. 'What did I tell you, Aeneas?' he cried. 'Helen's beauty is like a lodestone. It draws all manner of men along with it, whether they will or no. Paris, we have lacked your company. Come, take more wine with us. Or is it true what Eteoneus says – that you're finding Aphrodite's milk too strong for your head?'

'It will be the first time,' Aeneas laughed. 'There have been many nights when he's drunk me under the table.'

'But this has been a strange and powerful day,' Paris frowned.

'True,' Menelaus conceded. Already drunk, he was brimming with affectionate concern. 'Yet the shadow has passed from you now. We washed it away in the Bronze House of Athena. Be merry, my friend.'

Before Paris could find an answer, Helen spoke in a firm voice. 'Prince Paris is weary, husband, and not yet wholly himself. There will be other nights for merriment, but I think that now his need is for sleep.'

Menelaus made a gesture of disappointment. Blearily he studied Paris's pallid face. Always a straightforward man, he was some-times puzzled by the turbid shifts of emotion in his Asian friends. Then a thought occurred to him. He grinned up at Paris, gesturing with his cup. 'Cast your eyes about the room,' he demanded. 'There must be some woman here whom you would like to warm your bed tonight?'

'Were things otherwise . . .' Paris answered, hoarsely apologetic. 'But your lady wife is as wise as she is beautiful. I believe she reads my mind aright.'

Disappointed, Menelaus shrugged, and made a wry face at Aeneas, who was frowning at his side, perplexed by his friend's unusual demeanour. The Spartan king swayed a little as he got to his feet. 'Sleep if you must,' he said. 'But tomorrow – Aeneas and I have been making plans. Tomorrow we go hunting. We will camp out in the mountains together.' He closed his arms round Paris and warmly patted his back. 'A night or two of wild air will bring you back to yourself. Let's see if we can't find another she-bear to suckle you!' Menelaus was laughing at his jest when he caught his wife's eye. 'Dream well, friend,' he said more quietly. 'The Furies are gone. Your soul is cleansed. You are free to live your life as you wish once more.'

Paris was woken from heavy sleep late the next morning by a rough shaking of his shoulder. 'What's the matter with you, man?' Aeneas was saying. 'You were moaning in your sleep last night, and now with the morning half-over you're still lying here like a drunkard in the street. Menelaus is waiting for us. He's eager for the hunt. Rouse yourself or you'll offend our host.'

Paris dragged himself up from the bed with his head between his hands.

When Aeneas pulled back the drapes, fierce sunlight splintered at his fingers. Paris lifted a haggard face to his friend.

'You look like a gorgon's head!' Aeneas frowned. 'Are you sick or what?'

For a reckless moment Paris was about to confide in him, but he shook his head to clear it and saw that the time was not right. Aeneas was too frank and candid a soul. He was too close in his friendship to Menelaus and would not be able to conceal his trepidation if he knew what desperate plan was on his friend's mind. And if Paris failed to keep his own feelings under control, the King of Sparta would scent trouble soon enough.

'I don't know,' he groaned. 'My head is ringing like a gong.'

'There's a wench I know with a pitcher of water to pour over it. Come on, Paris, shape yourself. Menelaus was too gracious to comment on your behaviour last night, but I heard others remark on it – until Helen took you under her wing, that is. But the king means to hunt today and we're both eager to leave. Can I tell him you'll be ready within the hour?'

Eyes closed under the hand at his brow, Paris nodded. 'Give me time to wash and make my offering to Aphrodite,' he muttered, 'and I'll be with you.'

But when he came down to the hall he found a tumult of confusion there.

The air outside shook to the barking of dogs as they snapped and whined together, impatient for the chase, but a group of old women with faces gnarled as walnuts were moaning and keening in the hall and beating their breasts. Slaves were bustling trunks out to a wagon. Outside in the courtyard, farriers were backing a sprightly team of horses up to the yoke of Menelaus's chariot. The king himself stood in hurried council with Eteoneus and his other ministers, while Helen looked on, pale with anxiety, clutching her frightened daughter Hermione in her arms.

Aeneas crossed the hall to meet Paris at the foot of the stair. 'It seems we've picked a bad time to come,' he said. 'A messenger from Agamemnon has just informed Menelaus that King Catreus has died. He has to leave at once.'

'King Catreus?'

'He's their grandfather on their mother's side. A Cretan. His funeral rites must take place soon, so they have to sail for Crete tonight. The whole palace is in disarray.'

'What about Helen?' Paris demanded.

'Helen?' Aeneas seemed surprised by the question. 'What about her?'

'Will she go to Crete? Is she going with him?'

'I don't know.' Aeneas frowned. 'I'm not sure if it's been decided yet.'

Drawn by the sudden howling of the child, Paris turned to look back across the hall where he saw Helen in urgent consultation with Menelaus. She handed her wailing daughter to a serving-woman for comfort but the child was kicking and shrieking as the woman carried her away. Helen turned back to her distracted husband, evidently entreating him.

'We should offer our condolences,' Paris said.

Aeneas reached out to stop him. 'In good time,' he said. 'Can't you see the king has his hands full right now? He'll speak to us before he goes.'

So Paris had to wait and watch while, through constant interruption from his counsellors and stewards, Menelaus spoke softly to Helen, holding her by the arms and brushing a tear from her cheek with his thumb. Eventually he embraced her, looking about the hall as he did so until his eyes fell on his Trojan friends. With his arm about his wife, he crossed the marble floor to join them. 'Forgive me, friends, but grievous circumstances call me away.'

'We've been told of your loss,' Aeneas said, 'and our grief goes with you. It's clear you have much to attend to. Please don't

concern yourself about us. We shall shortly make our own preparations for departure.'

'By no means,' Menelaus demurred. 'I shall return within the
week and will bring Agamemnon back to Sparta with me. Then
we can give our minds to what most concerns us at this time.
In the meantime, Eteoneus will see to all your needs, and I have
asked my queen to show you royal entertainment. I cannot hunt
today, alas, but you certainly must. Listen – the dogs insist on it.'

He glanced, smiling, at Paris's pallid face. 'If you have the head
for it, that is! What is mine is yours. Make free of my home till
my return.'

'May your gods go with you,' Paris said, 'and give you comfort
in your loss.'

Menelaus nodded, clapped a hand about the shoulder of each
man, and turned to Helen, who glanced up at him in dismay.
'Be of good heart,' he said. 'I entrust my friends to you. Honour
them as you would myself.' Then, after making a few last arrangements with his ministers, he was gone.

Was Aphrodite so ruthless in pursuit of her ends, Paris wondered,
that she was prepared to kill off an old man so that a young
man's heart might thrive? Perhaps it was so. Perhaps King Catreus
had long been ready for the grave.

But what mortal understood the workings of a god? The only
certain thing was that Menelaus was far from his palace now and
his wife had said nothing to arouse his suspicion.

Paris feigned sick that day. He told Aeneas that he had no
stomach for the hunt, but the day was clear, the pack baying to
be freed, and the huntsmen ready, so Aeneas must certainly go.
'I know you're eager to discover what game these Spartan mountains hold. And I'll be well by the time you get back. Bring me
a bearskin to amuse Menelaus!'

After Aeneas had left, Paris remained in his chamber for an
hour that seemed endless before going down to look for her.
Helen was nowhere to be found. He came across the place where

the women of the house worked at their looms and spindles but he could see her nowhere among them, and the women giggled so much at his unexpected arrival in the weaving hall that he quickly withdrew. Nor was she walking in the gardens of the palace, or visible anywhere among the streets of the market-place.

By mid-afternoon, when the halls of the palace had fallen quiet in the heat of the day, he decided to risk entering the private rooms of the royal apartment.

He found the principal receiving room with its tall throne empty. A glance into a side chamber along the passage showed a plump serving-woman snoozing on a couch with the child Hermione in a cot beside her clutching a rag doll in one hand and sucking the thumb of the other as she slept. He pulled quietly away. The studded door to the next room was securely locked – Paris guessed that the king's treasury was here, or an armoury perhaps. Knowing that he must now be approaching the royal bedroom, he stole along the corridor scarcely able to breathe, and came to a trembling halt before the bronze-bound double door. He knew there was no excuse he could make if someone other than Helen was in there, sweeping the floor or changing the linen on the bed. But it seemed improbable at this hour and he could hear no sound through the door, so he threw the latch. It clattered in the still air. The doors swung open and he was looking into an airy chamber filled with light from a balcony that looked across the gardens to the river and the mountains far beyond. A huge bed built of cedar-wood, inlaid with gold and ivory, and with a pair of leopards carved at its head, looked towards the balcony. It was covered with plump pillows and gorgeously woven throws. A wooden chest stood at its foot. On the wall above the bed-head hung a tapestry of the Three Graces dancing together in a meadow of asphodels and violets. The other walls were painted in carmine, blue and gold. Against one of them, the iridescent hues of a peacock-feather fan shimmered in the breeze from the open window.

This was where she slept and dreamed. This was where her

husband made love to her each night. He had expected to be tormented by the thought, but he was now so certain of the invincibility of his own claim to Helen that he remained unruffled by it. Menelaus might have lain with Helen, and even sired a child on her. But the woman in his bed was not the real Helen of Sparta because Helen herself did not yet know who she truly was. How could she when the secret of her true life was known only to the goddess and himself?

Paris crossed the room to where a pair of inner doors opened on two separate closets, one of which was Helen's dressing-room. He could smell her perfume on the air. Many garments hung in racks there. He took the soft material of the nearest in both hands and clutched it to his face. Then he crossed to the table where her rich collection of cosmetics was assembled with the brushes, powder-puffs, files and combs neatly ranged beside them. There were posset-boxes made of sandalwood and many small apothecaries' flasks. Several caskets opened to reveal a small treasury of rings and bracelets, necklaces and earrings, finely worked armbands, brooches, diadems, jewelled hair-nets, clasps and fastening-pins. He looked for, but could not find, the jade necklace that was his token to her. Had she cast it aside, or put it somewhere secret for safe-keeping? But then his eyes fell on the silver scent-flask figured in the shape of Aphrodite holding a dove that Helen had prized among the other gifts he brought.

Clearing a space on the dressing-table, he lifted down the polished bronze plaque framed with dolphins that was her mirror, and laid it there. Then he took the stopper from the spout of the flask and in a thin drizzle of the perfume tried to write *I love you* across the face of the mirror, but the letters refused to keep their shape and began to evaporate on the air. Looking about he found a pot of the paint with which she must darken the lashes of her eyes. He took a brush, wetted it on his tongue, and began to write. The words were crudely done, and he had no time to worry, as he licked the brush again and again, whether or not the paint was poisonous. If it was, so be it: at least his message would survive him. And even his failure with the perfume proved a kind of success, for he had used so much of the costly stuff that the atmosphere of the closet had changed. It no longer smelled of Sparta, but of Troy.

When he opened the double doors of the bed-chamber to let himself out he heard the child whimpering in the nursery, a small noise but loud enough to wake her nurse. Furtively he slipped along the passage, peered through the hinge-crack of the half-open door and saw the nurse stooping to lift Hermione from her cot. She was tutting and shushing as she did so. Paris slipped quickly past the door and on to the end of the passage. He had just reached the foot of the stairs and was about to step out into the garden when a male voice behind him said, 'Was there something you wanted?'

Startled, Paris turned and saw Eteoneus frowning at him from the doorway that led to the kitchen quarters at the end of the hall.

'I was just . . .' Paris found the easy smile with which he had so often charmed the world, 'I was wondering where I might find the Lady Helen.'

'My lady understood that you were ill,' Eteoneus answered. 'She left instructions that you were to be visited every two hours if you did not appear. Her wise-woman Polydamna has been given care of you. She knocked at your door earlier. As there was no answer, she assumed you were asleep.'

Paris was on the point of agreeing that must have been the case, when he remembered he had been seen walking the streets. 'I was feeling better and thought I would take the air,' he said instead. 'That must have been when the woman knocked.' He smiled again. 'Tell me, where can I find her?'

'Polydamna is in the women's quarters. Shall I have her called?'

'I meant the Lady Helen.'

'Ah! My lady is at her devotions. She is making offerings for King Catreus, whom she greatly mourns. She would not wish to be disturbed.'

'And doubtless she prays for her husband's safe return?'

Eteoneus nodded, wondering a little at this puzzling Trojan's smile.

'I understand. Then I must patiently wait on her pleasure.' Paris glanced out into the bright sunlight. 'In the garden perhaps. I see there is a shrine to Aphrodite there. I too have devotions to make.'

With a courteous nod he turned away and walked across the pillared terrace into the garden. The grapes were fattening on the vine-trellis, and cypresses and tall plane trees shaded his way through oleanders and hibiscus to the distant myrtle grove where Aphrodite had her shrine. Entering the grove, Paris smiled at the statue of Priapus, a bearded, misshapen figure carved from fig-wood, who stood with his left hand resting on one hip, while his right hand held a flask of oil from which he anointed his impressively swollen member. Someone – a hopeful amorist presumably – had left an offering of pomegranates and quinces there. A blackbird chattered at Paris's approach. Then he was through into the sacred precinct of the goddess.

For a long time he knelt in silent meditative prayer where the small marble statue of Aphrodite overlooked a spring pouring from the rocks. The goddess stood on a plinth, dressing her hair amid the sharp, sweet scent of deep pink damask roses. Above her head, doves flapped loud wings from tree to tree across the glade or basked in sunlight murmuring. Somewhere in the distance a donkey sawed and wheezed its complaint against its load. But Paris was listening for Aphrodite to whisper encouragement and counsel in his ear.

After a time he got up to sit on the bench in a sheltered arbour woven from sweet-smelling myrtle switches. The sensuality of the place, the stillness of its scented air, the sound of water in the heat of the afternoon, everything conspired to fuel the desire for Helen that was aching through all his limbs. His prayer became a magical incantation. He was summoning her now.

But it was a child's voice that came to him through the trees, the voice of a little girl: Hermione! If Helen was walking her daughter through the garden it was unlikely she would bring the child here. Paris got to his feet. After a moment's hesitation he walked swiftly out of the grove, past the Priapus, in the direction where he could hear the child prattling.

He came out between two bay trees and saw Hermione romping in a patch of sunlight as she threw a ball to the fat nurse who stood across the grass from her. 'Catch it, Chryse,' she was calling, 'you have to catch it.' But the ball fell short. Sighing, the nurse bent to pick it up and when she threw it back, it came too high, passed between the child's raised hands, bounced once, and then rolled across the grass to where Paris stood in dense shade. With her eyes fixed on the ball, Hermione came running his way, calling back over her shoulder, and noticed him only when he stooped to pick up the ball. Laughing, he made to throw it gently back to her, but the child had come to a shocked halt, and was staring up at him as though a ghost was standing there.

'Catch,' he invited, bending a little, gesturing with the ball.

The child's face shrank with fear. She brought both clenched hands up to her mouth and let out a frightened cry. Dismayed by the response, he took a step towards her, but Hermione turned on her heels and ran back across the grass towards the nurse, crying out, 'Save me, Chryse, save me from the foreign man!' Then she threw her thin arms around the hips of the nurse. The woman put a hand down to the little girl's head where it was now buried in her skirts, and said, 'What's the matter with you, child?' Hermione raised her face briefly to glance back where Paris looked awkwardly on, and he was horrified to hear the child whimper. 'It's the man who kills children. I want my daddy, I want my daddy,' before she burst into a noisy torrent of tears.

The nurse looked up at the foreigner in dismay, made the sign to ward off the evil eye, then picked up the squalling child and hurried away.

Paris was left shaken in the garden's shattered peace.

★   ★   ★

He was still there half an hour later, utterly downcast by a chain of thought that had begun with the realization that for Helen to have a child was a far more complex matter than he had calculated, and all the more so as the child seemed possessed by an irrational fear of him.

He went back into the myrtle grove to contemplate his problem, but apart from the infant Eros, who was of quite a different order, he saw that Aphrodite had as little to do with children as she did with morality. She was the single-minded goddess of sexual passion and desire. Her duties ended where conception began. What possible help could she be against a hostile child?

Yet he found it impossible to believe that Aphrodite had brought him here and spirited Menelaus so swiftly away without some larger plan in mind. The alternative – that after such an auspicious start, a tearful five year old should stand as an insuperable obstacle between himself and Helen – was a torment too bitter to contemplate. Surely he had charm enough to win the child round?

He was considering how best to set about this when he heard the sound of someone approaching through the garden. Expecting Eteoneus to come with a disapproving frown across his face, Paris leapt to his feet from where he sat in the arbour and saw Helen striding across the grass towards him. Her face was flushed, her hair in disarray. His first exclamation of surprise turned into a wondering smile, but she had reached him before he could speak, was lifting her hand, and then she smacked him hard across the face with all the strength she could command. Paris stood, blinking back the tears that jumped from him, shaking his dazed head. The skin of his cheek smarted like fire.

Startled by the crack of skin against skin, a flight of doves were scattering their bright wings about the grove.

'How dare you?' she was gasping. 'How dare you?'

Against the ringing in his ears he said, 'I'm sorry, I'm so sorry. I didn't mean to frighten the child.'

She stared at him as though his mind was impaired. Her eyes

were flashing the fiercest glitter of sea-blue-green that he had ever seen outside a sunlit tempest off the Dardanian coast. He was trying to say that the child must have overheard something about him and misunderstood, but Helen erased his words with a furious gesture of her open palms across the air. 'To go into our private rooms, to finger my things, to leave the spoor of your absurd message for any chambermaid to smell! How could you? How dare you?'

Before he could stop her, she cracked her hand across his cheek again.

He pulled back, raising his arms to defend himself from further attack, and then he was laughing, laughing out loud through the sting of pain as he fell back onto the bench under the myrtle boughs.

She stared at him, appalled by his laughter, more beside herself with anger than at any time in her life before. 'If you ever dare to do such a thing again,' she hissed, 'I will stab you with my knife.'

The laughter stopped. They were both panting as they stared at each other across the trembling space between.

'Then do it.' Paris raised his open hands exposing his undefended chest. 'Bring your knife and kill me now, for if you will not love me I'm already a dead man.'

Her hands were both gripped tight – tight as knots, tight enough to hurt – as though only so could she restrain a fury that had already made her a stranger to herself and was now threatening to drag her, like the muscular currents of a flood, into a chaos beyond recall. If there had been a knife to hand in that moment she would certainly have used it.

As it was, all she could do was gasp – as much to herself as to the deranging man across from her – 'I would do it, I will do it.'

Again, after a shocked moment in which he realized that she was speaking her truth, he laughed.

Staring at him in incredulous rage, she said, 'I think you must be mad.'

'Believe me,' he answered at once, 'there is nothing I will not say or do to make you love me. If that is madness then, yes, I am mad.'

Helen pulled her body to its full height. Her heart was a mallet pounding her, strike by strike, like a stake into the ground where she was making her stand. 'I am Helen, Queen of Sparta,' she said, 'not some easy chit of a Trojan girl to lure into your bed. Do you believe I could ever love a man despicable enough to betray his friend while his back was turned?'

'Yes,' he hissed. And again, 'yes.'

'A man who would feign sickness and tell lies and steal about my house like a common thief.'

'Yes.'

'Then as well as a madman, you're a fool.'

'Then let it be so,' he said. 'But if I am mad, then I'm mad for love. If I'm a fool, I am a fool for love.'

Somewhere in the myrtle boughs around them, a dove clattered its wings.

She stood, trembling under the entreaty of his eyes. Knowing that he was gone beyond all reason and that if she remained longer in that glade she too might lose all dignity and control, she said, 'It would be best if you went from Sparta. But you are my husband's guest, not mine.' She heard her voice shaking as she added, 'If you choose to stay, do not expect to find me here.'

Helen drew in her breath and turned to walk away. But she had taken only three strides when he called, 'Why did you not tell him what passed between us last night?'

Had she walked on, a world might have been saved; but she stopped, and the accusation in his question caught her by the ankle like a hobbling rope.

She turned again to face him, fiery-eyed, 'Because you are his friend,' she said. 'Because Menelaus loves you and it would break his heart.'

'Yes—' he held her stare unflinching '—it will break his heart.'

For a time there was only the sound of water pouring between the rocks.

When he saw that she had not moved, Paris sat down on the bench in the myrtle arbour. Like a man suddenly exhausted, he rested his elbows on his knees and held his head between his hands. Hoarsely he said, 'It is the madness of Aphrodite. Lady, I have loved you since long before I came to Sparta. It is for love of you I came.'

She heard him at last. She heard the finality of his utterance. She heard its truth. But her will was protesting still. Bewildered, she reached for reason. 'How could you love me? You hadn't even seen me. You didn't know me. It's not me you loved but some fantastic dream inside your head.'

'You were the dream inside my head. The goddess put you there, and when she first whispered your name to me I knew you for my fate. The heart knows such things. And now that I've met you it's no longer a dream.'

For a moment she was held there, gripped by his eyes. She knew that it was imperative to turn now and walk away. She turned.

He whispered. 'Lady, you have been promised to me since the dawn of time. A whole world is turning on this moment.'

Her back was to him, and when she spoke, her voice was barely more than a murmur, as though it did not matter whether he heard or not. 'My world is here. I belong here, with the husband I love.'

He nodded, smiling as though in sympathy. 'I have watched you together and for a time I thought the love between you was such that the goddess must have misled me. Yet you have shown me otherwise.'

She rounded on him. 'How so?'

'Because there was more passion in the blows you gave me than ever you showed him. That was why I laughed – not to mock you, or out of crazy folly, but for the simple joy of knowing that you would never have struck me like that if I did not trouble your soul. I think you know me, lady. I think you knew me from the first moment we looked at each other. I think that you have begun to feel the madness of the goddess too.'

He had got up from the bench as he was speaking and taken two steps towards her. Helen backed away at his approach, but she had seen that what she had thought was arrogance might simply be a certainty so clear that it might be taken for a form of innocence.

'If there was passion there,' she said, 'it was no more than righteous anger. You have no right to invade my life like this.'

He said quietly, 'And if that life is finished? You can't go back to it now, not as it was. Menelaus is gone and there is no safety. Look for it again with him, and you will find only a tedium of years in which to wonder what might have happened if you had responded when the goddess called. There is a new life waiting for you. The life you have kept in hiding. Be brave and let it be.'

The terror of the words he uttered, the scent from the damask roses and the myrtle boughs, the narcotic whirr of the crickets in the heat of the afternoon, and the splash of water breaking from the rock – all these swirled inside her like the presence of a god. Helen turned her gaze to look where Aphrodite shamelessly dressed her hair, bare-breasted, the folds of her gown fallen about her hips, careless of everything but the sensual pulse of life delivered over into love. How many times had she studied that statue, restlessly aware that life must have more to offer than the repeated ceremonies of her daily round, the comforts of an undemanding role, and the easy sigh of satisfaction with which Menelaus consummated each swift and grateful act of love? But she had revered chaste Artemis when she was a girl, and now, as wife and queen, she honoured Hera and Athena. She told herself that it was better to choose Hera's bounteous ears of wheat, or Athena's loaded olive-trees, over the thorny roses of the Golden One. Better to resist the claims of passion than be swept away as its victim. Yet it was she who had placed this statue here.

And he was dismantling the world around her.

Helen shook her head. What was this mad Trojan asking of her? Could he really imagine that she would put all her life at risk for the sake of his devastating smile and these extravagant professions of immortal love? Was he anything more than a younger, more personable brigand of the flesh than Theseus had been – yet without that great king's glory? She recalled that day again – the heart-stopping terror of it, yes, but also the surge of exhilaration with which she had imagined herself carried off by a god in the moments before she came to her senses and saw an old man lusting over her.

'Such beauty must be less a blessing than a curse,' Theseus had murmured, and the words had pushed her soul so far into hiding that it remained beyond the reach of even her husband's considerate hand. Could this man really have fathomed those depths and seen it cowering there? Did he truly know how to call it forth? Why else, despite herself, was she trembling at his words?

And at the touch, tender and undemanding, of his hands at her shoulders?

His face was pressing softly into the hair at the nape of her neck. She could feel the stir of his breath. 'I know you have not yet had time to learn to love me,' he was whispering. 'But you can. You will.'

She pulled away. 'Hear me,' she said again, 'I love my husband. I have a husband who loves me. A husband who loves me dearly.'

He considered for a moment before saying what came into his mind. Then he uttered it quietly.

'A husband who steals from your chamber to another in the night.'

Her eyes widened, her nostrils flared.

'How can you know that?'

'Because I saw it with my own eyes. I came down on that first night to where we had dined together. I couldn't sleep for thinking of you. I saw him then.'

Drawing in her breath, she lifted her chin. 'Menelaus is king here. He has a king's rights.'

'What rights could possibly take him from your bed?'

'His right to a son,' Helen said, 'which is a thing I cannot give him.'

Paris stood winded by her answer.

With a kind of defiance the words burst from her. 'So yours is a barren dream, you see. A barren dream of a barren woman.' But before she looked away he saw the anguish in her face, and his heart went out to her. For a time their two vulnerable lives confronted one another across the still glade.

'I am so sorry,' he whispered.

And she looked up into a face so softened by compassion that she might have wept.

Who was this man? He had the appearance of a prince but there was such clear, uncourtly candour in his gaze that he might have been a country swain. So perhaps he was, simply, what he so passionately claimed to be – a man so far in love with her that he understood nothing else.

Unable to speak, to move, she was thinking, 'If my death is here then the goddess has sent it.'

But it was of life he was speaking – a life in which they might come to share the passion of the gods. A life such as only those elected into love could know, and of them only those who were prepared to offer everything.

He had reached out, tenderly, to touch her again. Immediately she pulled away as if she had opened her eyes to find herself on a chasm's edge and was reaching back for the safety of every-thing she knew. Though he had come no closer, she stretched out a hand in refusal, keeping him at a distance, repeating the word 'No' four or five times like a protective charm.

Gently, he shook his head. 'I think we are in the hands of the goddess now.' He reached out to pluck a damask rose from the bush. 'She means well by us.' He pricked the pad of one of his fingers on a thorn, and then pressed it softly to her lips till they too were smudged with blood.

Helen took another step away, open-mouthed. 'Do you blame the goddess for all the havoc that you wreak?'

Paris smiled down at her with the serene calm of a true believer. 'No.' Gravely he shook his head. 'I praise her.'

Moving closer again, he threaded the green stem through the tied-back tresses of her hair. 'I shall wait for you tonight,' he whispered. 'If you can deny what I have said, then leave me to pine alone and condemn us both to wither unrequited. Otherwise come to me.' Then he brushed past her shoulder and walked from the myrtle grove without a backward glance.

The Flight from Sparta

Aeneas's ship, the *Gorgona,* was the first to make landfall in Troy. The voyage home had proved less placid than the voyage out as a stiff gale blew up, forcing the ship to make way through rain against a heavy swell. Nor was the mood of Aeneas less turbulent than that of the sea he crossed. Already furious with Paris, he was convinced that his love-crazed friend had deliberately altered course in the dark of the storm to shake him off. So for days the *Gorgona* had battled the dirty weather alone, charting a course through the Cyclades, expecting at any moment to see an Argive warship overhauling them out of the dark horizon.

The odds were all against it, of course, for the Trojans would have been well out into the eastern sea before the news reached Menelaus in Crete. Yet the normally equable disposition of the Dardanian prince was so overwrought by his friend's treacherous behaviour that he lived in daily expectation of divine retribution. His crew, many of whom had grumbled at the hasty departure in foul weather from a port they had come to like, were already murmuring that Hera must have sent this storm against them.

Aeneas was not surprised, therefore, to find no sign of the *Aphrodite* in the waters of the Hellespont. In fact, as he muttered blackly to his sailing-master, he would have wagered all Dardania against a mouldy fig that if Paris's vessel was still afloat, it was laid up in some convenient bay while he cooed and dandled with the woman for whom he had put everything at risk.

As soon as he was ashore Aeneas hastened to his father's palace at the foot of Mount Ida to report on the disastrous outcome of the mission. Anchises listened, impassive as marble, from behind unseeing eyes as his son tried to make sense of Paris's insane behaviour.

'I blame myself for not having read the signs earlier. When I had half a chance to think about it afterwards, they seemed obvious enough. His manner at the banquet was so distracted that he came close to giving offence to our hosts.

'And I've never known him to be ill before – not even when he was drinking far into the night and tupping the palace-women like a randy ass. Yet two days after we arrived, there he was, complaining of sickness and headaches, and lying in bed when there was good hunting to be done. I put it down to the rigours of the cleansing ordeal at the time, but he's seen more than enough blood not to quail at the smell of it. He should have felt freed by the purgation, uplifted by it even. If I hadn't been so eager for the hunt myself, I might have suspected something dubious was happening when he hurried me off to the mountains as soon as the king's back was turned. I should have seen that . . .' Aeneas halted the rush of self-recriminatory thought. 'But he must have been so far out of his senses by then that I doubt I could have stopped him.'

'Not *out* of his senses,' Anchises said. 'Intoxicated by them. I recognized it in that youth a long time ago. His adoration of Aphrodite was always excessive. I tried to counsel him once in the wisdom of Apollo. But who was I to berate him for his love of the Golden One, when I have blighted my own life in her service?' Sighing, the old king pulled his cloak closer about his shoulders. 'Do not rebuke yourself. Aphrodite was always single-minded in her obsessions. If she has chosen Paris for the instrument of her passion, then nothing you or I or anyone could do would keep him from his fate.'

'But Menelaus was his friend,' Aeneas protested. 'The man even saved my life! And now I'm left torn between them. Zeus knows, I've always loved Paris – ever since that first day when I watched him bloody Deiphobus's nose. But I feel his treachery could scarcely be greater if it was *my* wife he had stolen.'

'Be thankful, therefore, that Helen was not your wife, for Aphrodite would not have spared you that betrayal.' Anchises's sigh was heavy with resignation. 'In any case, Paris has betrayed us all. You and he went to Sparta in search of peace. What he has done provides the Argives with a perfect case for war.'

'Unless someone more powerful than me can persuade him to give her up.'

'Do you think he will ever do that?'

Aeneas thought for only a moment before shaking his head again. 'No. He is gone beyond all reason. I don't believe he will.'

'But what of Helen?' Anchises said. 'Might she be persuaded to return?'

'Who can say what a woman might do in her circumstances? I tried to speak to her, I warned her of the consequences of her actions, but she was like a woman in a dream . . . except that there was a gleam in her eye such as I have seen only in the green stare of a wolf that knows it may die but will go down to the end enduring all.' Aeneas drew in his breath deeply. 'I think that Helen too must be possessed by a god. How else could she have let herself abandon her child?'

'She left her children in Sparta?'

'She has only one. A daughter, Hermione, a child almost as beautiful as Helen herself. For some reason – a prophetic instinct perhaps – the child had taken against Paris. And in the end Helen saw she must choose between Paris and her daughter. Had they tried to take Hermione with them, the child would have made the night loud with her screams. They could never have left the palace unseen.'

'Did you not challenge Helen on this score?'

'Of course I did! She answered that Hermione had always been her father's child, and that it would be more cruel to take her than to leave her behind. Whether she believed this or not, I cannot say. Certainly she is already suffering for the choice she made.'

'Passion always exacts a price. Paris will come to pay it in his time. But we must do what we can to make sure that all Troy is not made to answer for his crime.' Aeneas turned his blind gaze on his son and reached out a hand to draw him closer. 'We will speak with Antenor first – he has Priam's ear and is no friend to Paris. Then the three of us together will confront the High King with this news. It cannot be long before the sons of Atreus are hammering at his door.'

'And all Argos has sworn to defend Menelaus's right to Helen.'

'Yes,' Anchises sighed. 'I begin to fear that a still greater power than Aphrodite lies behind these events. If Sky-Father Zeus has decided that the time has come to cut a swathe through mortal men, then war might prove terrible indeed. We Dardanians must consider carefully how much we are prepared to risk for Troy.'

And what of the lovers meanwhile? Once they had found their way into each other's arms, they would have sequestered them-selves away for many days in an uninterrupted dream of love if they had been left free to choose; for in the few hours they were able to spend together that first night they were like astonished travellers entering a realm of the senses such as neither had known before. All trace of hostility between them had instantly dissolved, transformed by some subtle alchemy of love into a tender ferocity of desire to know the other more deeply in every crevice of their being, every gesture of feeling and of thought. And when the love-making was done, they lay side by side, talking and talking about their lives, as though their souls had always been intimate, though separated by the world for many years.

Gazing into Helen's eyes, Paris recalled how an ascetic priest visiting Troy out of India had once tried to persuade him that the human soul journeys through many lifetimes in search of peace. Though he had laughed off this philosophy as extravagant at the time, it now seemed easy to believe that he and Helen had known each other long before they met, in some other time, some other world. He whispered this into her ear as he lay beside her, and she smiled at him, saying, 'Perhaps it was in another life that I gave you that mark about your neck – unless some other woman has already set her teeth in you!'

'I remember nothing of any other woman,' he whispered. 'If there were any, they were only the vaguest dreams of you. But that mark has been with me from birth. My mother said it was as though I had been bitten by passion, and I swear I have never known true passion before. Perhaps you are right and Aphrodite left that sign for you to know me by. Come, let me lift your hair and brand you with the same mark, so we will know each other again in all the lives to come.'

'I believe I would know you,' she said as he raised his mouth from her, 'if I were deaf and blind, and an age of men had passed between this life and the next.'

'And I you,' he replied, 'if the sun were to die and there was only endless night.'

Yet at other moments, as they gazed into the unfathomable wonder of each other's eyes, the sense of accomplished union was so complete that there was no need for speculation – or of any words at all – to comprehend what was happening between them: the whole universe was simply and entirely love.

Yet if there were times when their hearts stood still that night, time itself would have no stop, and long before the first cock crowed, alarm was gathering in Helen's heart. Despite her lover's pleas and protests, she dragged herself from the bed just before dawn and hurried back to the royal apartment, fearful at every turn that she might be seen. Alone in her marriage bed, she shook at the knowledge of what had been done and what was now asked of her. Her mind refused all thought. She stared into the gathering light, knowing that any return to her former life was now impossible, and unable to see a way to any other.

When her child Hermione came running into the chamber to tell her of the bad dreams that had troubled her sleep, Helen could scarcely bring herself to speak. Filled with self-loathing, she longed for nothing more than to be free of the child for a few hours more and be clasped back in her lover's arms again. But she cast about for words of comfort and promised Hermione that her father would indeed be back in Sparta soon and would keep her safe from all her fears.

Of all the people around her, only one observed the change in Helen that day. Aethra, the former Queen of Troizen who had been her bond-servant and companion for many years, divined at once the agitation of her heart. It was her keen eye that observed the swift change in the colour of her face when Paris appeared in the reception chamber later that morning. And after Helen had vanished for hours that afternoon only to return flustered and distraught, her hair fallen and tangled like a storm-blown vine, it was Aethra, patiently waiting for her in the royal apartment, who looked up from her stitch-work and asked. 'So has the Trojan been thunderstruck by your beauty as my son once was?'

Helen saw at once that there was no point in denial. On the contrary, she felt an overwhelming surge of relief that here was someone with whom she could share the collisions of joy and fear in her heart – though her breath was shaking as she spoke.

'Paris loves me,' she heard herself say. 'Other men's eyes are arrested by this curse. He sees through it to the person beyond. If there were not countless other reasons, I would love him for that alone. And I do love him, Aethra. With Paris, I feel that I know who I truly am. I feel free to be myself.'

'As you do not with the husband who also loves you?'

Helen felt all the pain of the question and was amazed to find it far from mortal. 'I see now,' she answered, 'that I love Menelaus much as I would a friend. A good friend, the dearest friend I have, and, yes, as a good father to my child. And I know very well that is not how he loves me, and my heart grieves for it. But my love for Paris is of another order.' Helen looked up into Aethra's searching gaze, and a wistful smile broke like light across her face. 'For the first time I utterly understand why Penelope refused to give herself to anyone but Odysseus. She was always far braver than me. She was prepared to live alone if need be, rather than foreswear the honesty of her heart. And she was right. I'm only just beginning to realize how much of my own life I have mortgaged to fear. And I'm still afraid, but I believe that Paris's love is stronger than my fear. He has brought me from hiding, out into the elements where I can feel the wind on my face, where I can feel the fire burning under the earth. Aethra, there can be no going back on this.'

'So what will you do?' Aethra asked. 'Does he too mean to carry you away?'

Helen studied the bond-servant's regal face – a face which, many years earlier, had been ignited into life by a single night in the myrtle-grove at Troizen; a face in which a lifetime of womanly suffering through all the long years since was written clearly along the care-lines gouged into her skin. And when Helen spoke, it was as if in answer to a different question.

'But if I go,' she said, 'I go freely this time.'

Aethra considered the needle in her hand. 'Then you are decided?'

'Yes . . . No . . . I don't know.' Helen rocked like a logan-stone on her uncertainty. 'There are so many things that argue against it. Hermione is terrified of Paris. Can I abandon her in Aphrodite's service as my own mother long ago abandoned me for Zeus? Yet if I force her to come with me it will break her father's heart.'

'You have done that already,' Aethra said, 'though he does not know it yet.'

'I know it. Menelaus will go mad with grief when he learns of this.' Helen averted her mind from the thought. 'And I have my duties here . . . I am queen and priestess in Sparta . . . Aethra, what should I do, what should I do?'

'Why do you ask me,' Aethra said quietly, 'when you already know what you will do.' She looked up from the embroidery-frame again. 'Is it not so?'

'It is – may the gods help me,' Helen gasped, 'for they have given me this fate.' And because she could scarcely bear the gently complicit smile of reproach and understanding in the other woman's eyes, she turned her face away.

Then had come the difficult encounter with Aeneas, who returned from the chase wanting only to brag of the huge bear he and his comrades had hunted down. He was showing Paris the shaggy yardage of its skin, to which skull and claws were still attached, with its great maw wrinkled in a snarl, when his distracted friend begged him to be still for a moment and listen.

Secretly placed to overhear them, Helen waited, scarcely breathing throughout the long silence that followed Paris's frank confession of his love for her. Then she was appalled to hear the incredulous, heated oaths and insults that Aeneas heaped on her lover's head, and the merciless accuracy of the questions he shot at him, barb after barb, like arrows from his hunting-bow.

Impassively, Paris withstood it all, answering each question with a grim candour that sought neither exculpation nor extenuation, merely a simple acceptance of the agonizing fact that his love for Helen was such that he was left with no choice but to betray their friend and host by stealing away with his wife.

'Has that Spartan witch driven you out of your mind?' Aeneas demanded. 'Have you forgotten why we came here? Our purpose was to work for peace, not to start a needless war. Get hold of yourself! Think what your father will say to this.'

'I have my father's authority,' Paris answered, though with less certainty.

'To do what? Certainly he once spoke of making off with an Argive woman as hostage to exchange for Hesione if all else failed. But give my body to the dogs if he was thinking of Helen!'

Aeneas was shaking with frustrated rage. 'And all has not yet failed. Our mission is scarcely even begun. Menelaus means to help our negotiations with his brother. He must be preparing the ground right now in Crete.' Aeneas glared at his friend, wide-eyed. 'Or do you mean to betray your city as well as your friend? Would you set all the hosts of Argos against the walls of Troy for the sake of playing at love with a faithless woman?'

Then the two men were arguing so violently that Helen was terrified that someone else – Eteoneus in particular – must also overhear them. She stood trembling in her secret place as the friends all but came to blows.

'We should stop now,' Paris said at last, 'before something is said that cannot be forgiven or forgotten between us. Aeneas, you are my friend and I love you, but in this matter, believe me, my choice is made. I am no longer free to act as though it were not the case. The only question is, are you with me or against me? Whether you like it or not, you too must choose.'

Out of the tense silence of the private chamber, Helen heard the hoarse whisper of Aeneas's voice. 'Menelaus saved my life.'

'I know,' Paris answered, 'I know he did.'

'And this is how you would have me repay him?'

'I would have you do only what you must – even though my life is in your hands.'

'Come away with me now,' Aeneas urged. 'Leave the woman here. Get clear of her for a time. There is a gorge I know in the mountains where you can stand under a fall of melt-water and clear your senses. We will hunt together, and I swear not to speak a word unless it has to do with game or shelter or our life on the crags. Take time to think, and if, after a night or two in mountain air, your feelings remain the same, then I promise to do everything I can to help you.'

But when he looked up he saw his friend smiling so sadly at him that there was scarcely any need for Paris to utter the single, imperative syllable, 'Choose.'

           ★   ★   ★

The flight from the palace that night was covert and hasty, though it proved, in the event, less perilous than they feared. One of the attendants who had accompanied the Trojan princes to Sparta left the city openly on horseback in the early evening with secret instructions for the sailing-masters to ready the ships. As soon as the palace was asleep, others were sent to yoke the horses to the chariots and load them with the small amount of baggage that Paris allowed. Most of his own possessions were left behind to make room for Helen's needs, along with those of Aethra and a trusted handmaid, Phylo, both of whom were to flee Sparta with her.

Having made the choice and committed herself, Helen astonished Paris by her cool practicality. Though he assured her that Troy would provide all the wealth she could ever want, she insisted that much of the gold in the treasury was her rightful legacy from her father Tyndareus. The Queen of Sparta was not about to venture out among the hazards of the world without taking the means to provide for her comfort and security. As he watched her filling caskets with gold coins and precious stones, Paris was thinking wryly that, on his return from Crete, Menelaus would find himself lacking more than a wife – a considerable portion of his treasure would have vanished with her too.

It was Helen also who prepared the sleeping draught and mixed it with the jug of wine that Phylo took to the two men guarding the gatehouse that night. But when Paris went to check on the sentries later, he found one of them blearily stirring still. With a prayer to Aphrodite he slit the man's throat, and then, having killed one, he decided – with a ruthlessness that surprised him – that it might be as well to murder the other man too. But on his return to where Aeneas gathered weapons from the armoury, he told him only that the guards were asleep.

An hour had passed since midnight and everything was now in place, yet when Paris went to fetch Helen he found her collapsed in tears, having looked for the last time on her sleeping daughter. Worrying that all his plans must founder on her grief, he pulled her to her feet, whispering, 'Bring the child with you. We will fight our way out if she causes a stir.'

Still contending with her tears, Helen looked up into his gaze as though trying to ascertain whether this man who had over-thrown every stable thing in her life, was a demon or a god.

'You have been brave thus far,' he encouraged her. 'Be braver still. Our life is waiting for you.'

'But it can be won only at terrible cost,' she gasped.

'Yes,' he whispered, and the air between them strummed with that simple acknowledgement of an inescapable truth.

Helen glanced once more at the door of her child's chamber. Then she reached out to grip his arms so tightly that he might have winced at the pain. 'I know I cannot take Hermione with me. It is not her fate. But swear to me you will never forget that I made this sacrifice.'

In the vivid gleam of her eyes he saw the absolute gravity of the demand.

'On my life I swear it,' he whispered.

'Then come,' she said, 'it is time.'

The moon was big still, but its light across the Laconian plain was fitful under the passage of black clouds scudding inland from the sea. Yet only when they were some distance down the hill and out of hearing of the citadel did they climb into the chari-ots and make speed along the river road.

With the wind smarting at her face, and her cloak billowing behind her, Helen stood beside Paris, gripping the chariot rail with white hands while the landscape she had known since birth retreated swiftly around her into the relinquished past. Sparta was gone, Hermione gone, Menelaus gone, and only an uncertain future lay in wait beyond the mountain pass. The wheels jolted at speed along the rough road. Moonlight flashed like molten silver off the horses' backs. As she gulped on air that came at her mouth fast as the torrent of a spring, a surge of exhilaration thrilled through Helen's heart. She was already far gone beyond forgiveness or reprieve, and every fugitive cell of her being felt utterly alive.

There came another death in the mountains. The sentinel on watch at the fastness in the pass was about to call down in challenge when an arrow from Paris's bow took him in the throat. He crumpled at the parapet without a cry.

'That was the first death,' Aeneas muttered grimly within Paris's hearing. 'How many more will have to pay for this?'

But no one else stirred in that small, lax garrison, and minutes later, some four hours after they had crossed the Eurotas river and fled from Sparta, the chariots were through the pass and heading for the port without pursuit.

The ships were already afloat, the crews having been recalled, grumbling, from their various billets in the taverns and stews of the town. Two men who defeated all efforts to find them were left behind to meet whatever fate lay in store for them after the ships weighed anchor and dipped their prows into the swell. As the crew strained at the oar-benches, rain was already falling, cold and sharp, on the deck where Paris watched the greying headland slip away.

It had been agreed that, for safety's sake, the two ships would sail in close company, but as the storm got up and visibility worsened, that proved easier said than done. The whole world was in motion round them, the masthead tilting and plunging, the decks awash, the bow-wave clashing white crests of surf over inky green hollows, the sky a turbid race of blackening cloud. The *Aphrodite* had been toiling among the billows for less than an hour when Helen fell desperately sick.

She lay below decks, groaning in the salt-smell of the bilge, her face white as quicklime, crumpling again and again in drawn grimaces of pain. Out of nervous anxiety, she had eaten almost nothing for hours, and now she was retching on an empty stomach so that only malodorous green bile gushed vilely from her mouth. While Aethra wiped her soiled lips, and Phylo muttered to the sea gods at her side, Paris gathered Helen in his arms, where she panted like a dying dog.

Hours passed without the storm breaking and Helen's condition got no better. Afraid that he had stolen her away from land only to watch her perish at sea, Paris balanced the risk of being overtaken by pursuers against his lover's need to find haven from the turmoil of the storm. When he saw that she had lost even the strength to whisper, he ordered Skopas, his sailing-master, to put in at the first shore he could find.

They fetched up on a small island rising steeply from waters deep enough to risk running their keel into a cove. All around them, a stunned aftermath of fallen rocks lay in gloomy stacks where some casual heave of Poseidon's shoulders had long since scattered them. But the bald hill from which those stones had tumbled huddled its broad back to the storm. There was refuge in its lee.

Paris ordered the awning rigged across the mouth of a cave. A fire was lit from dried-out driftwood and chivvied to a blaze. With his own hand, he made a bed of cloaks and sail-cloth on a slab of rock above a standing pool. Then he carried his lady ashore into the stillness of a place that had, he promised her, never been known to move in a thousand years or more. Filled with love and anxiety, he watched her while she slept.

When he woke she was already bathing in a fall of fresh water deeper inside the cave. At first he thought it dawn, but there was a drenched, lemon glare to the light through the awning and the sky was singed with amber from a westerly sun.

Paris realized that this was still the first day of their flight. They must have slept throughout the afternoon from sheer exhaustion, having travelled all night and been worn out by the turbulence of the sea. But though the swell was still high, the storm had passed, and the woman who walked towards him, drying her slender limbs on a cape, was glistening like a nymph newly minted from the sea. He was famished with hunger and the sharp tang glancing off the briny light made him hungrier still. But his lady was smiling, however wanly. Her spirit was back inside her skin again. And there were other, more urgent appetites to sate.

Kranae – the rocky place – that was the name they gave to the nameless island where, for the first time in freedom, they consecrated themselves to the passion that was Aphrodite's fatal blessing on their lives.

For days, till the seas were calm again, they lived like the survivors of some rich wreck, banishing the others from their sight, feasting on fish and the squid they caught, and diving for sea-urchins, which they stripped back to the orange flesh with knives before swallowing down that vivid taste of sea. Gulls gleamed bright about their heads. The rocks which had once seemed gloomy through the drizzle of the rain were burnished to an ochreous red by sunlight now. They found figs and watermelons on the south-facing terraces of the hill, gasped at the chilly water from its springs, and squeezed the juice of lemons in their hair. They laughed and made love often, both by night and day, and during the drowsy afternoons they shared hot dreams of sleep.

When Skopas complained one morning that his crew grew restless, Paris gave them leave to visit the mainland shore that lay as a grey blur visible across the strait. Taking such store of food and wine as he and Helen might need, he gave orders that the ship return within the week, then the lovers stood together to watch the ship dissolve into the haze.

'And if they should not come back?' Helen said.

'Then we will live here forever,' Paris laughed. 'Here is our kingdom. The island kingdom of Kranae, which has no subjects, no slaves, no history, no worldly ambitions other than to remain itself, and only one law, which is love.'

'Yet we have enemies,' she said.

'Forget them. They will think us far away by now. Come, we will make of this whole island a shrine to the goddess. She is all the protection that we need.'

So under the hot sun, on the bare crown of the hill, they gave themselves once more to Aphrodite. And as an excess of wine dissolves the mind into oblivion, it was as if, through a glut of sensuality, they sought to erase from their bodies all memory of a world that must one day make them answer for this dream of liberty.

A Perfect Case for War

Outside the House of the Axe, in the sweltering heat of the bull-arena more than two hundred miles across the Cretan Sea from Sparta, Menelaus was bestowing prizes at his grandfather's funeral games when the news came.

The runner who had arrived sweating from the port was troubled by more than the heat. He waited anxiously while the chamberlain whispered in the ear of the Cretan king. Frowning at the interruption, Deucalion nodded and turned to Menelaus who was warmly congratulating the lissom bull-dancer into whose hands he had just thrown an opal ring. 'A ship has put in from Sparta,' he said. 'It seems someone has come with news. He wishes to speak privately with you'

Deucalion had been king in Knossos for more than thirty years now. It was he who had rebuilt the ancient palace of Minos after the labyrinth had been left in ruins by earthquake and the war with Theseus. But the power of Crete was a shade of what it had been for a thousand years before that evil time, and Deucalion felt far from easy that the death of one of his vassals should have brought the sons of Atreus to the island. It had once been among his ambitions to wed his son Idomeneus to Helen of Sparta, and thereby forge an alliance that would strengthen Crete against the growing might of Mycenae. But that hope had failed, so he had been forced to sit with Menelaus beaming at his side, while that crass bully Agamemnon cut a swathe through the palace-women, dreaming of a day when the whole of Crete might lie beneath his sway.

Deucalion caught the briskly disguised flicker of anxiety in his guest's face as Menelaus apologized and got up from his seat. Watching from the corner of his eye, he saw him tilt his head impatiently to catch the whispered message and was astounded to see how the colours changed in the King of Sparta's face.

The dense frown drained to a pallid white, then turned a fierce red as blood rushed back to his cheeks. Menelaus released an involuntary gasp, raised a clenched hand from his side and for a moment Deucalion thought he was about to strike the messenger. But the fist halted against the man's glistening shoulder, the fingers opened, and Menelaus was leaning his weight against the Spartan for support. Taking a few moments to gather himself, he shook his head, pushed back his ruddy locks of hair and glanced uneasily at the people near him. Then he uttered a single, sickly, incredulous laugh, and hissed something at the messenger, who took a step backwards, opening his hands in a helpless gesture of self-exculpation. Menelaus dragged the man further aside. There came a further clipped exchange of questions and answers before the uneasy runner pressed a fist to his brow as he bowed and backed quickly away.

Gathering his wits, unseeing, Menelaus seemed at last to remember where he was. Slowly he walked back to Deucalion. Around them the crowd was applauding the arrival of a new team in the bullring, so Menelaus had to wait for the din to die down a little before his voice could be heard.

'Forgive me,' he said, 'you must give me leave.'

Deucalion summoned a solicitous frown. 'Not bad news, I hope?'

'A matter that requires my urgent attention.' Hearing how hoarse his voice was, Menelaus turned abruptly away. 'Forgive me,' he muttered again, and left the stadium through the excited crowd, angrily demanding that his bewildered attendants let him be. The ground felt unstable beneath his feet. He might have been treading the sea's greasy swell. Alone in the dusty street, Menelaus, King of Sparta, stopped, leaning one hand against a tavern wall where someone had written in a wavering scrawl: *Clio is a whore.* He had to fight the need to vomit.

Two hours later, the sons of Atreus sat together in a private room of the mansion that had been put at their disposal while they sojourned in Knossos. The dark blue walls were painted with a procession of bare-breasted libation-bearers in flounced skirts, whose upraised arms were wreathed with snakes. During the quake that had wrecked much of the city, a crack had torn through their stately progress like a thunderbolt striking the field of irises through which they walked. Some jobbing builder must have been employed to stitch the masonry together again, but the repair had been painted over with a less costly blue. The chamber still stank of some cloying incense that had been burning there when they first arrived in Knossos. Outside, the sky was gravid with a storm that would not break and the light lent a lurid glow to the yellow blossoms dangling at the casement.

A big man, whose coarsely-haired chest was exposed under the loose gown he had slipped on to cover his nakedness, Agamemnon waited for the slave to set down the wine and leave the room before he spoke again. When he did so, it was in a low, throaty growl.

'The runner was sure about this?'

'He had it from Eteoneus. The words were exact. There can be no doubt.'

Agamemnon nodded. Preferring not to consider the raw evidence around the rims of his brother's eyes, he shifted his gaze about this unsavoury room with a casual indolence that belied the speed of his thoughts.

'Perhaps Eteoneus has got it wrong,' he said. 'The Trojan could have made off with her against her will. He might be holding her hostage for Hesione. I'm surprised Priam hasn't tried it before. It's what I would have done in his place.'

'Do you think I haven't considered that?' Menelaus snapped. 'It was my first thought – once I could begin to believe that this thing had happened at all. But there was no sign of struggle, no disarray in her chamber. Her favourite clothes and jewels are gone. And so is Aethra, and a body-servant she's particularly fond of. And if they had been mere brigands, out for what they could get, they could have forced my whole damned treasury! As it is, Eteoneus thinks she's taken only what she regards as her own.'

'How much would that be?'

Menelaus scowled across at his brother in disbelief. 'Do you think I give a fig for the money when all the light of my life has been put out?' He got up from his couch and crossed to the window where he looked down into the courtyard of the neighbouring mansion. A crate of quails had fallen from the tail of a wagon there and a number of giggling women were chasing the birds about the yard as they panicked on clipped wings.

'Then let's assume,' Agamemnon was saying, 'that your wife has proved wanton enough to run off with this Trojan friend of yours. What do you propose to do about it?'

Menelaus ran a hand through his hair. It came to rest at the back of his neck, which he gripped fiercely in his palm. 'I've already sent orders back to Sparta. They're to double the number of ships scouring the Aegean for them.' His neck and hands were sweating, his eyes closed. 'But they had a whole night's start – and that was three days ago. They could be in Troy long before we have sight of them.' His voice began to shake again. 'It's hopeless!'

Agamemnon snorted impatiently. 'Are you a son of Atreus or a lovesick swain? Pull yourself together, man, or you'll be the laughing-stock of all Crete!' He drew in his breath in a derisive sigh. 'Didn't I tell you that no good would come of fraternizing with these swindling Asiatics? They're about as trustworthy as a pool of crocodiles!'

Menelaus was as consumed by the appalling justice of the

remark as he was mortified by it. When he failed to answer, Agamemnon shrugged out another carefully considered, equally disdainful question. 'In any case, do you really want that Spartan bitch back after she's put a pair of horns on you bigger than any you saw in the ring today?'

This was too much. Menelaus turned on his brother, furiously red-faced. 'One more insult like that,' he snarled, 'and I'll cut your gizzard open and thrust it back down your throat!'

'That's better, that's better!' Agamemnon smiled. 'If you've been given horns, learn to use them. Rage is what you need. Good, clean, honest, dangerous rage! Enough rage to chase that handsome bastard all the way to Troy if you have to. Enough rage to knot his tripes round his windpipe and throw his balls to the dogs! And if you won't do it, I will. No one pisses on the House of Atreus and lives long enough to brag of it.'

'I can take my own vengeance,' Menelaus hissed.

'So it's not hopeless after all,' Agamemnon nodded, smiling. 'Telamon will be there for us. And don't I recall that our wily friend Odysseus got half the princes of Argos to swear some grisly oath before Poseidon that they would fight to defend your right to Helen?'

Agamemnon arched a thick eyebrow at Menelaus, who stood across the room, still trembling a little, clenching and unclenching his fists. Then he took a swig from his wine-cup, relaxed back on his couch, and chuckled. 'The Trojans may think they've got themselves a trophy, little brother. What they've actually got themselves is war!'

PART TWO

THE BOOK OF
Ares

The Gathering

News of Helen's flight travelled across Argos faster than a pestilence.

Sitting by the fire in their various strongholds, men remembered the dreadful oath they had sworn on the bloody joints of Poseidon's horse, and pondered what they would do when Agamemnon's heralds came – as come they must – to demand that their pledge be honoured. Menelaus' own immediate vassals were in no doubt. For them, the loss of Helen festered like a wound. She was their sacred queen, the priestess of their rites, the living heart of Sparta. She was their totem of beauty in an often ugly world, and it was hard for them to believe that such grace had willingly abandoned them. Witchcraft must have been at work, or some malice of the gods. Helen had been abducted by force or spirited away. Menelaus had proved to be a generous and kindly king, and now, in this adversity, he commanded their loyalty. If it would take a war to force the return of their Queen, then let there be war. Was there ever more noble cause for a man to lay down his life than the rescue of the Lady Helen?

Others beyond the Lacadaemonian hills awaited the call with less enthusiasm. Troy was far away across an unpredictable sea, somewhere east of common sense. They had troubles enough without bothering their heads over a younger brother's faithless wife. And, yes, they might indeed have sworn an oath before Poseidon's altar, but that had been to protect Menelaus from their envy, not to go chasing after a wanton who no longer wished to share the pleasures of his bed!

If a man failed to look to his wife, what was that to them? It had been folly to invite the Trojans into his house, madness to leave a beauty like Helen alone with them. Against such stupidity the gods themselves were helpless.

Such sentiments were not murmured in the High King's presence, but his spies caught wind of them, and it wasn't long before Agamemnon began to suspect that, with only his brother's interests directly threatened, mounting a force large enough to take on the power of Troy might prove harder than he had guessed.

Some of the difficulties had declared themselves even before the sons of Atreus left Crete. Once apprised of the situation, Deucalion had been fulsome in his sympathies for Menelaus – so much so that his manner drifted perilously close to gloating – but when Agamemnon sounded him out for support in their war against Troy, the Lord of the Labyrinth proved less immediately forthcoming. Yes, he felt in his own heart the gross insult that Troy had given to all Argos, but times were hard. He would have to think carefully before committing the already stretched resources of the House of the Axe to a distant campaign in which there might be much to lose. Since Theseus had reduced his country to a mere vassal-state of Athens, there had been little appetite for war among the barons of Crete. They already knew too much about its costs. At the very least, a council would be required, and though Deucalion would do what he could to sway its deliberations, the Atreides brothers must understand that the power of the Minoan throne was not what it had once been. For the moment, alas, he could promise nothing.

Agamemnon came fuming from the meeting. 'That old bastard is the rat-king of a rotten country,' he growled. 'Small wonder Crete fell so easily into Theseus' lap! But I've had my eyes open while we've been here! He may be the true heir of a degenerate father and a depraved mother but he's a lot less needy than he makes out. With Theseus gone, and only Menestheus to answer to in Athens, Crete is on the rise again. Deucalion has ships, and he knows we need them. But he's also thinking that if Argos and Troy wear each other out in a long war, then Crete might find scope to command the seas once more.' Agamemnon glared across at his brother. 'We'll have to teach him that he may have more to lose by staying out than by coming in.'

Menelaus nodded. 'But were you watching Idomeneus while we spoke? I'm sure he despises his father. We should talk to him separately.'

'You think we might set them against one another?'

'It could do no harm to try. Idomeneus and I are friends. He was among the first who swore to aid me. His father has lived too long, and he's been restless and ambitious for some time now. I think he might like a war.'

'I see you're learning, brother,' Agamemnon smiled. 'Hate is a mighty teacher.'

Shortly after his return to Argos, Agamemnon called his principal allies to a council of war in the great hall of the Lion House in Mycenae. Menelaus was there, bitter and gloomy still, having found his empty bedchamber in Sparta too desolate a place to bear. Nestor, king of Pylos, was among the first to arrive, already in his sixties but valiant and eloquent as ever. He was at pains to assure the Atreides brothers that, at this painful hour, they could rely on all he had to give in the way of wise counsel and military support. He was joined in those sympathies by Palamedes, Prince of Euboea, who was authorized to put the resources of his father Nauplius at the High King's disposal, and by the Argive hero Diomedes, who had always been so infatuated with love for Helen that he took her abduction as a personal slight. Like Menelaus, Diomedes was a devotee of Athena, and after the two men had wept together for a while, he told the bereft King of Sparta that the goddess had assured him in a dream of her special protection for the eighty ships he would commit to the war against Troy.

Others of the High King's vassals began to arrive through the Lion Gate. Some were openly eager for the venture, others discreetly kept their counsel, preferring to watch which way the wind was blowing. But on the whole, things seemed to be going well when news came of two unexpected setbacks.

Agamemnon had been counting on the warlike temper of Telamon to put fire into any of the princes who might query the wisdom of an assault on Troy. The old warhorse knew the city well. He had sacked it once and grown rich on the pickings. It was a sore blow, therefore, when news came from Salamis that Telamon had collapsed after a rowdy banquet on the night before he was due to cross to the mainland. Though his breathing was heavy and he had lost the power of speech, the old man was still alive. His son Ajax and his stepson Teucer were at his bedside, praying to Apollo the Healer for his full recovery.

The herald they sent in their place promised that the island would fit out six vessels for the venture. But Agamemnon cursed the ill luck that had deprived him of a man whose experience and forceful character was worth far more to him at that moment than a handful of ships.

The news out of Ithaca was still more dispiriting – so much so that the brothers went into private conference with Nestor before breaking it to the assembled warlords. The message came not with a herald but in a small bronze canister tied about a pigeon's leg. It came with the excuse that storms were blowing round the coast of Ithaca, and went on to tell how Odysseus and Penelope grieved to hear of their Cousin Helen's defection. They understood why, in his righteous anger, Menelaus might wish to take violent revenge on Troy, but wasn't it the case that the treachery had been the fault of a single man, not a whole city? Should any act of retaliation not be proportionate therefore? While their own loyalty to the High King was never in question, it was their considered opinion that the Atreides brothers would be wise to wait upon King Priam's response to their envoys before harnessing their power to a war that might prove long and arduous. Helen had acted rashly, yes, but that was no reason for her husband, who was always assured of their love and deepest sympathy, to do the same.

Agamemnon smacked the paper with his hand. 'The villain is looking to his own interests as usual. He got what he wanted when he came to Sparta. Now he thinks he can lie back, counting his blessings, and let the rest of us go hang.'

Still raw from the humiliation of his wound, Menelaus had listened touchily to the unwelcome homily out of Ithaca. 'Do we need him?' he frowned now. 'Ithaca's far to the west and hardly fit for goats to graze on. If our cousin doesn't want to come, let him rot at home.'

'It's not just Ithaca.' Agamemnon got up and began to pace the chamber. 'All the Ionian islands look to him. If the Lords of Same, Dulichium, and Zacynthus get to hear he won't come, why should they stir their stumps? This could cost us a thousand men. And Odysseus isn't just some bare-arsed sheep-farmer with more balls than brains. He's a thinker. A strategist. The best strategist we've got – with the exception of old Nestor here. Of course we need him!'

Nestor had been dandling Agamemnon's small daughter Iphigeneia on his knee as he waited for the rant to end. Now he took her fingers from his mouth and lifted his silver head. 'Odysseus doesn't actually say that he won't come,' he offered quietly. 'He merely suggests we wait to hear what your envoys report.'

'We know well enough what they'll say! If Priam's feeling strong, it'll be a defiant jibe about not getting much help from us in the matter of his sister. If he's not, then expect some appeasing diplomatic pribble-prabble. Either way, it's what I want to hear. There's never going to be a better time to take on Troy than this.'

'And Odysseus knows you think this way?' Nestor asked, stroking the small girl's curls where she nestled against him, sucking her thumb, with large eyes following her father's strides as he paced the floor.

'Of course he does. He's no fool. We've always shared intelligence on our raids. He knew what I was thinking a long time ago. But that was before he married and settled down and got lazy. I preferred him as a rogue and pirate! So did most of the princes of Argos, if truth were told. None of them much liked the oath he got them all to swear at the wedding but they admired his cunning!' Agamemnon sat down again, drumming the fingers of both hands on the table. 'The man has genius! He's wasted watching sheep on that barren rock. Somehow we've got to prise him out of that great bed he boasts of.'

'Then let me go and talk to him,' Menelaus said. 'After all, it was he who set things up so that I could marry Helen in the first place.'

'But it's hardly his fault if it went wrong!' Agamemnon scowled. Though Helen's defection had provided him with just the excuse for war that he had needed, he still felt the sting of humiliation that it brought on the House of Atreus. 'Odysseus didn't know you were going to let some Trojan stallion have the run of your house – any more than I did.'

At that point old Nestor looked up from the child whose smiling face had crumpled at the rising voices. He raised a magisterial finger, which silenced both brothers without offending either, then said, 'Would the sons of Atreus care to hear my thoughts on this matter, or shall Iphigeneia and I leave you to brawl at your leisure?'

'Speak up,' Agamemnon said. 'It's why I need you here.'

'Very well. Consider this. We all know that Odysseus is no coward! Something else must be keeping him at home. The last I heard from the island it was rumoured that Penelope was with child again. The letter says nothing of this, but if his wife is coming close to term, Odysseus would surely keep it to himself lest some evil fate cause yet another miscarriage.'

Agamemnon scratched his beard and looked across at the spoiled favourite among his own children, who had slipped down from Nestor's knee as he was speaking and was now trying to pull the old man away to play with her outside. 'Not now,' her father frowned. 'Be patient or I'll send you away.' He looked back up at Nestor. 'If you're right, and Penelope does bring the child to term, we could have a hard time winkling him off the island. What do you suggest?'

'My first thought,' Nestor answered, 'is that you say nothing to the other princes about this. Tell them only that the weather over Ithaca is foul and Odysseus saw no need to make the long journey to Mycenae at this time, but is content to wait for further instructions.' Nestor smiled and gave a suave little shrug. 'After all, it's not so far off the truth.' Holding the little girl gently by the slender stems of her wrists, he clapped her hands as she laughed. 'Then once the council is over, and they've gone back to rally their troops, let Menelaus go to Ithaca, but not alone. He should take someone guileful with him. Someone who can match wits with the wily Ithacan. I'm thinking of Palamedes. He's a young man still, but he's clever, and he's committed to the cause. He may be just the fellow we need.'

As the story now turns to Ithaca, I Phemius, may be forgiven for introducing a personal note, for though I cannot yet have been five years old when Menelaus came to our small island, I still recall the feast that Odysseus held to celebrate the birth of his son. That day my father, the bard Terpis, sang before the gathered people. I remember swelling like a bullfinch in my pride, and thinking that if one could not be a prince, then the next best fate was to be a poet and sing for men and gods. I remember the sunlight through the plane trees, and the thick caress of honey on my tongue. And I tell myself also that there is a picture of Odysseus in my mind, happiest of men that day, wearing vine leaves in his hair and dancing lightly to the throb of the lyre like a breathing statue of a god.

I cannot truthfully say that I remember anything about the

arrival of Menelaus and Palamedes. What I know of that fateful encounter I learned much later from the lips of Penelope when she told the story to Telemachus one day. He and I were almost young men by then and had long been friends of the heart. It was a grief to Telemachus that he had no memories of his father, and a greater grief that his mother was already under siege from several suitors. Angered by their manner, he had again demanded to know why his father had abandoned them alone on Ithaca to pursue the madness of the war at Troy. I was sitting beside him as his mother answered, and I think I learned the true tale of what happened when Menelaus and Palamedes came to Ithaca. It is a little different from the tale the people tell, for they attribute to a ruse of madness what was, in fact, a craziness of grief occasioned by an oracle.

That story tells how Odysseus was so unwilling to go to war that he tried to convince Menelaus he had lost his wits. Dressing himself like a peasant, he yoked an ox and an ass to his plough and began to sow his field with salt. Only when Palamedes snatched Telemachus from his mother and threw him in front of the ploughshare did Odysseus act in a way that betrayed his ruse.

The truth is subtler and more painful.

The whole island was so drunk with joy and merriment that day that the ship beating in off the mainland docked unnoticed for a time. As they climbed from the cove through the heat of the afternoon to look for Odysseus in the palace, Menelaus and Palamades heard the sounds of song and laughter drifting down the hill. They caught the hot smell of an ox roasting on the spit and knew that old Nestor had been right in his speculation: the Prince of Ithaca had an heir at last.

The feast itself, however, was more rustic than they would have guessed. Laertes, father of Odysseus and Lord of Ithaca, sat in state on a carved throne that had been carried out of the palace and placed under a vine-thatched awning, from where he stroked his beard and beamed on the happy throng. His plump wife

Anticlea sat beside him, nursing a swaddled, week-old infant in her lap as she chatted with the women who gathered about her, cooing at the sleeping babe. But Odysseus and Penelope were indistinguishable from the dancing shepherds and their wives. Only when the music stopped and the line broke up in laughter and applause did Menelaus recognize the short, bandy-legged man in a homespun tunic who stepped forward with his hands spread in welcome.

'The King of Sparta honours us,' he cried and the crowd's gasp became a din of excited chatter, while under the crown of vine-leaves, the eyes of Odysseus glittered with pleasure and defiance.

Penelope came to stand beside him, as graceful in her simple rural dress as she had been in her royal robes at Sparta. Though her thoughts had darkened at the sight of Menelaus, there was no sign of it about her face, which was tanned and glowing. Nor was there anything of Helen's sultry enchantment about her smile. She might have been a dairymaid had it not been for her unflustered poise in the presence of a king, and the regal lines of her high-boned cheeks.

'Be welcome in our house, my lords,' she said. 'You come at a happy time.'

'So I see, so I see.' Menelaus bowed towards Laertes and Anticlea, who dipped their heads in shy acknowledgement. Then he stepped forward to take Penelope warmly in his arms. 'My dear, I am so very happy for you at last. It was more than time that the gods favoured you.'

'But they have already blessed me with a loving husband and a good life here on Ithaca,' she answered. 'Now we have a son to make our happiness complete.'

Menelaus observed the hint of wariness in her smile but turned away from it to greet her husband. He clapped his arms about the smaller man's shoulders and squeezed him like a bear. 'You're a lucky man, Odysseus.' And at the unspoken contrast between the evident happiness around him and the bitter condition of his own marriage, a surge of grief and self-pity rose from his chest to his throat. For an instant, with his face pressed against that of his friend, the King of Sparta was blinking back tears.

Odysseus was the first to pull away. 'Surely you'll admit that I deserve no less?' he laughed. 'Come, you and your companion must wet the baby's head.'

'This must be his naming day. How shall we call him?'

'Telemachus,' Odysseus answered proudly.

'*Decisive Battle,*' Menelaus smiled. 'A good name and a good omen!'

With a reassuring glance at Penelope, Odysseus looked over Menelaus's shoulder at the vaguely familiar figure of a fashionably dressed young man, whose sharp, deep-set eyes were taking in the up-country, sheep-fair feel of the festivities. Menelaus gestured to his companion. 'You remember Palamedes, son of Nauplius of Euboea? He was with us in Sparta for the wedding.'

Smiling, Palamedes took the proffered hand. 'We seem to meet on lively occasions, Lord Odysseus. I was one of those you forced to stand barefoot on bloody horse-meat and swear undying loyalty to this fellow here.'

'I remember it well,' Odysseus smiled back. 'I also remember losing money at your game of dice and stones! And now I hear tell you've invented a new system of measures and weights on Euboea. Come, take some wine, and tell me about it. Where's young Sinon gone with the carving-knife? My friends here need meat. Make room at the benches there.' But neither man had missed the brisk chill of incipient hostility that passed invisibly between them, as though, for a moment, they had stood in each other's shadow and shut out the sun.

Late that night, Odysseus sat up with Menelaus and Palamedes on a balcony overlooking the cliff where they could hear the sea toiling on both sides of the narrow isthmus. A few merrymakers still sang at the benches under the trees. The baby had been washed and suckled and put down some hours earlier but Odysseus knew that Penelope would still be awake on the bed of olive-wood that he had built for them with his own hands when he first brought her to Ithaca. Weary as he was, he did not expect to see much sleep that night, but right now he was prepared to wait.

These men had sought him out. Let them begin.

Menelaus, who had been sitting with his eyes closed as he rubbed his knuckles across his brow, heaved a large sigh and stretched his legs. 'Need I say that we were disappointed by your response to Agamemnon's summons?'

Odysseus pursed his lips in an arch tilt of the head.

'We were counting on you for at least sixty ships,' said Palamedes.

'You have seen how small my island is,' Odysseus answered, smiling still. 'If you can find sixty ships here you may keep four fifths of them, with my blessing.'

'No doubt other ships await your word on Same, Dulichium and Zacynthus.'

Odysseus arched his brows. 'Agamemnon has all the hosts of Argos at his command. The Cretan fleet will almost certainly join with him since he's set Idomeneus against his father, and here you are with the might of Euboea and Sparta. So why would you need to trouble the peace of our dull sheepfolds?'

'You seem to be well informed,' Palamedes smiled.

'I try to keep my ears open.'

Menelaus cleared his throat. 'Be straight with us, Odysseus. It's you we need.'

Palamedes picked up the jug from the table. On the excuse that his stomach had been weakened by the sea-passage, he had drunk very little, but he poured more wine into his host's goblet now. 'Your reputation for courage and cunning reaches far across the Aegean. Where Odysseus goes, others will follow.'

'Then let them follow my example and stay at home.'

'I can't do that,' said Menelaus. 'I can't just let her go.'

Odysseus studied the anguish in his friend's eyes for a long moment. 'I know,' he said, 'and my heart bleeds for you. But surely there are better ways to catch a stray mare than setting fire to the forest? Surely this whole wretched affair could be managed through negotiation? Telamon can have no use for Hesione now that he's bed-ridden. It's time he saw reason. Let there be an exchange of hostages. That's the way to get Helen back.' He paused, remembering how proud Menelaus had been that day in Sparta: then added, '—if you still want her, that is.'

Menelaus took a swig at his wine and glanced away. 'It's too late for that.'

'Why?' Odysseus demanded. 'Because your heart is so badly wounded that only blood will heal it? Or because your brother's mind is set on war?'

When Menelaus did not answer, Palamedes said, 'The Trojans gave Menelaus their word that they came as friends to Argos seeking peace. This war is of their making. It surprises me that the Prince of Ithaca shows so little stomach for the enterprise. Agamemnon led me to believe that you and he have often talked together of taking Troy. Is that not so?'

'Yes, it's so. Just as I once talked with Theseus about sailing westwards round the coast of Africa just to see what was there! I was a younger man then, and full of idle dreams.'

Palamedes said, 'There is nothing idle in the thought of taking Troy. It has been done.'

'Yes, and Telamon never stops bragging about it! What he always fails to mention is that the Earthshaker had already flattened the city and salted the land with a great wave before he and Heracles came. And that was thirty years ago at a time when the Trojans were so desperate they were ready to propitiate the gods with human sacrifice. Things have changed since then. Priam has built a mighty city on the ruins of his father's town. And the Dardanians, Mysians, Lydians, and Lycians have all grown wealthy with him. He might even be able to call on the Amazons and the Hatti empire beyond the Red River further east.' Odysseus forestalled interruption. 'You're quite correct, my friend. I did think about taking Troy once – until I saw it for the madness that it was. Heed my counsel and stick to your dice – the odds are more in your favour there.'

Palamedes was eager to retort but Menelaus reached out a hand to restrain him. 'This isn't like you, Odysseus,' he said. 'I've never known danger or difficulties knock the heart out of you before.'

'My heart is strong enough. So is my brain. Also I have a wife now, and a son.'

'Menelaus also has a wife,' Palamedes said, 'and so do many men. If all of them thought as you do, then our Trojan friends would feel free to ravish their wives at leisure. Who knows but that your own might not be next?'

Odysseus narrowed his eyes. 'This has been a happy day, my lords, and we have drunk much wine.' He got to his feet. 'You are the guests of my house. I think it better that we sleep than that we quarrel.'

'We're not looking for a quarrel,' Menelaus said. 'It's your help I need. All Argos needs it. I thought you were my friend, Odysseus.'

'I am. And as your friend I counsel you against this madness.' Odysseus looked down to where the surf was breaking white in the moonlight at the foot of the cliff. Then he sighed, shook his head, and seemed to reach a decision. 'I knew you would be coming, and I knew what you would ask. Even before Agamemnon summoned me to Mycenae, I had taken the omens on this matter.'

'And what did they say?'

'That a war against Troy would drag on for ten years before it ended.'

Menelaus winced. 'Who gave you this judgement?'

After a moment's hesitation Odysseus said, 'It came to me in a dream.'

'Ah,' said Palamedes, 'a dream!'

'A dream which I took to the oracle on our island. The old priestess there serves Earth-Mother Dia. She has snake wisdom and second sight. It was she who read the meaning of the dream for me.'

Palamedes smiled into his wine-cup. 'Stranger and stranger!'

Menelaus said, 'My own soothsayers at the Bronze House in

Sparta have assured me that Helen will return. They said nothing of it taking so long.' He took in the shrug with which Odysseus looked away. Both men knew well enough that it was not unknown for priests to prophesy what their masters wished to hear.

In the silence Palamedes said, 'So will you share this portentous dream with us?' Odysseus looked away from him to Menelaus, who glanced up from his wine-cup with entreaty in his eyes. The Euboean added, 'Or must the princes of Argos be left to think that Odysseus stays at home because he has bad dreams?'

Without looking at him, Odysseus sat down again. When he spoke it was to neither of these difficult guests but to the night glittering above him and the dark sea below.

'In the dream I had yoked an ox and an ass to my plough and was scattering salt over my shoulder in the furrows as I worked the land. At the end of the tenth furrow I was stopped in my tracks by the sight of an infant boy that somebody had thrown before my ploughshare.'

There was a lull in the singing from the benches and the silence felt louder now. The two other men waited, but Odysseus said no more.

'That was it?' said Menelaus.

Odysseus nodded grimly.

'A droll dream,' said Palamedes. 'What did your wise-woman make of it? Not that Menelaus was the ox and myself the ass, I trust?'

Odysseus refused to rise to the jibe. 'Diotima knew without my telling her that war with Troy was much on my mind. She reminded me that the ox is Zeus's beast of summer and the ass the winter beast of Cronos. Each furrow in my dream stands for a year. To sow them with salt means ten wasted years.' He fixed his eyes on the two men. 'Diotima prophesied two other things: that I would shortly have a son, and that the decisive battle for Troy would not come until ten years had been thrown away. Her first prophecy has already come to pass.'

'So the dream also gave your son his name,' Palamedes smiled.

'A powerful dream, it seems, as well as droll – if your old lady of the snakes has it right.'

Odysseus said, 'I for one would not care to argue with the Earth Mother.'

'No more would I. But oracles and dreams are both notorious riddlers. What if the furrows represented not years but months? Might not ten summer months and ten winter months be encompassed within two years?'

Menelaus, about whom gloom had gathered like a pall, instantly brightened at the suggestion. 'Two years! That seems a more reasonable estimate for a campaign against Troy – especially with Odysseus there to help us win it.'

'And little Telemachus would hardly have gained the power of speech by then.' Palamedes glanced at Menelaus. 'I see his mother suckles him at her own breast, so all our friend would miss would be such pleasure in his wife as two years of sleepless nights allowed him.'

'When you are the shrine-priest at an oracle,' Odysseus said grimly, 'I may look to you for guidance. Meanwhile, I shall trust the earth-wisdom of my homeland gods.' But there was less confidence in his thoughts than in his voice.

Once again he got up and was about to bid his guests good night when Palamedes said, 'I have been thinking about your son.'

'What of him?'

'That one day he will be king here – and a brave warrior, one hopes.'

'I don't for a moment doubt it,' Odysseus said.

'But will it not be great shame for him when he sails to Argos then and hears the songs of the noble deeds that were done in the war at Troy by the fathers of other men, yet cannot call upon the harper to sing of what was done by Ithaca?'

Odysseus stood in silence, his head swimming with the wine. He stared down at the ground beneath his feet as though it was already turning to salt and he could see his infant son abruptly thrown beneath a ploughshare there.

Palamedes began to speak again, that dry, suavely insidious voice, through which an ironic intellect glittered like a blade. 'And will not those other kings have good cause to wonder why Odysseus dared to give his son such a proud name when he lacked the heart to honour the pledge that he himself had devised, and fight on his friend's behalf in the decisive battle?'

For a moment, such was the sudden blaze of rage inside him, Odysseus could have picked up this angular young man by the throat and thrown him over the cliff. But he heard the sea-surge sounding in his ears, and the ground might have been trembling under his feet. So he was held where he stood by the knowledge that, though he had never been counted among the contenders for Helen's hand, he too had been required to stand upon a bloody portion of the King Horse in Sparta. He too had asked Earthshaker Poseidon to bring ruin on his land should he fail to keep his oath to Menelaus. And he had done so at this man's urging.

A brief, self-mocking laugh broke harshly from his lips, and such was his sense of the irony of the gods that it was edged already with a bitter premonition of the anguish that was to come.

By the time he arrived in Mycenae, Odysseus was back in his right mind once more, but the interim had been a vertiginous descent to the bottom of his soul such as he was not to experience again till he began, ten years later, the long return from Troy.

In the end, I suspect, it was Penelope herself who freed him from the dilemma that was tearing him apart, though she never said as much. Always poised and self-possessed, she would say only that before Menelaus and Palamedes took ship for the mainland, her husband had pledged to bring a thousand of his Ionian islanders to Troy, and that honour required him to keep that pledge.

What she may not have known, however, was that Odysseus

would also bring, concealed inside the darkest chamber of his heart, a patient hatred for the clever young man who had brought him to this pass.

When the envoys that Agamemnon had sent to Troy reported back to Mycenae, they brought two surprises with them.

As expected, King Priam demanded to know what satisfaction he himself had been given in the matter of his sister Hesione. Why should the sons of Atreus expect him to act in the matter of which they complained when he had been demanding his sister's return in vain for many years? In any case, he had no certain knowledge that his son Paris was involved in the Queen of Sparta's disappearance as his ship had not yet returned to Troy.

'Then where in the name of Hades has he got to?' Agamemnon demanded.

The envoys could only report rumours that Paris and Helen had been heard of in Cyprus, Phoenicia and Egypt, but no actual sightings had been confirmed.

'Then they're lying low, hoping the storm will blow over,' Nestor said.

Agamemnon nodded. 'But they can't stay on the run for ever, any more than Priam can hide for ever behind his ignorance.'

'What about Aeneas?' Menelaus asked the envoys. 'Wasn't he in Troy?'

The envoys had seen no sign of the Dardanian prince. However, they had taken advantage of a private conversation with the High King's counsellor, Antenor, to question him on the whereabouts of Aeneas. They were told that, for some time now, both Anchises and his son had kept to their palace at Lyrnessus. Though Antenor had been careful to watch his words, hints were dropped of a cooling of relations between the courts of Ilium and Dardania, and the envoys were left with the impression that, if Prince Paris was never seen again inside the walls of Troy, Antenor himself would not greatly grieve.

If this news was welcome, the envoys' assessment of the powerful fleet Priam had built in readiness for war was less so. But the second surprise they brought back with them proved more encouraging. On the night before they were due to sail, they had been approached by a Trojan soothsayer named Calchas. As priest in the Thymbraean temple of Apollo at Troy, he had consulted the omens and could see no good future for the city. He now wished to take passage to Argos with the envoys and offer his services to the High King in Mycenae. Having decided that the man might prove useful, the envoys had brought him back and he was here in the Lion House now, eagerly awaiting an audience with the king.

'Then bring him before us.' Agamemnon said, 'Let's see if this soothsayer can bring us any better omens than did Odysseus's dream.'

While Calchas was being summoned, Palamedes said, 'They would have done better to leave the priest in Troy. A single friend behind the walls might have proved of more value than a whole company of archers on this side of them.'

'The priest serves Apollo,' Odysseus murmured from where he sat beyond Nestor to the left of Agamemnon. 'He knows the run of his own life-thread better than you or I. In any case, it seems we may have such a friend already. And he is powerfully placed – though he may take a little time to declare himself.'

'We do?' said Agamemnon.

'Odysseus refers to Antenor,' said Menelaus. 'He was the father of the child killed by Paris and has no love for him.'

'Do you suspect some connection with this priest?'

'Who knows?' Odysseus shrugged. 'We must see what emerges.'

At that moment Calchas was escorted down the hall. When he arrived before the Lion throne, he threw himself on the floor and lay there abased in the Asiatic manner with his arms outstretched and his forehead pressed against the tiles.

Agamemnon said, 'I don't much care for grovelling.' Calchas got to his feet, arranging his dark robes, and stood before the High King with his head lowered. 'Also I should warn you that

I mislike traitors,' the High King added, '– unless, of course, they can deliver my enemies into my hands.'

Calchas raised his face. Above the swarthy hollows of his cheeks, dark intelligent eyes looked back at the High King with no sign of fear or deference. Nor was there any arrogance in the voice that asserted quietly, 'We who serve Far-sighted Apollo in his temple at Thymbra answer neither to the High King at Troy nor the High King in Mycenae. We answer only to the god.'

'So I can rely on you no more than Priam can?'

'If you will hear what Divine Apollo, Slayer of Darkness, has to say, you can rely on my truth. If not,' Calchas opened his hands as if to let something fall, 'so.'

Agamemnon sat back on the Lion throne, studying the impassive face of the priest with his chin supported on one hand. 'Well, you're a bold enough fellow, stealing between the lines where more cautious men might fear to tread. My envoys tell me you've been taking omens. I'm curious to know what the God of the Silver Bow had to say to you.'

'That Troy will fall.'

At this confident announcement, Agamemnon turned to smile at his counsellors. Then he looked sternly back at the priest. 'This we know already, just as we know that Mycenae will one day fall, and Sparta will fall, and perhaps even one day all Argos and the high crags of Mount Olympus itself. The pressing question is when? And how?'

'There is a single answer,' Calchas answered.

'Then share it with us, friend.'

One by one, Calchas surveyed the princes around him, as if searching for some particular face among their number. Then he looked at the king again and said, 'I do not see the sons of Aeacus here.'

'Didn't the god tell you that old Telamon has fought his last battle, priest? He lies bedridden in Salamis, but his sons Ajax and Teucer will shortly join us, and the ships of Salamis will follow.'

Calchas nodded. 'And what of Telamon's brother?'

Nestor answered him. 'Peleus has not left his hall in Thessaly for many years. He is an old man who broods on the deaths that have shadowed his life. I think that the King of the Myrmidons longs only for his own death now.'

'We did not expect Peleus at this council,' Agamemnon said. 'Why do you ask about him?'

'Because there is a line of fate drawn between Aeacus and Troy, and it reaches across the generations. It was Aeacus who built the walls of Laomedon's city under the aegis of Apollo and with the guidance of Poseidon. It was to his son Telamon that Troy fell at the place where the walls were weakest.'

Agamemnon sighed impatiently. 'Telamon himself has told us this story many times. Why should we concern ourselves with it now?'

'Because the fate of Troy is bound up with that of two sons. The first of them is Priam's own son, Paris, who should have been killed at birth. Priam was warned by the priests of Thymbra that if the child was permitted to live he would bring destruction on the city.'

'And this is the omen that gives Troy into our hands?' Menelaus asked.

Calchas turned to frown at him. 'As you know from your own experience in Sparta, a wise king does not fail to heed Apollo's oracle – no matter what the cost.'

'You mentioned *two* sons,' said Palamedes.

Calchas nodded. 'The omens I have taken say that Troy will fall only after the seventh son of Peleus returns from the place to which he has withdrawn and joins the fray.'

Agamemnon turned an enquiring brow to Nestor. 'Do you know the son of whom he speaks?'

With a puzzled frown, Nestor said, 'To the best of my knowledge Peleus has only one son.'

'But there were six who died before him,' Odysseus put in. 'Achilles is the seventh son of Peleus.'

'Good,' said Agamemnon. 'Then Peleus must send us this son.'

But Odysseus was frowning now. 'I know the boy. The last time I visited Peleus a few years ago, Achilles had just returned from Cheiron's school. He was going on to be trained by Phoenix, the King of those Dolopians who chose to remain in Thessaly.'

'Then we will send to Thessaly for him.'

Odysseus shook his head. 'I doubt that you'll find him there. Peleus and Thetis have been fighting over him for years but he's of an age to make up his own mind now. I think you'll find that Achilles is with his mother and her people.'

'And where are they?' Agamemnon demanded.

'At the court of King Lycomedes on Skyros.'

'What difference?' Agamemnon brought his hands together in satisfaction. 'If that's the place to which he's withdrawn, then let's winkle the lad out and get on with winning this war.'

Odysseus knew the whereabouts of Achilles because he had been party to the decision to allow him to go to Skyros. It had happened this way.

When Achilles was almost eleven years old and still a pupil in the wilderness school on Mount Pelion, King Cheiron of the Centaurs passed away peacefully in his sleep. He was found on his litter of grass by Euhippe who had returned to live with the old man after Thetis had departed for Skyros. The little Centaur woman let out a deep-drawn, moaning wail that echoed throughout the dawn light of the gorge and was quickly taken up by her tribe.

Achilles was left utterly distraught by the death, but though he did not know it yet, he was about to lose far more than a much-loved teacher. The wider world was changing in ways that left little room for Cheiron's simple way of life, and when Peleus learned that the morale of the Centaur people had collapsed with the death of their king, he decided to bring Achilles back to his palace in Iolcus. At the same time, Patroclus was recalled by his father, Menoetius. These two boys, who had given each other a bloody nose at their first meeting, had become inseparable friends during their years on the mountain. Now they were being parted for the first time and neither dealt well with the separation.

In Iolcus things went badly from the start. The fair young face of Achilles reminded Peleus too fiercely of the wife who had burned his other children, while Achilles was shy with his father at first, and then increasingly dismayed to discover that the great king of whom he had often boasted to his friends was a morose and taciturn old man with a gammy leg. The boy wandered the halls of the palace uncomfortable in the princely robes that had been woven for him, missing the sounds and smells of the mountain woodlands and, above all, missing his friend. He grew fractious and bored. When he sensed that his father was reluctant to talk about the mother he had never known, Achilles pressed the issue. Eventually he learned what had been withheld from him earlier in order to avoid any suspicion of favouritism at the school – that Cheiron had not only been his teacher, he was also his maternal grandfather.

Already Achilles knew that he had loved the old Centaur as he could never begin to love this remote stranger who was his father. Now he began to believe that, in being separated from his mother at birth, he had been robbed of more than he had ever dreamed. Feeling wounded and betrayed by his father, he became increasingly importunate in his demands to meet Thetis – which was a thing that Peleus still could not countenance. When the subject was brusquely closed, father and son found themselves caught in a grim bind of mutual incomprehension and hostility. Yet Peleus cared deeply for the boy and was increasingly afraid of losing him to disaffection or mischance.

One day he came into his chamber after an exhausting afternoon of giving judgement to find that a table had been moved close to the wall and the great ash spear which had been Cheiron's wedding gift to him had vanished from the hooks on the wall where it had hung unused for many years. Furious that Achilles had taken his most prized possession without seeking his consent, Peleus went in search of the boy. He found him stripped to his breech-clout in the garden and using the trunk of an old plane tree for target practice. The spear was too long and heavy for his height, yet Achilles threw it with surprising accuracy from the distance he had set himself. Torn between his anger and his desire to congratulate his son on his marksmanship, Peleus said coldly, 'That spear you have stolen is a warrior's spear. Only a proven warrior has the right to wield it.'

Achilles stood flustered before his father. 'How shall I ever be a warrior,' he muttered sulkily, 'when you keep me cooped up here like a bullcalf in a stall?'

Sensing all the frustrated energy locked inside that stalwart young body, Peleus felt suddenly sorry for his son and ashamed of his own morose rage.

'Do you want to be a warrior?' he asked.

Achilles glanced away. 'I have watched the Myrmidons training on their field. I have watched them fighting together as if they hated one another and then oiling each other's bodies and dressing their hair afterwards, and I wondered whether they were men or gods. What else would I want to be?'

'Then you shall have your wish,' Peleus said. 'But I will keep my spear until I am sure I have a son who is fit to wield it.'

Already a skilled horseman, athlete and hunter, Achilles had never shown any concern for his own safety, and with hurt pride and anger prominent among his emotions now, he took to the volatile world of the common soldiery in much the same way that he had once felt at home among the Centaurs. Soon he began to acquire all the murderous skills of a professional fighting man.

One day his father came to watch him working with sword and spear on the practice field and was so impressed by his progress that he immediately agreed to make enquiries when Achilles asked whether Patroclus might not be allowed to come and train with him among the Myrmidons. Menoetius, who had run into similar difficulties with his own disgruntled son, readily consented, and the boys rushed to greet each other as though they had been deprived of air and light in the time when they were apart.

Over the next few years they grew ever closer – two young men united by a love so intense that they would gladly die, and kill, for each other.

Among their mentors was a commander named Phoenix, who had no children of his own, and to whom Achilles gave much of the affection that he denied to his father. Phoenix was one of the few Dolopians who had remained loyal to Peleus at the time when most of his people were migrating to Skyros, and though he was a Myrmidon warrior first and foremost, he had not renounced all the customs of his clan. So there was more than a touch of the old religion about him still. Fascinated by the blue tattoo etched into the skin of his thigh, Achilles was intrigued to learn that it was a mark of an initiation that Phoenix had undergone during the spring rites on his passage from boyhood into manhood. For a time he seemed reluctant to say any more, but Achilles reminded his tutor that he too had Dolopian blood through his mother's side and began to ply him with more questions about his tribal heritage. The answers came slowly at first and then, when Phoenix saw how much it mattered to the boy, more freely. The vague restlessness that still some-times troubled Achilles took on clearer form. He began to dream of his mother.

Odysseus visited Iolcus about this time and witnessed a violent argument between Peleus and Achilles. Peleus came away from it red-faced and distraught, calling for wine and complaining that Thetis was drawing their son away from him by some magical power with which he could not compete.

'But the boy has a right to know who his mother is,' Odysseus said, 'and he will soon be of an age to go whether you forbid him or not. Perhaps it might be better in the long run if he went with your consent.'

Peleus grimly shook his head. 'You've never met the witch who was my wife. You don't know the kind of power she has.

And Achilles is my only son and heir. I'm afraid that if I let him go to Skyros he might not come back.'

'Such things are for the gods to decide,' Odysseus answered, 'but one way or another he's going to have to get this thing out of his system. Why not allow the boy to go to Skyros but insist that he goes alone? After all, the strongest tie in his life is to his friend Patroclus. He won't want to be separated from him for long.'

Peleus eventually saw the sense of this and acted on it. Achilles proved so reluctant to be separated from Patroclus again that for a time it looked as though he might not go at all. But the draw proved stronger than the tie. He sailed for Skyros when he was fourteen years old. As Peleus had feared, he remained there for rather longer than Odysseus had anticipated.

Skyros is a windy island out beyond Euboea in the eastern sea, about half way between Mycenae and Troy. The people there have a picturesque tale to tell about the expedition that Odysseus made to the island to retrieve Achilles.

According to them, Thetis was an immortal goddess with prophetic powers who knew that her son's life must either be long, peaceful and obscure, or filled with undying glory and very brief. It was for this reason that she had decided to place Achilles far out of harm's way on remote Skyros.

When Odysseus came to the island he could see no sign of the boy anywhere among the young men who lived at the court of King Lycomedes. Realizing that only cunning would prise Achilles out of hiding, Odysseus returned to his ship and came back the next day disguised as a Sidonian merchant. Having regained entry to the court, he laid out his rich store of wares on the floor before an excited gathering of young women and girls. Most of the treasures he displayed were chosen to catch their eyes – embroidered dresses, bales of cloth, perfumes and cosmetics, necklaces, bangles and other fancy baubles. Among these pretty things, however, Odysseus also placed a sword and a shield which attracted no attention whatsoever until the chattering gaggle of girls picking through his delightful assortment of goods were startled by the sudden blast of a trumpet in the yard outside. When the cry went up that the island was under attack from pirates, the girls ran from the room in alarm – all that is save one, who reached eagerly for the sword and shield.

Smiling at the success of his ruse, Odysseus brought Achilles away to the war.

It's a good story, and no less good for the fact that much the same tale is told of the way their great heroes emerged into manhood by the people of the Indus far to the east and on Apollo's island of the Hyperboreans far to the north. But the truth as I learned it from Odysseus is somewhat different.

From the moment that his ship put in on the strand below the high rock where the castle of Lycomedes perched, facing the sea one way and the little town the other, it was clear that Odysseus would not receive a warm welcome on Skyros. The Dolopians had kept open their channels of communication with the mainland and they knew why he was coming. Odysseus was courteously prevented from seeing Achilles while Lycomedes reminded his guest that his people had chosen a different destiny from that of the other Thessalians and had no wish to become embroiled in a war which was none of their concern. Odysseus answered that he respected the choice they had made, but Achilles son of Peleus was no Dolopian. He was the sole heir to a great king in Iolcus who now required him to take up his royal duties and lead the Myrmidons to the war at Troy.

At that moment their conversation was interrupted by a woman's voice from the back of the draughty hall.

'A man's destiny is not determined only by the claims of his father.'

Odysseus turned to look at a tall, stately woman wearing a dark green robe shot through with colours like a peacock's tail. The derision in her voice was matched by the cold hauteur of her gaze. She must, Odysseus thought, have been very beautiful once, but those fiercely hooded eyes were more likely to exact obedience these days than adoration. He sensed at once that King Lycomedes was deeply in awe of her.

Beginning to understand for the first time why Peleus had found it so hard to deal with his wife, Odysseus declared himself honoured to have met Thetis at last, having already heard so much about her.

'But only from those who slander me,' she said.

'From those who respect your power, madam.'

'If that is true then you must know that I will not willingly give up my son again.'

'And if you are truly his mother,' Odysseus answered quietly, 'you will leave him free to choose for himself – as his father did.'

Thetis made a dismissive gesture with a heavily ringed hand. 'Achilles has already chosen. On this island he has learned the beauty of what he has hitherto been denied – the wisdom and consolation that is to be found only in the loving service of womankind. He is the chosen one of Deidameia, the daughter of King Lycomedes, and has already fathered a son on her. He has made his life here and is content with it. So go and fight your man's war if you must. My son wishes only to be left in peace.'

'I might believe it,' Odysseus said, 'if I were to hear it from his own lips.'

The lamplight cast a shadow on the hollows of Thetis's gaunt cheeks. An emerald necklace glistened at her throat. 'Achilles is preparing to take part in the spring rite tomorrow,' she answered coldly. 'He has no desire to see you.'

'But he knows that I'm here?'

'He has no need to know.'

'Surely that too is for him to decide?'

Thetis merely shrugged and glanced away.

'If you are not afraid of me,' Odysseus said, 'you will tell him that the friend who made it possible for him to come to Skyros wishes to speak with him.'

'I have no fear of you, Ithacan.'

Odysseus smiled. 'Then tell your son that I also bring word from his friend Patroclus. Perhaps he will speak to me when the rites are done.'

Odysseus was excluded from the inner mystery of the rite that took place on Skyros the next day but they could not keep him from joining the crowd that witnessed the procession afterwards. After hours of waiting in the sunlight he heard the clangour of approaching bells, and then the crowd were shouting and singing. His heart jumped as the procession rounded a corner of the narrow street and he was looking up at the huge, bear-like figure of a man hooded and caped in sheepskins, and with no face – for beneath the hood dangled only a featureless shaggy mask made from the flayed skin of a goat-kid. The man carried a shepherd's crook, and around his waist and hips were tied row upon row of goat bells which clattered and jangled as he danced along the street with a curious swinging amble designed to make all his bells ring. At his side danced what Odysseus took to be the veiled figure of a maiden wearing long, flounced skirts, but as more and more such figures appeared, he realized that these were in fact young men dressed in maiden's clothing.

Among them ran other, more comical figures holding long-necked gourds with which they made obscene gestures to the delight of the old women in the crowd. The air began to stink of wine and sweat. The din made by hundreds of bells was painful on his ears. But he was caught up in the noisy tumult of the cavalcade, wanting only to drink and dance and give himself over to the frenzy of the god. And then he became aware of one of the female figures faltering in the dance to stare at him with a shocked look of recognition, and he knew that hidden behind those veils and flounces stood the suddenly discomfited figure of the young man he had come to fetch from the island.

★   ★   ★

They talked together that night. Odysseus allowed Achilles space to tell about the life he had made on Skyros, of his love for Deidameia and their little son, whom they had called Pyrrhus because of his reddish-blond hair. He talked of the warm sense of return and homecoming he had found among his mother's people, and how Thetis herself had supervised his initiation into mysteries that had previously lain beyond the reach of his gauche, juvenile emotions. He claimed that never in his life – not even in the years at Cheiron's school – had he felt so at peace.

Odysseus listened with the kind of patience and sympathy that Achilles had never found in his father. He said that he was deeply glad that Achilles had found peace and joy at last. He said that he understood very well the things that the youth had been trying to tell him because he had known such a tranquil life himself on Ithaca. He too had a beloved wife. He too had a small son who was the delight of his life, and he knew how such things changed a man for the better.

'Then why have you left them?' Achilles asked.

'Because I am a man and I gave my word at the swearing of the oath at Sparta.'

Odysseus watched as the intense young man across from him frowned and shook his head. Then he added almost casually. 'Your friend Patroclus will go to the war at Troy for the same reason.'

'Patroclus is going to the war?'

'Of course. He was among those who contended for Helen's hand. He took the oath and will honour it – though that's not the only reason he will fight, of course. He and the rest of the Myrmidons are eager for the battle. They know that it will be the greatest war that has ever been fought in the history of the world. They know that there is such honour to be won there as will be sung of by the bards for generations to come. Even as I speak, a huge army is gathering not far from here at Aulis, on the other side of Euboea. Thousands upon thousands of men are arriving by land and sea. The harbour will be crowded with ships. All the great heroes of the age will be there – Agamemnon,

Menelaus, Diomedes of Tiryns, Ajax and Teucer, Nestor of Pylos, Idomeneus of Crete and countless others. Everyone who cares about the glory of his name.'

Odysseus smiled and shook his head as though amazed by the wonder of the thing. He allowed time for Achilles to respond but when the youth said nothing, he added, 'Your friend Patroclus wouldn't want to be left out of a gathering like that even if he wasn't bound by his given word.'

After a moment Achilles said, 'Did he not ask if I would come?'

Odysseus shrugged. 'He presumed that you would lead the Myrmidons – particularly as your father is in no shape to fight these days. Phoenix thought so too.' He looked up into the uneasy gaze across from him. 'But then they don't know how content you are here among these shepherds on Skyros.' Odysseus sighed. 'I could almost envy you, Achilles, knowing that you have a long and peaceful life ahead of you untroubled by the din of battle and the tumult of the world with its lust for deathless fame.' As though a new thought had occurred to him, the smile became a frown. 'Your father is bound to be disappointed. He was sure you would take his ashwood spear to Troy with you. He knows what a fine warrior you have become. He saw you winning all the glory that his wound has denied him. But it seems that you belong to your mother now.' Odysseus glanced out to sea. 'So shall I tell him that you've wisely decided that it's better to dance in maiden's clothing than to lie gloriously dead inside a bloody suit of armour?'

The Years of the Snake

They had agreed to assemble the fleet at Aulis, a rock-sheltered harbour on the narrow strait between Boetia and the island of Euboea. The Boeotian levies were already there, and neither their northern neighbours, the Locrians, nor the warriors of Euboea had far to come. By the time Agamemnon's own fleet of a hundred ships arrived in the port, Ajax and Teucer, the sons of Telamon, had also arrived from Salamis bringing the twelve vessels they had promised. Meanwhile, Menelaus had mustered sixty ships out of Laconia, and though there was no word from Crete as yet, the principal Argive allies rallied quickly to his cause. Diomedes brought eighty ships out of Tiryns while Nestor's flagship led ninety more out of Pylos round the many capes of the Peloponnese, and Menestheus sailed fifty Athenian warships around Sounion Head. More impressively, Odysseus and his allies out of the Ionian islands managed to launch only eight vessels short of the sixty that Palamades had mockingly suggested.

Even the distant island of Rhodes contributed nine ships, but King Cinyras of Cyprus was less forthcoming. When Menelaus sailed on a recruiting mission there, half-hoping that he might waylay Helen and Paris somewhere at sea, Cinyras promised to send fifty ships to Aulis. In the event only one Cyprian vessel turned up – though its captain did launch forty-nine model ships made out of earthenware in fulfilment of his monarch's pledge before he sailed away.

Menelaus was furious to have been duped in this manner, but perhaps he should have expected no more from a king who was also high priest to Aphrodite on the island of her birth. Worse still, the insult confirmed a suspicion that had haunted his jealous mind while he was on the island – that Cinyras had made a pact with Paris to conceal the runaways on Cyprus while he himself was there.

Agamemnon had set up his headquarters in the ancient fort on the rocky bluff overlooking the harbour where a vast fleet of around a thousand ships jostled each other as they made ready to cast off for Troy. The town below the fort had been over-crowded for some time now, and at night the watch-fires lit by the bivouacked troops stretched far along the strand. Standing beside Agamemnon one evening, the head of the college of Boeotian bards – a famous master of the art of memory – assured the High King that no one before him, not even Heracles or Theseus, had ever mounted an expedition on this scale. The Lion of Mycenae could scarcely manage his pride.

But various minor conflicts had already demonstrated the difficulty of holding together a diverse force that spoke many different dialects and harboured a number of old feuds and grudges. Agamemnon was under no illusion that so many men had been drawn to Aulis merely out of loyalty to himself and his brother. Yet whether it was greed for the rich spoils of Troy, or lust for land and trading advantage, or the mere love of violence and adventure that had brought them, this mighty host of warriors was now his to command, and the name of Agamemnon, King of Men, would live for ever in the songs of bards.

He was, however, engaged in the less glorious business of arguing with a hard-bargaining minister from Delos over terms for the provision of wine, oil and corn when word came that Achilles and his Myrmidons had arrived. 'Send him up at once,' he said. 'Let's see what this son of Peleus is made of.' Then he dismissed the Delian with orders to think of better prices and summoned his chiefs of staff into council.

Many ferocious warriors were oiling their spear-shafts and sharpening their swords among the host outside the fort, and Agamemnon was glad enough to have their weapons under his command. But the touchy youth that Odysseus had brought back from Skyros was an altogether different proposition. Resolute to demonstrate that he was a man among men, Achilles walked into the council with an arrogance that fell not far short of disdain and then he sat throughout most of its deliberations taut as a bowstring, observing the others in the room with a taciturn frown that could be construed as vigilant in some lights and as surly in others.

From the first there was no doubting that this young warrior had something of a god about him. Whether or not Thetis, his mother, had seined him with fire or dipped him in the Styx, a radiance of immortality already flashed like a nimbus off his hair and glittered from the keen grey metal of his eyes. And it did so with such ardour that even old Nestor, more than forty years his senior, found it hard to stop a wondering gaze straying towards his lithe, graceful presence. For there was – Nestor saw with both admiration and trepidation – a killer's glitter in that sheen.

Nor had he come alone. Though the invitation to join the council had been extended only to Achilles, a companion entered the room at his side, darker and slightly taller, but with much the same assured composure, as though the war had been arranged for their mutual satisfaction. When Agamemnon queried his presence, Achilles jutted his chin and said, 'This is Patroclus, son of Menoetius, grandson of Actor, King of Phthia. Where I go, he goes also.' And it was immediately clear that either both men stayed or both men left.

Seeing the blood flush in his brother's face, Menelaus hastened to remind him that Patroclus had been among the men who took the oath at Sparta, and Odysseus further defused the tension by remarking that the last time he'd seen Achilles and Patroclus together they had been six years old and scrapping like dogs beside the stream at Cheiron's school. 'If the two of you fight as hard now as you did then,' he said, 'the Trojans are in for a bad time.'

Having already reminded himself that Apollo had promised victory only if Achilles came to the fight, Agamemnon joined in the laughter and ordered that room be made for another chair.

When Nestor asked for news about his old friend Peleus, Achilles answered with the stiffness of a young man reluctant to speak freely about his personal life. 'My father regrets that he can no longer be of service to the cause himself, but the men I lead are his. Also he gave me the long spear which was Cheiron's gift to him and bade me use it well. Divine Athena polished its shaft with her own hand. My father prays that the goddess will bestow her favour on us.'

Diomedes and Odysseus exchanged glances at the youth's solemnity, but Ajax, who was cousin to Achilles, gave a good-natured laugh. 'And no doubt your father warned you about keeping on the right side of the gods as mine did me. But as I said to the old man when I left his bedside, any fool can win glory if the gods are with him. I mean to do so whether they're with us or not.'

'Well I for one,' said Odysseus wryly, 'will be glad of any help we can get.'

At that moment Agamemnon's herald Talthybius entered the room to announce the arrival of a Cretan legate, who was seeking audience with the High King.

'Only a legate?' Agamemnon frowned. 'Deucalion was supposed to send me ships. Where are they?'

Talthybius shrugged. 'There's no sign of them as yet.'

'Damn these Cretans and their lies. Let's have him in.'

Menelaus immediately recognized the legate from his visit to the island. One of Deucalion's shrewder ministers of state in Knossos, Dromeus had caught the drift of the changing wind and aligned himself with the dissident faction of young men that had gathered around Idomeneus. That it was he, and not one of Deucalion's minions that had come to Aulis, augured well. But where, Agamemnon demanded to know at once, were the ships they had hoped to see by now?

Dromeus chose to answer a different question. 'There have been changes in Knossos since the sons of Atreus graced us with their presence,' he said. 'Deucalion has crossed the river to the Land of Shades. His son Idomeneus now sits on the Gryphon throne.'

There came a few formal acknowledgements of regret for Deucalion's death before Agamemnon said, 'But were we not given reason to think that your new king looks on our cause more favourably than his father did?'

'That is indeed the case, Great King'

'Then I ask again. Where are the ships?'

Dromeus opened his hands, brought them together at his lips and smiled. 'The House of the Axe now stands ready to commit a hundred ships to this war.'

'A hundred! Excellent!' Agamemnon made no effort to conceal his pleasure.

He turned smiling to Menelaus, who exclaimed that this was more than they had dared to hope. The mood around the table lifted.

Then Palamedes said, 'So when can we expect to see them?'

Again Dromeus smiled. 'This is, as you acknowledge, a generous commitment. You will not be surprised, therefore, that it comes attended by a condition.'

Lifted by a breeze gusting from a courtyard down the hill, the distant shout of an officer haranguing his men entered the room. With an irritable flick of his hand Agamemnon shooed a fly that was buzzing about his ear. 'What condition?'

'That as leader of so large a force King Idomeneus should share supreme command of all the allied forces.'

Telamon's son, Ajax, an open-faced, broad-chested fellow with a frank manner, was the first to break the silence. He gave a derisive snort, slapped a hand across a sturdy thigh and said, 'The crown has gone to your new king's head! Go home and tell him that we already have the only leader we need.'

Still smiling, Dromeus fingered the curls of his beard and turned his gaze back to Agamemnon. 'I might point out,' he said, 'that Crete's hundred vessels are equalled in number only by the large squadron that the High King himself has brought out of Mycenae. Our ships are ready to sail. They await only your word.'

The stern young face of Achilles was also waiting for that word.

Agamemnon did not miss the quick sideways glance directed by Patroclus at his friend, but the cool, intimidating scrutiny of Achilles' gaze remained fixed directly on the king's frown, waiting to see how he would react.

Feeling the immediate need for decision, yet flustered by this unforeseen development, Agamemnon was, in those tense moments, listening for the advice of a god. When no voice entered the silence of his mind, he decided that though a hundred ships meant a great deal to him, his honour and authority meant a great deal more.

He was about to declare as much when Nestor straightened from where he had leaned to hear Odysseus whisper in his ear. 'Perhaps' – the old man cleared his throat – 'perhaps it might be wise for the council to deliberate upon this matter?'

Taken aback, Agamemnon observed Nestor's insistent nod.

'My own thought precisely,' he said. 'If the Cretan legate will excuse us . . .'

Bowing courteously to each of the counsellors, Dromeus backed out of the room, leaving a musky trace of perfume on the air.

As soon as the door had closed behind him, Ajax said, 'What is this whispering about? The High King is our commander. He has all the fighting force he needs.'

'Bear with me, friend,' Odysseus smiled, and would have said more but Palamedes intervened. 'This matter requires careful thought. Crete promises more than eight times the number of ships that Salamis could muster.'

'But at what price?' demanded Ajax. 'Any fool knows that a divided leadership can only spell trouble in the end.'

'I stand with Ajax,' declared Diomedes. 'It seems to me there's nothing to discuss. Like most of us here, Idomeneus was sworn to our cause at Sparta. A man doesn't make conditions when he swears before a god.'

Fortified to find his own instincts strengthened by such unqualified support, Agamemnon said, 'There's already too much scope for division in our forces. A hundred ships more or less will make no great difference to our strength. I'd rather do without them than lose control of the rest. If Idomeneus won't bow to our authority then let him stay at home.'

'Good,' said Odysseus. 'The only hard part being that's not what he will do.'

'What do you mean?' Ajax frowned.

'You heard what Dromeus said. His ships are ready to sail. If Idomeneus has scoured his island to mount such a considerable fleet, he's not about to let it rot in port at Knossos.' Odysseus turned his ironical smile on Agamemnon. 'A hundred more warships may not count for much in your reckoning, King of Men, but I've no doubt that Priam will welcome them with open arms.'

Ajax uttered an outraged gasp of dismay. Menelaus began to shake his head. 'Idomeneus was among the first to swear. I don't believe he would betray us.'

Odysseus shrugged. 'Is it unknown for Cretans to break their word?'

'But the man's my friend,' Menelaus protested. Then he saw that every man in the room was thinking the same bleak thought: that the open-hearted, younger son of Atreus had not proved to be the wisest judge of friends.

'Nevertheless,' Nestor dispelled the fraught silence, 'it seems that Deucalion's son has ambitions for his kingdom. Evidently he hasn't forgotten that there was a time when Crete ruled the seas and took tribute from many of our cities. With Troy's help it's possible that she might do so again.'

Diomedes said, 'Then what would he have to gain from joining us?'

'A large share of the spoils of Troy,' Odysseus answered. 'Unrestricted access to her trade routes through the Hellespont and around the Asian coast – gold, silver, grain, cinnabar, timber, amber, jade. All of this, along with recognition of his independent authority by every kingdom in Argos.'

'My friend Menestheus won't care for that,' said Palamedes.

Odysseus made a dismissive gesture. 'Then the Lord of Athens should have kept as tight a rein on his vassal as his predecessor did.'

Agamemnon grunted and sat back in his chair. 'Crete was on the rise again even before Theseus leapt from the cliff on Skyros. Idomeneus merely has more ambition than his father.'

'And more courage,' Menelaus put in.

Diomedes frowned. 'The more shame that his courage is not matched by his honour. I took him for a true man at Sparta, and a worthy contender for Helen.'

'But the question remains,' Odysseus insisted. 'Do we want his ten thousand Cretan spearmen inside our tents pissing out or outside them pissing in?'

A hint of a smile briefly crossed the face of Achilles.

Agamemnon caught it from the corner of his eye, and decided that the time had come to confront this arrogant young blood directly. 'The son of Peleus seems amused. What are his thoughts on this question, I wonder?'

'That it is a matter of indifference to me,' Achilles said.

Agamemnon frowned. 'How so?'

'With all due reverence to the gods, my trust is in my own strength and that of my friend.' Achilles smiled at Patroclus. 'Whether the Cretans are for us or against us, we will fight.'

'So will we all,' said Ajax. 'But who will lead? My obedience is to Agamemnon.'

'And mine,' Diomedes concurred.

Nestor rubbed a hand through the silvery-white curls of hair at the back of his head. 'Yet Idomeneus awaits an answer. I for one am wondering whether it may not be prudent to have his forces at our side.' He turned his grave eyes to Odysseus, who nodded and said, 'This war will have to be won at sea before it can be won on land. A hundred ships either way could make all the difference.'

Agamemnon stared at Palamedes, who said quietly, 'I agree with that judgement,' and glanced away across the table, where Menelaus fidgeted with the heavy gold signet ring that Helen had given him on their wedding day. He was frowning gloomily down at the rampant pair of leopards on its bezel when Palamedes asked, 'What does the King of Sparta say?'

The younger son of Atreus glanced uncertainly at the elder before answering. 'As I said before,' he murmured hoarsely, 'I consider Idomeneus to be my friend. I believe he will prove a valuable ally.' He fingered the ring which slipped loosely around his knuckle. Then he said, 'This thing is for my brother to decide.'

Again Agamemnon shifted in his chair, trying to gauge the feeling in the room. His face had reddened and his eyes were on the move, avoiding the silent faces round him, yet finding nowhere sure to settle. This was the first occasion since he had committed himself to this war when he knew he was faced with a decision on which the whole dangerous enterprise might turn. Yet which way to lean? Every muscle of his body insisted that he retain absolute control. Control over the forces he had gathered, control over this council, control over himself. And the two men in the room with whom he felt most at ease fully expected him to do so. But Ajax and Diomedes were men of action, not of thought. And the same was true of Achilles and Patroclus, young men both, driven by an invincible confidence in their own strength and prowess. Neither of them, he suspected, would hesitate for a moment. They would go down fighting sooner than yield an inch in pride. That was the warrior's way, the way of men, and he was Agamemnon, King of Men. But there was more to waging war than blood and fear and mindless valour amid the clash of chariots, and if shrewd old Nestor and that cunning thinker out of Euboea agreed with Odysseus on this, then more might be at stake than pride.

Agamemnon sat with his hand across his mouth, regretting that he had exposed his own position too soon. Were he to change his mind now, he might appear weak before those who most respected him. Yet if they were wrong . . . A hundred more ships . . . ten thousand more men . . . on one side or the other. He saw his whole proud fleet in flames around him and a Cretan pentakonter bearing down on his flagship with a gryphon at its prow and the double axe painted on its sail. An error made now might prove costly indeed when his ships were at sea.

But he could not vacillate for long under the impatient gaze of Achilles.

He was summoning the will to speak when Odysseus leaned back with a mildly incredulous air and said, 'Do I speak only for myself when I say that if there was disagreement between Idomeneus and Agamemnon, I would know where my own loyalty belonged?'

And before either of them had fully taken in the implications of the question, both Ajax and Diomedes, at whom his challenge was directed, had declared that he was certainly not speaking for himself alone.

Odysseus arched his brows at Agamemnon and opened his hands. 'It seems that we're in agreement then.'

Agamemnon narrowed his eyes and saw that a door had opened on his dilemma. 'Very well. On that clear understanding, let the Cretans come.'

But the Lion of Mycenae was feeling the full weight of the burden of command, even in the very moment when he was about to relinquish half of it.

Nor was he to know that Odysseus had no particular reason to mistrust the intentions of Idomeneus. But as the Ithacan said to his cousin Sinon afterwards when telling him how the meeting had gone, 'We need those Cretan ships and how else was I to persuade Agamemnon to give up half his command?'

As to whether or not divine assistance might be required, Agamemnon was more inclined to agree with Odysseus than Ajax, so he had set aside the day before the fleet was due to sail for prayer and acts of sacrifice to the gods.

All the principal commanders and their men assembled outside the town in a hollow where a thick-girthed plane tree, sacred to Hera, had stood for centuries. An altar had been raised in the shade of the tree beside a nearby spring. The priests invoked the almighty power of Sky-Father Zeus, and Calchas prayed for the wisdom and guidance of Apollo. Then Agamemnon offered the sacrifice.

He had just raised the knife from the kill when all the men standing in the hollow were amazed to see a huge snake slither out from under the altar. Agamemnon stepped back in shock, gazing down at the scarlet markings streaked along the mottled black scales of the creature's back. With astonishing speed, the snake writhed its long body towards the trunk of the plane tree and began to climb.

Calchas moved quickly from where he had been standing a little behind Agamemnon to observe the behaviour of the snake. He watched it make its way along a high bough to where a sparrow had made its nest. Though the mother-bird rose, fluttering her wings in alarm, she was quite powerless against the muscular strike of the great snake. Eight times it dipped its jaws into the nest, snatching out a fledgling sparrow at each strike. Then it raised its head upright, swayed for a time, watching the flight of the panic-stricken mother-bird. A last swift strike caught the sparrow by the wing and swallowed it whole. A moment later the snake stretched itself out along the bough and lay there so stiff and rigid that men later swore that it had been turned to stone.

A murmur of wonder and alarm ran through the assembled men.

Agamemnon stood with the sacrificial knife still dripping in his hand, looking to Calchas who threw the flat of his right hand to his forehead, cried out, 'We accept the oracle,' and stood with his eyes closed.

Silence settled across the glade. Not a man moved. Only the plane tree stirred a little in the breeze off the sea. Then Calchas lowered his hand, opened his eyes and smiled at the hundreds of men gazing at him with rapt attention. 'Argives,' he cried, 'the mighty intelligence of Zeus himself sends you this portent. We have waited long for it, and will have to wait long for its fulfilment, but the glory promised here will never die.'

Still dismayed by the shock, Agamemnon took encouragement from his words. 'Tell us, Calchas,' he said, 'how do you read the omen?'

'Does a serpent not renew its skin each year?' said Calchas. 'And are the leaves of the plane tree not reborn with every year that passes? Eight was the number of the fledglings in the nest. Their mother sparrow made the ninth, and the death of each bird speaks of the passing of a year. The sparrow is one of Aphrodite's creatures and Aphrodite fights for Troy. So for nine years you must fight to take Troy, but in the tenth year her broad streets will be yours.'

The priest's voice was exultant. He threw open his arms, gazed skywards, and then stood with his eyes closed as though in silent prayer. Around him the assembled men waited in silence, each locked in his own thoughts.

Agamemnon saw at once that more was needed. 'It is the will of Zeus,' he shouted. 'The god has spoken. Victory will be ours.' Then Menelaus and Ajax were quickly at his side taking up the shout, urging others on. Soon the hollow was loud with the cry of 'Victory will be ours'. It rose from the throng again and again, but as he joined the shouting, Palamedes, the prince of Euboea, became uncomfortably aware that only a few yards away across the glade, Odysseus of Ithaca was studying him with a cold, ironical regard.

The next day, to the accompaniment of a peal of thunder which was generally interpreted as a sign of encouragement from Zeus, the fleet set sail for Troy.

Two generations have passed since that day and many men have told the stories of the war many times. But memories grow confused with the passing of the years, so not all of the stories are reliable, and some chroniclers, for reasons that serve their own doubtful ends, have been known to tell downright lies. My own authority is the word of Odysseus, which I have found to be trustworthy in almost all respects, and he was quick to dismiss as nonsense the story put about by some that the fleet got lost almost immediately and made landfall in Mysia, where they launched a major assault, thinking that they had reached the coast of Troy.

Those who believe this fable offer divine intervention in explanation of the error. They claim that Aphrodite confused the navigators in order to stave off the attack on the city. But as Odysseus pointed out, Agamemnon was well-furnished with charts, Menelaus himself had already made a voyage to Troy without difficulty, and some of the most experienced rovers of the Ionian, Cretan and Aegean seas were among the captains of the Argive fleet. Odysseus was not the only prince who supplemented his wealth by piracy, and among his many other pursuits, Palamedes took a particular interest in the problems of navigation. So the story is most charitably understood as a muddled memory of a war that lasted for many years and involved many different campaigns not all of which took place beneath the walls of Troy.

It is true that when Agamemnon first conceived of attacking Troy, he had hoped to emulate the swift, devastating raid by which Telamon and Heracles had once breached the weakest stretch of the city's walls. But King Priam had strengthened his defences since then. He had also commissioned a new fleet of warships and had been engaged in serious, and successful, diplomatic activity to ready his many allies for the coming conflict around the western coast of Asia. The High King of Troy might have fewer ships at his command than the High King of Argos but he was not faced with the problem of transporting a hundred thousand men across the Aegean, and his fleet was quite large enough to guard the mouth of the Hellespont and offer support to his allies.

And his allies were many. As intelligence reports came into Mycenae from Agamemnon's spies, they proved ever more daunting. Of all Troy's friends, only the Dardanians had decided to stay out of the war. Having tried and failed to persuade Priam that Helen should be returned immediately to Sparta, King Anchises had declared that he would not embroil his people in a military conflict that had begun with Paris' perfidy and might end with the ravaging of all the lands around the Idaean Mountains. But neither would he lend support to the invaders, and all the other coastal kingdoms, from Paeonia and the Thracian Chersonese in the north to the Lycians in the south had swiftly rallied to King Priam's aid. The Phrygians, the Mysians, the Carians and the Pelasgians out of Larissa were raising armies, and Priam was also given promises of support from countries further east should the need arise. The Amazons, the Paphlagonians and even the distant Halizonians all stood ready to send forces to the defence of Troy.

In the face of such concerted opposition, Odysseus advised that a cautious war of attrition would be the wisest course of action. Troy might be more easily taken if they first wore down her allies through a campaign of naval blockades and raids on the weaker fronts. Until that ominous day at Aulis, no one except Odysseus had reckoned that the campaign might drag on for as long as ten years. But if such was the will of Zeus, he argued, then the princes of Argos must resign themselves to it, fortified by the knowledge that they would win in the end.

Agamemnon listened to this argument but his was not a patient temperament. He still nursed a hope that the sheer size of the force he had mustered would shock the Trojans into surrender and prove the reading of the omen wrong. When he expressed this view the council divided round him along the usual lines, with the thinkers among them – Nestor and Palamedes – supporting Odysseus. The rest argued for an immediate attack on Troy.

When he saw that he was outnumbered, Odysseus came up with an alternative plan. Very well, he suggested, rather than risk everything on a single throw while Troy was at her strongest, it would be wise to establish a secure bridgehead as close as possible to the city. The small island of Tenedos, rising from the sea off the Trojan coast, was perfect for their needs. From there they could either mount a direct assault on Priam's capital if it seemed likely to succeed, or they could blockade the mouth of the Hellespont and launch raids against Thrace to the north and southwards against the coastal strongholds of his other allies.

Everyone saw the sense of this and the plan was agreed.

By the time the fleet arrived near Tenedos, Agamemnon had decided to position most of his ships where they could hold an advance of the Trojan warships while the island was taken by a smaller force. He called a council aboard his flagship and was about to announce his decision to put Diomedes in command of the invasion, when Achilles demanded the honour of leading this first strike himself.

The day was sultry and close. There had been a delay in starting the council while the others had waited impatiently for Achilles to appear. The mood was now fraught with nervous anticipation.

Agamemnon hesitated. He had no wish to enter into open conflict with this volatile young man, but neither was he willing to trust the success of his first, crucial assault to a warrior who had yet to fight a full-scale battle. Before he could pick his words, Achilles narrowed his eyes. 'Calchas has warned you that this war can not be won without my help. If the gods are looking to me to seal the victory, they will favour me as I lead the first attack.' He spoke as though the full force of oracular authority lay behind his declaration, leaving no room for debate or contradiction.

News of the omen about the seventh son of Peleus had spread

quickly throughout the ranks, and Achilles already commanded the affection of the troops as well as their respect. His Myrmidons had always been prepared to lay down their lives for him, but so were many others now, and he was known among the common soldiers as the luck of the force. Well aware of it, Agamemnon had already bitten back his tongue on a number of occasions when the youth had spoken with arrogant presumption, but this time he was not prepared to yield.

'We commend your ardour, son of Peleus, and are grateful for your offer,' – he glanced down at the chart of Tenedos on the table before him – 'but our trust is in the experience of Diomedes, the veteran of Thebes. When you have proved yourself in battle as thoroughly as he, we will be glad to give you a command.'

Agamemnon cleared his throat and was about to progress the attention of the council to a discussion of tactics for the assault when Achilles said, 'The High King must think again.'

Agamemnon visibly swallowed his rage. 'Did I not make myself clear?'

Achilles rose from his seat. 'Quite clear enough. The insult you have just given me was quite as clear as the first I had to suffer at your hands.'

Agamemnon looked up in impatient bewilderment.

Anxiously old Nestor sought to intervene. 'Calm yourself, Achilles,' he said quietly. 'I feel sure that no insult was intended.'

'No,' Agamemnon growled, holding up a clenched hand so that the gold shone on the lion-seal of his ring, 'let's have this thing out once and for all. I shall be most interested to hear how the son of Peleus thinks I have insulted him.'

Achilles brought his fist down on the table. 'It's been clear to me from the first that you recruited me to this campaign only as a mere afterthought. Had Calchas not made it plain that Troy would never fall without my aid, you would have been content to leave me on Skyros and keep all the glory for yourself. Is that not so?'

Irritably Agamemnon said, 'If your fame had been greater we might have thought of you sooner.'

Achilles' nostrils flared. He was deciding whether to release his pent-up fury or to turn on his heel and walk away for ever, when Odysseus spoke. 'Achilles my friend, you're wrong to believe that the High King slighted you. Had I been quicker to come from Ithaca, you would have been called sooner to the cause. Such things are ruled by the gods, but if there is a fault here, it is mine.'

'And today?' Achilles demanded, barely mollified by the generous apology. 'Have I not seen my courage thrown back in my teeth?'

'No one doubts your courage,' Odysseus answered, 'but you ask a great deal.'

Menelaus shifted uneasily in his chair, sweating a little in the heat. 'My brother seeks only to secure the success of the landing.'

'Then am I to understand that the sons of Atreus question my prowess?'

Nestor smiled at him. 'No more than I do, and that is not at all. But there will be many opportunities for you to demonstrate your skill at arms, young man.'

'You are old, sir,' Achilles answered, 'and I respect your wisdom. But were you not once as young as I am and as impatient for fame?'

'It's your impatience that worries me,' Agamemnon scowled. 'I will not court disaster merely to feed your ambitions.'

Again Achilles bristled. Again Odysseus was about to intervene, but it was Idomeneus who spoke first. It had been one thing for the King of Crete to gain formal acknowledgement as joint-commander of the enterprise, but it had been quite another to make his authority felt in a council that had assembled around Agamemnon and evidently owed him its allegiance. His position was weakened also by the fact that he had brought twenty less ships from Crete than the hundred he had promised. But having observed this dispute with cool detachment, the suave Cretan now saw his first clear opportunity to assert himself. 'There is a way we might resolve this matter to everyone's satisfaction while at the same time advancing our business here today'. Gratified to sense that he had secured the full attention of everyone present, he kept them waiting a few moments longer than necessary. 'I agree with my royal cousin of Mycenae that Diomedes is the right man to lead this force. The conqueror of Thebes will surely make short work of Tenedos.' Achilles stiffened but Idomeneus smiled and raised a restraining hand. 'Be patient with me, friend.' When Achilles settled in his chair again, Idomeneus looked round at the others. 'Priam has, of course, anticipated our plans to seize the island, and has taken steps to fortify it. He knows that the only harbour large enough for the number of ships we will need is here.' He pointed to the place on the chart. 'One of my spies reliably reports that a number of large rocks have been placed on the cliffs above the harbour. In the event of attack, they will be rolled down, causing massive damage both to ships and men as they come ashore.' Agamemnon was about to demand why he had not been told this before, but Idomeneus spoke over him. 'This is my suggestion. Let Diomedes command the main assault on the harbour, but give Achilles command of a smaller force that will swim ashore under the cover of darkness, making for this cove here. From there he can storm the cliff positions from the rear. If he times his assault correctly, and conducts it with sufficient ardour, he will prevent the release of the rocks and allow the main force to come ashore unmolested.' His black eyes smiled across at Achilles. 'There is great honour to be won from such a perilous task. And this way the two commanders will act together – as Agamemnon and I act together, to mutual advantage and for the good of all.'

Odysseus and Nestor immediately commended the merits of the plan. When Diomedes declared that he had no objection to sharing that part of his command, Agamemnon gave the scheme his general approval so long as the details could be worked out to his satisfaction. But though the conflict between Agamemnon and Achilles had been contained, it had not been resolved, and

Odysseus came away from the council privately convinced that, whatever the oracles promised, the hostility between the High King and the dangerous young man he had brought out of Skyros might one day prove disastrous for the whole campaign.

Whenever Odysseus spoke about Achilles in later years he would always claim that there was a mystery about the youth that baffled understanding, for though his pride was impossible, his murderous efficiency as a warrior was matched by a degree of tenderness such as Odysseus had observed in no other man. In some respects, he suggested once, Achilles had more in common with Helen than with anyone else he knew. They had both grown up loving wild things in wild places – Achilles at Cheiron's school in the mountains, Helen in the wilderness groves of Artemis – and both had a certain feral quality about them, by which I think he meant an almost amoral air of innocence that was capable of ruthless action. It's true also that both of them had been injured by the human world at a crucial moment of their development and their destinies were shaped for ever by those wounds. Above all, however, they seemed kindred in the knowledge that though their bodies were mortal, their spirits were not, and everything about them seemed touched by immortal fire.

'Mother,' Achilles had said at last as he and Thetis parted, 'I was born to die soon, but Olympian Zeus owes me some honour for it.' And so he had come to the war, convinced that he would never return, and driven by so urgent an appetite for his destiny that he would let nothing stand in the way of his honour. Out of forces that once threatened to tear him apart – the bitter strife between his mother and his father, between the old religion and the new, between the claims of his peaceful life on Skyros and his need for glory – Achilles had forged himself into a weapon of war, and his whole being gleamed with warlike purpose.

This then was the young man entrusted with the leadership of the surprise assault on Tenedos, and his bristling new resolve to prove himself something more than a man among men generated such a degree of impetus that his small band of Myrmidons crashed into the rear of the Trojan defenders with terrifying ferocity. The cliff heights were taken with few losses, a signal was sent to Diomedes telling him to bring his ships ashore, and the raiding party advanced so far ahead of the main force that it was Achilles himself who thrust his spear through the breast of King Tenes, the commander of the island force, and then killed the man's father with a savage blow to the head.

Thereafter resistance quickly collapsed. Splashed with blood that was none of his own, his bright hair gleaming in the dawn light, Achilles stood among his cheering men, waiting for Diomedes to join him in the citadel. However soon his death might come, he felt certain now that his name at least would never die.

Once the bridgehead on Tenedos was established, Agamemnon decided to send ambassadors to Troy offering terms for the withdrawal of his forces. Menelaus, Odysseus and Palamedes were chosen to present demands which – it was clear to all of them before they set out – Priam must find unacceptable. The true purpose of the mission was to discover just how united the Trojans were behind their outward show of defiance, and with that intention in mind, Agamemnon's herald Talthybius had arranged for the envoys to be lodged in the house of Antenor while in the city.

They found the king's chief counsellor cagey and reserved at first, and far from at ease with the knowledge that he was responsible for their safety in a city filled with their enemies. Over a few goblets of wine, however, and at the subtle prompting of Palamedes, it was natural enough for Menelaus and Antenor to share some hard feelings about Paris, the man whom each saw as the destroyer of his happiness. Meanwhile, Odysseus worked his wry charm on Antenor's wife Theano, who needed little encouragement to express her undying hatred for the man who had killed her child and now threatened ruin on Troy.

For the first time the Argives began to gather a picture of the way events had unfolded in the city since Paris had left Sparta with his prize. They learned that Aeneas had lent his support to Paris during the flight from Sparta only because they were sworn friends committed to each other's aid, and not because he approved in any way of Paris's treacherous behaviour. He and his father Anchises had soon made it plain that the High King must not look to Dardania for help when the hosts of Argos came battering at his gates. According to Antenor, Priam had tried to make light of this rift with his cousin, saying that until his son returned, and he had heard the whole story directly from his lips, he would reserve judgement on the matter. Privately, however, the king's mind was already bent on war. He had known that it must come sooner or later, and was as ready for it as he would ever be. Antenor even remarked on a certain gleefulness in Priam's usually grave features when he considered the scale of the insult that his son had given to Argive pride.

But Priam had been forced to wait for several months before the *Aphrodite* returned to Troy, for Paris and Helen had sailed as far east as Cyprus in the hope of eluding all pursuit. Menelaus winced to learn that his wife and her lover had indeed been concealed on the island while he was there, and had sailed southwards into Egypt shortly after his departure. The weather was good at that time and the seas calm, so after making his devotions at the birthplace of Aphrodite, Paris had turned their flight into a prolonged voyage of love. He had calculated that a delay in his return would allow time for his father and brothers to accept what had been done and come to terms with it. Perhaps it might also whet the appetite of the Trojans for the fabled beauty of his abducted lover.

In that last respect, his calculations had certainly hit the mark, for as soon as the *Aphrodite* was seen approaching the city, a large crowd began to gather along the road from the harbour to the Scaean Gate, while yet others lined the streets. To further heighten the excitement and the air of mystery, Paris arranged for Helen and Aethra to be carried in curtained litters, so that they could pass from the ship to the palace without being exposed to the mob's coarse stare. They would have heard a few bawdy jeers from the back of the crowd, but they must also have sensed how the rich procession of retainers, slaves, animals and trophies was received for the most part with an exhilarated awe intensified by further expectation. Behind those gauzy curtains lay Helen of Sparta, who had now become, to the city's undying glory, Helen of Troy. It was as though a goddess had descended among them, one whose mystery must not be profaned. And Paris, the people's own prince – the bull-boy from the pastures of Mount Ida – could be seen riding proudly beside her litter. Who could argue when a beggar shouted that the age of wonders was come again upon the earth?

Antenor told how Helen's face had still been veiled when Paris finally brought his lady before the full assembly of Priam's family and counsellors in the great hall of the palace. 'It was a little like watching a sculptor presenting his master work,' he commented drily, aware of the pain on the face of Menelaus, whose sensitive imagination made him feel all the more a cuckold with each new fact he learned. 'We had waited for so long to see her that the entire hall was agog. And yes, I have to admit that Helen is a woman of astonishing beauty – though whether any woman is worth putting an army at risk is, in my opinion, quite another matter.'

'Or a city,' Palamedes said.

'Indeed.'

'Yet we are all reasonable men. Our enmity is with Paris not with Troy. It would be a great tragedy if thousands were to die for one man's selfish folly. Don't you agree?'

Aware that he was answering other questions than the one that had been put to him, Antenor said, 'Believe me, if my wife and I could see a way of avoiding war by delivering him over to you, Paris would return with you in chains this very night. But the High King is as smitten with Helen's beauty as he is indulgent of his son. And the war party on his council is stronger than those of us who would prefer a peaceful solution. So do not expect Priam to look with favour on any demands for Helen's return.'

When the Argive envoys presented themselves before Priam the following day, they found the atmosphere in the great hall even more openly hostile than they had expected. Paris himself was absent from the council, and Antenor did what he could to ensure a fair hearing for Agamemnon's ambassadors, but he could not prevent the gasps and jeers of outrage with which Deiphobus and Antiphus greeted their catalogue of demands. These included the immediate return of Helen, the surrender of Paris to answer charges of murder and abduction, the compensation of Menelaus for the injury he had received, the compensation of Agamemnon and Idomeneus and all the princes under their command for the massive expense to which they had been driven by Paris's actions, the establishing of well-defended Argive settlements in strategic locations on the Asian mainland, and free, unrestricted access to the Hellespont, the Black Sea and all the major trade routes with the east and north.

The monetary demands alone would have been sufficient to ruin Priam many times over, but the King of Troy heard Odysseus out, stony-faced, before silencing his noisier sons with a raised hand, and giving his response.

'As to the first point, we are hardly to blame if our royal cousin of Sparta failed to satisfy his wife. Unlike my sister Hesione, who has languished in captivity on Salamis for many years, the Lady Helen is here in Troy of her own free will. If it was her wish to leave, I would regard it as beneath my dignity to keep her here. Let the princes of Argos learn a simple lesson of courtesy in that respect.' Aware of the angry flush across the scarred face of Menelaus, he drew in his breath. 'As to your other demands, we have long been aware that the High King at Mycenae covets our wealth and power. And why should he not when his own domain is a mere hovel by comparison? Our message to him is also simple. Nothing awaits him in Troy but ruin and humiliation. Let him clear our waters of the infestation of his ships and take his pack of Argives home before all their wives find husbands better suited to their taste.'

Remembering the last time he had stood before Priam in this hall and the amicable manner in which they had parted, Menelaus found it hard to contain his fury. 'I see that your son lacks the courage to look me in the eye,' he said. 'If all your followers are as brave, King Priam, look to have your women raped, your city burned and pillaged, and your line extinguished. I will have my wife again. And you – you will rue the day that Paris shuddered from your loins.'

Odysseus put a restraining hand to his friend's arm, and then he turned to face Priam with a cool, disdainful stare. 'We will deliver your message to our king,' he said. 'Look to have his answer soon.'

The Argive ambassadors withdrew stiffly from the hall and returned to the house of Antenor. Not till long after they had left the city did they come to learn that, if Deiphobus and Antiphus had been given their way, the three of them might have been murdered in their beds that night. Only Antenor's outraged protests, fortified by Hector's sense of honour, had kept them from the crime.

The first assault on Troy turned into a brutal and inconclusive clash which left both sides damaged and thoughtful.

Things began well enough for the Argives when a night raid with blazing torches caused havoc among Priam's fleet, seriously weakening his ability to guard against invasion. But the same raid had warned the Trojans of the imminence of attack and by the time Agamemnon's ships approached the shore, a well-positioned army stood waiting to repel them.

To make matters worse, the Argive troops were troubled by rumours of a prophecy that the first man ashore was doomed to die. Even Achilles hesitated at the prow of his ship, reluctant to throw away his life with so little glory gained. Meanwhile the Trojans hurled rocks and stones at the crowded ships, keeping up an unnerving ululation that carried on the harsh wind blowing across the plain.

At last, stung by the insults coming from the enemy before him and from Agamemnon at his back, an old warrior called Iolaus who had once been charioteer to Heracles, gave a mighty shout and jumped into the surf. He was immediately surrounded and cut down on the strand before he could strike a single blow, but the man's rash courage was to win him undying fame. He was given the title Protesilaus – 'first to the fight' – and buried with great honour that night on the Thracian shore of the Hellespont.

But now that the first life had been lost, other warriors began to jump from the ships. Achilles and Patroclus were among the leaders, with Phoenix and the Myrmidons behind them. Odysseus, however, held back a while, watching how the battle developed. He had counselled against launching a land attack until more had been done to stretch Priam's resources, but Agamemnon had been so infuriated by the king's insolent reply to his terms that he was determined to force the words back down his throat. Now the price of his impatience swiftly came clear as more and more men fell under the volley of arrows that met them as they stumbled towards the shore.

By sheer force of numbers, the Argives forced a landing, only to find themselves embroiled in a fierce and bloody struggle all along the strand. The strongest resistance came from a sector of the front where a Trojan hero called Cycnus hacked his way through the invaders as if he was invulnerable. When Achilles saw what was happening, he shouted for Patroclus to follow and fought his way across the uneven ground until he confronted the Trojan giant. Cycnus laughed in his face, gesturing for the youth to come at him if he dared. A moment later he was astonished by the speed and ferocity of Achilles' attack. Even so, the fight was long and desperate, and might have gone either way had not

Cycnus stumbled over a stone as he sought to avoid a sword thrust. He fell to the ground on his back, pulling Achilles down with him. Both men lost their weapons in the fall, but Cycnus was winded by the weight of his opponent's armoured body. In a frenzy of violence, Achilles grabbed at the Trojan's throat and strangled the man with his own helmet straps.

When he stood up, gasping and exultant from the kill, it was to feel Patroclus pulling at his arm. All around him, as a trumpet sounded from Agamemnon's flagship, he saw the Argive warriors retreating from the shore.

Many recriminations followed the failure of that first attack, but the heavy losses he had taken persuaded Agamemnon that Odysseus had been right to insist that Troy would fall only after a long campaign of attrition. So the war entered a new, sullen phase of sporadic violence that dragged on for a year, and then another, until it became clear that, if Troy ever fell, it would not be until all the long years of the snake had passed.

Battles were fought at sea, and many ships were sunk, and many men burned and drowned before the Argives established their naval superiority. From their stronghold on Tenedos, they were now free to mount raids all along the Asian coastline. The island of Lesbos was taken, and mainland cities smaller than Troy fell before them. Priam's southern allies in Lydia suffered heavily from these attacks. Colophon, Clazomenae, Smyrna and Antandrus were all left looted and burning, but other important cities such as Sestos and Abydos on either side of the Hellespont held out under siege. So the years of warfare protracted themselves from season to bloody season, and all across Asia, from the Black Sea to Cyprus, even in places far from where the Argives had ever landed, the name of Achilles struck fear in men's hearts and kept children from their sleep.

There were also long periods of inactivity while both sides licked their wounds, or when fever, dysentery and pestilence robbed men of the will to walk let alone fight. Sometimes the troops could not be stirred in the torrid summer heat, and the dark winter months were always wretched and bitter. A maddening wind blew across the Trojan plain throughout much of the year but in winter there was ice on its breath. It left the springs frozen, the tents heavy with snow, and battle-hardened warriors groaning over chilblains and frostbite. And even when the weather was clement not a day went by without men questioning why they had ever got into this insane fight and wondering whether they would ever sit by their homeland hearths again. But those who deserted faced a long trek home through hostile territory and most of the Argives grudgingly decided that having endured so much, it made no sense to turn for home with little to show for their pains but wounds and stories. So the war went on.

In the ninth year, with Troy's western sea lanes cut, and many of her allies demoralized by constant raids, it began to look as though the war was finally moving Agamemnon's way. Late in the summer he decided to attack Mysia.

The Mysians are a Thracian people who had crossed from Europe a century earlier. Their king, Telephus, was a bastard son of Heracles who had gained the Mysian throne with Priam's help after marrying one of the High King's many daughters. His fertile lands were now keeping Troy supplied with wheat, olives, figs and wine that were carried along inland routes beyond the reach of raiders. Agamemnon had been convinced by Odysseus that if Mysia fell, then Troy might be starved into submission. So leaving behind him a force strong enough to hold Tenedos, he brought the bulk of his fleet to the island of Lesbos and used the harbour at Mytilene as a base for his assault on that part of Mysia around the mouth of the river Caicus which is called Teuthrania. But once again he miscalculated the strength of the resistance and the battle took much the same shape as his failed advance on Troy many years earlier. The landing was made more quickly this time but the Mysians had the advantage of the ground and by the time Agamemnon had seen half of his advance guard cut down, he was struggling to avoid a rout among his troops.

Again Achilles and the Myrmidons came to his rescue with a swift flanking movement that descended on Telephus behind his own front line and forced him to pull back along the river bank. Sprinting in pursuit of the fleeing king, Achilles hurled his spear and struck Telephus in the thigh, bringing him down among a tangle of vines. The battle might have been won in that moment but the king's lifeguards rallied to hold off Achilles while one of them pulled out the spear and carried the wounded Telephus away. Meanwhile, the Mysian warriors on the shore remained unaware that their king had almost been killed and fought on with such resolve that once again Agamemnon called a retreat.

Reluctant to return to Tenedos with such dispiriting news, he ordered the fleet southwards in search of weaker places to attack. Having burned a small town to the north of Smyrna, the weary leaders spent a few days bathing their wounds and easing their stiff limbs in the waters of some hot springs they found there. Ever afterwards those springs were known as the Baths of Agamemnon.

The weather was clear and it should have been a leisurely time, but the mood of the frustrated commanders soon turned as acrid and sulphurous as the steam rising round them. Achilles was still furious that his own brilliance on the battlefield had again been wasted merely because the Lion of Mycenae had failed to keep his nerve. He and Patroclus kept themselves apart from the others, finding comfort only in each other's company. Then, on the second evening, a quarrel broke out between Odysseus and Palamedes about whether they should persist with the Mysian campaign or concentrate their strength near Troy. Agamemnon's testy vacillation only made matters worse. Meanwhile, Diomedes grieved over the death of his friend Thersander, who had fallen as he led the advance guard against the Mysians, and Menelaus spent much time asleep or brooding alone.

Weary of the fractious company and feeling the need for fresh meat, Agamemnon decided to go hunting. Only Palamedes had the energy to accompany him. They dragooned a local huntsman into leading a pack of hounds pillaged from a burned-out estate and spent most of the day in a fruitless search for game. By mid-afternoon Agamemnon was ready to kill the sullen huntsman out of sheer frustration, but then the hounds put up a pretty white hart. Baying and whooping, they set off in chase with Agamemnon following in the lead as the deer weaved and darted among the brakes. Unaware of his surroundings and determined to make a kill, he plunged into a silent grove of trees, following the white flicker of the hart's rear-quarters until the panting creature was brought to bay. He hurled his spear. The hart staggered on its slender legs then fell bleeding in the glade.

Cursing that there was no one near to help, Agamemnon threw the carcass of the beast across his shoulders and carried it out of the wood. As he came out into the light, sweating and bloody, he saw Palamedes and the huntsman staring at him white-faced. Only then did he observe the offerings dangling from the boughs around him. He had killed the hart in a grove that was sacred to Artemis.

The next day they set sail for Tenedos but they had not been long at sea when a north-easterly gale gusted down on the fleet from the plains of Asia. The billows clashed and rose, the ships shook and dipped on the steep swell. In such treacherous weather the helmsmen were reluctant to put in on a hostile coast, so they tried to ride out the storm under reefed sails. But by late after-noon the rain slanting down against them was so dense that the ships could barely see each other. The sky turned dirty green, and then a malign, thunderous black. The tempest blew harder throughout the night, and by dawn the whole of Agamemnon's fleet had been scattered like driftwood across the turbulent eastern sea.

More than ten years later, I learned from Odysseus that my

father, Terpis, was in one of the ships that were lost in that storm, and there must have been many like him who died wretched, unwitnessed deaths at sea. As for the rest, one by one during the course of the next few days, the ships staggered into port, shaken and damaged, back where they had begun, nine long years earlier, in Aulis.

The Altar at Aulis

A woman who loathes and despises both her father and her husband is likely to want to prove herself a better man than either. This was certainly the case with Clytaemnestra, and even while her body was employed on the arduous business of providing the House of Atreus with an heir and two daughters, she turned her will and her powerful mind to the better management of affairs in Agamemnon's mighty kingdom.

Mycenae's massive walls stand on a crag that commands the mountain passes between the rich plains of Argos and Corinth. Various brigands had taken plunder there for centuries before the house of Atreus seized the stronghold and started to build an empire around it. As their power increased, tributes and loot poured into the city, and Agamemnon had not been idly boasting when he told Clytaemnestra that he was the wealthiest of the Argive kings. But his aptitude was for warfare and the brutal use of power, not for the dull routine of administration, so his queen had not been in Mycenae very long before her quick eyes saw how much of his wealth was draining away through poor management and corruption. She suggested that her husband place spies to watch over some of his principal ministers and tribute-gatherers. Shortly afterwards, those officials lost both their posts and their lives.

Faced with the problem of finding reliable successors, Agamemnon looked to the advice of his wife and was impressed by the immediate increase in his revenue. Thereafter he began to trust her judgement in other matters of policy. More appointments were made on her recommendation. Soon, in effect if not in name, the whole complex system of public administration was under her control.

Meanwhile, in those easy years before the war, reports reached Mycenae of the way that Helen and Menelaus were renovating the city of Sparta. From the first Clytaemnestra had felt uneasy in the gloomy palace that she had inherited. Its draughty chambers had witnessed murder, betrayal, incest, the unwitting slaughter of children by their fathers, and even – it was rumoured – cannibal feasts. When she had complained about the place to Agamemnon, he replied that money was hard to come by and he had better things to do with it than waste it on unnecessary luxuries. Infuriated by this mean streak in his nature, she shamed him into action by suggesting that his younger brother was now outshining him and everybody knew it. Agamemnon promptly gave her leave to spend as she liked on improvements.

Skilled architects, masons, sculptors and painters were commissioned and set to work. Under the queen's strict scrutiny, designs were drawn up and approved. Large quantities of Spartan stone – that curiously mottled porphyry for which her homeland was famous – were brought to Mycenae along with many tons of green and rose-coloured marble from quarries across the Peloponnese. Within a couple of years the haunted fastness in which Agamemnon had been born was transformed into a city that set a new standard for splendour among the Argive kingdoms and impressed the ambassadors who came from further abroad.

And Agamemnon liked what his queen had done. He was also happy to take the credit for it and, for a time, as his military power grew, and the reach of his tributes and trade agreements extended across Argos and the islands, he came to believe that the ancestral curse on the house of Atreus must have been lifted at last. The gods had smiled on what was already accomplished, and there was more to be done. But power is an appetite that grows with feeding, and the Lion of Mycenae had to face ever-rising costs – not least those incurred by his wife's majestic rebuilding of his city. Raids across the eastern sea brought back some of the gold, silver, slaves, cattle and other booty that he needed to feed his court, reward his retainers and keep his army equipped with horses, chariots and weapons. But when prices began to rise and the state's expenditure threatened to outrun her husband's income, Clytaemnestra saw that there might be much to be gained from a foreign war. Already she had cast envious eyes on the wealth of Asia, and she knew both from her own spies and from talks with the foreign legations that came to Mycenae, that the guardian of the gate to the eastern treasury was Troy. So it was she, before any of his comrades and counsellors, who first persuaded Agamemnon to contemplate the possibility that Priam's city might be taken.

The marriage between Menelaus and Helen was also Clytaemnestra's plan. She had been quick to point out that if anyone other than the High King's brother won Helen's hand, Sparta might pose a western threat to Agamemnon's power at a time when his attention should be firmly fixed on the east. With the shrewd help of Odysseus her plan had matured. So with the brothers of Mycenae wedded to the sisters of Sparta, and further plans in place for Clytaemnestra's son Orestes to marry Helen's daughter Hermione, the High King and his Queen could look forward with confidence to a time when the House of Atreus would be the undisputed ruler of the world.

And then Helen had astounded them all by running off with Paris.

At first Clytaemnestra had been furious with her sister for throwing her carefully thought-out ambitions into disarray, and it was some time before she could admit to herself that some part of her fury was attributable, once again, to envy.

What must it be like, Clytaemnestra wondered, to know a passion so great that you were prepared to stake your life on it? Only a god could be strong enough to wreak the havoc that Helen had wrought. So perhaps, like their mother Leda, Helen had been swept up on mighty wings and ravished into immortality, while Clytaemnestra sat alone among her children in Mycenae, constrained by the tiresome duties of a mother and queen, and hungry each day for news of the war her sister's lust had precipitated.

Nor had she imagined that the war would drag on for so long, for the years of the snake had passed slowly in the Lion House at Mycenae. Rumours came and went. Good news was followed by bad. In some weeks wealth flowed into the coffers, usually after some rich city had been sacked along the coast of Asia, and then, like the tide, it went out again to meet some new demand of this costly and seemingly interminable war. So as her husband fought his way from Thrace to Lycia and back again, and Troy showed no sign of falling, Clytaemnestra sat in Mycenae with all the instruments of power in her hands, and waited and watched.

One afternoon, Clytaemnestra was trying to wind up negotiations with a barely comprehensible sesame factor out of Mesopotamia, who was the last of the many people with whom she had dealt that day. The man was too long-winded and her mind had wandered, for rumours were rife about the fleet's unexpected appearance back in Aulis. Clearly the weather must have much to do with it, for such a storm as had blown in from the north-east had not been seen in years and fierce gales had continued to gust from that quarter for the past three weeks. But there were also alarming, if unconfirmed, reports that the storm had scattered the ships while they were beating back from a massive defeat in Mysia. Thersander, commander of the Boeotians, was certainly among the dead, and the whole land around Aulis was said to be in mourning. It was also reported that another great hero, Philoctetes, was suffering from so noxious a wound that no one could bear to be near him, and he had been abandoned to live or die, as the gods decided, on the island of Lemnos. A few days earlier King Nauplius of Euboea had sent Clytaemnestra a note of reassurance that the principal Argive leaders, including her husband and his son Palamedes, were all alive and well, though as yet the overall situation remained confused. But from Agamemnon there had been no word, despite his queen's repeated request for news.

This was worrying. And Clytaemnestra felt increasingly irritated by the sesame factor's obsequious manner. Outside, in the yard below the balcony, she could hear her children at work on a play that Orestes had written. He was also the director of the drama and had, moreover, claimed the role of Achilles, which he considered to be more glamorous than that of the High King his father, who was played by the fat son of the high priest in Zeus' temple. As usual, the girls were doomed to act the part of effeminate Trojans – twelve-year-old Iphigeneia making an unconvincing King Priam, and Electra a sulky Paris.

Their mother was thinking that if this war dragged on much longer, Orestes would be called upon to take up arms in earnest, but as far as the boys of the court were concerned, the war at Troy was going very well indeed that afternoon.

Now, however, Orestes and Electra were quarrelling, and if someone did not do something about it there would soon be tears. Clytaemnestra was about to get up and dismiss the ridiculous merchant when a herald entered the chamber and saluted her. She recognized the man as a junior on the staff of Talthybius, so the message must be from the High King. But why had Agamemnon not sent Talthybius himself, who had been appointed on her own recommendation, and from whom she might have gleaned answers to the many questions pressing on her mind – unless, of course, it was for that very reason?

Instantly her senses prickled. The factor was briskly dismissed. Clytaemnestra reached out to receive the bronze cylinder from the herald's hand and took out a scrolled sheet of paper sealed with the lion impress of her husband's signet ring. The message was not written in her husband's clumsy scrawl – it must have been scribed for him – but the tone was typically, and peremptorily, all his own. The demands it made astounded her.

Iphigeneia had not yet been five years old when her beloved father sailed for Troy. When she thought of him now it was hard to picture him at all, for her only memory was of someone big and very hairy, who sometimes swung her in his strong arms yet made her feel safe. What she knew was that he had been there for a time, and then he was gone, and all that was left of him was stories.

She knew what everyone else knew, of course – that her father was High King of Argos, that great men trembled before him, that he was leader of the mightiest army that the world had ever seen, and that one day soon he would return in glory with all the treasure of Troy to add to his stupendous wealth. But Iphigeneia found it difficult to conceive of such an awesome figure. It was too much like looking at the sun – one was left blinking at hot shadows.

And perhaps her brother Orestes felt the same way, she thought, for though he was older, and his memories clearer, and he used to brag about their father all the time, he was infatuated these days by the dashing figure of Achilles. Orestes insisted that Achilles was the greatest warrior the world had ever seen. He was the next best thing to a god, the terror of the Trojans, as beautiful as he was brave, and he would live for ever in the songs of men. In a year or two, when Orestes was old enough to go to the war himself, he would join the Myrmidons, and he and Patroclus would fight beside Achilles, leading the last assault on the Scaean Gate, and their valour would so inspire the rest of the Argive host that the city must swiftly fall. Iphigeneia, who dearly loved her brother, and was filled with admiration for him, felt sure that this was how it would be.

Regrettably, she would never be allowed to fight in the war

herself because she was only a girl, but as she listened to Orestes, she felt her soul swell with pride and glory, and longed for ways in which she could be of service to the cause. For she too believed that she was singled out for a special destiny. The dull womanly world of weaving and chatter and child-bearing was not for her. Her heart and her imagination were far too wild for that. And had not her mother already proved that a woman could serve the state as powerfully as any man? Well, Iphigeneia intended to find means to do that too, but in ways that would make people love her rather than fear her. She would be like her favourite goddess Artemis, who was virgin sister to Apollo, as she was sister to Orestes. She would keep herself pure, proud, single and free.

She had been thinking such thoughts even as she waited in the hot courtyard, wearing the silly beard that was meant to make her look like King Priam, while she listened to Electra telling Orestes that she was fed up with his stupid play and wanted to go indoors. The complaint had turned into a quarrel, with Electra in tears and no one else to take her part, so the play had been a disaster, which put Orestes in an angry mood. Iphigeneia was wondering what to do when, unusually, her mother had called down to her from the balcony of her chamber, and asked her to come up at once. And now she was waiting again in the ante-room, while her mother talked with her advisors inside.

Iphigeneia felt increasingly afraid. She was trying to remember what she could have done that would get her into trouble, and was frightened because she couldn't think of anything. So how should she prepare herself to deal with the cold tempest of her mother's rage?

Then the high door opened and the advisors came out and told her to go inside. But there was something strange in the way the old men looked at her, as though people had been telling tales behind her back, and they believed the lies.

Iphigeneia stepped inside the spacious room with its frescoed walls and pillars of mottled marble. She saw her mother standing in the light by the balcony with her back to the door, looking at a scroll. When she turned, there was a frown in her eyes but not the immediate release of anger that Iphigeneia had feared. After a moment, there was even, across those gaunt, rouged cheeks, a hint of a smile.

'Close the door behind you,' Clytaemnestra said, 'and then sit down.'

Iphigeneia did as she was told. She knew that, where her mother was concerned, it was wiser not to speak until you were spoken to, so she sat in silence, looking down at her knees in order to avoid staring too closely at the paint on her mother's eyelids and the heavy gold ornaments she wore.

'How old are you now, child?'

'I will be thirteen soon.'

'Yes, I remember – you made your offering to Artemis not long ago, so I suppose we must think of you as a woman now. Yet with your father at the war and all the cares of state on my head, I have scarcely had time to see you as a child. Stand up and turn around. Let me look at you.' Again, though more self-consciously, Iphigeneia did as she was bidden. 'Yes,' her mother said, 'you are more fortunate than Electra. She has her father's looks. You are more clearly mine. In a year or two you will be a beauty.' She nodded and sighed as though this too might be some kind of burden. Then she said, 'Sit down again. I have something to tell you. A message came from your father today. He is in Argos, at the port in Aulis. He wants me to bring you to him there.'

Iphigeneia raised her eyes in astonishment. Her breath shortened. She could feel her heart jumping at the thought of this important stranger returning to her life at last. But she was uncertain whether it did so with excitement, awe or fear.

'Will Orestes and Electra come also?' she asked, not knowing what else to say.

'This does not concern them. Only you and I will go, and we must go soon. So you will have to prepare yourself. You are going to be married, my dear.'

Iphigeneia was so used to unquestioning obedience in this formidable presence that she had almost said, 'Yes, mother, I will get ready at once,' before she realized what a momentous thing had been announced.

She sat in awestruck silence, clutching the edges of her seat, and wondered for a moment whether she was about to faint. Then she realized that some god must be present in the room, for the feel of the air had altered around her, and there was an unfamiliar tingling in her skin.

In the same moment it was clear to Clytaemnestra that the thought of marriage had never seriously crossed the child's mind.

'Have you nothing to say?' she asked, and when this unusual child did not immediately reply, she added drily, 'Do you not, for instance, wish to know who will be your husband?'

'Yes,' Iphigeneia whispered, 'I would like to know.'

'I think you will be pleased. Not of course that your feelings count for anything in this matter. Your father has made up his mind without even bothering to consult me, so your own wishes will be a matter of indifference to him.'

Clytaemnestra closed her eyes and for a time she was gone from the room, back into her own younger days, when her father Tyndareus had decided what was to be done with the precious thing that was her life. Suddenly, to her own surprise, and for all the authority and power with which she could now make truculent men tremble before her, she was experiencing with more intensity than for many years the ineluctable pain of a woman's life. Much sooner than she had anticipated, she and this strange, dreamy daughter whom she hardly knew at all, were entirely at one in their fate – for both of them were finally at Agamemnon's mercy, in this and almost all other matters. And that was no safe place to be.

Clytaemnestra opened her eyes and looked at the girl again. Though he had done well enough for the child, she was certain that Agamemnon's motives must have been shaped more by policy than affection, and she was furious that she had not been consulted

– so furious that only for the child's sake did she contain her rage. So furious that she might have wept, for there was grief in that fury – grief for herself, grief for the girl, above all grief at the injustice of things.

Perhaps Iphigeneia was right to preserve her silence. Why waste words where words could make no difference?

'You are to be married to Achilles,' she said at last. 'If the gods are kind, you may live up to the name we gave you and bear him a strong race of children. Now go. Marpessa will help pack your things. We leave for Aulis tomorrow.'

Almost three weeks had passed since the fleet took refuge from the storm at Aulis. Agamemnon had reckoned it would take them a week to render the stricken vessels sea-worthy, and then they would make speed for Tenedos in the hope that they would get back to the island before Priam realized that its garrison was unsupported. It might be a close run thing, but it could be done.

Yet once the repairs were made, the north-easterly gale that had driven them there refused to back. Agamemnon had risen each day at dawn with the intention of setting sail but the wind remained unseasonably fierce. Roof tiles were lifted, rotten trees smashed, vineyards wrecked. Sooner than bruise their heads against this gale, even the gulls huddled where they could. Meanwhile the crowded ships damaged each other again as they jostled in the greasy swell. Provisions in the hulls began to rot. The town stank of too many men sodden with rain. They were drunk and listless, thinking of their women not so many miles away, and of how wretched their life had been on Tenedos. And still the wind blew, a maddening bluster of air, banging at doors and casements, rattling blinds, crashing the waves against the harbour wall, obstinately locking the seas against them.

Soon, inevitably, someone murmured that a god's breath must be behind it.

Calchas took the omens and found that Divine Artemis was responsible for the wind. Someone in the host had offended her.

The contrary wind would continue to blow until the goddess was appeased. Palamedes, who was standing at Agamemnon's side in that moment, whispered. 'The hart,' and looked up into the High King's blanching face. 'The hart belonged to Artemis.'

The story of that unlucky hunt through the woods near the hot springs had been kept quiet lest it further disturb the army's already uncertain morale. But truth is the daughter of time, and time had passed, and now Agamemnon found himself answerable before both the goddess and his men. If disaster was to be avoided, some sacrifice acceptable to Artemis must be made at once.

Again Calchas was asked to consult the omens.

The priest was shaking when he emerged from his oracular trance. Sweat stood visible on his brow. He was already aware that Agamemnon mistrusted him. Now he was caught between the High King's anger and the anger of a god.

'Speak up, man,' Odysseus demanded. 'What did you see?'

Hoarsely Calchas said, 'As virgin mother to the creatures of the wild, Divine Artemis saw one of her young blasphemously killed in her own sacred grove. Only one sacrifice will be acceptable to her. The life of the killer's most beautiful child must be offered in return.'

Like everyone around him, Agamemnon stood transfixed. Then he clutched the hem of the cloak he was wearing, lifted it up to his mouth and began to back away. Wide-eyed, he shifted his gaze from the soothsayer to Palamedes, as though desperately seeking signs of collusion between them. 'No,' he was saying, 'this must not be.' Then he turned on his heel and walked away from them, still holding the cloak at his mouth.

But the oracular rites had been performed before too many witnesses and there was no denying what they had said.

That night Agamemnon locked himself away with his brother Menelaus, and the ghosts of the house of Atreus howled about their heads – children who were slaughtered, children who were murderers, innocence extinguished from the earth. Terrible things had been done in the time of their fathers and, whatever Agamemnon and Menelaus did to appease the fates, it seemed that the curse carried by those deeds crossed the generations and could never be escaped.

Agamemnon was in no doubt which one of his children the goddess had singled out. Iphigeneia had been touched at birth with something of Helen's beauty, though it was sharpened a little by the angularity of Clytaemnestra's face. Agamemnon remembered the child as he had last seen her, nine years ago, when she could hardly have been more than three or four and was still small enough to dandle on old Nestor's knee, or be swung about his own shoulders like a bundle of thistledown. He remembered thinking how slender her wrists were. He remembered the delight that had shone in her eyes. She was the only one of his children ever to lay large enough claims on his heart to keep him for more than a few moments from the things that really mattered to him. And now, as Menelaus mixed more wine in a golden bowl they had looted from some king's palace across the sea, Agamemnon raged to see his most tender feelings chopped up and served as a bloody dish that he must force himself to eat.

But Clytaemnestra would never permit this atrocity. He had already snatched one child from her breast and ordered its death. Never would she allow him to kill another, not if all their wealth and power should hang upon the death. She might not be the most tender mother that the world had ever seen, but if she learned what was asked of him, she would take the whole brood of his children and flee with them to furthest Scythia sooner than let this terrible thing happen.

It could never be done.

Yet the wind still clamoured at the latches on the casement of the room. The ships still rotted in the port, a garrison on Tenedos waited for relief, and if the fleet did not get there soon, the island must fall, the bridgehead would be lost, and all the long years of the snake would have been endured for nothing.

Either way, he could see only disaster from which he might never recover.

That night Agamemnon drank himself into a stupor of unconsciousness and woke before dawn, sweating from his dreams. Yet for all his fervent prayers, there had been – he heard it at once – not the slightest lessening of the wind.

Later that morning, the warlords came to his room. He sensed that they had already been arguing among themselves, but Palamedes had insisted that the High King must be told of the murmurings among the men. A number of men who lacked heart for the war had already deserted, but Palamedes claimed that most of the rest were willing to fight on for victory so long as the fleet was not delayed in Aulis much longer. If it was, then Agamemnon might soon face a full scale mutiny. Already some voices were saying that the High King had brought this trouble on his own head. If he was not willing to placate the goddess and lead them to Troy, then they were ready to look for another leader.

So what did he intend to do?

The High King intended to rage against the injustice of both men and gods.

Had not Apollo promised him that if he held out for nine years, victory must come in the tenth? Had not Calchas given him that oracle in this very place? Had they not all seen the snake for themselves? Had the god's promise not sustained them all throughout the long years of the campaign? Was he now to call Apollo a liar? Or was it rather that duplicitous Trojan priest he must mistrust? Could he even count on the loyalty of his own generals any more?

His generals shifted uncomfortably as he raged. Not one of them seemed ready to speak. Palamedes frowned impatiently at his colleagues then turned to face the king again. Calmly he pointed out that there need be no conflict between the two oracles. Yes, Apollo had promised victory all those years ago, and that promise might still be kept. But Apollo was brother to Divine Artemis and if the god was forced to choose between loyalty to a mortal and loyalty to his offended sister, then that promise could also be swiftly revoked. It was for men to win the favour of the gods, not the other way round. And that could be done only by making the proper offerings at the proper time.

Odysseus turned away in disgust. 'Palamedes seems as ready to trust the divinations of a Trojan traitor as he is to listen to complaints among the men.'

'I have merely reported what the High King needs to know,' Palamedes retorted. 'My own loyalty is not in question. Do you dare to suggest otherwise?'

'Gentlemen, gentlemen,' old Nestor sought to restrain them. 'We are all bewildered by this development. Let us not darken counsel further.'

Agamemnon turned to Odysseus for support. 'What are you saying?'

Almost in a gesture of despair, Odysseus shook his head. 'Don't I recall that this whole quarrel between the Trojans and the Argives began in the days when Laomedon offered his daughter up as a human sacrifice? And much good it did him. What I am saying is that I, for one, want no part in the killing of a child.'

'Nor I,' said Ajax. 'Haven't I said all along that any glory I win will be my own achievement not a mere favour from the gods?'

Achilles nodded. 'I stand with Odysseus and Ajax on this.'

'Then you must argue with the wind, gentlemen,' said Palamedes.

'At least its sound might be cleaner in my ears.' Odysseus scowled at Palamedes, who merely shrugged and glanced away, whereupon Odysseus got up and left the room. The wind scattered papers in his wake. Immediately Achilles got to his feet and went out after him. A moment later, Ajax and Diomedes glanced at one another, and they too stepped outside, gathering their cloaks about them.

Agamemnon turned to Nestor, who sat with his head in his

hands, staring at the floor. 'What do you say, old friend?'

Nestor looked back at him with haggard eyes. 'For once in my life, I find myself at a loss for words. It seems that both sides are right in this matter. Yet how can they be? Forgive me, but I don't know what to say.'

Agamemnon turned his anguished gaze on his brother. 'Menelaus?'

'My heart grieves for you, brother . . . but . . .'

'But what?'

'I am thinking of what this war has already cost us all across the years. I am thinking of the men we have left on Tenedos . . .'

'And of the wife you lost, no doubt.'

Menelaus looked away from the hot glare in his brother's eyes. Agamemnon released his breath in a growl of pain so fierce and baleful that it made the others wince. And when the cry had exhausted itself the room was utterly silent but for the moaning of the gale outside.

'Only the king himself can consent to this sacrifice,' said Palamedes after a time. 'It is for him to decide.'

'You have no children. It is an easy thing for you to say.'

The four men sat together listening to the wind. After a time Nestor said, 'In such a pass as this it may be that a man can do nothing but cast himself on the mercy of the gods.'

'What do you mean?' Agamemnon demanded.

Nestor opened his hands in a hopeless gesture. 'If the High King declared his willingness to make the offering by bringing the child here to Aulis, it might be that the goddess would be moved to take pity on her.'

For a moment Agamemnon stared across at his friend with a glimmer of hope, but then he remembered. 'Her mother would never consent to it,' he said, shaking his head. 'And you cannot ask me to drag the girl screaming to the altar from her mother's arms. It is impossible. Hear me.'

Again, but for the noise of the wind, silence closed down around his words.

But Palamedes had sensed that Agamemnon's refusal was no longer absolute, and his quick brain was at work.

'Then we must look for a pretext,' he suggested quietly.

Old Nestor frowned. 'Say more. I don't follow you.'

'We must find a reason that will compel the queen to bring the girl to Aulis.'

Palamedes looked back at the king. 'How old is your daughter?'

'Twelve, thirteen? I don't know. I can't remember.'

'But old enough to be given in marriage. Why not tell your queen that the girl is to be married? That you have decided to give her in marriage as a reward for gallant service.' A half smile touched with admiration for his own ingenuity spread across his face. 'Why not tell her that she is to be married to Achilles?'

Perhaps Iphigeneia was doomed to die long before her father's sacrilegious act of killing a hind within the grove of Artemis? Perhaps she was already doomed to die when Agamemnon killed the infant child of Clytaemnestra's husband Tantalus? So dark are the workings of the gods that she may even have been doomed to die a generation before her own birth when Atreus slaughtered the children of his brother Thyestes. The wisest among us are only mortal, and none of us can know the answer to such questions. But this much I would claim to know: that a man cannot go to war in quest of power and wealth without doing mortal harm to some portion of his soul, and once the soul is damaged and impaired then all kinds of madness follow.

By the time Iphigeneia arrived in Aulis, all the women were weary after the long journey from Mycenae against that gruelling wind. The servants who had accompanied the girl took her aside into the apartment that had been prepared for her. She went readily enough, filled with thoughts of the next day, wanting to bathe and rest herself so that she would be at her best, and sorry only that there had been no time to see her father, who was, she was told, busily engaged about the business of the war. But when

Clytaemnestra demanded to set eyes on the bridegroom that her husband had chosen for their daughter, Agamemnon glanced uneasily away. He opened his mouth to speak and could not do so. Menelaus, who had entered the chamber at his right hand, was left to explain as best he could the hard fate that had fallen on the elder son of Atreus.

There was a time of silence. Then the tempest that broke about the High King's head came at him stronger and more dangerous than the storm outside. All the years of hatred and anguish that had festered since that dreadful day in Pisa were unleashed at once, and their mouths were full of curses. Even as the king's brother pinned her arms back against the wall, Clytaemnestra was sucked deeper into the vortex of her frenzy, weeping with fury, and spitting imprecations across his shoulder. If Menelaus had not been there, using all his strength to restrain her, she would have torn the eyes out of Agamemnon's head. As it was, the King of Men stood for a time with his head bowed like a man tethered to a flogging frame and waited for the storm to pass.

It did not pass. There was one moment as Clytaemnestra paused to catch her breath, when he murmured, 'Do you not think that I am as a dead man already even to contemplate this thing?' But she had only a huge, accumulated capital of hatred and derision for the impotent appeal in his bleak eyes.

With a voice that chilled his soul, she hissed, 'It would gladden my heart to see you die in agony a thousand times sooner than let you touch a hair of my child's head with your butcher's hands.'

And she had gone too far for him.

If there had ever been a shred of tenderness anywhere between them, they might have found some means of escaping the trap that fate had sprung for them. They might have said, 'Let the gods and the world do as they will, there is nothing more precious to us than our daughter's life, so let that be an end to it.' But there was no such tenderness, and the longer and more cruelly she railed against him, the more sullenly ready he found himself to commit the act she was determined to prevent.

She saw it suddenly in his eyes. She read it in his hostile silence.

Clytaemnestra sagged in Menelaus' grip. For a moment both brothers thought that her fury must have burned itself out in despair. But as soon as Menelaus let go of her arms, she made for the door with the intention of rescuing her child.

Outside the door the guards were waiting for her.

There are bards who will tell you that Iphigeneia was not killed at Aulis. They say that Achilles was so outraged to learn how his name had been abused that he hastened to the girl's protection. They say that even as Agamemnon raised the sacrificial knife, a clap of thunder rent the skies, and Achilles drew his sword at the command of Artemis, took the girl from the altar and carried her away. One of these stories says that he sent her to safety in Scythia, where man-slaying Artemis is first among the gods. Another bard claims that Achilles did marry Iphigeneia after all, and that she, not Deidameia, was the mother of his son.

Such bards are mere romancers who dare not contemplate the cruel truth of things. Let them tell their stories. I believe what was told to me by Odysseus many years later, for he was certainly there in Aulis, and like it or not — and he liked it not at all — he was party to the dreadful thing that was done that day.

Woken by the wind, Iphigeneia leapt into consciousness filled with excitement and trepidation. The palace women came to bathe her and robe her in a knee-length saffron tunic, chattering as they fussed about her clothing and dressed her hair. But of her mother there was as yet no sign.

After a time, an old man with silver hair came into her chamber and dismissed the women. He smiled at her mildly and said in a soft, slightly croaking voice, 'You look very beautiful today, my dear.'

'Are you my father?' Iphigeneia shyly asked.

'No,' the old man smiled. 'Don't you remember me? I'm Nestor, the King of Pylos. I used to dandle you on my knee when I came to visit your father in Mycenae. You were always a favourite of mine. It was me who sent you the little Thessalian pony to ride . . . But it was a long time ago. Perhaps you don't remember.'

'I remember the pony. Electra had him after me. Where is my father?'

'You will see him in a little while, child.' Nestor pulled his cloak closer about him against the draught. 'But there is something he has asked me to tell you first.'

'Is it to do with my wedding?'

'Yes, in a manner of speaking it has.'

'Then may I ask you something first?'

'Of course.'

'Is it true what Orestes says – that Achilles is the next best thing to a god?'

Nestor sat back in surprise, wanting to smile, but so sick at heart that the thought of smiling seemed an abomination. 'Listen to me, my dear,' he said after an uncertain moment. 'You are not to be married to Achilles today.'

Iphigeneia's heart sagged in her breast, in part with disappointment, but mostly – she saw it at once – with relief.

'Then when?' she asked. 'Must I take off this dress?'

'No, you may keep on your dress because something else is going to happen.'

Nestor glanced away across the room. It felt as though his tongue had turned to stone. What price his reputation for eloquence now? He could wish that his mouth had been stitched up with twine for ever rather than saying what he had come to say.

'Does my mother know?' the girl asked. 'I wasn't sure whether she was happy for me to be married or not.'

'Your mother knows,' he said. 'But . . . I was just thinking about what you said . . . about Achilles. And yes, I suppose Orestes is right – Achilles is the next best thing to a god. And that is why what will happen to you today is better still. You are not to be given to Achilles, my dear. You are to be given to a god.'

'To a god?'

And when Nestor nodded, she said, 'Which god is it that wants me?'

'Artemis, my dear. The Lady of the Animals. It is she who wants you.'

A smile broke across the face of Iphigeneia, 'But Divine Artemis is my favourite among all the gods,' she cried. 'Am I to be her priestess then?' And before he could answer, another swift thought stumbled from her lips. 'Am I to be a virgin for the rest of my life?'

Nestor stared at her, nodding his head as old men do when they sit alone, pondering on the refractory nature of things. He was looking for disappointment – even for defiant refusal – in her face, but he found none there. Rather, this strange girl was staring upwards with an expression in her eyes that seemed close to rapture, as though some vital realization was coming clear to her, and everything had begun to make perfect sense.

'I think I have always known this,' she whispered. 'I think this was why I wasn't sure I wanted to be married to Achilles, even if he is almost a god.' She looked into Nestor's anxious eyes and smiled at him shyly. 'Above all things I have always loved to dance for Artemis. I think I always knew that I belonged to her.' Then, astoundingly, she gave a little laugh. 'But why didn't my father come and tell me this himself? Was he afraid I'd be disappointed? But then he doesn't really know me, does he? And he needn't have worried at all!'

Iphigeneia walked towards the window and looked out across the town. And then another thought occurred to her. 'In which temple will I serve the goddess? Will it be here, in Aulis?'

'Yes,' Nestor answered hoarsely, 'it will be in Aulis.' He closed his eyes. 'But you don't yet understand.'

'What?' she asked, puzzled. But his tightly wrinkled eyes stayed shut and she began to worry that he might not be feeling well. 'What don't I understand?'

The words came out almost impatiently. 'It is your life the goddess asks.'

'I know that,' she answered, smiling. 'I do understand. Once I give my life to the goddess there will be no going back. But I'm ready for that. It will give me great joy to live just for her.'

'Listen to me, child,' he urged almost impatiently now. 'The goddess does not want you to live for her. She wants you to die for her. You are to be made a sacrifice on her altar. It will happen today.'

A goose-feather from her pillow lifted on the draught from beneath the door, floated for a while, then fell back to the floor. Outside, the wind barracked at the shutters. Somewhere further beyond, down by the crowded wharf, the ocean boomed.

'Do you understand?' old Nestor said.

'But why?' she whispered. 'Why does the goddess want me to die?'

'It is,' he began, ' – it has to be – for the good of all of us. That is what your father wanted me to explain.' He faltered, avoided her eyes, tried to gather his thoughts. 'Do you hear the wind outside? Do you know how many weeks it has been blowing now? That wind belongs to Artemis. As long as it blows our ships cannot put to sea. Yet the whole course of this war depends on the High King returning soon to Troy. If he fails to come there in time, then all will be lost. Many men will die. Our enemies will flourish and your father will be defeated in the eyes of his men. If that happens, then it cannot be long before he loses his throne. Mycenae will fall to some other powerful prince. Your father will die and all your family – you, your mother, your brother and sister – will die with him. This is the terrible truth of what must happen unless that wind ceases to blow.'

He could see the impact of this catalogue of disasters on her face, but even as he listed them he was appalled how abstract and empty they sounded beside the warm, bewildered presence of this child.

'But why?' she whispered again. 'Why is Artemis so angry with us?'

Again Nestor looked away from the appalling innocence of those eyes.

'It is not for us to question the wisdom of the gods,' he said at last. 'But once we know their will, it is our duty to accept it.' He glanced quickly back at her. 'Your father is ready to do his duty, child. May I tell him that you are ready to do yours?'

All the host in Aulis assembled to watch the sacrifice that day. They had raised an altar down on the quay so that it could be seen from the streets and from the cliffs above and no one need be left in doubt that the High King would discharge his debt to the goddess. Though many of the troops had been ready to mutiny only a few days before, they waited there in solemn throng, and not a man among them murmured as the warlords gathered by the altar where Calchas was already burning incense and invoking the presence of the goddess. Each alone with his own thoughts, they watched.

Agamemnon stood among them, cloaked against the wind, with Menelaus at his side. He was staring out beyond the ships at the race of breakers hurtling off the strait. The island of Euboea was a mere blur across the water, and Troy lay a further two hundred miles away across that impassable horizon. Around his head, the turbulent sky was loud with the tinkling of mast-heads and the creak and groan of yards and timbers as the wind plucked and buffeted his ships.

Under the gaze of thousands of men, each of whom might one day lay down his life for him, Agamemnon knew himself to be the loneliest man alive.

They brought Iphigeneia in procession from the temple to the altar, with priests and priestesses swinging censers and carrying the holy things before her under their covers. She was accompanied by young men and women singing the hymn to Artemis, though the girl herself, whose singing voice had been known to make men weep, was silent now. They sang about the way the strong heart of Artemis quickens to the chase among the mountain shadows and on the summits of the wind. They sang how, when the goddess has taken her quarry, she unstrings her bow, and goes to the house of her brother Apollo and takes first place among the dancers when the dance begins. And as they approached the altar, the hymn ended and there was only the noise of the wind.

Iphigeneia had been given a cloak to keep her from the cold, but one of the women unfastened it now, and they saw how the skin of a fawn had been tied about her shoulders, and her hair was bunched and piled at the crown of her head so that her neck stood clear and white. When Odysseus spoke of that day he said that the girl had been almost smiling as she walked steadily through the throng with her head tilted. He thought at first that it was because, in her innocence, she was content to lay down her life on behalf of all the great heroes of Argos, and the thousands of men around her. Later, however, he wondered whether she had, in fact, been listening to the voice of the goddess.

Whatever the case, in the moment when her cloak was removed, Iphigeneia saw the altar and began to tremble, and Odysseus saw in her eyes that it was as much with fear as from the cold.

Immediately, Agamemnon dropped his own cloak and stood before the girl in all his golden regalia. He was so evidently the High King that Iphigeneia looked up at him shyly and said in a voice so slight that it could hardly be heard above the wind, 'Are you my father?'

Trembling now himself, Agamemnon nodded. For a stricken moment, he gazed down into the beautiful young face that gazed back at him in expectation of an embrace or a fatherly kiss. But he must have felt that the thing he was about to do revoked all rights a man might have to such consoling gestures of affection. He turned his head away, darting his eyes at those who stood ready to help him. Two men stepped forward; Iphigeneia let out a startled cry as they swept her off her feet and spread her body across the altar. Someone pushed a horse-bit into her open mouth and gagged it with his hand. Another man pulled back her head so that the chin was raised. Agamemnon cried out, 'Great Artemis, accept the offering,' and with a swift stroke of the knife that had been slipped into his palm, he cut the breath out of his daughter's throat.

Quickly he turned away. Her ankles jerked and quivered for a time. Then they were still, and above the boom of the surf, and a momentary sagging of the wind, rose the low moan of an army looking as if for the first time on death.

The Wrath of Achilles

Point by point, the wind shifted. The fleet put to sea, and as the laden ships coasted along the straits of Euboea, every man aboard was gloomily aware that if the sacrifice of Iphigeneia had been the first death of the last phase of the war, there would soon be countless others.

They found the garrison on Tenedos weakened and half-starved, but it had held out. With his bridgehead still secure, Agamemnon knew the time had now come to plan a final assault on Troy but after years of stalemate he was uncertain how to approach it. Even before the warlords had sailed from Aulis there had been unsettling disagreement on the matter and the argument revolved around the neutrality of the Dardanians.

For some years Agamemnon had been persuaded by those who insisted that the decision of King Anchises to stay out of the war must work to the Argives' advantage. As leaders of this party, Menelaus and Odysseus argued that the task of taking the city would be made far more difficult if the Dardanians were provoked into bringing their forces to its defence. Palamedes disagreed. The city would fall faster, he insisted, if Agamemnon opened a second front by attacking it from the south across the Dardanian lands. Achilles, Ajax and Diomedes tended to support this aggressive policy, while Nestor and Idomeneus hovered uncertainly between the two positions. But after the failure of his first frontal assault on Troy, Agamemnon was worried that a further ambitious move might precipitate disaster. So the debate had been carried by the more cautious counsellors and Agamemnon's main effort had been concentrated on keeping the Trojans confined to the city while the Argives weakened their allies around them.

But now the main force was back on Tenedos, the tenth year of the snake had begun, and the argument was renewed with increased urgency.

Still Agamemnon vacillated. These days the Lion of Mycenae was like a man usurped by his own ghost, with only his stubborn will to drive him where once there had been ambition and fire. The truth was that the ghost of his daughter hung like a curse over his every thought. Yes, the wind had shifted with her death, and the fleet had sailed, but Agamemnon was left unnerved by guilt. And once Achilles had learned how his proud name had been used to lure Iphigeneia to her death in Aulis, his contempt for Agamemnon became an inveterate hatred. By the end of that terrible day Agamemnon knew that he had gained the undying hostility both of the wife on whom he had come to rely at home and of his army's best-loved champion.

Achilles had played almost no part in the councils of war since then, so Palamedes remained the main spokesman for an incursion on Dardanian lands. But Agamemnon had grown increasingly mistrustful of the Prince of Euboea. It had been Palamedes who had told the others about the sacrilegious death of the hart. It had been Palamedes who argued most obdurately for the sacrifice of Iphigeneia. It had been Palamedes who had thought up the means to bring her to Aulis. It was even Palamedes' name that had been murmured most often, when the host thought of looking for another leader. Of all his generals, therefore, it was Palamedes whom Agamemnon most loathed and feared, and his was the counsel that the High King least wished to hear.

One morning, after yet another inconclusive argument,

Palamedes left the king's tent angry and frustrated, and sought out Achilles to complain about Agamemnon's dithering. Already frustrated and bored with inaction, Achilles called Patroclus and Phoenix into a brief council of his own, then ordered his Myrmidons to board ship. They crossed the strait to the mainland where they beached the ships under guard and advanced into the mountain pastures of the Dardanians. By the end of the day they had cut down the herdsmen, driven off a large herd of cattle, and stormed the royal settlement of Lyrnessus.

Taken by surprise, Aeneas tried to mount a force to repel the invaders, but his warriors were no match for the battle-hardened Myrmidons. The Dardanians were quickly routed, Aeneas and Anchises were lucky to escape with their lives, Lyrnessus was left in flames, and Achilles' storm-troopers returned in triumph to Tenedos with the cattle, women and other booty they had taken.

When Achilles presented himself before Agamemnon's tent to bring the High King his rightful share of the spoils, the common soldiers were already cheering their champion as though he had won a major victory. Agamemnon was left with no choice but to congratulate the insolent young hero on his success and grant him his wish to keep for himself a beautiful young woman called Briseis whom he had taken captive.

Only subsequently, in conversation with Odysseus, did the High King admit that the unlicensed raid had given fresh impetus to the war. The Dardanians would fight alongside the Trojans now, but the road to Troy could be cut open across their lands.

Within days Agamemnon launched a major assault. He posted his archers and slingers to keep the enemy at bay while his main force landed, and throughout the day there was some fierce fighting, but by dusk the Argive ships were safely beached in three rows along the shore of the bay. Fresh troops were brought up to guard them, and on the next day a stockade was raised for their defence.

As he watched his army pitch camp, Agamemnon thought to himself that things had gone well – better than he had feared, for he seemed ever more dogged by a truculent pessimism with every fresh decision he had to take. Palamedes and Achilles urged him to drive on at once towards Troy, but the landing had been costly and he was reluctant to push his luck. Also winter would be on them soon, so Agamemnon gave the order to dig in.

With memories of blizzards etched into their skins, the Argive soldiers hunkered down for a further test of their endurance. Troy, the city they had come to take, was now under siege.

If it was not the harshest winter they had endured, the snow-laden wind driving across the Trojan plain was bitter enough to leave the Argives feeling envious and resentful whenever they looked on the tiled roofs of the beleaguered city. The walls themselves seemed unassailable, and it was clear to everyone that the next act of the war must be played out on the open ground of the Scamander plain between the city and the ships, where stood the great barrow-mound of Priam's grandfather King Ilus. Either the Argives would overwhelm the Trojans there and besiege the city, or they would be driven back on their ships and see their fleet burned. That catastrophe must be prevented at all costs, so the men were set to work digging a defensive ditch around the camp, and fortifying its mound with a stronger palisade. It was guarded by wooden towers and furnished with gates through which the chariots would advance to battle.

Inside that perimeter an improvised city of huts and tents grew up, where archers practised at the butts and foot-soldiers were put through their battle-drill. But as the winter hardened and the wind bore down on them, stinging their faces with rain, hail and snow, and chilling their bones to the marrow, men brooded on old feuds and grudges. Quarrels and fights were frequent around the camp-fires and some of them ended in death. Nor was there much warmth among the leadership, which was held together only by a common – if sullen and obstinate – sense of purpose.

Agamemnon and Menelaus kept close company together, often morose and frequently drunk. Sometimes they dined more cheerfully with their old friends, Nestor, Odysseus, Ajax and Diomedes, but Idomeneus was happier among his fellow Cretans. Achilles, meanwhile, kept himself apart with Patroclus and his Myrmidon comrades, and during those harsh winter nights he became ever more tenderly attached to his beautiful young captive Briseis. She was the first woman to whom he had made love in all the long years since he had left Skyros, and though she had been afraid of him at first, the Dardanian girl eventually responded to his shy, surprisingly gentle approaches. Only when he was sure that he had her consent did Achilles take her to his bed, and soon they began to feel safe in each other's arms. Even Patroclus, who was no stranger to his friend's capacity for love, was surprised by the tender way he made a lover of his captive. Indeed, he was relieved to see how the too often embattled spirit of Achilles took comfort as well as pleasure from her increasingly affectionate embrace.

In these circumstances, Palamedes found himself ever more isolated. Though each preserved a malevolent respect for the other's intelligence, he and Odysseus had detested each other for a long time. At many difficult council meetings, their colleagues had looked on with bewildered awe as the two men clashed intellects with the same animus that most men reserved for less subtle weaponry. Only rarely did it seem they might come to blows, but that point was reached around midwinter when the supplies of corn in the camp ran short, and Odysseus' ships returned empty after a failed foraging expedition along the coast of Thrace. Morale was already low, and it took a steep plunge when he reported that the harvest had been poor and the Thracian granaries had yielded nothing.

'Either that,' Palamedes sneered, 'or this is another example of Odysseus' lack of enthusiasm for the war. Perhaps he would rather be at home, filling his belly and pleasuring his wife, than fulfilling his duties here?'

Had Odysseus been wearing a sword at that moment he would have run the man through. As it was, he leapt across the ground, closed his hands round the Euboean's throat and would have strangled him there and then if Diomedes and Ajax had not managed to break his grip and pull him away. Agamemnon was shouting at both men to get control of themselves, while the others looked on in dismay.

'If you think there's corn to be found,' Odysseus shouted, 'I defy you to go and get it. Otherwise keep your weasel mouth shut in the presence of better men.'

'Somebody is going to have to find it,' said Agamemnon, pulling his cloak closer about him, 'or we shall soon be starved out. Palamedes, I suggest you take up his challenge.'

Palamedes stalked out of the council tent, fingering his throat.

Before putting to sea, he went to pray at the temple of Apollo in Thymbra, a sacred site outside Troy which was recognized as neutral ground and where those seeking to worship the god from either side of the lines could enter without harassment. This was not the first time Palamedes had gone there and his devotions seemed to have found favour, for three days later his ships returned to the camp, low in the water with the weight of grain they carried.

Once again, as the hungry soldiers set to work, grinding the wheat and lighting their ovens, Palamedes was a name that commanded popular acclaim. But Odysseus was left suspicious that the Euboean should have succeeded so easily where he had failed. He decided to share his suspicions with the king.

What happened after that remains, I concede, a doubtful affair. The facts, such as I have been able to garner them, were as follows. Some time after Palamedes had returned with the grain, a Trojan spy was found outside the camp with an arrow through his heart. A brisk search of the body turned up a note in his wallet signed by King Priam, agreeing to the price demanded by Palamedes for betraying the Greek camp. A time was appointed for payment at the temple of Apollo.

Palamedes was immediately arrested and brought before the council. When he heard the charge against him, he furiously denied it and claimed that he was the victim of a foul calumny.

Odysseus calmly suggested that the matter could easily be settled one way or the other. Let the king send a trusted man to the temple of Apollo of Thymbra, claiming to be there at the behest of Palamedes. If he returned laden with Trojan treasure the case would be proven.

And that, despite Palamedes' outraged insistence on his innocence, was what transpired. The bags full of Trojan coinage were displayed before the troops. Publicly denounced as a traitor, Palamedes was stoned to death by the whole army. But his last words left many of them convinced that Agamemnon and Odysseus had indeed colluded against him. 'Truth, I mourn for you,' he cried in the moments before the stones were cast, 'for you have predeceased me.'

Odysseus would never speak of the matter except in cursory and dismissive terms. The Prince of Euboea was a traitor, he declared, and met a traitor's end. And that, on the surface at least, appears to have been the case. But King Nauplius of Euboea, the grieving father of Palamedes, would never believe it, and he found a devious way of taking his revenge on those whom he was convinced had traduced his son. He visited their wives and told them that their husbands intended to replace them with their favourite concubines on their return.

If truth is, as men say, the first casualty of war, one thing remains beyond all doubt however: the war at Troy may have been a bloody feast of masculine violence, but again and again the quarrels broke out over an abducted woman. In violent times the scale of a king's standing is ratified not merely by his wealth and power but also by the quality of the women he rapes. Thus Hesione is abducted by Telamon, and the long quarrel between Troy and Argos begins. Clytaemnestra is wrenched from her beloved husband Tantalus, and Mycenae gains a calculating queen. Helen is carried off first by Theseus, then by Paris, and the world goes to war. During the course of that war, Briseis is plundered from her home by Achilles, and then – as if to demonstrate that he too is still a formidable male animal – Agamemnon launches a raid on the small settlement of Thebe and takes captive Chryseis, the daughter of Apollo's priest in that town. And it was the seizing of this girl that led to a quarrel which eventually threatened disaster on the whole Argive host.

The quarrel began when Chryses, the father of the abducted girl presented himself at the gate of the Argive camp bearing the sacred chaplet of a priest of Apollo and carrying his golden staff. The dignified old man was admitted to the assembly ground under divine protection and made an eloquent plea before Agamemnon that, out of due reverence for the divine will of Apollo, the High King should allow him to ransom his daughter.

The priest's appeal was so moving, and the ransom he offered so generous, that the general feeling in the assembly was that his wishes should be respected. But Agamemnon had been drinking heavily for days and a thick head had left him in a truculent mood. He told Chryses bluntly that Chryseis was the captive of his spear, won fairly in battle. He claimed to have taken to the girl and, far from letting her go, he had every intention of carrying her home to Mycenae and settling her among his palace women. 'So be off with you, old man,' he growled, 'and stay clear of my camp. If you bother me again you'll find that your staff and chaplet give you scant protection.'

Chryses looked up into the High King's sullen face and saw that there could be no reasoning with him. Conceding nothing in dignity, he nodded, drew in his breath and walked out among the silent soldiery without a word.

Within days pestilence struck the camp. It began among the dogs and mules first, but soon spread among the men from tent to tent. As more and more men fell sick and died, and the mingled smells of putrefaction and burning flesh drifted across the camp by both day and night, the morale of the army began to fail.

On the tenth day of the plague, Achilles exercised his right to demand an assembly. Standing before the host with the sacred sceptre in his hand, he argued that Sminthian Apollo, the bringer of pestilence, must have been offended by a broken vow or by some failure to observe his rites. He insisted that omens should be taken to see what could be done to placate the angry god before the Argive host was so depleted by sickness that it would be forced to give up the war and sail home.

A murmur of assent rose from the gathering. Calchas stepped forward, saying that he had already taken the omens but was prepared to divulge his findings only if Achilles solemnly vowed to protect him from the anger they might arouse. When Achilles swore that the soothsayer need have no fear of retribution, Calchas declared that there was no question of broken vows or neglected rites. The wrath of Apollo was the direct result of Agamemnon's refusal to allow the Trojan priest to ransom his daughter. Chryses had invoked the aid of the god in his cause. The god had listened. The pestilence would not be lifted until Chryseis was returned to her father without payment of any ransom.

Immediately Agamemnon leapt to his feet, his eyes red with menace as he scented collusion against him. He turned his fury on Calchas first. 'Every time you open your mouth you bring some evil down on my head. Can't you ever prophesy good fortune for me? I've come to rue the day that brought you to my side.' He would have raged on but he raised his eyes from the priest's face in that moment and saw the gathered host glowering at him. 'If I refused a ransom for that girl,' he shouted, 'it wasn't to defy the god but because I've grown fond of her. That's why I want to keep her. It would grieve my heart to let her go.'

The wind gusting across the plain caught his words and scattered them. In not one of the hundreds of faces around him could he find any sign of sympathy. He was left feeling like a drunkard grumbling in the street.

'But when a god is against a man what can he do?' he shouted into the wind. 'If releasing her is the only way to end this pestilence, then of course she must go. She'll be returned to her father at once. And I'll forgo the ransom.'

He took in the grim nodding of heads. He had given them what they wanted because fate had left him with no option, and he hated them all for it. Why was it that every way he turned, it seemed he must be the loser? And how many such defeats could his leadership sustain? There must be some way of turning this thing round, of emerging from it with a degree of self-respect. Then his eyes fell on Achilles and he saw the contempt in that insolent young face.

The host was shifting and about to disperse when Agamemnon spoke again.

'But it can't be right that your leader has to give up his prize when lesser men are allowed to keep theirs. If I'm going to surrender Chryseis on behalf of you all, then I should be given some other woman in compensation for my loss.'

The crowd began to mutter at this. Agamemnon looked for support to Menelaus, who frowned and glanced away. Nestor murmured something about the spoils already having been fairly divided.

Then Achilles stepped forward again.

'It can only cause grievance if the king claims what is not rightfully his. No one but you is in question here. Obey the god's demand and give back the girl. Once Troy has fallen you'll have all the recompense you could want.'

But this was too much.

'Since when did Achilles have the right to tell the High King what he may and may not do? I've already said that the girl will be released. You can take her back to Thebe in your own ship if you like, along with whatever sacrifices are needed to propitiate the god. But I expect my loss to be made good, and if the army doesn't give me satisfaction in this matter, then I'll seize a woman for myself.'

Agamemnon was trembling with rage as he spoke. Achilles held his stare for a moment then glanced at Patroclus with a look that communicated his incredulous scorn for the blustering fool who had led them to this war.

Agamemnon did not miss it. His face darkened with menace. 'You would do well to show more respect, son of Peleus, or I might just help myself to the woman I allowed you to keep after that raid you made without my consent.'

All the anger that had smouldered between Agamemnon and Achilles for years now combusted to a blaze. 'What kind of leadership is this?' Achilles demanded. 'How can you expect any man to follow you into battle if he knows you're likely to seize for yourself any spoil he takes? As Apollo is my witness, these Trojans have done me no harm. They've never lifted my cattle or ravaged my lands. Nor have they harmed most of us here. The truth is, we came to this war to help you and your brother gain satisfaction for your loss, and now you turn on us, demanding that we surrender our own lawful prizes to your greed. You even dare to threaten me – Achilles, son of Peleus, I who have born the brunt of the fighting from the first. If it hadn't been for me and my Myrmidons you'd still be sitting on Tenedos. Well, I've had a bellyful of fighting for an ungrateful fool who makes enemies of his friends and puts his own pride before the good of the host. I see no further point in dirtying my sword to win plunder for you when I get nothing but insults in return.'

Agamemnon had listened to this tirade white-faced, knowing that his leadership was now at stake. 'Take to your ship then,' he bellowed before Achilles could turn away. 'Go home and graze your sheep on Skyros. I have friends enough to fight at my side without suffering your insolence a day longer.' Breathing noisily, he narrowed his eyes in a baleful glower. 'But no one defies the High King and gets away with it. I'll have that woman off you before you go. The host shall see which of us is mightier – the stripling Achilles or Agamemnon, King of Men.'

In that moment, driven by the impetus of his rage, the hand of Achilles reached for the hilt of his sword. He was about to draw it and run the king through when a voice inside his head restrained him so powerfully that it felt as if an invisible hand was tugging at his hair. It was the voice of the goddess Athena bringing him back to his senses, promising that a day would come when he would be amply recompensed for this outrage.

Achilles stood for a moment, wide-eyed, scarcely breathing, attending to the whisper. Then he pushed the sword back into its scabbard, turned his gaze on Agamemnon, and snatched the sceptre from his hand.

'You're a drunkard and you're a coward,' he said with cold, dismissive menace. 'Not once have you dared to lead your men into battle. You'd sooner skulk in your tent and wait for bolder men to win your spoils for you. Well, others may lack the heart to stand against you, but I swear by this sceptre that a day will come when you'll be crying out for my aid in the heat of battle, and we'll see then how mighty you are, when Hector is cutting his way through the Argive ranks while you eat out your coward's heart with remorse for having disgraced the bravest of your warriors this way.'

He threw down the sceptre at Agamemnon's feet and would have walked away but Nestor rose from his chair and caught him by the arm.

'Shame on you both for hot-headed fools,' the old man shouted. 'Priam and his Trojans will dance for joy when they get to hear about this. I may be an old man – a lot older than either of you – but I've fought alongside better men in my time. Theseus and Pirithous were my comrades – great kings both and shepherds of their people. Not one of you here could have stood against them in battle. And if heroes like that were ready to listen to my counsel then so should you be.' He looked up where Agamemnon was still trembling with rage. 'Remember your dignity. There's more to be lost here than a mere woman. And you, Achilles, curb your truculent manner. Remember that the king's authority derives from Zeus himself. He deserves your respect both as your lord and as the better man.'

Agamemnon shook his head. 'This arrogant young thug doesn't know the meaning of respect.'

Achilles came back at him at once. 'Because I see nothing worthy of it in your drunken folly.'

Again Nestor intervened. 'The girl was given to you at the

king's own hand, Achilles. He is within his rights to take her back again.'

Achilles stared from Nestor to Agamemnon with all the contempt that youth reserves for the stupidity of the old. 'So now we see what Agamemnon's word is worth,' he said. 'Very well! Let all men note it. But if he tries to take a single other thing off me I swear my spear will run black with his blood.' Then he turned away and walked off through the silent host with his friend Patroclus stiff and angry at his side.

Seeking to recover command of the situation, Agamemnon immediately gave orders for Odysseus to take ship and return Chryseis to her father, along with a generous number of cattle to be offered as sacrifices to the god. He then retired to bathe himself and offer his own sacrifices to Apollo on an altar by the shore. But the rage was on him still. He stood in the smoke blowing from the roasting ox-thighs, knowing that he would lose all authority if he failed to force Achilles to bow to his will.

Two hours passed and the girl did not appear. At last he summoned his heralds and told them to go to Achilles with a demand that he hand over Briseis at once.

The heralds found Achilles still passionate with rage where the Myrmidon ships were propped on stakes along the westward reaches of the strand. Patroclus sat beside him, throwing stones at the sea, angry and incredulous at the way his friend had been treated. The Myrmidons stood round them, feeling their leader's shame, muttering together, and glowering at the heralds' approach.

Aware of the injustice of his mission, Talthybius found it hard to deliver his master's demand, but Achilles sensed his apprehension and quickly dispelled it. He asked Patroclus to bring Briseis out of his lodge, and then turned back to the herald. 'Be my witness here before the gods, Talthybius. I have done as that madman commands, but never again will I raise my spear and sword to come to his aid. Tell him to remember that when his host is fighting for its life among the ships.'

Briseis was weeping as she came out of the hut. Achilles had always treated her well and everyone present knew that the girl could expect nothing but humiliation at Agamemnon's hands. But of all the players in the conflict she had the least power over her own fate. She could only pray to the gods for her protection as she was led away by the heralds. The cries were lifted back to Achilles on the wind.

Before she was out of sight, he turned away and sat for a long time alone, watching the waters break against the shore. His eyes smarted with the fury of his injured pride as he thought of the deathless fame and honour he had hoped to win by fighting in this war, and there was such hatred for Agamemnon in his heart that he could scarcely breathe for it. The gods had promised him that if he came to Troy his life would be brief but glorious, yet he had suffered the ignominy of Agamemnon's insults and had now banished himself from the coming fight. And what glory could there be in this recalcitrant isolation? There was, it seemed, as little justice among the gods as there was among men.

But then he remembered how Athena's voice had come to him in his rage, and he recalled the promise that the goddess had made him. Surely his life must still be singled out for a glorious purpose? Sooner or later he must be vindicated.

A Duel in the Rain

After nine protracted years of war, the army of Agamemnon had now endured another bitter winter, witnessed the stoning of Palamedes, suffered a debilitating onslaught of pestilence, and seen the ardour of its champion extinguished in a disgraceful public brawl. The murmurs of mutiny which had already stirred in Aulis were sounding even louder now, and they found a rancorous spokesman in an ill-favoured soldier named Thersites.

This fractious rabble-rouser was a distant kinsman of Diomedes, but while the fleet had been stuck in Aulis he had become vociferous in his support for Palamedes as a man of shrewder qualities of leadership than the vacillating and ill-tempered elder son of Atreus. It may well have been Thersites who started the rumour that Agamemnon had conspired with Odysseus against Palamedes, but in any case his seditious influence now began to thrive with every performance he gave of his satire show about the squabbling leaders. The common soldiers watched it, laughed and applauded, and came away increasingly convinced that this whole expedition against Troy was badly led and would finally prove futile.

Only an optimistic fool could have imagined that an army in such a state would be eager for the coming fray. Agamemnon was not the wisest of men, but neither was he a fool. Nor, since the sacrifice of his daughter, was he left with any degree of conviction that this war would go well for him. He was amazed, therefore, to jump from his sleep early one morning, having dreamed with startling clarity that the gods had promised him a speedy victory.

Immediately he summoned his captains and told them of his dream. A figure had appeared to him there in the form of his most valued counsellor Nestor, demanding to know why he lay sleeping when Zeus himself had opened up the way to Troy. He swore that the dream had left him in no doubt that the Argives should arm themselves immediately and profit from the good will of the gods, for their golden chance to take the city had come at last.

His commanders stood about him, listening in astonished silence. Even Menelaus was taken aback by the abrupt change in Agamemnon's mood, for he too had been oppressed by his brother's irascible fits of gloom. Yet here he was, restlessly striding his tent as he talked, and filled with a brash confidence that seemed justified by nothing in the circumstances of yet another grey day in which a gritty wind, heavy with the threat of rain, blew over a camp still recovering from sickness.

Agamemnon stared back at their bewildered faces in frustration. 'What's the matter with you all? Do you only believe in evil omens? The wind has changed, I tell you. The gods are with us again. The time to strike is now.'

Privately flattered that the god had chosen to manifest in his own form, Nestor was the first of the counsellors to respond. 'I think everyone is as surprised by this as I am, and I have to admit that . . . well, in our present circumstances, if anyone else had come to me with a dream like this, I would have been hard pressed to take it seriously.' He turned, smiling, to his colleagues 'But this is an extraordinary day, gentleman. Zeus, the greatest of gods, has given this dream to our chief of men. Can we afford to question it? I say we should marshal our forces at once in the knowledge that the gods now favour us.'

Odysseus gasped with incredulity. 'Have you seen what's going on out there? If you ask that rabble to pick up their weapons and fight they're more likely to make a run for the ships. Some of them are still sick. Others are close to mutiny. Get out and listen to what that scurrilous rogue Thersites is saying to them. It's obvious they're in no shape for battle.'

Caught between the dream and that grim reality, Ajax and Diomedes glanced uncertainly at one another. Idomeneus was frowning at the floor.

'Can I count on no one here except Nestor and my brother?' Agamemnon demanded. 'I thought I'd brought leaders of men with me, not a craven pack of curs. But look what happens — Palamedes betrays me, Achilles skulks off and sits sulking in his tent. And now you, my closest friends start backing off just when I need you most! All right. Go home then, if that's how you all feel. I'll fight this war on my own if I have to. At least I know the gods are with me.'

'No one's talking about going home,' said Odysseus quietly, 'dearly though some of us would like to do so. We're merely asking for a realistic appraisal of our circumstances.'

'And you think you're a better judge of that than the gods themselves? Is that it? Well forgive me if I beg to differ. Nor do I intend to waste my time listening to a mongrel like Thersites.' Agamemnon turned impatiently away, ordering his squire to bring him his cloak and staff. Then looked back at his discomfited generals. 'Before you prate to me of caution, consider this. We have reliable intelligence that some of Priam's Asiatic allies left for home during the winter months. So we almost certainly outnumber him now. Yes, there's still sickness in the camp but the worst of the pestilence has lifted since I made the offering to Apollo, and we can't sit about licking our sores for ever. Nine years we've already given to this war — *nine years* — but it was prophesied that in the tenth year Troy would fall and the tenth year has come. The omens are in our favour at last. And now the gods have sent a dream that gives me warranties of victory. If you are men, and leaders of men, you will get out there and rally your troops. Troy can be ours by the end of the day – if you have the heart for it!'

There was a fire in Agamemnon's eyes and a fervour in his voice that none of them had seen for a long time. Menelaus was exhilarated by this sudden renewal of his brother's passion for the cause. Ajax and Diomedes felt their spirits lift at his defiant challenge, and rather than split the leadership at this crucial moment, Idomeneus nodded his assent. Only Odysseus was still shaking his head as he left the tent praying to Athena for inspiration.

The nine heralds went about the camp calling the Argive host to assembly. When all but Achilles and his disaffected Myrmidons had taken their places on the benches, Agamemnon stepped forward, holding the great staff which had been made by Hephaestus and passed down from Zeus to Hermes, and thence to Pelops and his son Atreus. Agamemnon had seized that staff when he took the throne of Mycenae, and all his authority as High King of Argos was vested in it. His army listened in disgruntled incredulity now as he proclaimed his intention to launch an assault on Troy that very day, and when he had finished speaking, the assembly ground fell silent except for the buffeting of the wind.

Then the jeering voice of Thersites rang out from the ranks. 'Well, we know that Achilles will stay tucked up at home in bed with Patroclus, but does the High King intend to come with us on this expedition – or will he appoint some other poor bugger to do his looting for him?'

Coarse laughter rippled throughout the host.

Nestor got to his feet and shouted out for silence and respect.

'Respect!' Thersites shouted back. 'Find me ten men in this army who have any respect for the leadership we've got and I'll sack Troy with them myself.'

Agamemnon could feel the blood beating behind his eyes.

'We cannot all be kings here,' he bellowed. 'I have the authority of almighty Zeus to lead this army, and I swear by his thunder-bolts that I mean to lead it to victory this day.'

'On the other hand,' called Thersites, 'we could all go home!' The laughter was louder this time. Encouraged by it, Thersites said, 'I for one have had enough of parading up and down the coast of Asia to no purpose but filling your coffers with plunder! What about the rest of you?'

A rumble of agreement rose from those immediately around him. A scattering of calls lifted across the crowd. But many of the foot soldiers were as surprised by Agamemnon's renewed show of vigour and confidence now as his commanders had been earlier, and the rebels were not yet carrying the whole host with them.

Then someone shouted, 'Let's hear from Odysseus. What does he have to say?' And the cry was taken up.

Of all the leaders, Odysseus was held in most affection and esteem by the common soldiery. Palamedes had curried their favour, teaching them to play his dice game, and listening to their grievances, but Odysseus had always commanded their respect. They liked his piratical air, and they approved of the fair-minded way he always made his judgement count, whether in debating great affairs of state in the assembly or in settling petty disputes among his men. He was still distrusted by those who had been of Palamedes' party, but Palamedes was dead, and most of the troopers assembled there had thrown one of the stones that killed him, so they looked to Odysseus for guidance now.

Holding his cloak against the pull of the wind, Odysseus rose to speak. He waited till the throng was silent, and was about to begin when Thersites called out, 'Palamedes once trusted this Ithacan sheep-shagger, and look what happened to him! Watch out, lads, or he'll have the skin off your backs.'

When the laughter had died down, Odysseus said, 'Thersites has a nimble wit. He has a nimble tongue too, and I promise him that if he doesn't teach it better manners soon, I'll have it out by the roots! As for his suggestion that you all go home –

well, it sounds reasonable enough. I miss the pleasures of my wife's bed as much as any man here, believe me.' He looked across into Agamemnon's apprehensive frown and then away again. 'If I thought it made any sense,' he resumed, 'I'd take ship for Ithaca tomorrow. But I've heard my sheep bleat better arguments than our foul-mouthed friend over there. Just think about it for a minute. You've already stuck this war out for nine years – nine long and sometimes terrible years. Years in which you've taken wounds and watched old comrades fall in combat or vomit up their guts with pestilence. And yes, you've taken some plunder in that time, and those of you who haven't squandered it on dice or women could go home tomorrow richer than you came. But just over the other side of that wall sits the richest city in all Asia. It's fat with treasure and it's ripe for the plucking! Can't you smell the women in there? Can't you hear the rustle of their silks? Ten years we were told it would take before that city fell. You were all in Aulis. You all saw that serpent eating Aphrodite's sparrows in the tree. And I was given much the same omen myself even before I left Ithaca, so you can understand why I thought twice before setting out on this Trojan junket! My boy Telemachus will be ten years old this year, and I've yet to hear him talk, let alone watch him string a bow, so those years have been as long for me as for anybody. But do you think I'm going to throw them all away by heading for home before the job is done? What kind of sense would that make – to go back empty-handed when, with a little patience and courage, I could take a handsome share in all the golden treasure of Asia with me? You wanted to know what I have to say – well, this is it. This is the tenth year of the snake, comrades. The gods have promised us that Troy will fall. Those among you who have any heart will do as I intend to do – take up my spear and sword, and follow our King out across that windy plain of battle and right on through the gates of Troy!'

Though he had seemed to begin haltingly, his voice had gathered power as he felt the host warming to him, and when his peroration rose to a climax at the end, his words were swallowed in a great assenting roar. Odysseus surrendered the sceptre to Nestor, and then stepped back, wondering what he had done.

But old Nestor built on what he had achieved, reminding the throng how, on their first departure from Aulis all those years ago, Zeus had sent a flash of lightning to hail them on their way. He too was roundly cheered, so by the time Agamemnon came to issue his commands, the whole mood of the army had lifted. The men fell to with a will – sharpening their weapons, checking shield-straps and harness, yoking the horses to the chariots, and assembling in battle order. Attended by his commanders, Agamemnon sacrificed an ox to Zeus. The sacred grain was scattered, the libations poured. As smoke rose from the altar fire, Agamemnon offered up a prayer that the Lord of Olympus not let the sun go down until he had vanquished the army of Priam and over-run his halls and palaces. Then the heralds shouted for the army to advance, the gates were opened and the army of the Argives marched out onto the plain.

Dense cloud scarfed the summits of the Idaean mountains that day, driving a bitter drizzle down across the Scamander into the faces of the advancing host. Horses shied against it. Men marched in silence with their heads down, hearing the sound of their own progress in the creak of leather, the jingling of harness and the chink of metal against metal above the tramp of their feet. The drizzle was not yet heavy enough to make the dust lie, so it rose around them in gritty swirls, darkening the air, and as they began to fan out in a wide front across the field, they heard a withering sound, like the noise made by a huge flock of migrating cranes, drifting towards them on the breeze. When they raised their eyes, they saw the Trojan host advancing from the city to meet them, ululating as they came.

A low moan rose from the Argives as they saw the size of the forces ranged against them along the ridge of the high mound that was known as Thorn Hill. Odysseus ordered his chariot ahead of the line to get a better view. He could see a tall figure wearing a high-plumed helmet parading in his chariot before the massive battalion of spearmen at the Trojan centre, and knew that it must be Hector. He recognized Aeneas and the Dardanians standing to his right, and beyond them shone the shields and standards of the Phrygians, the Mysians and the top-knotted warriors of Thrace. On the left flank were the Lycians, Carians and Pelasgians out of Larissa, but there were other, more exotic forces gathered there too – Paeonian archers with their curved bows, Paphlagonians from the eastern lands south of the Black Sea, and even a contingent from the distant Alizones. Agamemnon's hopes that Priam's strength had been depleted suddenly seemed as doubtful and insubstantial as his dream.

The wind was gusting too, blowing the dust back into the men's eyes, but when Odysseus looked back along the Argive lines he sensed something of the trepidation that Priam's host must also be feeling. Even without Achilles and his Myrmidons – whose presence might be sorely missed before the day was done – those lines were long, deep, and well-armoured. And once battle was joined, the Argive warriors would have no choice but to drive forward, for with their backs only to the sea, there was nowhere else to go.

Odysseus wheeled his chariot round and cantered his team across the rough ground to join Agamemnon and Idomeneus where they stood in conference at the centre of the line. 'They have the advantage of the rise,' he called. 'Hector's not about to come at us, so we might as well grit our teeth and take it to them.'

Agamemnon gave a dour nod. 'I'm going to advance the Locrian bowmen first. Idomeneus will do the same with his Cretan archers. That should thin them out a little where they stand.'

'There's a mist gathering too,' the Cretan said. 'It could give us some cover.'

'Then we just push and pray,' Odysseus smiled. 'Good hunting, gentlemen.' He was nodding to his driver to turn the chariot round again, when Agamemnon said, 'Hello, what's this?' All three men squinted against the glare of the drizzle towards the Trojan lines where a single chariot was rattling swiftly down the slope, raising dust and stones in its wake and cheered on by the host behind. It was pulled by a sleek pair of blacks adorned with scarlet crests that matched the tall plume of the driver's helmet. Clad in a panther's skin, with a bow at his back, he carried a sword in the scarlet baldric that crossed his breastplate, and two spears were fixed to the rails at his side. 'It looks like someone's out to make a name for himself,' Agamemnon muttered. 'Does anybody recognize him?'

The others shook their heads. Then another chariot broke free of the Trojan lines to follow the first down the hill. At the foot of the rise both teams pulled up, and there was a brief exchange between the drivers before they advanced slowly, side by side, across the open plain.

'The second man's Hector,' Odysseus said. 'I watched him marshalling his centre just now.' He turned at the sound of a chariot clattering along the Argive line and saw Menelaus speeding towards them from his place at the head of the Spartan levies, steam rising from the dappled haunches of his team. Dust skidded from the wheels as the horses were reined in, panting and snorting. He saw a fierce ardour in the King of Sparta's eyes.

'The blacks are driven by Paris,' Menelaus shouted. 'I'd know him anywhere. I think my hour has come, brother.'

Without taking his eyes off the approaching chariots. Agamemnon nodded. The wind shuddered through the tall sweep of his horsehair plume.

Paris halted his chariot about fifty yards in front of the Argive commanders, but Hector came closer, holding his plumed head high. Damp sunlight glinted off his shield. A shout came from somewhere down the line. Then a stone was thrown at him. It missed by a yard or more but his team whinnied and shied. Another stone followed, falling closer still. When Hector reined in his team, the horses shook their heads close enough for the Argives to see their eyes roll and their nostrils flare.

'Stay your hand there,' Agamemnon shouted down the line. 'This is a prince of Troy. Show him some courtesy before we drag him through the dirt!'

Hector pushed back his helmet so that he could be better seen and heard. 'Do I have the honour to address Agamemnon, son of Atreus, the Lion of Mycenae and High King of all Argos?' he shouted above the gusting of the wind.

'You do.'

'Then I bid you welcome to Troy. I'm glad to see that you have found the will to match your might against my own at last.' Briefly he looked up and down the Argive line and then back, smiling, at Agamemnon. 'Though I regret we lack the pleasure of Achilles' company today.'

'Then you will miss him more than I do,' Agamemnon scowled. 'But I came here to fight, not to bandy words. Say what you have to say and let us get to it.'

'Very well! My brother, the noble prince Paris stands here at my back ready to meet any of your champions in full and final settlement of this conflict. He freely concedes that his actions is the cause of this great quarrel, and has no wish to see many good men die needlessly on his account. So let it be agreed that all other troops lay down their arms while the duel is fought, and that whoever wins the fight will keep the Lady Helen along with all her wealth, while the rest of us swear in blood to honour a pact of peace and friendship.'

A damp gust of wind ruffled the manes of Hector's horses. One of them champed at the bit. Its bridle jingled. Along the line men strained to hear.

Agamemnon leaned his weight casually against the chariot rail. He was about to declare that he had not brought the whole fighting force of Argos half way across the world merely to watch a duel, when his brother Menelaus spoke out. 'This is my time, brother. Let me accept this challenge. I have the right.'

Agamemnon saw the confidence in his brother's eyes. He had no interest in pacts of friendship but nor could he deny Menelaus this chance for vengeance. He nodded and Menelaus urged his chariot forward of the line. 'You know me of old, Hector!' he shouted. 'We have met on better days than this. I have broken bread and mixed wine with you, and we have worshipped the gods together. I remember a time when we spoke of friendship, you and I. But if you are the honest man I believe you to be, you will acknowledge that I am the injured party in this quarrel. It was my trust that was abused. It was my hospitality that was violated. It was my friendship that was dishonoured. And the villain who did these things stands at your back growing pale as I speak.'

For a moment Menelaus held Paris in his glare, and then dismissed him from existence with a derisive shift of his eyes.

'What you say is true,' Menelaus added, '– only one more death is needful now, and the gods have already appointed it for him. He and I will shortly settle accounts once and for all. You and I can perhaps speak of friendship again when I am standing over his lifeless body.'

Agamemnon made as if to intervene, but Menelaus held out a hand to restrain him. 'Bring two sheep to the sacrifice!' he called to Hector. 'A black ram and a white ewe – and we will do the same. Then fetch your father, King Priam, out of Troy, and let him take an oath on this agreement, for I have been given little reason to trust the word of any of his sons.'

Hector looked to Agamemnon who heaved an uncertain sigh before nodding his assent. A murmuring rose from the opposing armies on both sides of the plain. Hector and Paris withdrew, and while a herald was sent to summon Priam, and the sheep were tethered for the sacrifice, the charioteers and archers pulled back from the front, and the infantrymen lowered their spears and shields.

Throughout all the difficult years she had lived as an exile inside the walls of Troy, Helen's heart had never been heavier than in the moments when she stood on the parapet above the Scaean

Gate watching Paris drive his chariot out onto the plain to confront the massed ranks of the Argive host.

Earlier that morning she had beseeched him not to do what he intended to do. But as had increasingly been the case in recent years, he had chosen to ignore her pleas, for his pride was more susceptible to taunts from his brothers than his heart was to Helen's complicated feelings. And what made things all the harder was the knowledge that, adoring her as he did, Paris could not understand why she did not simply want him to go out there and triumph over the man from whom he had taken her all those years ago.

For Helen those years had been far from the dream of love that had drawn her out of Sparta. Revered by some in Troy and reviled by others, she had soon found herself to be a lonely stranger in a foreign city. Thankfully, Aethra was there to keep her company. Otherwise she would have been reduced to utter dependence on Paris's love for her, if King Priam had not also proved to be as infatuated by her beauty as his son. In many ways she felt that the father saw her more clearly, for Priam had known enough suffering in his time to recognize the wounds behind her beauty. He understood how she was hurt and oppressed by the envy and backbiting of the women around her. Above all, he understood the melancholy and guilt that overwhelmed her whenever she thought about the child she had abandoned – a child who must now be older than Helen had been when Theseus and Pirithous abducted her. He understood why Helen could never be truly happy in Troy.

And Priam understood these things as Paris did not. From the first, Paris had inhabited a self-sealing dream of love, seeing things only on his own enraptured terms. And Helen had been drawn deeply into that dream with him, living her life at a pitch of intensity such as she had never previously known. It was as though that love elevated them to a visionary realm beyond the ordinary, a realm whose landscapes were reflected in the blue, dolphin-crowded waters of the seas they crossed, in the fragrant enchantment of Aphrodite's temple on Cyprus, and among the hot dunes of Egypt where their passionate adoration for each other felt entirely at one with the timeless love of Isis and Osiris. But then they had come back to Troy, and after the first elation of their triumphal entry to the city, the world had gradually closed down round them. And how could it have been otherwise when the world was at war and their love was the cause of it?

For life inside Troy had been harder in recent years than the Argives camped in their rough lodges outside could ever have guessed. As the cities of their allies were attacked and burned, the Trojans lost both markets for their manufactured goods and sources of supply. Prices had risen with the war, and the luxuries to which the people had grown accustomed were much harder to come by. Food was rationed. Anxiety grew, and when the Argives made their first successful landing on the Dardanian shore, panic gripped the city for a time. In the middle of all this, Paris and Helen, who had once been icons of the city's grandeur, were now perceived as the principal cause of its grief. Increasingly they were isolated figures, and isolated with a love that had lost the rapturous intensity of an illicit passion and yet found no other, more substantial way to be. It became hard for them not to blame each other for the losses they had suffered.

There had been nights when they lay side by side, tense and unspeaking in their bed, like prisoners confined together for a crime they could neither repent nor condone. There had been dawns too when, after grieving far into the small hours for her child, Helen woke to look at the lax, vulnerable form of the familiar stranger sleeping beside her and wondered how she could ever have felt it right to put a whole world at risk just to be with him, to love and follow him, and dissolve her body in his embrace.

And now, on this day, when she must stand on the parapet watching him go out to fight with Menelaus to the death, it felt as if all the love and tenderness in her life was about to be subsumed within the mutual violence of the two men she loved most in all the world. And she knew that the man she had deserted must feel only hatred for her now, while the man for whom she had deserted him had left their chamber that morning, flustered and angry that she could not simply pray for him to win.

King Priam stood beside Helen at the parapet, his cloak blowing in the wind that swept across the plain where the might of the Argive army was ranged against his city. These days he was an old man who had seen much of the confidence with which he had prepared himself for war with his enemies evaporate across the years. Like Agamemnon, he too had once dreamed of a quick conflict in which his own assembled powers would settle the issue once and for all, but this long war of attrition had drained both his strength and his coffers. As news came in of city after city burned, of brief successes followed by immediate setbacks, of ships sunk and armies laid low by pestilence, of friends and allies killed and their wives ravished, increasingly the mood of the old king had veered between outraged defiance and long fits of gloom in which he was haunted by dark pictures from his youth. He would wake in the night, remembering how both the priests of Apollo and his crazed daughter Cassandra had prophesied ruin on his city, and he would see again and again the torn body of his father Laomedon slain by Heracles in the citadel of Ilium, while women screamed and the palace burned.

He had asked Helen to join him on the parapet that morning, for her presence was a constant consolation to his harassed mind, but as he asked her to point out each of the Argive heroes who had been no more than names to him before, he was confronted by the imminent gravity of his situation. It was not just Agamemnon and Menelaus, Ajax and Diomedes, Odysseus and Idomeneus that he saw, formidable in their war-gear though each of them might be: he was appalled by the sheer scale of the anonymous host assembled round them – thousands of warriors drawn from the cities, mountains, plains and islands of Argos and far beyond, for the single purpose of tearing down the high walls round him, slaughtering his people and plundering his city of every last jot of its wealth. What had taken years of skill and cunning and perseverance to build might be reduced in a day to no more than a stinking rubble of smoke and ash.

Yet Priam had prayed to the gods and made his offerings, and he too had great powers gathered at his side. And there had been encouraging reports of sickness and disaffection in the Argive camp, and everyone in Troy had rejoiced to learn that Achilles, son of Peleus, that ferocious young killer whose name and reckless deeds had long since chilled even the bravest of hearts, had withdrawn his forces from the fray. So there had been hope in Priam's thoughts that morning as well as trepidation.

And then the herald came with the news that the issue was to be settled in single combat between Paris and Menelaus, which had never been his own intention. No one had said anything of this to him before they left the city. Priam's trust was in the power of his forces and the strength of his walls more than in the skill and courage of his son. So what could have happened out there on the field that Hector should have agreed to put everything at risk on a single throw? It could only be that the same rash heart that had occasioned this war was rushing to bring it to a quick conclusion now.

Priam turned to Helen, who only moments before had been naming the enemies who had once been contenders for her hand, and saw her trembling in the wind beside him. 'Did you know about this?'

'I feared it.' Her voice was barely a whisper above the wind. 'I have feared it from the first.'

Priam turned away and summoned Antenor to his side. 'How can we stop this madness?' he demanded. 'Our army has advantage of the ground. There is every good chance that it will win the day. But if Paris loses this fight . . .' He broke off, shaking his head. 'It makes no sense. It must be prevented.'

Gravely Antenor said, 'This thing lies with the gods.'

Priam glanced back at him in suspicion. 'I know you have no love for Paris.'

The counsellor did not flinch before the accusation. 'But there can be no doubt of my love for my king and for my city,' he answered quietly. 'If Paris has already put the challenge, we cannot force him to withdraw without bringing humiliation on us all. The Argives will take heart from what must seem cowardice to them, and our own forces will be dismayed by it. I feel the gods at work among us, my Lord. Let this war end where it began – in the hands of your son.'

Agamemnon and his commanders watched as Priam rode out through the Scaean Gate of Troy with Antenor standing in the chariot beside him. They saw his men roundly cheering as he passed along the Trojan lines, stopping for a time to speak to the leader of a company of bowmen, and then with Hector and Paris, whose chariots fell in behind him. Then he advanced with his heralds across the plain to where Agamemnon's standard was snapping and blowing in the wind.

The two kings came together where the sheep were tethered ready for the sacrifice, and stood eyeing each other for a time, knowing that the burdens of kingship gave them more in common with each other than with any of the thousands of men who watched them as they raised their hands in mutual salute. Priam looked older and wearier than Agamemnon had anticipated, while the High King of the Trojans suspected that the Lion of Mycenae's wits were probably as slow as his body was strong. Yet both knew that the other might hold the power to extinguish both his rule and his life for ever, and there was, for a few silent moments, a grudging respect between them.

Agamemnon broke the silence. 'Our heralds have agreed the terms of this conflict. Do you assent to them?' And when Priam merely nodded, he added, 'Then let us perform the rites.'

The two kings descended from their chariots. After water had been poured over their hands, Agamemnon grabbed one of the sheep, cut some locks from its head and passed them to Talthybius who distributed them among the watching captains. Then the High King of Argos raised his head and arms towards the cloudy mountain range of Ida. 'Father Zeus,' he cried, 'greatest and most glorious of the gods, you who watch over the fate of men from Mount Ida, I call on you this day, as I call on the great Sun who sees all, and on the Earth and the Rivers of the Earth, and on the Powers of the underworld who hold men answerable for their words. Bear witness to the oaths we swear before you now and ensure that they are kept. If Paris kills Menelaus in this fight, then let him keep the Lady Helen and all her wealth, and we, for our part, shall sail away from Troy and leave her in peace. But if my brother Menelaus should vanquish Paris, then the Trojans must surrender his wife Helen and all her treasure back to him, and make such ample restitution to the Argive host that future generations shall know the price of treachery and remember it for ever. Moreover, if Paris should die and King Priam fails to make such reparation, then I shall remain here with my army and fight on till the full measure of the bill is paid. To this I solemnly swear.'

Agamemnon lowered his arms and shifted his eyes back to Priam. The King of Troy held his gaze for a time and then simply said, 'To this I also swear.'

The heralds tipped the bleating sheep off their feet, the two kings drew their knives across the animals' throats, and hot blood splashed across the ground. Moments later it mingled with the libations of wine that were poured, and Agamemnon was saying, 'May the brains of whichever party breaks this sacred oath be spilled on the ground as this wine is spilled, even to the second generation.' Then both kings stood with their heads bowed in silent prayer, and around them the opposing hosts stood witness as the damp wind blew the words away.

Menelaus raised his head first and stared across the ground at Paris, taking his measure, thinking that the Trojan had put on weight since he last saw him. His face seemed softer and pouchier about the cheeks and jaw. He took strength at the sight, but Paris stared impassively ahead, refusing to let his eyes be caught.

Brushing back the white hair from his face, Priam turned to Agamemnon. 'I feel the weight of years on me and have no wish to watch these men battle for their lives. I will return to my city certain that the immortal gods already know whether it is my son or your brother who will shortly meet his doom.' Raising an arm in salute, he turned to grab the rail of his chariot, and he and Antenor sped back along the road to Troy.

While the heralds cleared the ground and measured out the distance from which the spears would be thrown, Odysseus put two lots into his helmet – one marked for each of the combatants. He crossed to Hector, who took the helmet from him and shook it until one of the lots jumped out. Odysseus bent to pick it up and held it for those close by to see. Then he shouted out across the lines, 'The right to make the first throw falls to Paris.'

The rain was gusting harder as Paris and Menelaus stood among their supporters for a time, removing their cloaks, dry-throated, glad of the wine and water they were offered, half-listening to words of advice as they adjusted their armour, even trying to joke a little. Then the sons of Atreus briefly embraced each other, and the sons of Priam did the same. Both donned their helmets and took up their stations, each with a sword slung at his side, his shield gripped in one hand and a long spear in the other. Ragged shouts of encouragement broke out from both sides of the front line. Then there was only the noise of the wind.

Paris balanced the spear in his hand, flexed his thigh muscles and tested the ground beneath his feet. Feeling as if the entire trajectory of his life had been directed towards this fateful moment, he turned his cheek to the wind, trying to calculate its strength. He whispered a prayer to Aphrodite, looked up and fixed his gaze on the armoured figure standing across from him only a few short yards away. Menelaus's face and flowing red hair were hidden inside the bronze curve of his helmet but Paris knew them well enough. He recalled how often and easily that face had laughed during those hours in Troy and Dardania when they had still been friends. He recalled how Menelaus had stood over him in his bloody apron in the temple of Athena and how freely he had welcomed him to Sparta. All the accumulated fury of the years since then must now be compressed inside this man to a single point of unmitigated hatred. And who could blame him for that? And who could blame either of them for loving Helen? Perhaps, Paris thought, with a sudden lurching of the heart, all three of them had been no more than playthings of the gods, who were looking down from Mount Ida now at the one thing that in all their immortal lives they could never experience for themselves – the fear, and the fact, of death.

In a single fluid movement, Paris raised the shield on his left arm, dropped the balanced weight of his body onto his right leg, and uncoiled his sinews like the spring of a snare. The long spear hummed and wobbled as it travelled through the air, reached the highest point of its trajectory, then plunged swiftly down to bend its bronze point against the layered strength of the King of Sparta's shield. Menelaus staggered for a moment under the shock of the blow, but the weapon fell harmlessly away. He laughed out loud, sure now that he had not deluded himself when he caught the smell of victory on the wind.

The earth felt lively beneath his feet. He could taste the rain on the wind. Menelaus drew a deep breath through his nostrils and whispered a prayer to almighty Zeus that he be given justice at last against the man who had so sorely wronged him. Then he focussed all his senses on the detested figure across from him, raised his shield-arm, and hurled the spear with all his might.

So great was the power of unleashed emotion behind the throw that the head of the spear struck Paris' shield and pushed right on through. It would have shattered the bronze plate over the Trojan's heart had he not instinctively swerved aside, so the point only tore through the tunic at his flank, scoring the skin there and making it bleed. Unbalanced by the weight of the long shaft stuck in his shield, Paris saw that the head had come too far through to be released. He had no choice but to cast it aside as Menelaus leapt across the ground towards him, brandishing his unsheathed sword as he came.

Neither man had heard the great moaning roar that went up from the lines. Neither man had time to realize that the rain was beating harder against their faces and that a thicker damp mist was drizzling round them now. Paris lunged aside so that Menelaus's armoured onslaught took him on, panting, past. In the same frantic moment, he was drawing his own sword, but Menelaus swiftly turned again and all but knocked him off his feet with a great buffeting blow of his shield. Roars and shouts were blown on the wind from both lines but the rain began to drive so densely down across the plain that it became hard for the troops to make out what was happening. Paris was stumbling back on the defensive now with only the bronze blade between his body and the advancing strength of Menelaus. Two or three times he contrived to parry the swingeing blows, but then a thrust of Menelaus's shield knocked him backwards again. Instantly Menelaus raised his sword and brought it down with tremendous force onto the ridge of Paris's helmet – only to see the bronze of his own blade snap and shatter under the impact.

Paris staggered to his feet again, almost concussed by the blow. Cursing his ill-luck, Menelaus threw the useless sword-hilt at his opponent, grabbed him by the horsehair plume and pulled him off his feet. Shrugging off the shield, he threw his weight down onto Paris's body, and for a time the two men were tussling on the ground like dogs as the rain swirled and gusted round them, turning the ruts to rivulets and the dust to mud. Then Menelaus pushed himself upright, and through the veils of the rain it was seen that he had caught Paris by the chinstrap of his helmet and was dragging him bodily towards the Argive lines.

As if the clouds had been shattered by the shout rising from the Argive host, the heavens opened and rain came shafting down across the plain so sharp and hard that men dipped their heads and covered their faces with their hands. The sky flickered with a livid glare. Horses whinnied and trembled all along the lines. The whole world had turned to water, and for a time neither army could see the other across the turbid distance between them. As for the two men, they might have been struggling alone on some remote island where they could see barely a yard in front of their faces. And then Menelaus lost his footing. His whole body tipped and sagged, his feet slipped in the mud, and he was down on the ground, staring in bewilderment at the finely-worked leather chinstrap that had snapped off in his hand.

Half-strangled, bruised and bleeding, Paris slithered away through the mud and stumbled to his feet. Before Menelaus could recover from his fall, he turned and ran towards the Trojan lines, looking for the place where he had left his chariot.

Afterwards, men said that, for reasons best known to himself, Cloud-gathering Zeus must have permitted Aphrodite to send that storm. Only divine intervention could have protected Paris from the death that was waiting for him if Menelaus had managed to drag him to where a weapon might be found. There was also, some said, a kind of justice in it – for Zeus had answered Menelaus' prayer for victory over his enemy, and Aphrodite had swept away her devotee back to the chamber where Helen waited to give him succour. But the truth was that, though many men had fervently hoped for a time that the issue might be settled between Paris and Menelaus, few of them had ever really believed in the deeps of their heart that Agamemnon would simply go home after seeing his wronged brother lying dead in the dust, or that Priam would yield up the wealth in his coffers along with the slaughtered body of his son.

So it seemed that the immortal gods as well as mortal men had their minds set on war, for how else to explain the strange way that the storm had veered out to sea as swiftly as it came, leaving only a lurid-yellow light behind it in which the solitary figure of Menelaus could be seen striding about the field shouting out his angry demand that the proven coward Paris come again and stand against him?

Nor was that the end of it, for an archer called Pandarus seized that moment to step out of the Trojan lines, draw the great bow he had made from the horns of an ibex, and release an arrow at Menelaus where he stood shouting on the plain. The younger son of Atreus was saved from death in that moment only because the head of the arrow was deflected by his belt buckle, so much of its force was spent by the time it penetrated his corselet and leather jerkin to puncture his skin.

Agamemnon saw his brother stagger and fall. Outraged by this treacherous violation of the truce, he shouted for his surgeon, whipped up his horses and drove quickly across the ground to where Menelaus lay bleeding with the arrow still protruding from his flesh. So much blood was flowing through the gash in the jerkin that both men thought the wound fatal. Agamemnon stood up roaring with grief and rage, cursing the Trojans and vowing bloody vengeance. But having recovered from the first shock, Menelaus probed the wound with his fingers and realized that no organ was damaged. He was already reassuring his brother when the surgeon Machaon came up with a company of guards, who ringed the fallen warrior. Agamemnon watched as Machaon exposed the flesh and pulled out the arrow. He was cleaning the wound and applying healing ointments when Agamemnon looked up and saw that the Trojan lines were preparing to attack.

Immediately he set off to rally his forces. All of his commanders stood ready for action except Diomedes of Tiryns whose men were far out along the line and had not clearly seen what was happening. But Diomedes responded to Agamemnon's angry commands and swiftly advanced his men so that the two armies clashed with a great shout all along the lines.

Antilochus, one of Nestor's sons, was the first Argive to the kill. The spear he hurled struck a fully-armoured Trojan through the forehead, shattering his brains inside his helmet. On the other side, Antiphus threw a javelin at Ajax, which missed its mark but caught another man in the groin. Then blood was flowing everywhere, and the Argives had been so angered by the wounding of Menelaus that the impetus of their rage pushed the Trojans back up the hill.

Seeing what was happening, Hector drove his chariot to the fore, rallying his warriors by reminding them that Achilles was not in the field. Trojan spirits lifted at his shout, then the plain belonged to Ares, god of war, with his two sons Phobus and Deimos, Fear and Panic, raging round him, and men at their bloody work, hacking and stabbing, warding off blows with their bucklers, or dropping to their knees, clutching at their entrails, as the last cry left their throats and darkness shut down round them.

Both Agamemnon and Idomeneus proved their worth as leaders on the field that day, but when men were bathing their wounds afterwards and talking over the brave deeds that had been done, it was generally agreed that, of all men, Diomedes had distinguished himself by his ferocity and valour. Agamemnon's rebuke at the start of the battle must have stung him to prove his mettle, for his chariot smashed straight through into the Trojan lines, spreading panic before it. Even when his shoulder was pierced by another bow-shot from Pandarus, he asked a comrade to wrench the arrow out, called on Athena for aid, and hacked his way among the Trojan charioteers, slaughtering drivers and warriors alike.

When Aeneas saw that this furious assault might start a rout among the Dardanians, he summoned Pandarus up into his chariot and they bore down on Diomedes together. But the Lord of Tiryns heard a warning shout and swerved so that the long spear hurled by Pandarus glanced first off his shield then off his armour. As Aeneas's chariot hurtled past, Diomedes threw his own spear. Its point struck Pandarus in the jaw, smashing down through his teeth to cut off his tongue at the root. The force of the blow knocked him bodily from the chariot. Instantly Aeneas reined in his horses and leapt out to stand over his fallen friend. Diomedes jumped from his own chariot, picked up a rock from the ground and threw it at Aeneas, striking him on the hip-bone with such force that he fainted from the pain. Aeneas would surely have died in the next moment if a surge of the battle had not come between him and his assailant.

So strange and powerful were the events of those moments that men felt the presence of the gods among them. Some said that Aphrodite leapt to protect her son with her own body so that it was the goddess herself who took a wound in the arm from the point of Diomedes' spear as she sought to carry Aeneas away. They say that Ares came to her rescue then, sweeping her up into his chariot and taking her from the battlefield to where her mother Dione could comfort her and heal the wound she had taken. Meanwhile Diomedes fought on, furiously trying to reach Aeneas in the fray, and was prevented from doing so only by the intervention of Divine Apollo, who warned him of the danger that must come to any mortal man who dares to take up arms against the gods.

Certainly the tide of combat seemed to lurch in that moment. Diomedes fought on so fiercely that men said he would have cut down Ares himself if he had come across him in the field, but Hector held grimly on at the centre and the Trojan flank found the strength to throw the Argives back elsewhere. And so the battle rolled on across the plain all day with the advantage seeming to shift from one side to the other at different points along the line.

Menelaus rejoined the fight, disregarding his wound, and was hurtling in pursuit of a wealthy young warrior called Adrestos when he saw a wheel of the Trojan's chariot snarl on the branch of a tamarisk bush. The chariot veered and tipped, its yoke-pole snapped and Adrestos was thrown to the ground. As the screaming horses galloped away, Menelaus leapt from his own chariot to spear the winded man, but Adrestos clutched him by the knees, begging him to spare his life and promising that his father would pay a fortune in ransom for the son he loved. Menelaus was about to summon an aide to escort his prisoner to the ships when Agamemnon came up, demanding to know what kindness the Trojans had ever shown his brother that he should be soft-hearted with this youth now.

'Why think about ransom when you'll be able to take all his family's treasure soon enough?' he growled. 'Be done with him.'

Menelaus pushed Adrestos away. He was still staring down into his terrified eyes when Agamemnon lifted his spear and thrust it deep into the young Trojan's side. Gasping out a cry, Adrestos fell backwards on the ground. Agamemnon put a foot on his stomach, pulled the ash-spear out, and turned to shout his men on.

Towards the end of the day, when both sides were exhausted by their efforts, there came a lull in the fighting. Seeing that his fellow Trojans needed fresh heart, Hector stepped out between the lines, shouting out a challenge of single combat, but so fear-some was his reputation as a warrior that none of the Argive champions immediately rose to meet him. Menelaus would have done so, but he was restrained by his brother, so Nestor got to his feet berating this younger generation of warriors for its lack of spirit. Stung by the old man's reproaches, nine of them leapt up, including Diomedes, whose shoulder was stiffening from the wound he had taken earlier in the day. Lots were drawn for the honour of fighting Hector, and the lot fell on Telamon's son, Ajax, the Prince of Salamis.

So the day came to an end, as it had begun, with two heroes facing one another between the lines. But right from the first the fight seemed more evenly matched this time. Though both men took wounds, neither would concede victory to the other, so they fought on, grunting and panting in their armour, stum-bling as their blades swung and fell, until the plain began to darken round them. Eventually, by mutual agreement, the two heralds – Talthybius of the Argives and Idaeus of the Trojans – intervened with their staves to push the exhausted men apart.

'Clearly, you are both beloved of Cloud-gathering Zeus,' said Idaeus. 'But the light has gone. Give up the fight now.'

'Hector issued this challenge,' Ajax panted. 'I'll only lower my sword if he gives the word.'

Hector thought for only a moment before lifting off his helmet. 'There'll be time enough for us to find out which of us is the better man, but what Idaeus says is true. This battle has been long and hard, the light is poor, and we're both too tired to fight at our best. Let's agree to call it a day.' He took in Ajax's nod, and they were smiling at one another in mutual respect.

'We should exchange gifts in honour of each other's prowess,' Hector said, 'so that our friends can say that both of us fought well and neither returned defeated from the field.' And when Ajax gladly agreed to this offer, Hector gave him the sword with which, for the past hour, he had been trying to kill him. Ajax studied the fine work on its silver-studded hilt for a moment, and then unslung his own intricately decorated purple baldric and handed it over to the Trojan prince. Then, weary but elated, the two heroes parted friends that night. Yet as they returned to celebrate among their comrades, neither man was aware of the part that those gifts would later come to play in the circumstances of their deaths.

An Offer of Peace

Hector returned to the city after his duel with Ajax knowing how close he had come to losing that hard fight. His shoulders were bruised, blood was clotting at his knee and he was filled with trepidation that the Trojan host could not withstand many more days such as this. His push to drive the Argives back upon their ships had failed, and they had recoiled with such ferocity that many of the women gathered by the oak-tree at the city gate would not find their husbands, sons and fathers among the warriors returning home. Already the streets were loud with grief, and this was the first day of fighting that Troy had endured in a long time.

So when he looked back into the dusk where kites and vultures were gathering above the unburied bodies, it seemed to Hector's weary heart that the weight of favour among the gods had lain with the Argive invaders that day. They had called on Athena for aid and the goddess had answered.

Something must be done to restore the balance.

He went first to embrace and reassure his wife Andromache, and to comfort his little son Astyanax who was frightened by the sight of his blood and bruises, and cowered away from his father when Hector, who was still wearing his high-plumed helmet, leaned over to kiss him. Then, when he had bathed his wounds and thoroughly cleansed himself, Hector made his way across the citadel of Ilium to the temple of Athena.

The priestess at that temple was Theano, the wife of Antenor, a woman who had once been beautiful but whose face had hardened over the years to match the austerity of her soul. She watched as Hector made his offerings and poured the libations. She listened to the fervour of his prayer that Athena lift the force of her wrath from the city, but then she shocked him with her response.

'Divine Athena will not hear you,' Theano said, 'no more than she would hear your mother this afternoon. For the time being, the goddess is deaf to our pleas.'

From where he knelt, Hector looked up into her cold eyes. 'I could feel her power working against us out there on the plain. It was as though the goddess herself was driving Diomedes' chariot. What have we done to offend her that she turns against us so?'

Theano gazed up at the impassive statue of Athena. 'Why should the goddess listen to us when we give our loyalty to one who has insulted her?'

'You mean my brother Paris?'

'He alone has brought Athena's rage upon this city.'

Hector looked into that severe face. Her mouth no more than a peremptory line drawn down towards her chin. He said. 'I know you have had no love for my brother since the death of your child. How could it be otherwise?'

'There is nothing in my heart for him but hatred.' Theano's voice was as calm as it was forthright. 'I have never denied it, and the hate will never leave me. But this is a matter quite apart from the grave harm he has done to me. This thing lies between Paris and the goddess. In some way I do not understand unless it began with a disparaging of her rites and stature, your brother has earned for himself the unremitting enmity of Athena.' For a cold moment Hector felt he might have been looking into the face of the goddess herself and he saw no possibility of remission there. 'He has brought that enmity upon this city,' Theano said. 'It falls there, and will continue to fall until reparation is made for the injury he has given her. And it must come from the one with whom the fault lies. It is not enough for you or your mother or King Priam himself to make the offering. Paris is the author of our ills. It is he who has neglected the service of Athena and derided her power. Her quarrel is with him. Let him pay the price of it.'

Paris had found his way back to the city through a daze of shock and humiliation.

His vision was blurred and uncertain. He was bleeding where the point of the spear had seared his side. The chinstrap had scorched the skin of his neck, and every bone of his body felt bruised from the battering he had taken. He was drenched and dirty, and shamed by the huge silence across the Trojan lines as they parted to let him through on the road back to the city.

The same silence waited for him where the women were gathered by the gate. His chariot wheels clattered on the cobbles of the empty street leading up to the citadel. He could hear rainwater gushing along the runnels there. And because of the rain driving into his face and the droplets spilling off his hair, it was impossible to tell that he was weeping, but weeping he was as he entered the silent mansion where he now lived with Helen. He unbuckled his breastplate and greaves, and let them crash to the floor, then threw himself down across the embroidered coverlet of their bed, careless of the mud drying on his arms and legs.

A slave came in to attend to him and was angrily dismissed.

Inside the painted room, the silence grew larger round him until he realized that the rain had stopped. Through the casement came a brilliant rinsed light. It fell across the great tapestry where Ares and Aphrodite lay in each other's arms. In the boughs of the almond tree outside the window a bird began to sing.

Paris had scrambled away from that defeat with his life intact and little else. His pride was gone. His honour was gone. His nerves were shattered – so much so that he jumped when a great shout went up from the distant battlefield and shuddered on the wind. On any other day he would have climbed up to the roof to see what was happening, but he knew already that, whatever that shout might mean, the continuing endurance of the men struggling across the plain spelled only shame for him. He thought of the panther skin in which he had set out that day. It must be lying somewhere in the mud. It would have been better by far to stay out there and die. So why had he not done so? Why?

He could still smell Menelaus' sweat pressing close against him. He could hear the malevolent effort in his grunts. He could see, through the narrow visor of that bronze helmet, his fierce, reviling eyes. And then, as he had been dragged by the throat across the rough ground, choking on the point of suffocation, the world began to shut down round him into a small, airless chamber where for evermore he would see only the menace and loathing in the King of Sparta's face.

So when the chinstrap snapped and his head fell suddenly free, his first and only thought had been to get away. And once he had begun to run there was no stopping. He would, he knew, always be running now, for the rest of his days.

Meanwhile, Helen had been keeping silent company with King Priam in the vast hall of his empty throne room, where he had chosen to sit because he could no more bear to watch the duel than could she. They had sat in perfect silence together, each thinking their own thoughts, and finding no consolation in them, but taking a kind of comfort in the other's unspeaking presence.

In the stillness of that marble space all they could hear of the roaring of the hosts watching the two men fight outside was a distant susurration like the murmur of the sea. Then the light from the windows had darkened as the clouds gathered and they heard the rain rattling down onto the tiles. They had glanced at each other in that moment, and though neither spoke, Priam wanted to confess how he had left orders that if his son was killed in the fight, Menelaus must not be allowed to walk in triumph from the field. He wanted to tell the beautiful, silent woman sitting across from him that if both her husbands died, then he himself would care for her till his dying day. Yet he was afraid that she might recoil from the knowledge, so he kept his peace, and waited, as Helen waited, to learn what fate the wisdom of the gods had chosen for them.

Then Cassandra had come into the hall, white-faced, her hair in disarray, her face and clothing drenched from the rain. She was laughing a little and clutching the damp folds of the gown she wore as though she had been running through the storm. Priam and Helen looked up in alarm as she came in. Of all the people in the city, this half-crazed girl was the one they least wished to hear from in those tense moments.

'Do you smell it yet?' she said, 'the smoke that writhes around this house? It will come soon. This place will burn while Helen and I wait to see who comes to claim us. Didn't I warn you, father? Didn't I say you should never have taken that she-bear's foundling back into your house? And see what a wretch he turns out to be, flying from the field without his helmet and shield and panther's skin. Aphrodite's spoiled darling, weeping and beaten and looking for succour at the soft breast of his Spartan whore.'

'What of Menelaus?' her father demanded.

'Struck down by treachery. But living still for all your schemes. The gods will not be cheated, father. This city has burned before and it will burn again. Soon enough the red-haired son of Atreus will stride through this hall to claim his own.' Cassandra turned the black glamour of her eyes on Helen, whose heart quailed. 'And will you warm to him once more? I think you will, I think you will. And like a dog at his vomit he will lap you up again.'

Priam and Helen stared in silence as she walked out of the hall. Then they were left looking at each other like hostile strangers, each seeing the other's gift for treachery nakedly revealed, and recoiling inwardly from the sight.

'What have you done?' Helen demanded. 'Would you have seen them both killed? Is there no honour left in Troy?'

Priam lifted his hands in a vain gesture which seemed to say that honour was a thing no longer to be found anywhere.

And Helen had got up, saying, 'I must go to my husband,' but even as the word left her mouth she was uncertain of which man she spoke. Her breath shook with the growing understanding that there was now nowhere safe to go.

When she entered the bed-chamber of the gilded house that Paris had furnished for her with all the spoils of the east, Helen saw him lying in his filth on the bed. Glancing quickly away, she pulled a shawl about her shoulders as though against a draught. Paris opened his mouth to speak but could say nothing.

She said, 'Helice tells me that she offered to draw your bath but you refused it. Shall I call her again or do you mean to lie as you are?'

Still he could not speak.

'I think that your wounds need attention.'

He said, 'There is a wound here that only you can heal.'

'There are some wounds that no one can heal.' Helen turned away from him and walked towards the casement where she stood listening to the din of battle on the wind. At this distance the noise might have been no more than the shouting of a crowd at the games, yet men were fighting and dying out there, and both of them knew that their love – that sad, abraded, and now almost extinguished love – was the cause.

But in that moment, strangely, he was hardly thinking of her. His talk of a wound that only she could heal had brought someone else to his mind. He was thinking of Oenone. He was remembering what the girl had said to him on the day when he first left the mountains to come to Troy. He was remembering how she had warned him that one day he would take a wound that only she would be able to heal. Her words had come back to him and, for a deranging moment, it felt as though he had directed his appeal to the wrong woman.

And that woman was almost as much a stranger to him now as the rough boy who had once bravely fought off the Argive raiders with his bow. Alexander they had called him, *Defender of Men*, and who would ever have thought that such a boy would end up lying inside this beaten body on this silken bed in a perfume-scented chamber in the royal precinct of a city that might soon burn because a bear had suckled him once and he had grown up to betray a friend?

And it was unnerving that he could no longer read the once intimately known thoughts of the woman who stood across from him gazing out towards the plain.

'Why don't you ask me about it?' he said to her now.

She looked at him. 'Speak about it if you wish.'

Paris glanced way towards the window. 'There was such hatred in him. I looked into his eyes and saw myself as he must see me, and it filled me with such a numbing sense of the wrong I had done him that I couldn't stand against him.'

Helen studied his anguished frown for a moment before turning away. He could see the nape of her neck beneath the piled hair, and the graceful sweep of her back as she murmured, 'I think if you had killed him, it would have killed me too.'

He stared up at her in bewilderment.

'Whatever I have done,' his voice entreated, 'I have done it only for you.'

She turned to look at him again and saw the truth of it. They were alone in all the world, the two of them, exiled for ever in their passionate delinquency. And the only hope for understanding lay in each other's eyes. She felt a surge of pity rise inside her – pity for him, pity for Menelaus, pity for herself, pity for all who had ever trusted love to lead them through a loveless world. And perhaps only there, she thought, in the compassion of the injured heart, was there any solace to be found. Certainly, if there were wounds that might never be healed then they were left with no kinder choice than to tend them for each other.

'Come,' she said, 'the water has been heated. Let me bathe your wounds.'

So she led him to the bath and dismissed the slaves who stood ready to serve him, for neither of them could endure the company of others. He lay with his eyes closed in the tepid water as she washed the blood and filth from his limbs. Then they returned to their chamber and lay down together, and when he became aware that she was weeping silently, he too began to weep.

Reaching out a hand to stroke the dark fall of her hair, he said, 'Do you remember our small kingdom of Kranae – where there were only the two of us?'

She nodded, lifting her cheek to the soft brush of his finger-tips.

'It was a place of the heart,' he whispered. 'We don't belong in Sparta or in Troy. We belong to Kranae and we are traitors only when we betray that place, for there were no armies there, and no quarrels, and all this din and clash of weaponry is not of our choice, not of our making.'

He closed his arms about her. She lowered her head against his chest, and though both of them knew that every word he uttered was falsified by a world that was locked in mortal conflict round them, they gave themselves once more to Aphrodite, and returned for the last time to their island kingdom of the heart.

It was Hector who woke them. The slaves had told him they were in their chamber so he hammered at the door until Paris came to open it. A robe was draped loosely round his shoulders and the smell of sleep and sex hung about him still. Hector studied his dishevelled brother with incredulous contempt.

'Is it not enough for one day,' he said, 'that you should set an example in cowardice before all the host, but that you must now lie pleasuring yourself in bed while men fight and die out there in your name, for your cause?'

Of all his brothers, Hector was the only one for whom Paris had ever felt unqualified affection. It was Hector's gaze he had most feared to meet when he ran for his chariot. But a thousand times worse than that was to confront the scorn in Hector's eyes now. Better to have taken a thousand wounds from Menelaus' sword than to have to endure that withering glance.

'Forgive me, brother,' he cried. 'Not all of us have your strength.'

'You are no brother of mine – not unless you're man enough to prove yourself as gallant on the battlefield as you appear to be in bed.'

From where she stood at the back of the room with her hair tousled and a robe wrapped about her naked body, Helen said, 'Will you not come in and speak privately, Hector?'

'No, madam, I will not,' Hector snapped back at her. 'This city is grieving the loss of many sons right now, some of whose poor bodies are still lying out there on the plain. I have no time to sit and bandy words with you. But this much I will say – if you have any shame left, you will tell this paramour of yours to come to the council chamber right now and speak for himself as a man among men. And you may tell him also that it will not be enough to restore him in my sight unless he also shows himself ready to take his place beside men who are not afraid to fight – and for a nobler cause than your right to sport together while we die!'

As Paris hurried along the corridor to the council chamber he could hear voices raised in argument but they all fell silent as he entered. He stood in the doorway for a moment seeing that all the princes and nobles of Troy were assembled there along with their principal allies. Conscious of Hector's glare and of the cold reserve of his former friend Aeneas, with whom he had exchanged only a few formal sentences since his return from Sparta, he crossed the marble floor to take his place at the left of the throne where Priam sat gravely with his head leaning to one side and his jaw cupped in a gnarled hand. Paris made a brief obeisance before his father, who gestured for him to rise, and then he turned to face the hostile faces round him.

'Forgive my tardiness,' he said. 'I have been half out of my mind this day. And no one here can shame me more than I have already shamed myself, so do not spare your words on my account.'

Above the murmuring in the hall, Priam said, 'You have heard my son, Antenor. Speak your mind.'

Antenor stepped forward, holding the speaker's sceptre. He tilted his gaunt chin, gathering his words before he spoke. His cheeks were flushed, his knuckles white about the sceptre.

'Trojans, Dardanians, loyal allies,' he began, 'most of us fought bravely today and together we withstood the first assault of the Argive host. But we know to our cost that there are many who did not return from the plain, and many more too badly injured to fight again. Already our numbers are not what they were, and tomorrow yet more will die. How long, I wonder, can we continue to endure such losses? And for what good cause? For make no mistake, we are fighting not just against men here, but also against gods. Athena is against us. Hera is against us. And even Apollo, who has always been revered in this city, warned us long ago that Troy would fall if one who stands among us now was allowed to live.'

For a space a pensive silence filled the hall. Then Antenor continued in a lower, more fervent voice. 'That warning was ignored, and I have more reason than most to rue it. All men here know that my wife and I have no cause to love Paris. We know also that he has broken an oath of friendship, violated the laws of hospitality and the sanctity of marriage, and brought long years of war and hardship on us all. Yet it is not for those reasons alone that I impugn his presence among us. I do it for the good of our city. I do it because it is what the gods require. He should have died many years ago when Apollo demanded it. He might have died honourably today, and would have done so had he not lacked the courage to take the fate that lay in wait for him. So he cowers now behind our walls, and as long as he is allowed to do so, the Argive host will batter our gates and give us no rest until his life is in their hands.' Antenor drew in his breath and raised his voice for emphasis. 'Let us give it to them now, therefore. Let us deliver Paris back to the wronged man before whom he fled today. And let him take the Spartan woman with him, along with all their wealth. For his treachery has made traitors of us all. A pact of friendship was broken many years ago and it was he who broke it. A truce was broken today and it was we who broke it. Justice is no longer on our side and those who fight without justice call down the anger of the gods.' Antenor was trembling as he spoke. He looked across at Priam who was gazing up at the blue ceiling as if his thoughts were elsewhere. 'But if my lord the king feels it too much to deliver his son into the hands of his enemies, at least let him be forced to part with Helen and her wealth. Let us restore to Menelaus what is rightfully his, and end the long travail of this war.'

Antenor had not looked at Paris once as he spoke. Now he withdrew from the floor and his friends gathered round him in a murmur of assent. Paris waited a few moments to see whether anyone would rise to speak in his defence, and when no one did so he stepped forward into the silence of the hall.

'My royal father, friends,' he began, 'there is some truth in what Antenor has said, and I confess myself guilty of the charges he brings against me. It is true that I was to blame for his young son's death and I have rued it all my days. It is true that I broke a vow of friendship and that I violated the laws of hospitality while I was in Sparta, and it is true that in doing so I occasioned this long war. None of this do I deny, and if you think my life should be made forfeit for it, you have it in your power to deliver me over to the vengeance of the sons of Atreus.'

Pausing, he raised his hands at his sides and opened them as if to show himself weaponless and vulnerable. 'But this much I would say in my own defence. Firstly, this war was coming long before I set eyes on the Lady Helen. My deeds might have been the spark that lit that fire, but the tinder had been lying dry for years. And there are those in this hall who sought this war more eagerly than I.' Paris glanced briefly at his brothers Deiphobus and Antiphus before continuing. 'Secondly, as all men know, there are more gods than Athena and Hera, great though they are in their divine power, and what I have done was done in the service of another goddess, one who is quite as powerful as they. King Anchises will tell you that once a man's life is taken within the embrace of Aphrodite he is no longer free to act as other men do. It is the goddess who acts through him and if her works are sometimes dreadful in their power, they are driven by the living force of love, which is a law unto itself. That law has its own court and its own trials, and in the eyes of that court I am innocent of all crimes except the failure to love well enough. But let no man doubt that the love I have for Helen is so great that I will never betray it. Take my own life if you will. Take all my wealth and hand it over as reparation to the Argives and I will murmur no word of objection. But I will never surrender my wife to any man.'

For long seconds after Paris had finished speaking, the air of the hall was still tense with the passion in his voice. Then, to his amazement, Deiphobus stepped forward and said, 'I stand with my brother Paris on this,' and after a moment, Antiphus was nodding beside him.

Antenor stood frowning, shaking his head, and then the whole hall was a murmur of uncertain debate until King Priam rose from his throne to speak.

'I have heard the words of my counsellor Antenor,' he said, 'and I have heard the words of my sons. Now hear my word on this. We will keep a watch about our walls as usual tonight. Tomorrow the herald Idaeus shall go to the Argive camp and convey the offer of Prince Paris to return to Menelaus all the treasure that was taken from Sparta except the Lady Helen. To that sum shall be added the greater portion of his own wealth in reparation. If the sons of Atreus accept this offer, well and good. If not, we shall fight on and let the gods decide between us.

And that was how it was left, though no one in the court believed the issue could be resolved this way. Hector left the council filled with gloom and returned to his apartment in the palace where his wife Andromache anxiously waited. She knew at once from his face that the war must go on, and she railed against Paris for a time until Hector stilled her. 'He spoke well for himself,' he said, 'and he no more wishes to give up the wife he loves than I would wish to surrender you.'

'So he will cling on to her even though you must die for it? Haven't I suffered enough in this war? My father was killed by Achilles in the attack on Thebe, and all my brothers died with him. Must I now lose my husband too, and my child his father, for the sake of Paris and his Spartan woman?'

'This war was never just about Helen,' Hector said.

'No,' Andromache looked back at him with accusation in her eyes, 'it was always about men's love of power and their appetite for violence. What do I or Helen or any woman really matter in this mad world except as spoils of war? And there would never have been a war were not so many of you men eager to fight it. I think you are all in love with war, that you take pleasure in its cruelties, that you find a surer proof of your manhood in killing other men than in caring for a woman's love.' She looked up and saw the hurt in the eyes of the man she loved. Hopelessly she shook her head. 'Didn't you see how our little son shuddered when he saw you in your battle-gear today? You were all such children once, yet none of you will rest till you have turned your sons into men of violence. You are fools, blind fools, all of you. Paris may be a fool for love, but those of you who fight for him and die for him are greater fools by far.'

'So what would you have me do?' Hector said. 'Would you have me run for my life as Paris did today?'

'Yes,' she cried, 'yes, why not? Your life doesn't only belong to you. It belongs to me and to our son. Or do you find it easier to die for Paris than to live for us?'

'Nothing of this is easy,' he said. 'And if I die it will not be for Paris, but in the effort to keep the Argives from our gates. This war is with us whether I will have it or no, and all the burden of it falls to me. Twice I have tried to prevent it – first by urging Paris into single combat, and again in the council tonight. But it seems it's not the will of the gods that things should end that way. So what am I to do?'

He got up from the couch and paced about the room. 'My greatest fear is that Agamemnon and his horde will come running through our streets and into our houses and that some Argive man-at-arms will kill my son and drag you off to slavery. I will fight and fight and fight again sooner than let that happen.'

Andromache stared up into the haggard appeal of her husband's noble face. 'But must you always fight in the most dangerous place?' she begged. 'Must you always be out there in the front line, trading blows with their charioteers and spearmen? Why can't you watch with us here on the wall, keeping guard over its weakest places so that the Argives can be held at bay?'

Hector shook his head. 'Don't you see what a comfort it would be to the enemy if they could say, "Look how the Trojan hero Hector cowers among the women at the walls"? And how could I expect my comrades to fight bravely if they knew I was keeping myself safe with you? The gods know that I wish only to live at peace with you and watch my son grow up to be a better man than his father. But for that to happen I must live out this fate that falls to me.' Hector gathered his wife into his arms and tried to smile down at her. 'I will have more strength for that, my love, if I don't also have to fight with you.'

Early the next day the herald Idaeus presented himself before Agamemnon's council to inform the Argive leaders that Paris was unwilling to return Helen to Menelaus but would pay the greater part of his wealth in compensation. The sons of Atreus merely glanced at one another and shook their heads in refusal.

Still fired by his deeds on the battlefield, Diomedes spoke up for the rest of the captains. 'The Trojans wouldn't make such an offer if they didn't already fear that their fate was sealed. Why should we be content with what Paris chooses to give us when all Troy is ours for the taking?'

'You have our answer,' Agamemnon said.

'Very well,' Idaeus replied, 'but do not underestimate the strength of our resistance. Meanwhile King Priam observes that many dead lie unburied on the field. He will assent to a day of truce so that both sides may do them honour.'

Agamemnon readily agreed to this and wagons were sent out to collect the bodies that lay strewn across the plain. All that day the sky was black with the smoke rising from the funeral pyres, and the air men breathed was foul with the smell of burning flesh. But the Argives also took advantage of the temporary armistice to strengthen the fortifications they had built to defend the ships, and when the Trojans saw this, they were confirmed in their belief that there was no hope of saving the city except to drive the invaders back into the sea.

The next day broke under a gloom of cloud swirling down from Mount Ida. All morning the two sides fought. Both sides sustained heavy losses and neither gained much ground. And then, around noon, the storm-clouds broke in a violent stroke of lightning so close that the instantaneous volley of thunder stunned the ears. The bolt fell among the Argive lines, singeing the air with a stink of sulphur and spreading terror and confusion among both men and horses. For a moment even the Trojans were dazed by the shock. But Hector recovered quickly. 'Zeus has spoken,' he shouted. 'Zeus is with us,' and urged his forces forward to take advantage of the confusion in the enemy line.

The Argive centre, which had been closest to the strike, fell back first, and all Agamemnon's ravings could not rally it. Then Idomeneus pulled back, and soon, the line was buckling all along its length as men panicked and turned round to run. Before old Nestor could turn his chariot to retreat, Paris released an arrow which struck his trace-horse in the head and sent it crashing to the ground. Nestor leapt out of his chariot to cut the horse free and would have been ridden down where he stood had not Diomedes seen Hector's chariot bearing down upon him and hurled his spear. It struck Hector's charioteer in the chest and the weight of its long shaft pulled him down among the horses, making them shy. As Hector struggled to gain control of the reins, Diomedes pulled Nestor up into his chariot and carried him off to safety. But the whole line had broken round them. They had no choice but to join the rout with Hector hurling insults at their back. As they fell back towards the palisade, they could hear Agamemnon bellowing and cursing through the rain as he shouted out his orders, calling up archers to break the Trojan advance. Ajax and Teucer, were among the first to respond, taking up a position where Ajax defended his brother with his great ox-hide shield, while Teucer swiftly released his arrows at the oncoming Trojans. Some men fell, and the advance would have shuddered to a halt, but the impetus of those following up behind was so strong that the Argives were driven further back toward their ships.

Only the palisade and ditch prevented them from being completely overrun. But once they were off the open plain and could take cover behind the rampart, the commanders halted the rout and pushed their men back into a bloody struggle around the ditch and gates. All afternoon men fought and died there, hand to hand, in a slither of mud and rain. The killing stopped only when the light from the overcast sky was so poor that Hector could no longer see along his lines to keep control of the advance and decided to pull his weary men back.

But the hearts of the Trojans had been lifted by the day's success. They were strengthened further by Hector's elated presence among them, promising them victory on the morrow. He gave orders that his army should camp out on the plain, keeping the Argives pinned between the palisade and the ships. So the besiegers became the besieged that night and the watchmen looking out from behind the stockade saw a thousand watch-fires burning across the plain and knew that fifty warriors were gathered around each one of them, and that on the next day the Argive army might find itself trapped between the ditch and the sea.

The Price of Honour

Though his ships were beached far to the west of the line, some distance away from where the fighting had taken place, Achilles was well aware that the Argive host had barely escaped disaster that day. He was not surprised that evening, therefore, when Phoenix came down the strand to where he sat with Patroclus, playing his lyre, and said that Odysseus and Ajax wished to speak with him.

Achilles got up to greet them. 'It's been some time since I had visitors, and the two of you are the ones I'm happiest to see. Come, let's drink some wine together.' He permitted himself another wry smile. 'You must be hungry after your day's work. Why don't you stay and eat with us?'

The guests made themselves comfortable in the thatched lodge of rough-hewn timber that Achilles shared with Patroclus while the wine was mixed and joints of meat were roasted on spits across the fire. Patroclus threw the ritual portions into the blaze as offerings for the gods, and when they had eaten and refilled their cups, Odysseus said, 'I don't suppose you need any explanation of our visit.'

Achilles merely shrugged and sipped at his wine.

Odysseus sighed. 'Let me be frank then. We're in an almighty mess out there. If we hadn't managed to hold on till the light had gone we'd have been completely overwhelmed today. You must have seen for yourself that Hector's army controls all the plain between the palisade and the city. He can't wait for morning to come. And when it does, there's a good chance he'll push us right back into the sea.'

Still Achilles said nothing. Patroclus sat with his palms together at his chin, listening but revealing nothing of his feelings. By the firelight Odysseus could see old Phoenix tugging at his beard. He could also sense Ajax's agitation at his side. 'Two nights ago,' he went on, 'our glorious leader had a dream that Zeus was promising him a quick victory, which is why he's been putting everything at risk since then. We took huge losses yesterday and a lot more again this morning. And if that wasn't bad enough, a thunderbolt fell among our lines this afternoon. It got the Trojans convinced that Zeus is on their side, and we lost so many men in the ensuing rout that Agamemnon is confounded by the same thought. It won't surprise you to hear that he's been thrown into another violent fit of gloom. It was all Diomedes and Nestor could do to prevent him ordering us back into our ships – though it would have been a massacre if he'd done so. Hector was ready for it. His Trojans would have been down on us like a landslide while we ran.'

Lips pursed in a half-smile, Achilles stirred the embers of the fire with the skewer he held. They could hear the boom of the surf outside.

'So morale is lower than it's ever been and there's only one thing that can lift it.' Again Odysseus drew in his breath. 'We need you back among us. We need you to put some fight into the men.'

Achilles lifted his cold eyes. 'I thought I made myself clear.'

'You did – but things can change.' Leaning forward, Odysseus spoke more urgently. 'There's no need for this quarrel to go on. Agamemnon has begun to see things differently. He's prepared to back down. You can have Briseis back untouched – he swears that he hasn't laid a finger on her since he seized her. Seven other women that he took on Lesbos come with her. Then there's ten talents of gold on offer and twelve prize horses swift enough to win you all the cash you could want.' When he saw that Achilles was about to interrupt, Odysseus quickly raised his voice. 'And if that's not enough to soothe your hurt pride, he wants to make you his son-in-law when we get back. You can take your pick among his remaining daughters. She'll bring a huge dowry with her, including the lordship of seven handsome towns with all their lands, flocks and cattle.'

Achilles glanced away. 'I seem to recall that Agamemnon makes free with my name when he thinks of marriage for his daughters.'

Odysseus, who had always considered that element in the offer injudicious, expressed his embarrassment now by opening his hands in a wry, deferential gesture. Ajax said, 'Think about it, cousin. All this is yours for the taking. All Agamemnon asks in return is that you come back and fight at his side.'

Achilles flicked a hot ember from the fire and smiled across at Patroclus. 'Anyone might think that the King of Men was desperate!' Then he turned his cold gaze on Odysseus again. 'Does Agamemnon think I'm a mere bondsman to be bought and sold?'

'He knows you're not. He thinks that . . .'

But Achilles interrupted him. 'If there's one thing I loathe above everything else, it's a man who thinks one thing and says another, so let me be straight with you – as he has never been with me. You brought me here, Odysseus. You know what I've done for the Argive cause. You know how many battles I've turned, how many cities have fallen before me, how much plunder I've brought back and laid at Agamemnon's feet. You also know what I've been given for my trouble. I've been humiliated before the host. I've seen my woman taken from me and put to his foul uses. And who cares if she was a captive of my spear? – I loved Briseis dearly and her loss to me was as grievous as the insult to my honour.' He turned his fierce gaze on Odysseus. 'Have the sons of Atreus forgotten why we set out on this misbegotten enterprise? Wasn't it to help one of them recover the woman that was stolen from him? Do they think they're the only men who care about their wives? No, my friend, I've seen the Lion of Mycenae for the ungrateful and false-hearted oaf that he is.'

'The man has his faults,' Odysseus conceded. 'I'm not about to deny it. But so do we all. Isn't that why we need each other – to compensate for each other's weaknesses?'

'Then if he wants to save his ships he must look to you and the other lords to help him. As for me and my friends – tomorrow we put to sea. With luck, three days should see us back in Thessaly. So tell this to your king – it was he who first broke faith with me and if he offered me all the treasure of Egyptian Thebes, I wouldn't serve him. I want no part of his bribes.'

Odysseus nodded and sighed. 'I told him you would say that, and I'm glad to see I was right. But aren't you forgetting something yourself? Didn't you come to Troy in quest of honour? It seems a pity to leave with little of it gained.'

'At least it's not lost,' Achilles answered stiffly. 'So don't ask me to sully it again by fighting at his side. I am for home, gentlemen. If you're wise, you will cram your ships with spoil and follow me.'

Fat crackled and spat among the embers of the fire. The wind off the sea shook the leather flap over the door. Otherwise there was only silence.

Odysseus had known that this was how it would be. He knew that Achilles was no more likely to accept these terms than Agamemnon had been inclined to accept Priam's offer of the previous day. Now he was cursing quietly to himself in the knowledge that he was surrounded by obdurate men who would watch the world burn sooner than admit that they were wrong.

How condignly Achilles and Agamemnon deserved one another, he thought, in their differing postures of stupidity. But if disaster was to be avoided, there was still a job to be done, and for the moment he could see no way of doing it, for he could find no chink in this young man's armoured pride.

To his surprise it was Phoenix who broke the silence.

'I've listened to you, Lord Achilles,' the old Myrmidon said quietly, 'and I've kept my silence. But I've known and loved you since you were a boy and I believe my love earns me the right to speak. I understand your anger. I've shared it with you. But a time must come for it to end.'

Achilles sought to silence him. 'This is not the time, Phoenix.'

But the old man would not be deterred. 'A man should be wary of refusing an apology when it's offered. He can offend the gods that way and bring a worse fate down on his head. I think you would do better to think less of your hatred for Agamemnon and more of your love for your friends. Stand beside them in battle again and they'll give you more in love and honour than the Lord of Mycenae could ever take away.'

Odysseus saw the flicker of irritation and uncertainty in Achilles' eyes. Sensing a shift, he gave another push. 'The truth is, I have little more respect for Agamemnon than you do these days, but Phoenix is right – come back and fight for your friends, not for him, and they'll honour you like a god.'

Achilles frowned. 'My friend Phoenix would do well to remember that I place no great weight on the good opinion of the Argives. His duty is to stand by me.'

Phoenix lowered his eyes and withdrew into the shadows. Odysseus looked to Patroclus who avoided his eyes and glanced uncomfortably away. Thinking quickly, he made one last throw. 'Well, I understand your position – but it seems a great pity. If ever there was a chance to win immortal glory, it must surely be now when Hector thinks there is no one in the Argive lines to stand against him.'

For a moment he thought he had caught him. Achilles hesitated. The pupils of his eyes were moving quickly, and Odysseus could almost hear the fierce young man recalling the prophecy that his life would be short if he fought at Troy but his glory would live for ever. He tried to project into Achilles' mind a picture of him standing in triumph over the body of Hector, but there were already other pictures there – of Agamemnon smirking as Achilles returned to the battle, of the humiliation of going back on his word before the entire Argive host.

Achilles frowned impatiently. 'I have said what I have said. Not unless Hector comes against my Myrmidons and my ships will I raise my weapons against him.'

Ajax, who had sat in apprehensive silence, released his frustration now. 'Come, Lord Odysseus,' he snapped, 'we are clearly wasting our time here. We should get back and think what dispositions we must make now that Achilles has failed us.' He got to his feet and stared down, shaking his head, at the proud young man. 'I've always loved and admired you, son of Peleus, but this stubborn petulance baffles me. Even in cases of murder, men will accept blood-money to end a feud, yet here – in a stupid quarrel over a woman – you turn your back on your friends and refuse to hear reason. Well, so be it. I'd rather go down fighting in defeat than stand here pleading a moment longer.'

Shortly afterwards, Odysseus and Ajax returned to report the failure of their mission. They left a prolonged and uneasy silence in the lodge of Achilles.

So prodigal were the terms of Agamemnon's offer that he had not contemplated the possibility that Achilles might reject it, and the news of the refusal left him aghast at first. But when Diomedes castigated him for having tried to make concessions to the intransigent young man, the shock tipped him out of gloom into a vainglorious ecstasy of rage. Let the next day come – he would show that arrogant little shit how a true fighting man comported himself when the odds were against him.

His spirits were lifted by the events of the night. A Trojan scout was captured and, working on information forced out of him before his throat was cut, Odysseus led a marauding raid on a loosely guarded stretch of the enemy lines, broke through a corral and ran off an entire string of Thracian horses. So Agamemnon armed himself for battle next day fortified by the knowledge that the enemy's mobility would be significantly impaired. But he knew that his situation was still so desperate that only an over-whelming counter-attack could redeem it. To inspire his forces he would have to lead it himself, so he steeled his nerves and urged his chariot at the Trojan host with mindless courage.

Having smashed his way through the volleying spears, he came across the chariot in which Priam's son Antiphus was driven by his bastard half-brother Isus. Isus went down under Agamemnon's spear and then his sword crashed into the side of Antiphus' head with such force that he was knocked out of the chariot. As if possessed by a vision of his own invulnerability, Agamemnon pushed on, with his infantrymen shouting at his back. They drove the Trojans off the high ground and half-way back towards the city walls before Hector managed to rally them. But the Argives were within sight of the Scaean Gate and Agamemnon was roaring at the smell of victory when he was caught unawares by a spear thrust through the arm.

For a time not even that wound could deter him. He struck down his assailant and pushed on, hacking at the enemies around him until the muscles of his arm suddenly seized and he was forced to order his driver to pull back. Above the din of the struggle he shouted to his captains to fight on, but the impetus of the attack had been driven by his reckless battle-ardour, and the force went out of it when the Argives saw their leader in retreat. Hector gave a great shout of encouragement to his own men and led them in such a powerful counter-assault that almost everywhere the Argives were thrust back across the plain.

All along the line, men were on the run, scrambling and stumbling, dropping their shields in the rush to get away. Some were crushed by the chariots as they ran, others fell under blows that darkened their eyes for ever. Odysseus leapt from his chariot and tried to halt the rout near the burial-mound of Ilus. He was joined there by Diomedes who caught sight of Hector and hurled his spear. The point struck Hector's helmet with a glancing blow that left him briefly dazed. Once again the battle might have turned in that moment, but Paris had returned to the field armed with his favourite weapon. He put an arrow to his bow, released it, and thought it was about to fall short until he heard Diomedes shout with pain. The arrow had pierced him through the foot, pinning him to the ground. Odysseus sprang to protect his comrade while the wounded man pulled out the arrow and limped into his chariot to be carried away.

Odysseus was now isolated with his small company, and fighting like a bayed boar to hold off the ring of Trojans who were threatening to encircle his position.

He had cut down five men before a spear penetrated his shield and tore through his armour to cut a gash in his side. Wincing with pain he managed to pull out the spear and hurl it back at his attacker, but then he was forced to give ground with blood streaming down his thigh. His cousin Sinon sprang at once to his defence, but Menelaus, who had taken command of Agamemnon's Mycenaeans on his left, had also seen him take the wound. Calling to Ajax for support, he drove to the rescue of the struggling Ithacan and pulled him up into his chariot while Ajax and his brother Teucer held the Trojans back.

Three of the Argive commanders were now out of the fight, and as each of them was carried away from the front, the men around them lost heart. Ajax held his ground as long as he could but he was exposed and outnumbered, and his nerve was shaken when he looked around and saw that it couldn't be long before the whole Argive host was thrust back over the ditch and through the palisade. In all the long years of the war their position had never been so desperate.

Knowing that if Agamemnon's forces were routed, they might soon be fighting in defence of their own ships, the Myrmidons had been keeping careful watch on as much of the battle as they could see from the western end of the palisade. When Achilles saw Nestor driving his chariot from the field at great speed, he decided to send Patroclus to get a report on how things stood with the Argive cause.

Glad of the chance to act, Patroclus ran along the strand to Nestor's lodge, where he found the old man caring for the army's chief surgeon Machaon, who was bleeding profusely from an arrow wound in his thigh. 'Paris did this to him,' Nestor panted. 'I had to get him away. We're going to be in dire need of his services. Agamemnon, Diomedes and Odysseus have all taken wounds. Ajax is trying to hold the Trojans back but it can't be long before they're at the wall.' He looked up from the wound with an angry scowl. 'No doubt your friend will take satisfaction from the news.'

At that moment there was a great shout at the main gate of the stockade and a panic-stricken body of men came bursting through. Even as their officers urged them up onto the parapet to defend those coming after them, some of them made a run for the ships. Nestor looked up at Patroclus, white-faced. 'Hector must be near the ditch. We need your help, son of Menoetius. Your father is my good friend, and I know he would die of shame if he saw you standing idle while your comrades are cut down. We need the Myrmidons. Go to Achilles. Tell him what's happening. If you speak, he'll listen. Tell him that if he doesn't bring his aid to us now, he will live to regret it for ever.'

Though he shared his proud friend's sense of injury, Patroclus had stayed out of the fight only from a fierce loyalty to Achilles. He had been biting his tongue with frustration when Odysseus and Ajax came on their mission to the lodge, for like Phoenix, he believed there was now far more at stake than wounded vanity. He knew that he was not alone among the Myrmidons in wanting to forget the quarrel and get back to the fight, but Patroclus was also troubled by the knowledge that, unlike Achilles, he had taken the oath at Sparta. He was sworn to the aid of Menelaus as Achilles was not, and the quarrel with Agamemnon had opened a deep divide in his loyalties.

That divide had suddenly become too wide for him to bridge. He nodded to Nestor now, gave him his word that he would do all he could to persuade Achilles to order his men back into the battle, and sprinted back down the strand.

Not long after he had left, Agamemnon, Odysseus and Diomedes staggered across to Nestor's lodge to find out what was happening beyond the wall. All three of them were in pain from the wounds they carried, and when Agamemnon learned how far the situation had deteriorated, his nerve failed him once again. For a stunned moment, the others listened in silence as he shouted that the gods were against them and they must do what they could to avoid destruction. 'We should at least get the first line of ships out to sea. They can stand off the coast until we see how things are going.'

Odysseus said. 'If the men see you taking to the ships they'll panic and the Trojans will be all over them.'

Diomedes nodded his agreement. 'I haven't fought here for ten years merely to forsake my friends at the end.'

'Nor I,' said Nestor.

Agamemnon turned away, clutching his wounded arm and staring at the ships.

For a vivid moment earlier that day, he thought he had broken through. He could see his glory in front of him like a bright torch urging him on. Proud men had fallen before him. He had seen their chariots smashed, heard their horses scream, watched them die in agonies of disbelief. And then, out of nowhere, that spear thrust had sapped his strength and once again he was confronted by ruin. It seemed that everywhere he turned he must be blocked and opposed – if not by the enemy, then by his own fractious captains, and if not by them, then by the capricious gods themselves. He might have stood on the strand bellowing like a wounded bull had he not been conscious of the three men staring at him.

'Those ships are full of booty,' he said. 'At least if we get them away we can fight again.' But seeing only contempt around him, he looked away. 'If anyone has a better plan, I will be pleased to hear it.'

'There is only one honourable course,' Diomedes answered, 'to fight and keep on fighting, as Menelaus and Ajax are fighting. Wounded as we are we can't do much ourselves, but we can at least urge on our friends with our presence at the wall. And if it's the will of the gods that the Argives are defeated, then we can stand and die with them between the Trojans and the sea.'

Even as they were talking, the great double-gateway through the palisade was being closed against Hector's advance. Many retreating Argives were left trapped outside the gates, out-numbered and desperate, and they were swiftly cut down. The Trojans began battering at the gates and though the timbers splin-tered and groaned, the bar behind them held. In an inspiration of fury, Hector lifted a huge boulder and hurled it at the gate. One of the hinges broke and the gate at that side sagged far enough for the attackers to get a purchase on it. Minutes later the gate was down. With a huge shout of triumph, Hector stepped through and when the Trojan warriors followed him the Argives fell back like men in fear of an oncoming flood. Moments later they turned and ran for the ships.

A detachment of Locrian archers had been posted by the ships as a last line of defence. They raised their bows now and released a volley of arrows that brought the advancing Trojans to a stag-gering halt. But Hector had gone unscathed. He turned to urge his troops on, shouting that they would break through the wall of men confronting them just as they had broken through the wall of wood. Heartened by his cry, the Trojans charged again. At different points along the buckling Argive line, Idomeneus, Menelaus and Ajax rallied the ranks to meet them, and the ground between the palisade and the ships shook under the convulsive impact of thousands of men.

Achilles had been watching the progress of the battle from the stern of his ship. His heart was agitated by the din and he was aware of his Myrmidons glancing towards him as they chafed against their involuntary idleness. From somewhere far down the strand he heard a cry of dismay rise from the Trojan lines – one of their heroes must be down in the fight, but among that confused mass of men hacking at each other hand-to-hand before the ships, it was impossible to make out who it was. Then he saw Patroclus hurrying back towards him along the strand, his tunic stained with blood. It took a little time for Patroclus to catch his breath and when he looked up to where Achilles gazed down at him from the high side of the ship, his eyes were running with tears.

'Our friends are falling,' he gasped. 'Diomedes, Odysseus and Agamemnon are all wounded. I've just bound up a gash that an arrow opened in the leg of my friend Eurypylus. He asked me to do it so that he could get back to the fight.'

Achilles looked away along the strand towards the battle where the Trojans had recovered from whatever loss had briefly shocked them and were now attacking the beached ships as though each one was a citadel. 'Eurypylus was always brave,' he said without emotion.

'He made me ashamed,' Patroclus shouted up at him. 'In the name of the gods, Achilles, we are needed out there. If we don't send them help the Argives will be pushed into the sea. It is happening now – even as we stand here.'

When Achilles merely nodded impassively, Patroclus lost all patience with him. 'You're my friend,' he cried, 'and I suffered for you when your pride was injured. Since then I've stood beside you in your stubborn anger as I've stood beside you in battle many times. But I won't dishonour myself for you.'

Still Achilles said nothing.

'What's happened to you?' Patroclus bitterly demanded. 'Is it just hurt pride that's keeping you from the battle or have you lost your nerve?'

Achilles eyes widened. His nostrils flared. 'You know why I withhold myself from this battle, and that I have just cause.'

'Just cause, yes,' Patroclus retorted, 'and may you take much satisfaction from it when all your friends are dead, and people are saying, "There goes Achilles, son of Peleus, who might have been a great hero but wouldn't fight for his comrades at Troy, and because of that the war was lost and many good men died – though he claims he had just cause!"'

Achilles turned his face angrily away only to see Phoenix and the whole company of his Myrmidons staring up at him in silent reproach.

In that moment a despairing moan was carried along the strand by the wind beating off the sea. All of them shifted their eyes that way and saw the first of the ships catch fire. The flames gusted and flickered against the grey afternoon sky before the blaze took hold and the air around the high prow blackened with smoke. They could hear men screaming. They caught the smell of burning pitch.

'It has begun,' said Patroclus. His eyes flashed at his friend. 'I'm going to join the fight, and I believe that your Myrmidons will come with me. Lead us, Achilles.'

Achilles stared down into the stern entreaty of his eyes. For an anguished moment, he was recalling the day when they had first met as boys on the mountain in Thessaly – how they had quarrelled over something that neither could now remember, and beaten each other with bare fists till their noses bled and their limbs were bruised. Never since that day had they quarrelled again. If need be, they would have stood together against the world. Yet the world was forcing its way between them now.

Urgently Patroclus beseeched him again. 'Lead us.'

Achilles swallowed and shook his head. 'I have sworn that I will not fight for Agamemnon.' He heard the muttering of the Myrmidons about him. 'But whatever else men say, let it not be said that I stood between a friend and his honour. Go to the fight, Patroclus. Take as many of my men as will go with you, and may the gods be with you all.' He would have turned away then, but his friend had not yet done with him.

'It's you that the Trojans fear,' Patroclus shouted up at him. 'If you won't come with us, at least lend me your armour so that when I lead the Myrmidons into battle, Hector and his brothers will think that Achilles has returned to the field.'

Achilles smiled wanly down at him. He was thinking that if he could have his wish it would be that Agamemnon and the rest of that Argive rabble had taken to their ships, and only he and Patroclus and the Myrmidons were left to take the city. That would have been a day for poets to sing of till the end of time. But he drew in his breath and raised his voice so that all could hear him. 'Take my armour. Take my chariot and my horses. Take my men into the battle with you and do for both of us what I wish I was free to do with you. Drive the Trojans back beyond the wall, and when it is done, come back to me unharmed.' Then he turned to the Myrmidons. 'As for the rest of you, go out and fight as though you fought for me, and give my friend a great victory today.'

Afterwards, at the end of that terrible day, men spoke in hushed voices of the deeds that had been done. They told how the hearts of the Argives fighting by the burning ship had lifted at the shout of the Myrmidons coming to their aid. They told how Patroclus had launched his assault at the Paeonian spearmen, killing their king, and shaking the hearts of his followers with the fear that it was Achilles himself who had returned to the fray. They told how, at the shout of that dreaded name, the Paeonians fell back, pushing others with them, so that their recoil began a confused retreat that quickly became a rout as Menelaus, Ajax and Idomeneus took advantage of the shock to push their own troops forward.

Having come within yards of burning the whole fleet, the Trojans were now scrambling to get back out of the killing-field through the gate that they had forced. But they had already been fighting for the best part of that long day, and their weary arms and legs were no match for the fresh strength of the Myrmidons bearing down on them. Within minutes the trench beyond the stockade became a writhing pit of screaming men, smashed chariots and wounded horses.

With the charioteer Automedon at his side, urging on the mighty horses of Achilles, Patroclus led the charge beyond the wall, slaughtering everyone who came within his reach. As one Trojan charioteer strove to turn out of his path, Patroclus speared him through the side of the jaw, smashing bone and teeth, and then, using the spear as a lever, he swung the man up over the chariot rail to drop him in the dirt like an angler gaffing a fish. The terrible sight spread terror among the men around him. In the confusion only Sarpedon of the Lycians found the courage to confront the Argive champion. He hurled a spear which flew wide of Patroclus but struck his trace-horse in the neck and as the animal stumbled, its comrades reared, snorting and screaming, hooves flashing at the air. Automedon slashed through the outrigger's traces till it fell away, and then struggled to regain control while Patroclus balanced himself and hurled his long spear. It burst through Sarpedon's rib-cage. And not even Hector could now stop the Trojans in their frantic scramble for the safety of the city walls.

When he was again capable of thought, and had listened to the hushed account of how his friend came to die, Achilles thought he knew exactly what must have happened in those moments. He had led too many such charges himself not to know that when a man sees a confused mass of warriors fleeing before him, his head swirls and blazes with the intoxication of his battle-ardour. At such a time, though he may be only minutes away from death, a man can begin to feel immortal. He can believe, as Patroclus must have come to believe, that if his men are with him, all things are possible, and that precisely because he believes, his men will follow. And so, forgetful of Achilles' instructions that he should return once the Trojans were pushed back beyond the wall, Patroclus advanced against Troy as if the city might be taken single-handed.

He leapt out of his chariot near an old fig tree at the place where the walls of the city were known to be weakest. Three times, with the Trojans hurling missiles down at him and calling on Apollo for aid and protection, he tried to climb the wall and three times he was thrust back down. He was recovering from his third fall on the flat ground below the ridge when Hector sallied out through the Scaean Gate leading a counter-attack, and came careering towards him.

Looking up, Patroclus saw the horses bearing down on him through the dwindling light. Instinctively, he picked up a stone and hurled it at Hector's driver with such accuracy that it smashed into his head and sent him toppling backwards from the chariot. As the horses swept on past, Hector leapt from the chariot and the two heroes were joined in fierce hand-to-hand combat for a time until a surge in the press of men fighting around them pushed them apart.

Moments later, Menelaus glanced up from the man he had just killed and saw Patroclus a few yards away. Through the stones and arrows falling round them, he saw him lurch forward with his arms flying up as though he had been struck in the back. Yet no one was standing close by, so men would say later that Patroclus must have been pushed by Apollo. The high-crested helmet of Achilles fell from his head to roll away beneath the hoofs of a panic-stricken horse. Patroclus seemed stunned and winded by the blow. As he stood shaking his dazed head, a Dardanian foot-soldier came up behind him and thrust a spear between his shoulder blades. With a sickening wrench, the man pulled out his spear but was knocked aside before he could strike again.

Menelaus saw his wounded friend fall slowly to the ground. As Patroclus turned, gasping, trying to push himself back up, his glazed eyes must have focussed briefly on the looming figure of Hector. He collapsed back beneath him and, for a few seconds, it was as if all the din of battle stopped to witness the moment in which Hector raised his spear and thrust it down into the belly of the fallen man.

Almost an hour later, Achilles was standing in the failing light, gazing out across the dark stretch of the bay towards Tenedos when he heard someone running down the strand towards him. All through the late afternoon, his chest had been heavy with trepidation. His fears had darkened with the day, and now, when he looked into the mask of grief and foreboding which was the face of Nestor's son Antilochus, he knew at once what he was about to be told.

The ground felt unstable under his feet. His breath stuck fast in his throat. From a long distance, as though the sound was distorted by the wind, he heard Antilochus speaking. Patroclus was dead. A spear-thrust in the back. Then another, from Hector, through the stomach. Antilochus was sobbing as he spoke. Patroclus was dead. The armour was being stripped from his limbs when Ajax and Menelaus had come up to make a stand over the body. They were determined not to yield an inch of ground and the fight had still been unresolved when Antilochus was told to run from the field and bring the news to Achilles. Patroclus was dead.

The wind gusted under a turbid sky. Somewhere the sea was chanting out its grievances.

Achilles' legs sagged under him. He was on his knees, staring down at the dark sand. Forearms crossed, fists clenched at his shoulders, he was rocking his body as though to soothe some wounded thing he clutched to his chest. Then his hands opened. He reached down, grabbed at sand to fill them, and poured it, again and again, in a thick, choking cloud over his hair and neck.

He could hear Antilochus sobbing. And then word spread among the captive women who had lived with Patroclus and learned to love him, and one of them began to wail. Soon the gloom was hideous with their keening. For a time only Achilles was silent. Then the breath shuddered out of him, struggling to free a sound that was locked inside his throat. When at last the cry came, it began as a primitive, creaking moan that widened to a howl and became a bellow of anguish. For Achilles, son of Peleus, sacker of cities, slayer of men, had learned at last the price of honour.

The Gods at War

The body of Patroclus might never have been recovered if Achilles had not found the will to convert his grief into a savage ritual of violence. Hearing the din of battle come closer through the dusk, he climbed one of the wooden towers in the palisade and looked down on the toiling mass of armoured men. Everywhere across the plain the Argives were in retreat, pushed back towards their ships once again by a Trojan army that had drawn new strength from the killing of Patroclus. Where the clash was fiercest, he could just make out the figures of Menelaus and Ajax desperately refusing to give ground, and he knew that they must be fighting to protect the dead body of his friend.

From a place far beyond the reach of reason, Achilles fetched so loud a shout that it rose above the noise of combat and echoed out across the lines of fighting men. The shout was a single protracted word – 'Hector!' – and when he repeated it, louder and more urgently, the men struggling above the body of Patroclus looked up to see whence this great shout had come.

What they saw was a dark figure at the high point of the parapet with the last rays of dying sunlight shining through his hair.

Immediately the name of Achilles ran in an awe-stricken murmur along both lines. As though it were some great engine seizing up, the battle stopped in its tracks. Again the shout of Achilles boomed out through the reddening dusk like the voice of a god. It filled the Argives with fresh heart and the Trojans with dread. Again the battle turned. Hector was forced to give ground, and in the thickening gloom, Menelaus and Ajax were able to carry the body of Patroclus from the field.

Hector had already stripped the body-armour of Achilles from that poor corpse. Now they took the torn and bloody tunic from him and washed the dirt and blood from his body. Then they anointed him with olive oil and stopped up the gashes of his wounds with unguents and laid him out on a bier covered with a soft sheet and a white mantle. Achilles and his Myrmidons gathered about the body, and all night long men passed before it, weeping with grief.

Menelaus and Ajax came to Achilles with their stories of how bravely his friend had led the host against the foe, and how they had held the ground above the body so that Hector should not have it. Achilles listened to them unspeaking and, already in a place that none of them could reach, he remained silent later when Odysseus came to him, seeking to give what comfort he could.

Throughout the night he looked down on the body of his friend, recalling the countless times they had fought side by side, covering each other with shield and sword, delighting in their triumph as the enemy ran before them, and then washing and binding each other's wounds when the fighting was done. There had been a time once when Achilles was laid low by fever, thrashing about for days in a delirium of dreams, only to wake at last and see the face of his friend looking down on him, haggard with anxiety, and then softening suddenly into a smile of relief. And there had been the doldrum days when for one reason or other Agamemnon lost the will to fight, and Achilles and Patroclus had vented their impatient scorn together, or withdrawn with the women who loved them, to sing and dance and make love as though, out of a prophetic certainty that neither of them would live for long, they must cram each hour with passionate intensity.

The memories only intensified his grief and the grief intensified his rage. So as he sat beside his friend's body throughout that night, Achilles forged himself into an instrument with a single purpose. As a boy at Cheiron's school, many destinies might have been possible for him. His singing voice was among the most beautiful that had ever echoed around the gorge and he might have grown up to become a bard, singing of the deeds of other men. Under Cheiron's tutelage, he had shown a gift for healing and acquired a wide knowledge of the medicinal power of herbs, so he might have spent his life tending wounds rather than giving them, saving life rather than taking it. He was a fine hunter and dancer too and if Odysseus had not brought him to this banquet of violence which was the war at Troy, he might have passed a tranquil life on Skyros in the arms of his first love Deidameia, watching their son Pyrrhus grow to manhood.

For Achilles also had a huge talent for love. He had loved both his parents but life had torn his heart apart between them. He had loved his time on Skyros with his wife and infant son but life had stolen him away from them. He had loved Briseis, the captive of his spear, but she too had been taken from him. Above all, he had loved Patroclus, and now Patroclus too was gone. So there was, in the whole desolate landscape of his heart, no longer any place for love. He would become, utterly and completely, what the world had always most wanted him to be. And then he would be done with it.

During the course of that night the rain began to fall. It carried on falling into the day, heavy and wind-driven.

Not having slept at all, Achilles rose from the chair where he sat and took out from the coffer where it was stored, the richly worked suit of armour which had been his mother's last gift to him. A craftsman skilled in the service of Hephaistos had fashioned the corselet and greaves in bronze and tin, and worked them with gold and silver until they seemed forged from light. The helmet fitted closely about his temples, the cheek-pieces were intricately blazoned, and it was ridged with a golden crest. And the shield that Thetis had given him was a masterwork of the armourer's art, which portrayed within its glittering broad circle, images of the whole pattern of life that his mother had once wished for him. For between the rim which depicted the River Ocean surrounding the world, and the central boss where shone the sun, moon and stars, Achilles could contemplate a vision of the human realm in which war was only one activity among many others, and where the larger part was given over to the peaceful arts of ploughing and reaping, of tending flocks and cattle, of harvesting the vintage, of music and dance.

The armour had been intended for ceremonial purposes, not for fighting use, and many times Achilles had imagined himself wearing it as he entered Troy in triumph. But Patroclus had taken the less ornate armour that he wore for battle out onto the plain with him, and Hector had stripped it from his bleeding body, so now his mother's gift must be put to grimmer work.

Achilles was arrayed in that armour when he stepped out of his lodge and crossed the strand to where Agamemnon and his warlords sat in council under an awning raised against the rain. All of them had been desolated by the death of Patroclus and by the failure of his tremendous effort to crush the Trojans against the city walls. Some of them were still recovering from their wounds and few had slept. Now, in this unremitting rain, none of them had much heart to return to the field. So they looked up at the approaching figure of Achilles with both awe and trepidation in their eyes. Agamemnon, who was still in pain from the spear-thrust in his arm, could scarcely look at him at all.

'Son of Atreus,' Achilles began, 'it seems to me that no one has profited from our quarrel but Hector and his Trojans, and it's time we brought it to an end. Summon the host to arms once more and let me find out whether any of the enemy dare stand against my spear.'

The awning flapped in the wind, spilling the rainwater that had gathered there. The air felt damp against their faces and, beyond the ships, the morning was no more than a rainy grey blur of sky and sea. Somewhere a horse whinnied and they could hear the noise of hammers against metal where the smiths and carpenters were repairing the broken axles and linch-pins of the chariots.

Agamemnon rose slowly to his feet. His arm was still strapped in a sling, and he glanced only briefly at Achilles before speaking, but his voice was loud enough for all to hear. 'I know that some among you have blamed me for this quarrel, but I think that on the day when I stripped Achilles of his prize, Zeus and Fate and blind Fury must have darkened my mind. And when such gods decide to act what can a mortal man do to prevent them? But I now understand that my judgement was blinded by the gods and am willing to make amends.' He turned briefly towards Achilles, though his gaze remained slightly askance. 'You shall have everything that was promised when Lord Odysseus came to your lodge. My servants will bring it from the ships immediately and lay it before you.'

He was about to turn and give the order when Achilles said, 'That can wait a while. We have more urgent matters on our hands. The Trojans are making ready to fight even as we stand here talking. We should go out to meet them.'

Agamemnon groaned and sagged back on to his seat. Grey-faced, he looked up at Odysseus who stood beside him, carrying his weight on a spear-shaft to relieve the pressure on his wound.

'It's good to have you back among us, Achilles,' Odysseus said, 'but the men are still weary from yesterday's battle and they haven't eaten yet. There'll be time enough to fight. So why don't you let Lord Agamemnon have his gifts brought before you and we can celebrate your reconciliation with a feast?'

Stiffly Achilles said, 'I cannot think of eating while my friend lies dead and the bodies of our comrades are still out there on the plain. Let the men fight first and eat later. That is my way, and they will follow me.'

But when his urgings failed to move the other leaders, Achilles retired to his lodge while the others feasted on the boar that Agamemnon offered to Zeus. The morning was far advanced before the horses were yoked to the chariots, and Achilles at last raised his battle-cry and led the Argive host in the charge across the plain.

There had been times during the course of the war when the balance of power between the two forces seemed so poised that the bards watching the battle claimed that Zeus had forbidden the gods to lend their weight to either side. On that day, however, the violence unleashed itself across the battlefield with such savagery that it was clear the gods themselves must have come to war. They were present in the loud rolling of the thunderclouds. They were present in the driving rain with which both men and horses contended. They were present in the cries with which men urged each other to greater effort, and in the prayers they stammered out when they caught sight of death approaching in the eyes across from them.

But Achilles gave no thought to the gods. He was far beyond thought, in the pure realm of unreflecting action where his only concern was with the work of slaughter as he fought his way through the Trojan ranks in search of Hector. Twenty men fell to his spear in the first onslaught, the last of them, clasping him by the knees, trying to offer a fortune in ransom even as Achilles lifted his spear and smashed it in the man's face. At one point in the fight he was confronted by Aeneas who stood up against him as few men had dared to do and cast his spear. It struck the great shield but failed to penetrate it, and Aeneas was about to join the number of those whom Achilles had killed when a surge in the line pushed him away. Achilles turned and saw a young Trojan warrior, barely out of boyhood, staring at him through the rain.

It was King Priam's youngest son, Polydorus, a bastard half-brother to Hector, who had come into the field against his father's wishes. Turning swiftly on his heel, the youth began to run, but Achilles' spear was swifter. It caught him in the small of the back and sent him headlong in the mud.

From his own position twenty yards away, Hector saw the boy die. Throwing aside all caution, he pushed his way through the throng till he confronted Achilles. In the same moment, a volley of thunder rolled about the sky and the rain thickened, driving down with torrential force. Hector hurled his spear but it flew wide. And then neither warrior could see the other so fierce and dense was the storm against their faces.

Achilles raised his voice in a terrifying shout, urging his Myrmidons to drive the Trojans back to the city. They responded at once with a push of their spears and saw the enemy fall back before them, making for the ford in the Scamander by which they could cross the river and get back to Troy. But the ford was narrow and many men were trying to cross it all at once, and such was their terror of Achilles that men began to jump into the deeper waters of the swollen river where they were swept away amid a wreckage of chariots and swimming horses.

When he saw what was happening, Achilles ordered the Myrmidons to outflank the fleeing enemy, and they moved quickly enough to trap a large body of men in an ox-bow bend of the river. They were mostly Carians – warriors who went into battle jingling with gold ornaments like girls – and they had no choice now but to trust their jewelled limbs to the deep, muscular currents of the river or face the swords of the Myrmidons.

Achilles led the assault against them. The world had wanted him to be a killer and he was going about his work swiftly and cleanly, without thought or feeling and with a butcher's practised skill. Blood splashed all around him. His arms and legs and face were streaked with it. Things that had once been men became soft bags of air and blood and excrement that burst before him and expired. The noises of their dying blurred with the racing of the river through his mind. He was deep inside a trance of killing, slashing and thrusting and pulling out his blade with no more hatred or disgust than if he had become his own golden suit of armour hacking his way through the ranks of death towards immortality.

As he cut his way through to the river bank a warrior struggled up out of the mud at his feet. Achilles recognized the face of Priam's son Lycaon who had escaped his sword once before on the battlefield. This time there would be no escape. When he raised his sword, Lycaon grovelled beneath him begging to be spared. 'None of us is spared,' Achilles answered. 'Patroclus wasn't spared. Nor will I be spared when my time comes. This world is turned into a killing-field. So be brave, friend, and take this brotherly touch from one mortal to another.' As Lycaon stared up at him, he brought his blade down through the Trojan's neck into the collarbone. Then he kicked the body back into the river and watched the brown current carry it away.

So the slaughter went on. He might have been wearing a mantle of invincibility, so easily did he pass among the spears and swords without taking a wound. Yet the dead and dying lay piled around him, and soon the only men left to kill were struggling to save themselves from drowning far out among the river's rocks. As though each life was an obstacle to be removed before he could come through to Hector, Achilles plunged into the river after them and was surprised how fierce the current's grip about his thighs. But he strode on through the bloodied water and had already killed three more men before he sensed that the accelerating flow of the Scamander might sweep him off his feet.

Several miles away, high among the chasms of the Idaean Mountains, a dam formed by trees that had fallen in the storm had given way under the pressure building behind it. That water was flashing down the mountain now and racing between the banks with such strenuous force that it drove boulders and drowned animals and smashed boughs along with it.

Hearing the river roar, Achilles glanced upstream and saw a

turbulent white wall of water hurtling towards him. He turned and was striding to get back to the bank when his wrist was gripped by a hand that reached up from below the surface. As he struggled to break free, he could make out the man's bearded features staring up at him. The arm which had grabbed him was sinewy and muscular, and holding on so tightly that its white fingers might have locked there and seized. Then the flood crashed into both of them, the drowning man was swept away, and the armoured body of Achilles was dragged under into a world of vigorous brown shadows, each of which seemed possessed by the desire to hold him down till his lungs had consumed the last available gasp of daylight air.

Then, for a time he was with his mother in the watery realm of the Nereids, breathing water, thinking water, dreaming water, as the river sought to swallow him by being swallowed. And when Thetis asked him why he was weeping so, he told her how the death of Patroclus had made futile his own quest for glory, and that the death of his friend could be redeemed only by the death of Hector. 'But once Hector is dead,' his mother was saying, 'you too must die,' and Achilles was answering that nothing could come closer to his wishes when he broke through to a harsh dazzle of consciousness again, and was coughing up brown river water. He looked up and saw Phoenix gazing anxiously down at him. Instantly two thoughts blazed across his mind: he was still alive; and so was Hector.

From the walls of Troy, King Priam had seen his army routed. He had seen how many of his warriors fell before the first onslaught of Achilles and the Myrmidons. He had seen how the whole battalion of Carians was trapped and slaughtered in the ox-bow bend of the Scamander, and his old heart was shaken by the sight of the brown torrents of flood-water sweeping men away among a violent trash of trees and stones and broken chariots. He had given the order that the gates be opened so that those who escaped from the fury of Achilles could flee within the safety of the walls, and they had crowded in like sheep driven to a pen, not stopping to care for those carrying wounds. But when Hector remained outside the gate, ushering the stragglers in, Priam guessed that the noblest of his sons must be debating whether he too should withdraw from the field, or stay to confront the man who had struck such terror into the hearts of the Trojan host.

There had been many times over the years when Priam had woken in the night wondering whether he had been out of his mind to waste the treasure of his kingdom and risk the lives of his sons in this brutal war. But now, for the first time, he was contemplating the possibility of utter defeat. And with Achilles back in the field, only Hector could rally the Trojan forces to their city's defence. His life must not be thrown away.

Priam turned to Deiphobus, who stood at his side bleeding from a gash in his arm, and ordered him to bring the Queen to the wall. Then he looked back down over the crenellated parapet to where Hector stood in his chariot at the foot of the ramp that led up to the Scaean Gate. The storm had blown over at last, though the birds flying above the watchtower were still buffeted by the wind. Further out across the plain, by the flooded banks of the Scamander, kites and vultures swooped among the dead. Elsewhere the Argive army were taking advantage of this lull in the fighting to regroup, dress their wounds and carry the injured away. Finding it incomprehensible that a day which had begun with such elated hope should have shifted so swiftly to disaster, Priam called down for Hector to come back inside the walls.

'The day is not yet done,' Hector answered. 'They must come against us soon.'

'I know it,' Priam answered, 'but I can afford to lose no more sons – least of all yourself on whom all our hopes depend.'

Without answering him, Hector looked back across the plain. He tilted his chin as though sniffing at the wind that ruffled his helmet's tall plume, and though outwardly he seemed poised, his thoughts were in turmoil. There had been a critical moment earlier that day, when his line was shaken by the onslaught of Achilles, and his captains had counselled him to lead the army in an orderly retreat back across the plain so that they could take shelter behind the city walls and give thought to the changed situation. But Hector's blood had been on fire after the successes of the previous day. He had decided to stand and fight the Myrmidons, and the ruinous consequences of that decision were evident to all.

His proud spirit balked now at the thought of skulking back behind the walls to meet the recriminations of those who had paid the cost of his folly in lost husbands, brothers, sons and friends. Better to mount a stand here at the Scaean Gate, making a defiant show of Achilles' own suit of armour, in the certain knowledge that the son of Peleus was still out there and must soon come looking to avenge his friend Patroclus.

Above his head, he could hear his father calling to him still, but Hector did not turn. One of his pair of greys snorted and its harness jingled. He saw how blue reaches of sky had begun to appear and the light was glancing across the plain with the freshly rinsed glare that often follows a storm. Over by the mountains, Iris, the goddess of the rainbow, shimmered her veil among rags of cloud. Hector wondered if his little son Astyanax had seen her. How good it was, he thought, simply to be alive.

Then he heard the anguished voice of his mother the Queen calling down to him, begging him to come back inside the wall. 'Think of your wife and your son,' she was crying. 'And must I who gave you life watch it taken away by that fiend Achilles? Come inside, I beg you. Come back inside and let us close the gate.'

For a moment Hector dithered, thinking of his wife working at her loom to steady her nerves, and longing again for the peace they had once known together. Surely the Argives were as weary with blood as the Trojans were? Both sides had taken terrible losses, yet Troy still stood impregnable on its windy ridge and could not be starved into submission. Who could possibly want more long years of bloody stalemate? So if he stripped himself of this armour and went to meet Achilles unarmed, offering to return Helen to Menelaus along with half the treasure of Troy, might the offer not be accepted now? Wouldn't any man in his right mind gladly grab at such a settlement and leave in peace?

But Achilles was no longer in his right mind, and the Argives would not leave, not with the son of Peleus back at their head, insatiable for slaughter. And Achilles would desist from fighting only when either he or Hector was dead. These were the brutal facts of the case, and when Hector glanced up out of his brief trance of hope, he saw a stir among the Argive lines, and the chariot of Achilles advancing towards him across the plain.

He heard an anxious moan rise from the walls behind him as the Myrmidons moved in behind their lord.

'Hector,' Deiphobus called down, 'we must close the gate.'

Hector nodded. His horses stirred fretfully at their yoke-pole. He heard another urgent voice shout that he should come inside – the voice of Paris with whom all this bitter quarrel had begun – and still he did not turn. Then there was a loud commotion at his back, a shouting of orders, a voice countermanding them from the parapet, and a brief time of argument. But with a creaking of timber against its huge bronze hinges, the great Scaean Gate began to close.

Now he was alone between the city and the plain, and Achilles was advancing alone to meet him.

Hector was thinking how strange it was that a man's fate should be written from the hour of his birth and yet no man could know what his fate might be until the deathless gods unfolded it before him. As for himself, he had revered the gods, honoured his parents, loved his wife and son, served his city and fought its enemies with skill and courage. And yet all of that might be obliterated in the coming minutes.

He saw Achilles brandishing his spear. And then a shaft of sunlight shone through the drenched air of the plain, dazzling off Achilles' helm and shield with so fierce a lustre that the figure at the reins of the chariot careering towards him might have been more than a mortal man.

Hector's heart began to shake like an awning in the wind.

Too late he saw that he was not ready to die. Yet the gate was shut and barred behind him, and while he shouted for it to open he would be struck down like his brother Polydorus in the back. His mother was still wailing from the wall. Now he must either fight or run.

Hector whipped his horses and urged them away from the oncoming chariot, past the ancient fig tree by the gate, and out onto the wagon track at the foot of the city wall. A great jeering shout went up from the Myrmidons, but louder still he heard the clatter of Achilles' chariot wheels among the ruts and stones close behind him. He could smell the steam rising from those horses as he drove his own team past the hot springs and the ancient stone troughs where the women used to chatter over their washing in the days of peace, and then on round the steep curve of the city wall, as if these were merely games in which he and Achilles contended, and one of them might emerge laughing as winner from the chase.

Three times they circled the walls and the whole world circled round them – the dark sheen of the Hellespont, the palisaded coast of the bay where the Argives had beached their ships, the distant shadowy island of Tenedos, the banks of the Scamander still strewn with corpses, and the cloud-wrapped crags of the Idaean Mountains from where the gods gazed down. The whole landscape of Hector's birth and youth and manhood was spinning around him as the chariot jumped and lurched across uneven ground. His horses sweated and strained before him as if in flight from the terror in his heart. When they passed the Scaean Gate and approached the troughs once more, he glanced back to see Achilles gaining on him, and in that moment his right wheel struck against a stone.

Thrown from his feet, Hector clutched at the rail while the

spokes splintered, his team reared and shied, and the chariot skidded to a halt with its broken axle dragging through the dust.

Hector staggered out of the wreckage, reaching for his weapons. Blood flowed from his mouth where he had bitten his tongue at the shock. He looked up to see Achilles dismount from his chariot, holding his long spear. The sun was bright at his back. Hector wiped the blood from his mouth with the back of his hand and stood, panting, as he tightened his grip on the strap of his shield and balanced his own spear in his hand.

Achilles came to a halt a few yards away. Almost nothing of his face was visible inside the bronze hollow of his helmet – only the grey eyes that were fixed on his quarry with an implacable stare.

Hector raised his voice. 'Let there be an end to it then, son of Peleus. But swear with me that the victor will treat the body of the vanquished with respect.'

There came not the least flicker of response.

Hector was about to speak again but, with the sharpened senses of a man fearful for his life, he saw the muscles flexing in Achilles' spear-arm. Ready for the throw when it came, he crouched down so that the spear flew over his bent back and lodged in the earth with its shaft quivering from the force of the strike.

'May the gods grant me better fortune!' Hector said and moved round to get the sunlight from his eyes, balancing his spear in his grip. Achilles moved with him, waiting for the throw. When it came, the spear struck the shield with a clang of bronze on gold, but the shield had been forged from so many layers of metal and hide that though the spear-point stuck, it lacked the power to break through.

Unbalanced by the weight of the shaft, Achilles threw his shield aside. Hector reached to draw his sword. In the same moment he realized that his circling movement had brought Achilles back within reach of the spear he had thrown. Hector leapt across the ground between them, but his assault was not quick enough to prevent Achilles from grabbing for the spear-shaft. In a single deft movement Achilles twisted the spear upwards and shoved its point deep into what he knew to be the one weak place in the armour that Hector wore. Then, with a twist of his wrists, he wrenched it out again, and saw Hector sag to the ground with a runnel of bright blood bubbling from a gash in his neck.

Hector fell first to his knees, hung there a moment as though in prayer, and then slumped forward onto his chest. With a flick of his foot Achilles kicked him over onto his back to look down on the dying face. The eyes were losing focus and blood was spurting from his neck, yet Hector managed to gasp out a last plea that Achilles allow his body to be ransomed.

But the voice that came back at him was merciless.

'You would have hung the head of Patroclus from the walls of Troy if his friends hadn't fought over him, so ask no favours of me, Hector. It's my pleasure that you should die knowing that your father will never look on your face again.'

The words were lost in the rush of blood in Hector's ears, and his mind was already merging with the blood-red dusk that was closing down round him. Moments later, with no more than a hoarse sigh from the torn passage of his throat, the life passed out of him.

Achilles lifted his head and shouted at the sky.

High on the watchtower, King Priam looked down, tugging at his hair, as he watched the Myrmidons stabbing at Hector's limbs with their spears. Beside him, Hecuba was keening out her grief, and all along the wall the citizens of Troy looked on in shock as the Myrmidons stripped Hector's body of its armour.

Thrusting his men aside, Achilles picked up the purple baldric that had once belonged to Ajax, knotted it round Hector's ankles and dragged his mutilated body across the rough ground towards his chariot, where he fastened the baldric to the rail. Then he leapt into the chariot, urged his horses to a gallop and dragged the body of Hector round the walls of Troy with his head jolting among the stones and his long hair trailing through the dust.

★   ★   ★

When he returned to the Argive camp that night, Achilles untied the battered corpse from the rail of his chariot and threw it down by the bier where the body of Patroclus lay. But he felt less like a hunter returned with his kill than an awkward boy seeking to make clumsy reparation for some unrightable wrong he had done.

Achilles collapsed weeping over the body of his friend.

After a time Phoenix approached him, putting a gentle arm across his shoulder, and bidding him come to the bath that had been prepared for him, and to eat with Agamemnon and the other Argive lords. But Achilles pushed him away, and got up to sit alone by the dark shore staring at the sea.

The sea was a darkness lapping at darkness, and there was scarcely a star to be seen in the dark sky. Grief was what Achilles had become – a grief so immense that it was like a black chasm into which he had thrown Hector's body and the bodies of countless other men, yet its darkness would never be filled even if he were to exterminate the whole Trojan host. Grief was all there was, and nothing now would ever change.

The body of Patroclus was burned the next day. Each of the Myrmidons cut a lock from his hair and placed it on the body, and from his own head Achilles cut off the lock that his father Peleus had asked him to leave uncut till he came back home to Thessaly where he would offer it in grateful sacrifice to the gods. Now he placed that lock in the palm of his dead friend, and the men mourning round him knew that Achilles no longer had any intention of returning from Troy.

Then a torch was put to the immense pile of wood. The tinder caught but there was no wind that morning and the unseasoned wood was still wet from the rain. Though a few flames flickered and guttered for a time, the fire refused to take.

Achilles stared in despair at the immense holocaust he had made for Patroclus whose motionless body still hovered between the world of light and the world of shades. Again men tried to light the pyre, and once more it yielded no more than a few list-less wisps of smoke.

Weeping with frustration, Achilles asked everyone but his Myrmidons to leave. Then he sat by the pyre, praying for guidance to far-sighted Apollo. After a time he went into the lodge he had shared with Patroclus, and brought out the two-handled golden drinking cup. Filling it with wine, he turned first to the north where he poured a libation to Boreas, the god of the north wind. Then he turned to the west and poured a libation to Zephyrus. And having asked both those Thracian gods to lend the strength of their winds to the fire, he waited throughout the heat of the day for his prayer to be answered.

Towards evening, a breeze got up, blowing in across the bay towards the pyre. Again a torch was lit and put to fresh tinder, and this time the flames thrived. They licked along the oil that had been poured onto the wood until, with a hoarse suck of air, it combusted. The flesh of the sacrificed animals began to smoulder, fat sizzled and dripped. Soon the air around the pyre wobbled in the heat as the blaze twisted higher and a reddening pillar of black smoke billowed in the breeze off the sea, blowing hot sparks through the dusk across the plain to Troy.

When the fire had died and the ashes cooled, they collected the charred bones of Patroclus and sealed them in a golden urn. Achilles took the urn into his lodge and placed it where it would wait until the day when his own ashes were mixed with the remains of his friend. Then the Argives raised a revetment of stones around the site of the pyre and built a high mound of earth above it as a monument to the name of Patroclus.

Achilles declared that he would give rich prizes for the funeral games to be held in honour of his friend, but he watched only listlessly as the contenders raced before him on foot and in chariots, and wrestled and boxed together, and drew their bows and threw their spears. Nor could he find any solace now in the company of Briseis, who had been returned to him by Agamemnon, for she reminded him too painfully of the times they had spent together with Patroclus, and Achilles believed himself no longer capable of love. So he gave the girl her freedom and sent her, weeping, back to her people. By night he slept alone in the hugely empty lodge, and morning after morning, in an increasingly futile ritual of vengeance, he dragged Hector's still unburied body around the mound of Patroclus only to find that the god of his grief remained unassuaged.

There came a night when he dreamed that he saw the ghost of Patroclus gazing tenderly down at the broken corpse of Hector as if in mourning for him, and when Achilles reached out to clasp his friend in a last embrace, he found that it was Hector's broken body that he was clutching to his breast.

He woke, crying out in the night.

During the next day he decided to visit the sanctuary of Apollo at Thymbra where he might beseech the god to show mercy on the shade of Patroclus. Though he barely spoke to Laocoon, a son of Antenor who now served as priest in that temple, Achilles must have found some consolation in the tranquil silence of the place for he returned again a second time.

On his third visit he saw a young Trojan woman, perhaps fifteen years old, standing beside the priest. She wore the garb of a priestess, and as he made his offering she stared at him with an expression both of modesty and trepidation in her eyes.

When the offering was made, Laocoon spoke uncertainly in the silence of the temple. 'This is Polyxena, a servant of the god. She wishes to speak with you.'

Achilles stood uncertainly. He had come here for the solitude and wished to speak with no one but the god, and after what had been done about the banks of the Scamander and before the walls of Troy, he could not see how he could talk easily with a young woman who might be the daughter or sister of one of the many men he had killed.

Her voice was shaking as she said, 'You are Achilles, son of Peleus?'

He nodded and glanced away from the accusation of her eyes.

Seeming to draw strength from his dismay, Polyxena said, 'It was you who slew my brother Hector.'

Though the words passed through him like a spear, he stood motionless. It was she who started a little as his grey eyes flashed fiercely back at her. 'You are King Priam's daughter?' And when she nodded, he said hoarsely. 'If you have come to curse me, you should know that my life is already cursed. Nothing you could say can add to my woes.'

He was some ten or eleven years older than she was, and his name alone had terrified her heart since she had been a little girl, yet she found herself looking at a strangely unanticipated figure now. The glare of ferocity was gone from his face and much of the light gone with it. His blond hair was already greying a little here and there, and his whole presence seemed shadowed by an almost famished aura of hopelessness such as she had never encountered before. Polyxena had come to the temple trembling that day, hoping at best that she might touch this man's mind with some scruple of shame. But her dread was diminishing now. And perhaps it was the abiding presence of the god in this holy precinct, or perhaps it was some deficiency of loyalty in her own soul, but she was amazed to discover a kind of pity in its place.

'You are grieving for the friend you loved,' she said.

Again he could only nod, for the tide of that grief was building inside him again and might overwhelm him at a single word.

'As I am grieving for the brother I loved,' she dared to say.

He could not bear to look at her now. He wanted to turn away, to stride across that cool marble floor, to go out onto the plain and cover his hair with dust as he had done when he first heard that Patroclus was dead. But he could not move.

Nor could his eyes flee forever from the reach of hers.

When he looked up he found himself thinking that this must surely be King Priam's youngest daughter, that she could have been no more than an infant when this war began. How many such girls had grown up knowing only war? Then he remembered Iphigeneia, the girl who had come to Aulis thinking that he was to be her bridegroom only to find that she was marrying death. And Deidameia also came into his mind, holding their infant son at her breast, and he remembered the feast of the shepherds on Skyros when he had dressed as a girl in service to the goddess and had sensed in the ecstasy of the dance the dark, strangely familiar wonder of a woman's condition. How would it have been if he had been born a woman then? If instead of becoming a killer he had been fated like them to wait in the knowledge that some day some brash foreigner smelling of sweat and blood might burst through the door with rape on his mind?

Either way it seemed that there lay at the end of everything only the inescapable fact of grief.

Polyxena said, 'You are not as I thought to find you.'

In the stillness of the temple, he said, 'I am not as I thought to find myself.'

'Yet Divine Apollo knows who you are.' Her voice took on greater confidence. 'It is in his name that I have a thing to ask.'

'Then ask it of the god, not of me. I no longer know who I am.'

'But you know your grief. You know your loss.'

Again he had to fight to prevent both overwhelming him.

'My father also knows such grief,' she said. 'He too knows such loss. You grieve for a friend. He grieves for a son. And you are enemies, I know. But in the place of grief you and he are one and the same.'

With a lurch of the heart, he knew then what she was going to ask of him.

The thing was done in secret. Without the knowledge of his master Agamemnon, the herald Talthybius consulted with King Priam's herald Idaeus at the Thymbraean temple under the sign of Hermes, herald of the immortal gods, and the arrangements were duly made. Yet the mission might still have proved impossible if both armies had not been glad of this lull in the fighting, and if the ships of Achilles had not been drawn up on the beach far to the west of the line, where only Myrmidons were posted at the watchtowers. As it was, on a moonless night a wagon might pass unseen across the plain.

Achilles had just finished eating with his friends Phoenix and Automedon when the arrival of Idaeus was announced. 'Let the herald enter,' Achilles said, but when he looked up at the door, two men came in and Idaeus was not the first. The other was a slightly stooped figure who stood with his face lowered in the gloom and with the thick folds of his cloak covering his head. He turned to Idaeus who took the cloak from his shoulders. White hair glinted in the light of the oil-lamps, and when the stranger turned, Achilles and his friends started with amazement for they were looking into the careworn features of King Priam.

The old king stood uncertainly for a moment fingering the grizzled curls of his beard. Automedon was the first to move, but knowing that his friend was reaching for a sword, Achilles restrained him with a gesture. Priam lifted his hands so that they could see he was weaponless.

'May we speak alone?' he said and nodded for Idaeus to leave. A moment later Achilles gestured for his friends to follow, and the young warrior and the old king were left staring at one another uneasily across the dirt floor of the lodge.

Achilles said, 'This is not as I expected.' But he was thinking that the mutilated corpse of this man's son still lay at the back of the compound outside the lodge like a dog thrown on a midden.

'Nor I,' Priam answered, 'but when a god commands a mortal must obey, and I value my life as nothing since you killed my son. In any case, I wanted to be quite sure that you would keep to the agreement.'

Achilles stiffened. 'I am a man of my word. I vowed before Athena to kill your son and I killed him. I told your daughter that I would return his body and it would have been done. I am not some Trojan whose honour might fairly be questioned.'

For an instant the hatred of the old man for the young warrior who had slain his son gleamed between them like the blade of a knife. Achilles sensed that if it had been within the old man's power, Priam might have tried to kill him in that moment. And he knew too that he would have caught the frail hand holding the blade and bent it back into the old man's heart. But the moment passed and they simply stared at one another in the bewildered awareness that, whatever their own desires, the gods had larger claims on them.

King Priam sighed and shook his head. When he held up his hands in a gesture of remorse, Achilles saw that they were trembling. Then the old king crossed the floor towards him and fell to his knees like a supplicant.

'Forgive an old man his frailty,' he said. 'Think of your own father, Lord Achilles. He and I must almost be of an age. He too faces only the wretched prospect of the decline towards death. Yet he has a consolation that I lack. He has a son who will support him in his weakness.'

'You too have sons. The traitor Paris still lives. No doubt there are others.'

'But the best of them – the only one on whom I could rely – is gone.'

Achilles stood stiffly above him. 'Hector was killed in fair fight. His death is not on my conscience. The Daughters of the Night do not visit me on his account.'

Priam lowered his face. A moment later he astounded Achilles by reaching out to take his hand between both of his own and pressing it to his lips. When Achilles pulled his hand away, Priam looked up with an expression of abject desolation in his eyes. 'I have done what no man has done before me. I have kissed the hand that killed my son. Now be you merciful, son of Peleus, and give his body back to me.'

Achilles realized that he too was trembling.

'Stand up,' he said, 'I pray you.'

The thought of his own father had already made his heart heavy. Now he could scarcely breathe for the turbulence and confusion there. Helping Priam to his feet, he said, 'You were brave to risk coming here. And you have suffered greatly. Come, sit down with me. You must be weary. Eat something if you will. Let you and I talk together for a while.'

His voice had been gentle enough, and the offer was sincerely made, but the old man's pride bristled at it. 'I cannot think of that while Hector's body lies unburied. A fortune in ransom waits for you in the wagon outside. Take it, and let me leave with my son.'

Achilles stiffened again. 'Do you think you're alone in grieving? I assure you, you are not. And I doubt that my father will ever look on my body as you shortly will on that of your son. So do not insult me by thinking that I have any interest in the ransom you will pay. I will take it only to repay my followers for their sufferings in this war. But I am a man of sorrows as you are, King of Troy. As you grieve for Hector, I grieve for my friend who was killed by your son. We are alike in grief, you and I. We should treat each other with respect and courtesy.'

Chastened by a man that he had thought closer kin to a wolf than to his own noble son, King Priam stood abashed. Like a great wave striking him from behind, exhaustion overcame him. Achilles saw it in the sudden pallor of his face. He heard it in the voice that whispered, 'Forgive me. It was my grief that spoke.'

Achilles reached to pull up a chair and the old king sat down with his head in his hands. Achilles stood across from him. His eyes were closed as he spoke. 'I could never have killed Hector as I did if he hadn't been wearing my own armour. I knew its weakest place. But when I thrust the spear, it felt as if I was pushing it into myself. And if I despoiled your son's body, it was because I loathe my own that it still stands here, living and breathing, like a useless thing, when it should be ashes and dust and I should be with Patroclus and Hector among the shades. It is I who should beg forgiveness of you, King of Troy, but I am not a man who was born to beg.'

When Achilles opened his eyes he saw the silent tears that were pouring down the old man's face. A moment later – almost as though they were indeed father and son grieving together – he too began to weep.

After a time Achilles went out of the lodge and gave orders that the body of Hector should be bathed and anointed with oil and dressed in a clean tunic and wrapped in a mantle so that the old man would not have to look upon its wounds. Then he came back inside and persuaded the king to eat something with him and to rest his old bones on the bed that was prepared for him before making the journey back across the plain to Troy.

Achilles did not sleep at all that night, and he woke the king before first light so that he could pass back out of the Argive camp undetected. With his own hand he helped King Priam to climb up into the wagon that now carried the body of Hector on its bier. Idaeus climbed up beside his king and took the reins. He was about to whip the mules into motion when Achilles said, 'Tell me how long you mean to devote to the funeral.'

Priam shook his head. 'It is hard for us cooped up in the city. It will take time to gather the wood we need for Hector's pyre.'

Achilles nodded gravely. 'Tell your men that they may go to the mountains freely to fetch wood. They will not be troubled by our warriors. I promise you that the memory of your son shall be held in honour among us.'

'Then know that we Trojans will mourn him for ten days. Then we will perform his rites. By the twelfth day we will be ready to fight again.'

Already faint streaks of light were breaking in the east. Achilles said, 'You have my word that the Argives will not take to the field before that day.'

King Priam leaned forward and offered his hand. Achilles reached up to grip it firmly, and when they pulled apart, Idaeus whipped up the beasts into motion. Priam sat huddled in his cloak against the cold and did not look back, but Achilles stood for a long time watching the wagon roll slowly away into the dawn mist that was rising off the river.

Murder at the Shrine

Helen was woken from her sleep by the sound of Cassandra's wailing in the square outside the palace. In the bed beside her, Paris stirred in the depths of his opium dream, but he did not wake. Helen could smell the sleep on him. She could taste the fetor of wine and poppy on his breath. The air about her head felt thick and cloyed.

Softly, so as not to waken him, she slipped from the bed, pulled a wrap about her shoulders against the dawn chill, and crossed to the casement where she could look down onto the broad square of the citadel. Cassandra was mopping and mowing there, oddly beautiful in the dawn light, like a scrawny dancer miming some ritual of grief. A wagon had come to a halt beside her and – to her amazement – Helen saw the herald Idaeus helping King Priam to climb down, a little shakily, from the driver's bench. Only then did she take in the mantle-covered shape laid out in the back of the wagon, and know that Hector's mutilated body had come home.

Helen wanted to weep and could not do so, though her heart felt it might break open like an ill-made dam. People were appearing in the street, some of them only half-dressed. The women among them began to raise once more their desolate keening moan. Any moment now Andromache must come running from the house where she had grown thin from mourning since the day of her husband's death. And then Hecuba would be there too, with Polyxena at her side to prop her failing strength. Helen knew that their cries would rend her heart as surely as they would rend the morning sky. Troy was now the capital city of grief, and feeling herself to be all the cause of that grief, she desired nothing more than the oblivion into which Paris had increasingly withdrawn since he had watched the death of Hector.

And still he slumbered, for all the inconsolable noise outside, and she could not bear it. Helen crossed the room and pulled the rich throw off his naked body. His hands crossed quickly at his shoulders as though clutching against the cold. He snorted and shook his head, but his eyes came open only when she smacked her hand across his face as she had done once before in Sparta, long ago.

Paris jerked awake from his dream, staring wide-eyed, expecting to confront the derisive scowl of Menelaus, and saw instead the drawn face of Helen staring down her perfect nose at him.

'Your brother has come back to haunt you,' she said, and turned away.

Then he heard the keening in the street and knew what must be happening.

'It seems your father has had the courage to do what you didn't dare, Helen said as she sat down at her dressing table, staring with distaste at the face reflected back at her from the mirror's polished bronze. 'He has confronted Achilles and persuaded him to give back Hector's body.' She could hear him stirring across the room but she was speaking to the mirror now. 'Only once in all the time I've been here did Hector ever reproach me – even though my being in this city put his whole world at risk. And it seems to me now that with Hector dead, everything that was noble is quite gone from Troy.'

'And how long will it be before you are gone?' His voice came at her with more cruelty than she had ever known before. 'Do you think I'm not astonished each morning to find you still here

– that you haven't slipped away in the night to throw yourself on Menelaus's mercy?' And by now his despair was so intransigent that he added, 'You found it easy enough to betray him once. Why shouldn't you betray me too?'

Helen stared at him aghast, amazed by the hatred in his eyes and voice. The shock could hardly have been greater if he had picked her up and thrown her across the room.

Was it possible that they had begun to hate each other then? Was it possible for such an ecstasy of love to turn against itself like a famished creature gnawing its own limbs? How could they have diminished themselves to this?

And outside the women of the city keened their grief and pain.

Paris turned away from her, locking himself in silence.

She stared at the shadows along his back, and when he failed to turn, she looked into the mirror and was appalled by the frigid stranger waiting there.

For ten days the city mourned its fallen hero. On the eleventh day they raised a burial mound around the golden urn that held his ashes, and so great was the noise of lamentation that men said it stunned the birds of the air.

Throughout those days of mourning the Argives left the Trojans in peace while they mended their wounds and gathered their strength for what they now hoped would prove to be the final push against the city. Hector, the great champion of Troy, was dead, and the morale of the beleaguered Trojans at its lowest ebb. Surely the end of this misbegotten war must soon be in sight?

That anyway was how the warriors encouraged each other when they armed themselves to fight once more. But they had not reckoned with King Priam's indomitable will, for even in the dark hours of his grief he had been making dispositions. When the men had gone out during the truce to gather wood from the mountains, messengers had gone with them. They had reached

Priam's half-brother, King Tithonus at Susa in Assyria, begging him to send the aid that had long been promised. The answer arrived by carrier pigeon, and Priam was quick to let it be known that a regiment of Ethiopians was crossing Phrygia out of Armenia on its way to Troy under the command of Memnon, a black warrior who was reputed to be the most handsome man on earth.

So the struggle was resumed but with a grim weariness that left both armies in poor heart. Even Achilles was no longer seen to fight with the fervour that had once terrorized the Trojan host and some of his friends began to believe that he was looking for only one thing on the Trojan plain, which was his own death.

Only once was he seen to flash with the same murderous anger that had carried him through the killing field at the bend of the Scamander. It was directed against one man, and he a member of the Argive host. Achilles was returning across the plain at the end of a day's fighting when he saw Thersites using the point of his spear to gouge out the eyes of the Amazon Queen Penthesileia, who had been dragged from her silver chariot and slain that day. Overwhelmed with fury and disgust, he leapt down from his chariot and knocked the man violently aside with his shield. A few moments later Diomedes found Achilles sobbing beside the corpse of the maiden warrior, and rebuked him for shedding tears over the enemy. The two warlords would have come to blows if their friends hadn't pulled them apart, but the animosity did not end there. When Achilles heard that Diomedes had ordered Thersites to throw the body of the Amazon Queen into the Scamander, he crossed the plain to retrieve it with his own hands. He had just pulled the body back up the bank and was tenderly wiping the mud from her face with his cloak when Thersites shouted out that Achilles must truly be desperate if he was ready to pleasure himself with a barbarian woman's corpse.

Achilles brought the blade of his sword down into the man's skull with such force that it sent the teeth scattering from his mouth. Infuriated by the murder of his kinsman, Diomedes felt his resentment grew even more bitter when Achilles ordered his Myrmidons to bury the gallant woman with great reverence.

Two days later Memnon and his Ethiopians came up to Troy, and though they were held at bay for a time, they managed to fight their way through to the city. To the weary eyes of Agamemnon and his commanders, the high walls of Troy began to appear more impregnable than ever. Disputes among them were now frequent and rancorous, Diomedes claimed that it had been madness to allow the Trojans a time of truce rather than pushing home the advantage of Hector's death. Achilles refused to answer him but Ajax roundly defended the cousin whose ruthless courage he had come to admire with a passion since the bloody slaughter at the oxbow bend. Nestor as always strove to hold the ground between the contending parties, while Idomeneus and his Cretans grew impatient with their squabbling allies, and Odysseus wearily dreamed of home.

Achilles took to spending more time at the shrine of Apollo in Thymbra, hoping that he might meet Polyxena there again. In his desolated mind she had come to seem the one uncorrupted thing left anywhere across the corpse-strewn plain of Troy. But time after time he came there without seeing her, and with each disappointment the need became more urgent until he brought himself at last to ask the priest why the girl no longer came to the shrine.

Uneasily Laocoon glanced away. 'Her father the king believes it too dangerous for her to leave the city.'

'And if I gave my word that no harm would come to her?'

'Can the son of Peleus speak for all the Argive host?'

'I can speak for myself. My word is protection enough.'

The priest nodded. 'And if I were to speak to Polyxena, what should I say when she asks why the son of Peleus wishes to see her?'

Achilles frowned into the marble silence of the temple. 'Tell her,' he said after a time, 'it is because we remain one in the place of grief, she and I.'

Disconcerted by the unguarded innocence of this terrifying man, Laocoon nodded again. 'Come again tomorrow,' he said. 'I will talk with the king and see what can be done. Now make your offering to the god, son of Peleus.'

But there were forces at work around Achilles of which his proud heart had no knowledge. Still rankling over the murder of Thersites, Diomedes sought out Odysseus one evening and asked him whether he was not suspicious of the way that Achilles, like Palamedes before him, was spending too much time at the shrine of Thymbraean Apollo.

'Palamedes was a traitor,' Odysseus answered. 'Achilles is not.'

'How can you be so sure of that?'

'Because the mind of Palamedes was devious and subtle, while Achilles is as straight as his father's spear. Why would you think otherwise?'

'Did it never strike you as strange,' Diomedes said, 'that Achilles should have insisted on permitting the Trojans all that time to mourn Hector rather than sending in his Myrmidons to overwhelm them while they were at their weakest?'

Odysseus had indeed found it so strange that he had spoken privately to Achilles about it at the time. At first Achilles had tried to fob him off with pieties about how it behoved warriors to honour the death of a hero on whichever side he fought. But Odysseus had observed the shiftiness in his honest eyes, and pressed him further until he learned the story of how Priam had come secretly to the Argive camp. Astounded that such a thing could have happened, Odysseus had agreed to say nothing of it to the other leaders, but he was left uneasy by the knowledge that secret channels of communication existed between the Myrmidons and Troy. He was further unsettled now by the questions that Diomedes had put to him, but he was also aware of the hostility that had sprung up between the two Argive leaders.

'Are you really suggesting,' he asked drily, 'that Achilles is looking to make a separate peace with the Trojans?' And when Diomedes muttered something to the effect that Achilles showed so little enthusiasm for the fight these days that it wouldn't greatly surprise him, Odysseus said, 'Dare you suggest as much to his face? Even Ajax would tear you limb from limb if he heard you call his hero a traitor.'

'I have not gone so far,' Diomedes answered. 'I merely suggest that these frequent visits to the Thymbra give grounds for suspicion. I seem to remember that there were men who denied that Palamedes could be a traitor when you voiced the same suspicions about him.'

Now Odysseus was on uneasy ground. 'So what do you mean to do about it?' he asked.

'I thought it might be wise to keep watch on him when he next goes to the shrine. Don't you agree?'

Odysseus shrugged. 'I think it's as likely that Achilles is a traitor as that you are, my friend. But if it will put your mind at rest, by all means do so. However I think that Ajax and I should come along with you. We needn't say anything to Ajax about your suspicions – merely that we feel Achilles is taking unnecessary risks in exposing himself outside the camp this way, and that his friends should be discreetly at hand in case of need.'

When Achilles made the journey to the shrine on the following afternoon, he was followed by Diomedes, Ajax and Odysseus, though they kept at a far enough distance for him not to be aware of their presence. He entered the cool silence of the temple, paid his fee to the attendant, and then was kept waiting for longer than he would have expected.

After a time the priest Laocoon appeared. 'The person about whom you asked is here,' he said, 'but she remains in some anxiety about seeing you again.'

'She need have no fear,' Achilles answered. 'I only wish to speak with her for a while.'

The priest nodded uncertainly and withdrew again. Achilles

waited alone, wondering at the impulse that had brought him to the shrine. How could he have imagined that the young woman would ever look with kindness on her brother's killer? What had he been dreaming of? What could he possibly have to say that Polyxena would wish to hear? Flushing suddenly, he was about to get up and leave when he heard a stirring from the inner door and Polyxena was there. Wearing a pale blue gown and holding her hands clasped tightly together, she stared down at the marble floor.

Achilles flushed again. 'Thank you for coming,' he said hoarsely.

She did not look up as she said, 'I don't understand why you wished to see me.'

'To talk a little. There are things that lie heavy on my mind.'

'You mean the death of my brother?' Coldly she added, 'It was gracious of you to return his body.' And when she glanced up at him, he saw only fear and hostility in her eyes.

He said, 'But you would rather I was dead in his place.'

She did not answer him, merely turned her anxious gaze to where the bronze statue of Apollo gazed serenely down across the temple.

Achilles said, 'Hector and I were enemies. Don't you think that he would have killed me too if the gods had been with him?'

'I'm quite sure he would. But he had good cause. No one asked you to come here and attack our city.'

He said, 'My friend Menelaus was also given good cause.'

Polyxena looked up at the heat in his voice, but she merely shrugged before glancing away again. And he had no wish to wrangle with her. Quietly he said, 'It was a hard fate that brought Argos into conflict with Troy.' He paused uncertainly, then added, 'And I have been thinking also that it must have been a great love between Prince Paris and the Lady Helen that they were ready to plunge the world into war for its sweet sake.'

She glanced up at him then, surprised at the tenderness in his voice, but she said nothing.

He had to think for a time before speaking again. 'I know that you must see me only as a man of blood. How could it be otherwise? But since the death of my friend Patroclus all sense has gone from my life.' He looked up at her in a kind of entreaty. 'I've grown weary of killing, Polyxena. I've grown weary of a world which takes from me everything I love so that I might better become an instrument of hate. I no longer wish to live this way.'

Polyxena looked nervously about her, as though discomfited by this naked honesty and uncertain what might be done with it.

She brought the clenched knuckles of her hands up to her mouth. 'Then leave,' she said, 'be gone from Troy. Leave us and let us live our lives in peace.'

'If I were free,' he answered, 'I would take ship tomorrow. But I have a debt of honour to my friends.'

'And so you will stay and carry on with the killing. And the people you kill will be my friends. What am I to say to that?'

He was in such a trance of concentration on what he most deeply wished to say that it was as if she had not spoken. 'If I were free,' he said again, '. . . I would ask you to come with me.'

She stared at him wide-eyed. Was he mad that he could even think of this? How could she ever feel anything but dread for the violent man who had slain her brother and countless others?

Yet he looked utterly vulnerable before her now.

She looked up in appeal at the statue of the god – the serene, far-seeing presence that presided in silence over this strange, unconscionable meeting.

And the god spoke through her. 'It cannot be me that you want,' she said. 'I think it must be your own lost soul you are seeking.'

He frowned at that. He became aware of himself as she must see him – a pathetic figure looking for love among those who, of all people on the earth, had most reason to hate and fear him. He too looked up at the statue of Apollo and found neither sympathy nor comfort there. Achilles was alone in a foreign land, gone far beyond the place where his friends could understand him. And his own acts had left him for ever exiled from the common human bond he thought he had sensed in his meeting with King Priam, and which he had dreamed of finding again in the presence of this girl.

Achilles stared up at Polyxena and felt her flinch under his gaze. It was clear that she wanted nothing more than to be gone from his presence. Why then had she come? No matter – he would trouble her no longer. With a swift, involuntary catch of the breath, he turned on his heel and strode across the marble floor.

He had reached the door when she called out his name, just once, fiercely, as though in alarm. He stopped and was about to turn, but he had seen that there could be no point in further words between them, so he shook his head to clear it and then walked on, out through the temple door into the glare across the plain.

Achilles was at the top of the steps when the arrow pierced the back of his leg. He stumbled as though he had been kicked from behind, but did not fall at once. Only when he leaned over to look in puzzlement at the thing which had wounded him did he lose his balance, and then he was tumbling like a drunkard down the flight of marble steps.

From where they sat in the shade of the grove outside the temple, the three Argive captains thought at first that he had missed his footing, but when they leapt up to help him they saw the shaft of the arrow protruding from the lower calf of his right leg.

With a cry of 'Treachery!' Ajax ran to make a stand over the fallen body of his cousin. He arrived at the foot of the steps as two men appeared at the door of the temple above him, one of them holding a curved bow. When they saw Odysseus and Diomedes hurrying to join him with their swords already drawn, the men glanced quickly at each other and ran back inside the temple.

Ajax and Diomedes hurried up the steps in pursuit of the Trojans, shouting out for them to stand and fight. Odysseus leaned down over Achilles, who was studying the arrow with a dazed expression on his face.

'You were lucky that his aim was bad,' Odysseus said. 'His hand must have been shaking at the thought of slaying the great Achilles!'

Achilles looked up in bewilderment at his friend. 'I don't understand,' he murmured. 'What are you doing here?'

Odysseus drew the knife he wore in the scabbard at his belt. 'Ajax was worried about you coming out here alone. He was afraid that something like this might happen.' Glancing at the ground around them, he added, 'Let me find a stick for you to bite on while I cut this arrow out. Are you all right there?'

When Achilles nodded, Odysseus stood up and walked back to the grove where he broke off a twig thick enough for his friend to bite. He came back, sat down on the steps beside Achilles and cut a strip of fabric from his own tunic ready to bind the wound when the arrow was out.

'A couple of feet higher and he would have hit you in the arse,' he grinned. 'Now come on. Have a chew on this.'

He offered the stick to Achilles who gazed up at him with a sickly smile on his face, shook his head, and then reached his own hand down to the shaft and wrenched it from his leg. The barbs tore the flesh into a vivid red gash as the head came out followed by a swift spurting of blood. Odysseus swore, reaching down to staunch the brilliant flow of blood with the piece of cloth.

'You and your damned pride,' he said. But when he looked back up into Achilles' face, he saw that there was something awry about his eyes, and that the fixed smile on his face was deteriorating into a squint.

'Poison,' Achilles whispered. 'The arrow is poisoned.'

Quietly, like a man sharing a private joke with the universe, he began to laugh.

Odysseus stared down at the wound in horror. Quickly, with

the point of his knife, he cut further into the flesh of the calf to increase the flow of blood, hoping that to draw the toxin out with it. Achilles gasped at the sudden flash of pain, and then shook his head again, smiled blearily at Odysseus, and let his body fall back against the flight of steps. He lay there with one arm lax at his side and the other propped upwards from the elbow, watching the sky swim about his head. He was muttering something to himself, and when Odysseus leaned closer he could just make out the words, 'Far-shooting Apollo has done for me too.'

'You're not done for,' Odysseus said with tears starting in his eyes. 'We'll get you back to Machaon. He'll soon put you to rights.'

But Achilles was mumbling over him. 'Do you remember what Apollo said when he slew the dragon Typhaon? *Now rot you right here on the soil that feeds mortal men. You at least shall live no more to bring your monstrous evil on them.*' The words ended in a wry, ironical laugh and a trickle of spittle from his lips. Then his head tilted to one side and he was looking past Odysseus as though he could see someone approaching.

Alarmed by the dilation of his eyes, Odysseus was urging him to hold on to consciousness when Ajax and Diomedes came out of the temple above them.

'The bastards got away,' Ajax called down, red-faced with fury. 'They had a chariot out at the back of the temple. There was a woman with them. It must have been some sort of trap.'

'The one with the bow was Paris,' Diomedes said, sheathing his sword. 'I think the other was Deiphobus, but I can't be sure.'

Wiping the sweat from his brow with the back of his hand, Ajax came down the steps saying, 'How is he? Did you get the arrow out?'

Odysseus blinked up at them, biting his lip. 'The tip was poisoned,' he said in a taut gasp of breath. 'I think he's dying.'

Ajax stared down at him in disbelief, and then, as he looked into Achilles' face, a grunt of anguish broke from his muscular frame. His upper lip pulled back so that his teeth were bared. He bent down to take his cousin's limp hand, but let it drop after a moment like a useless thing.

When he stood up, Ajax, son of Telamon, who had once boasted that he had no need of help from the gods, was shouting curses at the sky.

The news that Achilles had been killed brought jubilation to the streets of Troy.

After the death of Hector, the people had huddled behind their walls, wretchedly preparing for the siege. Even the arrival of Memnon and his Ethiopians had not greatly cheered them, for though their help was welcome, the African warriors had also brought another regiment of mouths to feed from the city's dwindling stores. But now that Achilles was dead, surely the heart must have been knocked out of the Argive host? It could only be a question of time before they gave up this vain struggle.

And it was Paris, the cause of all Troy's woes, who had proved to be its salvation. He had done what was needful in a desperate time, and the city was ready to hail him as a hero.

Yet as he stood in the citadel of Ilium smiling down on the cheering crowd with his father and Deiphobus beside him, Paris already knew how empty his triumph was. Helen had refused to appear beside him, and still would not come from her chamber even when the crowd summoned her by name. Antenor had shrivelled him with a glare of utter contempt, and though Priam stood beside his son before the public gaze, when he turned away into the palace, his face was grim and austere. The royal company was about to disperse, when Priam summoned Paris and Deiphobus into his withdrawing room.

'Why was I not informed of this plan to ambush Achilles?' he demanded quietly.

Deiphobus said, 'We thought you might forbid us to put our lives at risk.'

'So you chose to act without my knowledge and consent?'

'For the good of the city,' Deiphobus answered. 'Have events not justified us?'

Priam studied him with weary eyes. 'Can anything justify the profaning of Apollo's shrine? The Far-sighted One has long protected this city. How long do you think he will choose to do so if we commit murder in his sanctuary?'

'We waited till Achilles had left the temple,' Paris said. 'It was why I used the bow.'

Priam shifted his gaze to study him. 'Or was it because you dare not stand against him man to man?'

Paris recoiled into anger. 'Don't I recall that even your beloved Hector ran before Achilles? Be content that he is avenged.'

Sharply Priam drew in his breath. 'It demeans both names to hear them on your lips.' He turned away, shaking his head. 'A poisoned arrow fired from a place of concealment! Did your hand tremble so much that it spoiled your aim?'

'The arrow would have gone straight to his heart if Polyxena had not pushed at my arm.'

'I have spoken with Polyxena,' the king's voice was shaking as he spoke. 'It was she and the priest who told me the shameful facts of the case. Is there no honour left among my sons that they could use their youngest sister so?'

'What matter?' Deiphobus put in. 'Achilles is dead. That is all that counts.'

'You think so?' Priam answered. 'Is that what these long years of war have done for us? There was a time when I was proud of my sons. There was a time when I believed that right was on our side and that the gods would therefore wish us to prevail. But look what we have become. It sickened me to perform that charade of triumph before the people.'

'Would you rather Achilles had lived to burn your city?' Deiphobus snarled. 'Perhaps you would rather he had been born your son?'

Priam glanced away, 'I would rather my sons had been such a man as he was, that is all. Now get from my sight, both of you. I have grieving to do for the death of honour in the world.'

Helen was sitting by the window casement combing her long hair when Paris came in. Aethra, frail and ancient now, was working at her tapestry frame across the room.

'Why didn't you come when the people called for you?' he demanded.

Quietly she said, 'Because I had no wish to share in your disgrace.'

'The city was doing me great honour.'

'The city does not know what the women of the palace know.' With her head tilted away from him towards the light from the window, Helen resumed the combing of her hair.

Paris glowered across at the old bondswoman. 'Leave us.'

'Aethra, stay,' said Helen.

Aethra hesitated uncertainly between them.

'Evidently the hero of Troy thinks we've been deficient in respect for him,' Helen said. 'How shall we honour the man who slew Achilles, do you think?'

He saw that she had been drinking wine.

'If there's shame in what I've done for you,' he said, 'you have an equal share in it. What I did was done for your protection.'

She could deny neither her horror at what he had done nor the truth of what he had just said. They were as close in shame as they had once been in love. And still that love laid claims on her, even now as she fought against it. The conflict shadowed Helen's face, but all he saw of it was a cold stare, from which he turned away in pain. Then he was looking at the rich hangings of the room and the many beautiful objects they had collected there – things brought back from Cyprus and from Egypt, gifts that had come from friends and admirers all across the east, pieces they had commissioned together from the finest craftsmen and artists of Troy. All the memorials of a now defeated love which had once filled every moment of their lives. He had wanted only to be at liberty with her, to adore her as he adored Aphrodite. Yet somehow, almost without seeing it happen, he had lost her, and he could not see how he would ever win her back again.

'There was a time when you were proud to love me,' he said.

'There was a time when you . . .' she began. But lacking both the will and the desire to wrangle with him, she shook her head and looked away.

'Say it,' he demanded, 'say what you were going to say.'

When she looked back at him, there was neither reproach nor dismissal in her eyes, only an infinity of regret. 'If I had any hope I would say it.'

'But you have no hope?'

His voice was harsh with accusation, but his eyes were those of a man standing in a last court of appeal, still hoping to refute the evidence. Unwilling to pass sentence, Helen reclined back against the casement and closed her eyes.

Paris said, 'You think there is no hope for us.'

He saw her black hair shining in the light. And when she still declined to answer, it was as though one of them, either he or she, was drifting helplessly out to sea, far beyond the other's reach.

Paris glanced uncertainly at Aethra, who lowered her eyes to her work. And when he looked back at Helen again he saw that the light might have turned her into a marble statue of herself, as beautiful as she had ever been, but bereft of speech, and passionless, waiting for the dark to fall.

For a time Agamemnon wondered whether his army would ever recover from the death of Achilles. Day after day they mourned their dead champion and not even the ardour with which the men contended in the funeral games could ease the brutal sense of desolation. Hard-bitten veterans who had stared death between the eyes for years were unmanned by this loss. Achilles had seemed as close as a man might come to being a god — he had never been known to show fear for his life, he had taken the life of others with a god's relentless indifference, and his followers had begun to believe him immortal. It made no sense to them that he should have fallen ingloriously to an assassin's arrow on holy ground. All of the commanders – even Diomedes – were left shocked and incredulous, and the grief of Ajax in particular knew no bounds.

Unable to forgive himself that he had been lounging in the shade eating figs when only a few yards away Achilles was struck down, Ajax had carried him unassisted all the way back to the Argive camp, hurrying to find medical help. But by the time he laid his burden down, Achilles was dead, and this further failure added to the already intolerable sum of his guilt.

The grief of Ajax turned rapidly to rage. Shouting that the greatest warrior of the age had been struck down by treachery and that his shade cried out for vengeance, he went out onto the plain and began to hunt down with appalling savagery any Trojan unlucky enough to cross his path.

The war had already shattered the nerves of many men who sat about the camp weeping and trembling until someone lost patience with them and put them out of their misery, or they were smuggled aboard a returning supply vessel and shipped home. But the madness of Ajax began only as a still more fanatical commitment to the struggle, and at first it went unrecognized. Men said that he was trying to emulate Achilles, fighting as his cousin had done in the bloodbath at the Scamander. But when he came back from a raid one day wearing a necklace of severed ears, Odysseus began to fear for Ajax's mind.

On the last day of the funeral rites that were held for Achilles, the hero's ashes were mingled with those of Patroclus and the golden urn was buried under a great mound that was raised on the headland overlooking the Hellespont. The funeral games were over and nothing remained to be done except to decide who should inherit the marvellous suit of armour that had been the gift of Thetis to her son.

The decision fell to Agamemnon, and it was a hard one, for all the commanders coveted that trophy, both for its own rich sake and for the memory of the man who had worn it. Agamemnon decided that the principal contenders must be those who had been with Achilles at his death, and of those three men it seemed wisest to give the armour to the one on whom he most depended – Odysseus.

The decision was unacceptable to Ajax. Was he not the man who had tried hardest to hunt down the murderers of Achilles? Had he not carried the body back in his own arms? Had his exploits since the death not shown that he was the true successor to Achilles as the terror of the Trojans? By every right the suit of armour should be his. Were Achilles alive, he declared, Agamemnon would not dare to dishonour him by offering it to any lesser man.

But Agamemnon had made his decision and would not go back on it.

Not even his half-brother Teucer could comfort Ajax for this further loss. Shouting that there was justice neither among men nor among the gods, he withdrew from the assembly in a black frenzy of rage.

Calchas declared that Athena had inflicted him with madness for having insulted the gods once too often and advised Teucer to see that he was confined to his hut until his senses returned. But Odysseus watched Ajax walk away convinced that, like many others, he was simply unable to sustain the long strain of this war.

Whatever the case, Ajax was discovered that night, flailing about with his sword among the penned cattle and sheep that had been lifted from the Dardanian pastures. The animals were screaming and moaning around him as he cut them down, shouting curses on the names of Agamemnon and Odysseus. No one dared approach until he collapsed at last from exhaustion.

Ajax came to his senses, not on the battlefield where he had believed himself to be but under a dark sky in a grisly butcher's yard of dead sheep and oxen. Refusing all offers of help, he got to his feet and staggered away. When Teucer called after him, he shouted back that Athena had told him to wash himself clean of blood in the sea. But when he was down by the shore Ajax must have found only a blackness there that corresponded to the darkness in his mind, for he took the sword that had been Hector's gift to him, fixed it in the earth and threw himself on to the blade.

A quarrel broke out over what should be done with the body. Teucer insisted that Ajax should be shown the honour due to a great warrior. But he had died by his own hand, not on the field of battle, and Menelaus said that his body should be left where it lay for the kites and vultures. As the son of Telamon, who had always been Agamemnon's friend, Teucer brought his case before the High King. Finding himself caught between loyalty to Telamon and fear of offending the gods, Agamemnon could not make up his mind what to do for the best. Odysseus urged him to permit the funeral rites and offered to help with them himself, but Teucer proudly declined this offer. The matter was finally settled by Calchas who said that Ajax had forfeited the right to a hero's funeral pyre, but his body might be buried in a suicide's coffin rather than left to the birds of prey.

By the end of that dismal funeral Agamemnon had fallen into another fit of gloom. Once Hector had been killed, he had believed that the war was finally going his way, but after the murder of Achilles and the madness and suicide of Ajax, everything seemed to be falling apart again. To add to his anxieties, the Trojan army had been reinforced by the arrival of the Ethiopians, and the walls of the city remained as unbreachable as ever. Uncertain which way to turn, he took Odysseus's advice and asked Calchas to take the omens.

Calchas returned from his prophetic rites with the encouraging news that Paris had incurred the wrath of Apollo by his sacrilegious act. Troy could no longer rely on the support of the god but two things were necessary before the city would fall. 'Firstly, a new warrior must be brought to lead the Myrmidons.

We must send to Skyros for Pyrrhus, who is the son that Deidameia gave to Achilles.'

'The boy can scarcely be twelve years old,' Diomedes objected.

'He is the son of Achilles and the grandson of Peleus,' Phoenix answered. 'The Myrmidons will follow him.'

'Then let him be brought,' said Agamemnon. Then he looked warily back at Calchas. 'What is the other thing?'

'Troy once fell to the might of Heracles,' said the priest. 'The city will fall again when his great bow is brought to the war.'

'And where in the name of Zeus is that to be found?'

'Not far away,' Odysseus answered. 'It's on Lemnos where Philoctetes still nurses his wound.'

Remembering the sickening stink of decay that had been given off by that wound, Agamemnon frowned. 'Will he let the bow go?'

'I doubt it,' said Odysseus, 'but surely we can bear with his stench if it means the city will fall?'

As the island of Lemnos was only fifty miles west of the Trojan coast, the vessel carrying Philoctetes was the first to return. The wound in his leg still festered but Agamemnon immediately set his surgeon to cutting away the putrid flesh and his physician to treating it with poultices of healing herbs. Their reports were good. The patient would soon have the use of his leg again.

Odysseus and Menelaus came to visit Philoctetes as he lay recuperating, and after they had chatted for a time, Odysseus picked up the great bow of Heracles that stood beside the litter on which Philoctetes lay. 'We were wondering if you're still as sharp with this as you used to be.'

Philoctetes smiled. 'Give this leg another day or two to heal and I'll show you.'

'That's good,' said Menelaus. 'That's very good. You know that Paris fancies himself with the bow. We thought you might challenge him to a duel.'

'Do you think the coward dare stand against me?'

'He's the oldest son that Priam has left,' said Odysseus. 'He's the hero of Troy these days. He won't dare to refuse a public challenge.'

Paris was drinking wine alone when a herald brought the news that there was a challenger outside the walls summoning him to a duel. When he demanded to know who it was, the herald could say only that the challenger was carrying a great curved bow and a quiver of arrows, and had never been seen outside the city before.

Then Deiphobus was at the door. 'It's Philoctetes, the greatest of their archers. He has the bow of Heracles. You'll have to stand against him.'

Though they had fought side by side out on the plain of Troy, and had conspired together, after the death of Hector, to assassinate Achilles, Paris knew that this brother had never forgiven him for breaking his nose in the boxing match all those years ago. That blow had knocked Deiphobus's face awry in a way that lent a further twist to the smile with which he studied Paris now.

Paris got to his feet and was crossing the room to fetch his bow when, with a lurch of his heart, he saw that Helen had been standing just behind Deiphobus.

He had always known that his brother lusted after Helen but until recently she had kept herself distant from him, and whenever she spoke of him it was with an edge of scorn. But that had begun to change. Paris sensed a different kind of tension between them, an almost sensual animosity in which her despair mingled with his brother's desire in ways that sickened and humiliated him.

Helen stared at the floor unspeaking, waiting to see what he would do.

Paris had no wish ever to fight or kill again, but this war that he had started refused to let him go. He looked across and saw the taunt in his brother's eyes. Without saying a word to either of them, Paris turned away to look for his bow.

★   ★   ★

Less than twenty minutes later, his servants carried him back into the chamber. His left eye had been put out by an arrow that had deflected upwards off his armour. Another arrow protruded from his thigh and a third had entered below his rib-cage on the right side. The surgeons were afraid to remove it, so he lay watching his father and mother weep over him as he tried to comfort them with a weary smile.

Uncertainly Helen approached the bed. She forced herself to look down where Paris lay, half-blinded, bandaged to staunch the flow of blood, and still transfixed by a shaft so slender one could scarcely believe that it could do him harm. And she thought that she might faint.

'It seems you were right,' he whispered, smiling up at her. 'For us there was no hope.'

And there was such loss in his disfigured face that she could not bear it. Yet for a long time she sat beside the bed, holding his hand in hers, and unable to speak because she too was transfixed by anguish so complete and unendurable that all the available resources of her body were consumed by it.

And he could take no comfort in her presence, for each time he looked at her he saw only the magnitude of his loss. So after a time, as though out of consideration for her, he said, 'Leave me now. We have suffered together long enough.'

Dusk came. They lit the room with oil-lamps. Only his mother and her women were grieving now beside the bed. And it was taking so long to die that he began to feel afraid. Like a hunter lost in a dark wood, he was casting about among his memories, looking for a way through, back into the light. Then a thought came to him, and with it came a flickering of hope. Paris reached out for his mother's hand and pulled her closer. 'Aeneas,' he gasped. 'Ask Aeneas to come to me.'

More time passed. The night grew darker. At last Aeneas came and stood uneasily beside the bed. Paris gathered his strength, but his voice was scarcely more than a whisper now. 'We were friends once, you and I,' he said, 'and if that friendship failed, the fault was mine. I beg you to forgive it.'

Aeneas felt his heart flood with compassion as he said, 'A man must follow his fate. You were in the power of the goddess, as my father once was.'

Paris tried to smile again. 'And see how Aphrodite blinds us.' He shook his head. 'Who would have thought a Dardanian bull-boy could bring such trouble on the world?' Then Aeneas felt his hand firmly gripped. 'There is a thing I must ask. Do you remember the girl you saw at the healing shrine at Sminthe – when Menelaus made his offerings there?'

He saw Aeneas frown. Wincing, Paris gathered his breath to speak again.

'Her name is Oenone. She loved me once. She said that if ever I was wounded, I should send for her . . . that she had the power to heal me.'

Doubtfully Aeneas nodded.

When Paris opened his mouth to say more, he began to cough. Blood dribbled at the corner of his mouth.

Aeneas said, 'Lie still now.'

Again Paris gripped his hand. 'Will you bring her to me?'

Again Aeneas frowned. 'It was a long time ago.'

'Hers was a truer love than mine,' Paris said. 'It will have lasted. She will come. I know she will come.'

He held on throughout that night and into the next day, but for much of that time he was lost in delirium and if Helen came to his bed again he did not see her.

Aeneas returned the following evening, alone and apprehensive, and as soon as Paris looked into his friend's face he knew that his last hope had failed.

'She would not come?'

Aeneas shook his head.

'Did she send no word even?'

Knowing that he could never bring himself to pass on Oenone's bitter message, Aeneas was about to say that Oenone could not be found, but he saw that Paris would know at once that he was lying. So he stood in silence, watching the past drift across those damaged features.

After a little while, in a brief, choking gasp of blood and spittle, Paris turned his face to the wall and died.

Hours later, agonized that she had let her pride overwhelm her charity, Oenone came to Troy. The guards would not open the gate for her. When she explained why she had come, they merely shrugged and said that she had come too late.

A Horse for Athena

Twelve years old, restless with boyish vigour and big for his age – almost big enough to fill his father's armour – Pyrrhus, the son of Achilles, came to Troy. He put fresh heart into the Myrmidons who called him Neoptolemus, the new warrior. Agamemnon decided that his luck was in, the Argives took to the field once more, the two armies fought each other to a bloody standstill, and still the war dragged on.

Then the weather turned foul again, the bitter wind driving rain down across the plain, and stirring the sea to such a steep swell that the supply ships could not make it into port. Wretched and drenched, the Argive host huddled by their fires and grumbled. Only the dreadful weather prevented many of them from packing up and taking to the ships.

One afternoon, after a skirmish with a small band of Dardanians who surrendered to him surprisingly quickly, Odysseus was approached by their leader, a man who claimed that he was kin to Aeneas. He brought a message from Antenor offering to open secret channels of communication, and naming a time when Antenor might be found at the Thymbraean temple of Apollo.

Odysseus said, 'I seem to recall that we Argives have been given good reason not to trust the sanctity of that place.'

The Dardanian nodded. 'You may also recall that Antenor has reason to hate the one who violated its sanctity. Also the priest at the shrine is Antenor's son. Laocoon knew nothing of what Paris and Deiphobus had planned and was outraged by the sacrilege. Antenor also reminds you that you were once his house-guest. That bond still holds. My own life is hostage for it. I look to be free again after you speak with him.'

Accompanied by his cousin Sinon, Odysseus made the journey to the shrine where Achilles had been murdered. He found Antenor waiting for him there, alone and unarmed. While the wind howled outside, the two men talked together for a long time. Antenor informed Odysseus that King Priam was a broken man who had lost all heart for dealing with affairs of state. Deiphobus had now taken command of the Trojan forces.

'But there is much dissension in the city,' he said. 'Many of us are desperate for the war to end and I'm far from alone in thinking that Helen should be returned to Menelaus as part of an immediate peace treaty. Aeneas and his father are with me – too many Dardanians have already died in a war that none of them wanted. But Deiphobus is heir to the throne and he still has many supporters.' Antenor glanced away. 'There's another thing you should know. Helen is now living with Deiphobus.' He looked back and saw the shock in Odysseus's face. 'And there's no way he'll surrender her. He still thinks this war can be won. His trust is in our walls and he doubts that your troops can stand another winter on the plain.'

Odysseus said, 'He may well be in the right of it. But winter is many weeks away and there's plenty of time left for senseless killing.'

'Then can we not come to terms,' Antenor urged, 'as reasonable men?'

Odysseus raised his brows. 'I've long since lost all faith in human reason.'

But they talked on, discussing possible terms for an armistice, and by the time Odysseus left the temple he had promised to do what he could to find a way of ending the war.

'So it seems our spies were right,' Sinon said as they climbed back into the chariot. 'It looks as though both Antenor and the Dardanians are thinking more about survival than victory these days.'

Odysseus smiled wryly at his cousin. 'Let's hope that some similar vestige of sanity is to be found behind our lines, otherwise we'll never get back to Ithaca.'

Menelaus was so sickened by the news that Helen had now given herself to Deiphobus that he sat in morose silence throughout the long council meeting at which Odysseus reported what he had learned. As for the rest of the warlords, the divisions in the Argive leadership almost exactly mirrored those among the Trojans and their allies. Odysseus and Idomeneus were ready to settle for sensible terms, but Diomedes declared it madness to have fought for all those years, and to have lost so many friends, only to give up before the city fell. Neoptolemus agreed with him. Speaking with a grave, implacable air that reminded them all of Achilles, the young warrior declared that he was not about to leave Troy until all those who had conspired to murder his father were dead.

Odysseus listened to the boy speak with a heavy heart. He was thinking of his own son, Telemachus, who was almost the same age, and wondering whether the dreadful patrimony of this war must one day be passed on to him too, like a curse casting its shadow across the generations. Meanwhile, old Nestor dithered somewhere between the two camps, aware of the futility of the war, yet knowing that none of the heroes of his youth would ever have settled for less than total victory. Agamemnon listened to the arguments through a surly blur of alcohol. Tempers were rising. It would not be long before insults flew.

Then Menelaus looked up from his wine. 'This war began with an injury done to me. At Sparta all of you swore before Poseidon to defend my right. You are still bound by that oath.' His voice was heavy with menace. 'I expect you to honour it.'

Even Agamemnon was astounded by his baleful vehemence. Struggling to keep the incredulity from his voice, he said, 'Are you saying you still want her back?'

'I want Deiphobus dead as Paris is dead,' Menelaus answered. 'I want to watch this city burn.'

There was a long silence in which each of the assembled company stared into a future black with death and smoke.

'You heard my brother,' Agamemnon said at last. 'This war goes on.'

Odysseus woke from a dream of blood that night wondering whether he too was going mad. And then he saw the cause – Menelaus had brought back the vile memory of the oath that he had sworn at Sparta. To the best of his knowledge no one had thought about the oath for years. However this war might have begun, it had long since developed an insane logic of its own that kept them all locked inside it. And yet at the very moment when they might have negotiated a way out of the long nightmare, Menelaus had raised the spectre of that oath again. Small wonder it had returned to haunt the dreams of its deviser!

Recalling the dream, Odysseus shuddered. He had watched the bloody joints of the horse that had been sacrificed at Sparta rise up and come together again. The horse was reassembled, and one by one the Argive leaders were forced to climb into its belly until they were all shut up inside that grisly cave of blood.

He shook his head to clear it of the dreadful image. Then he lay for a long time, aching for his wife, remembering how she had been as a girl in Sparta, how they had sailed for Ithaca at last, glad to leave the ambitious bustle of the world behind them, wanting nothing more than the joy of living together on their own small island. Yet Menelaus and Palamedes had come and they had brought with them the memory of that dismembered horse to haunt him there.

And Palamedes, Patroclus, and Ajax – each of whom had sworn on the joints of the king-horse with him – were all now dead; and Achilles, Hector and Paris were wandering the asphodel fields in the Land of Shades with them. And still it seemed the curse of the horse would not let him go.

Odysseus yearned to touch his wife again. He wanted to feel her soft weight in his arms. He wanted to breathe the fresh, herby smell of her body. Somewhere there must still be a world that that did not stink of men's sweat and fury and fear. A world where a man might think of other things than killing and dying.

Wearily, dreading that he was locked inside this world of blood for ever, never to see Penelope and his son again, Odysseus rose to meet another intolerable day.

His head was still heavy with the dream when Menelaus came to visit his lodge. He brought with him a small, grey-bearded man with a gammy leg and a canny glint in his eyes. Odysseus couldn't recall having seen him before.

'This is Prylis,' Menelaus said. 'He's a farrier with the Lapiths. He's come up with an interesting idea. I want to discuss it with you.'

Inwardly, Odysseus groaned. The malevolent energy of Menelaus' renewed appetite for the war figured large among the many things he found hard to bear these days. He remembered the younger son of Atreus as he had been all those years ago on his wedding day in Sparta – open-hearted and generous, tender with love for his bride, at pains to compensate for his brother's aggressive manner, magnanimous in his hour of triumph. Of all the contenders for Helen's hand, Menelaus had been the worthiest to win her, and it grieved Odysseus to reflect on what life had made of his friend.

He gestured for the two men to sit down. 'So what is this idea?'

'One that might win us this war,' Menelaus smiled.

Odysseus studied the small man dubiously. 'I'm ready to listen to anything that might get me home,' he said.

Flattered to have the attention of these mighty men, and made garrulous by it, Prylis told how he had been a pirate and soldier-of-fortune in his younger days. He had sailed eastwards with Pirithous and Theseus, through the Hellespont and into the Black Sea, where by ill chance he had been taken captive and sold into slavery. But like all Lapiths, he was skilled with horses and had proved his worth as a horse-breaker.

'I got this leg from a Scythian brute of a stallion,' he said, 'but I held on anyway, and he came round sweet in the end.'

Prylis told how he had been sold on three times, moving south and eastwards every time, till he was taken into the service of a general in the army of a warlike people called the Assyrians, who lived between the rivers Tigris and Euphrates at a big place called Babylon.

Yes, Odysseus had heard of the people, but where was this leading?

The Assyrians were great warriors, he was told, and they had invented clever engines of war such as had not yet been seen in Argos or Crete. These engines were for use against fortified cities such as Troy, and there was one of them that had taken his fancy because it was called the Horse. The thing was built like a lodge on wheels and covered with dampened horse-hides to protect it from fire. The men who travelled under its shelter would push it along till they reached the gate of the city they were attacking, and then they would wield a huge battering ram against the gate until it fell open before them. If the Horse was built strongly enough the people on the walls could do nothing against it.

Prylis himself had seen a great city fall this way, and he would have gone on to say more but Menelaus interrupted him eagerly. 'Surely it's not beyond our powers to build such a horse?' he exclaimed. 'If one great city should fall to an engine like that, why not another?'

Odysseus' cousin Sinon had been listening with interest to what the Lapith had to say. 'It wouldn't be too difficult to build such a thing,' he said. 'There's plenty of timber in the mountains and we could soon flay a few horses.'

'Troy could be ours within the week,' Menelaus put in. 'What do you say?'

Stroking his beard, Odysseus gave the matter thought. He had been puzzling for years over how they would ever break through the massive walls of Troy yet such an idea had never occurred to him. Could it really be so simple? He began to play out the pictures in his mind.

Then he quickly saw the difficulty.

'I can imagine cases where the thing might work,' he said, 'but consider the site on which Troy stands. For the ram to burst open a gate the horse must first come within reach of it. The Trojans are still strong enough to keep us from the wall with their chariots and foot-soldiers. And even if they weren't, how could men push a heavy wooden engine up that steep ramp? It would have to be pulled not pushed, and how could that be done while under attack from the walls?' Smiling, he shook his head. 'It's an interesting idea, but I don't see how we could make it work – not yet at least. Not till the Trojans are much weaker than they are today.'

Prylis frowned with disappointment, and Menelaus tried to argue for a time, yet both men only had to look at how steeply the walls of the city beetled on their ridge to see the strength of the objection.

Odysseus put a hand to the Lapith's shoulder. 'Who knows, friend Prylis, the time of your horse may still come. But there's a lot of hard fighting to be done first.' He looked up wryly at Menelaus before adding, 'If we still have the stomach for it.'

That night he dreamed again. The goddess Athena came to him in his dream, fully armed and helmeted, wearing the aegis over her armour and carrying a golden staff. He gazed up in awe at her mighty figure and saw her grey eyes studying him with an expression of rebuke and disappointment. He could see Penelope and his son Telemachus cowering behind her, like hostages held beyond his reach.

'You offered a horse to Poseidon, Odysseus,' the goddess said. 'Why do you not offer a horse to me?'

Odysseus jumped awake and could not sleep again. He lay on his bed pondering the dream.

Once again he considered what Prylis had said about the wooden siege-horse of the Assyrians, but he could still find no way round the objections he had raised to the idea. If the ramp had been less long and steep, and if the gate had not been so well guarded by its bastions, it might have been done. The way into Troy could have been battered open. But as things stood . . .

Not for the first time, Odysseus cursed old Aeacus of Aegina for having done such a good job of rebuilding the walls of Troy. He turned over in his bed and closed his eyes, looking for sleep.

And then he remembered the other dream. Again he saw the Argive captains climbing inside the reassembled body of the horse that had been sacrificed to Poseidon. Again the horror of that image kept him from sleep.

Eventually he got up and went to walk along the shore where the breakers were rolling in off the heavy swell of the bay to scatter their force against the strand. By the time the dawn light began to break across the turbulent eastern sky, Poseidon's horse and the Assyrian horse had come together in his mind and Odysseus knew what must be done.

Several weeks later, as a fresh breeze from the east blew the early grey daylight across the plain of Troy, the watchmen on the tower of Ilium rubbed their eyes at an astounding sight. Apart from a seaward drift of smoke where fires were burning out, there were none of the usual signs of activity around the Argive camp. The curved prows of the ships that had lined the coast of the bay beyond the palisade for the best part of a year had vanished. Nor could the two watchmen see any vessels riding the waters of the Hellespont beyond.

For a moment they looked at each other in disbelief. Then one dared to say out loud what both were thinking: 'They've gone! The Argives have gone.'

Deiphobus was lying asleep with one arm stretched out across Helen's breast when his two surviving younger brothers, Capys and Thymoetes, came to wake him. Heavy-headed, and still bad-tempered from having discovered Helen too far gone with opium the previous night to be more than a desultory partner in his bed, he found it hard at first to take in what he was being told.

'Are you sure?' he demanded. 'It could just be some sort of stratagem to lure us out beyond the walls.'

'The scouts say not,' Thymoetes insisted. 'The lodges are burned, the ships are gone and there's no one in the camp. It looks as though they've taken the chance to get back home now that the weather's turned.'

Allowing himself to begin to believe, Deiphobus uttered a little laugh. 'Didn't I tell you they couldn't stand the thought of another winter out there? We've beaten them. In the name of all the gods, we've beaten them!'

But Capys was frowning. 'There's one strange thing about it.'

'What's that?' Deiphobus demanded, immediately suspicious.

'They've left something behind them on the beach. A horse, the scouts said. A great wooden horse.'

'What do you mean – a wooden horse?'

'Just that. It's a huge thing by all accounts, made of wood, in the shape of a horse. The scouts said they'd never seen anything like it before. They say there's an inscription carved on it, but none of them can read. We're about to go down to the coast to take a look, but we thought you'd want to see it for yourself.'

Helen had been disturbed by the voices outside the chamber. She stirred uneasily on the bed when Deiphobus came back to finish dressing, and asked what was happening.

'It looks as though your Argive friends have seen sense at last.'

Helen sat up, holding her head between her hands. 'I don't understand.'

'Their camp's empty. The ships are gone.' Turning to look down where she lay with the richly woven throw gathered across her breast, Deiphobus caught the moment in which her disbelieving eyes began to flicker with alarm. 'You don't find the news to your taste? Perhaps you were hoping that Menelaus might come and carry you back to Sparta with him?'

When Helen turned her pallid face away, he saw how close to the mark his jibe had come. 'What a faithless bitch you are!' he said. 'But I'm afraid you're going to have to think again.'

Watching him stride out of the chamber, Helen found herself appalled by the thought of spending the rest of her days inside this city. She could hear the murmur in the streets outside as people came from their houses, roused by the news. Amid the barking of dogs a man was shouting somewhere. A woman began to sing one of the songs with which the whores used to taunt the Argives from the walls and her voice was soon joined by others. People were laughing and cheering everywhere.

It must be true then. Menelaus and Agamemnon had wearied of the cost of this long war. They had cut their losses and made off for home, leaving her alone among the Trojans, a worthless thing. Panic seized her then. Her mind filled with dark images. She could see what would happen. As time and wine and the drug erased her already jaded beauty, Deiphobus would tire of her. He would cast her off. She would be left to survive as best she could, passed on like a drab from man to man, because there would always be someone eager to brag that he had taken his pleasure with Helen of Sparta, Helen of Troy.

Helen got up from the bed, shivering in the morning light and crossed to the casement. From that high place in the palace buildings of the citadel she could see across the wall out to the plain where people were already running to dance in triumph on what remained of the Argive camp.

For ten years the people of this city had suffered the anguish of war on her account, and now their trials were over. But Paris was dead and Hector was dead, and Antiphus and Polydorus and countless others were dead with them. And King Priam was a broken man, trembling and rheumy, and all but dumb with grief. Yet the people would sing and dance and make merry with wine now because they had survived, and they need no longer wake up each morning wondering whether they would be dead or widowed before the end of the day.

The war was over, and it had been neither won nor lost. It had merely ground to a halt like the derelict thing it was. And, for now, she – the chief cause and prize of all those years of struggle – was forgotten in the shocked relief of its ending.

She was alone with her terror.

Beyond the palisade, the camp was a squalid tip of burned-out lodges, broken chariots, discarded equipment, and half-eaten bits of food over which the vultures and the pie-dogs squabbled. Smoke drifted across the mess, gusting in dirty billows along the beach where they could see the tracks carved into the sand by the keels of the Argive vessels as they were pushed back into the sea. The charred hulk of the ship that had been fired when Hector broke through the palisade and stormed the camp, still lurched on its props like something that had been disembowelled. In the growing heat of the morning, a fierce stink was lifted by the breeze across the strand from the open ditches of the latrines.

And over everything loomed the enigmatic figure of the horse.

Built of trunks and planks from the fir trees of the Idaean Mountains, it stood on thick splayed legs, each of them the girth of a tie-beam from a barn. The shipwrights or master-carpenters – whoever had constructed this astounding beast – had smoothly jointed the thighs into the sinewy bulges of its shoulders and haunches, and the great swag of its belly curved like a barrel between. The sweep of its tail reached down to the platform on which the horse was mounted, acting as a counterweight to the forward thrust of the arched neck and the long, princely head,

which hung some thirty feet high where the carved mane bristled between its ears. Its eyes were bulging, its hollow nostrils
flared. There was a spring and vigour to its lines which seemed
to lighten the inert tonnage of wood from which it had been
hewn. And the sheer scale of the thing compelled silence for a
time, as though this horse had broken loose from some paddock
in the realm of the gods to cast its majestic shadow over the
world of mortal men.

An inscription had been carved along one flank. King Priam,
who had insisted on being carried down to the beach to witness
the dereliction of the Argive camp, read the words aloud: *Offered
to Divine Athena that she may favour us with a safe journey home.*
Then he turned, smiling, to Deiphobus. 'It seems you were right.
The Argives are gone at last.' Tears broke from the rims of his
eyes. 'Would that my son Hector had lived to see this day.'

Impatient that the old man should think first of his dead brother
when this hour of triumph was entirely his own, Deiphobus
turned away and saw Capys looking up at the massive horse with
suspicion.

'What about this thing?' Capys said. 'Why would they leave
something as improbable as this behind?'

'It speaks for itself,' Deiphobus answered. 'It's an offering to
the goddess. The Argives always looked to Athena for help and
protection.'

'Then why should we trust it?' Capys asked, 'I think we should
burn it. I think we should make a burnt offering of it and cleanse
our shore of the last trace of them.'

A murmur of assent rose from the people gathered round the
royal party. What better way to be rid of these long years of war
than an immense bonfire in which the horse would be inciner-
ated along with the rest of the rubbish polluting the shore? They
would burn their air clean.

'But the horse belongs to the goddess,' Thymoetes said. 'Might
it not be an unlucky thing to desecrate her property?'

King Priam frowned up at the huge, noble head of the horse.

'It is a thing of great beauty,' he said uncertainly.

'And it's the emblem of our triumph.' Deiphobus jumped up onto the platform of the horse and stood by one foreleg to address the crowd. 'If they're lucky, Divine Athena may grant the Argives a safe journey home, but she's denied them victory here. I say we should keep this horse and bring it inside the walls so that our children's children may look on it and remember how we Trojans fought to save our city.'

The mood of the crowd shifted at his words. Here was the new order in action.

Everything was possible once more.

Deiphobus turned to look at his father, who was nodding his old head beside him. 'The gods have favoured us,' Priam said, 'and we should be thankful for it. We will take this idol to the temple of Athena and consecrate it to her there.'

But the thing was easier said than done. Logs were pulled down from the Argive palisade and used as levers and fulcrums. With enormous effort the front edge of the platform was lifted high enough for the first of many rollers to be slid under it. Thick ropes were made fast about the horse's neck and extended with knots until two long lines of men could get a grip on them and begin to haul the horse across the strand towards the dismantled gateway of the palisade.

Yet the thing was immensely heavy, and as the sun rose higher, the heat of the day increased. Hour after hour, the horse jerked clumsily forward on its rollers, but the ground was uneven and progress slow. Men were often hurt in the scramble to replace the rollers and keep up such momentum as they gained. At each upward gradient, the weight of the horse increased, and where the land sloped downhill, it had to be restrained from behind rather than dragged from the front. Not till the middle of the afternoon, after sustained effort by changing shifts of men, did it stand at the foot of the ramp leading up the ridge to the Scaean Gate. By then it was already evident that they would never be able to haul the horse to the top of the ridge unless an efficient system of winches and pulleys was installed. Even, if they succeeded, the crenellated parapet above the gate would have to be demolished to accommodate the height of the horse's head.

For some time many among the haulers had been grumbling that the whole enterprise was insane and not worth the trouble it was costing them. But Deiphobus had been determined from the first that the horse should be brought into Troy as a symbol of the city's strength and his zeal had kept them going far into the day. Now even he was disheartened by the scale of the effort still required.

Capys looked up at his brother from where he panted above a water-skin. 'We should have burned the thing in the first place, like I said.'

'Or we could just leave it out here on the plain,' Thymoetes suggested.

Feeling his own arms aching from the strain of the turn he had taken at the ropes, Deiphobus imagined Agamemnon and Odysseus laughing over this struggle to drag the horse inside the city. He frowned up at the great weight of wood that threatened to defeat him. Perhaps his brothers were right.

Yet to have got the thing so far only to give up at the last push . . .

He was still trying to make up his mind when he became aware of a stir beyond the horse and a muttering among the crowd. When he stood up he saw the priest Laocoon approaching at the head of a small band of Dardanians who were pushing and shoving a prisoner along the road. Since the sacrilegious murder of Achilles at the shrine there had been only hostility between Deiphobus and the priest who stood before him now, stony-faced. That tension was still palpable as Laocoon said, 'This Argive was found skulking near Apollo's shrine.'

The man was pulled forward in front of Deiphobus, where he stood, staring at the ground. His wrists were bound, he was dirty and dishevelled, and clearly in fear for his life. Under question, he said his name was Sinon, that he was an Ithacan, and that he had fled from the Argive camp the previous night.

'Why would you do that?' Deiphobus demanded.

'Because they were going to offer me up in sacrifice to the Winds. They've been wanting to sail home for weeks but the weather was against them. Calchas said they should offer a blood sacrifice to the Winds, and Odysseus made sure that the lot fell on me.'

'A fellow Ithacan? That seems surprising. Did he have a grudge against you?'

Sinon looked up, narrow-eyed. 'He was afraid of me. I was the only one left who knew how he'd set up Palamedes to look like a traitor. He was looking for a way to get rid of me before we went back home.'

'Yet here you are,' said Deiphobus.

'Only because I was lucky. They were preparing the altar last night when the wind changed and there was a mad rush for the ships. I managed to get away in the confusion.'

Deiphobus wrinkled his lips, still unconvinced. 'If what you say is true why didn't you just tell Agamemnon what you know about Odysseus and throw yourself on his mercy?'

With the air of a man who has seen enough of the world and its corruption, Sinon shrugged. 'Because he didn't want to know. None of them wanted to know. They all took part in the stoning, didn't they? They weren't about to encourage talk of Palamedes' innocence. The only person who cares about it any more is Palamedes' father, King Nauplius, back in Euboea. He's already suspicious about what happened, and if he gets certain proof he'll come looking for his vengeance. Odysseus knows that – which is why he wanted to keep me quiet.'

Impressed by the way Sinon's story squared with what he already knew of Odysseus's devious mind, Deiphobus conferred in whispers with his brothers.

Capys turned to Sinon and said, 'So what were you doing out at Thymbra?'

'It seemed the best place to find sanctuary until the ships were gone. I was hoping to get back to Argos overland and make the crossing to Euboea. Once Nauplius knows what I know, he'll take good care of me – and of Odysseus!'

At that point Antenor spoke up from the walls where he stood beside the frail figure of King Priam. 'Tell us more about this horse.'

Sinon looked up at him and then back at Deiphobus. 'That's all down to Calchas again. When everything started going wrong in the past few weeks, he took the omens and told us that Athena had turned her face away from us. Achilles had always been her favourite, he said, and any chance we had of taking Troy had died with him. Calchas said that things were now so bad that if we even wanted to get home safely, we were going to have to propitiate the goddess with a major sacrifice.'

'But why offer her a horse?' Capys demanded.

'That was Odysseus's idea. He said it came to him in a dream. This whole war started with the offering of a horse to Poseidon at Sparta. Odysseus said we should end it by offering a horse to Athena at Troy.'

Antenor said, 'Why not a real horse then, such as was offered to Poseidon?'

Sinon gave him a contemptuous glance. 'After so many have been killed here already? Dead horseflesh is cheap on the plain of Troy, or hadn't you noticed?'

Misliking the man's tone, Deiphobus smacked him across the face. Sinon put a hand to his cheek and stared down at the ground.

'Say more,' Deiphobus demanded.

'I don't know what else to say. I think that Calchas took the omens again. He must have done because he said that Athena wanted an idol raised to her.' Sinon shrugged again. 'We had only wood to make it with.'

'But why did you make it so big?' Capys asked.

'So that you couldn't get it into the city, of course.'

'Explain.'

'Calchas said that you Trojans might try to win Athena's favour by consecrating the horse at her temple. If you succeeded, then the tables might be turned, and it might not be long before Troy was invading Argos.'

The crowd had been listening attentively to the prisoner's story. Now they began to talk among themselves. But they fell silent again when Laocoon raised his voice. 'Why should we believe a word this man says? These sound like lies concocted by Odysseus. The Argives have never impressed me with their piety. I have no trust in them, least of all when they leave us gifts.'

A woman's voice called down from the walls. 'The priest speaks truly.'

Deiphobus looked up and saw Cassandra standing at the parapet with the strands of her black hair blowing about her face. 'That horse will bring destruction on us. It carries death in its belly. Believe me, brother, I see Menelaus standing over you. I see you lying in a bed of blood.'

'Take her inside,' Deiphobus shouted. Impatiently he muttered to his brothers that Cassandra saw destruction everywhere. Convinced now that Laocoon was out to spoil his triumph, he turned to confront the priest. 'And you,' he said, ' – it's no secret that you have no love for me. Nor have you shown much stomach for this war. Not until now when all the fighting's done. You would have done well to demonstrate your hostility to the Argives sooner.'

Laocoon turned his face away from him. 'I speak as the god bids me speak.'

'Then go and pray for more auspicious omens on this happy day.'

Antenor made plain his displeasure at the way Deiphobus was treating his son. He turned to the king and said, loudly enough for all to hear him. 'Laocoon is speaking wisely. It would be foolish to ignore him.'

'But I think that my own son has more courage,' Priam answered testily.

At that moment another voice – that of Aeneas – joined the discussion. 'Nevertheless,' he said, 'my father Anchises and I share the feelings of Antenor.'

Worried that these dissenting opinions might turn the day against him, Deiphobus moved to a higher place on the ramp from where he could address the uncertain crowd of men gathered about the wooden horse. 'You all heard what this Argive had to say,' he said. 'Clearly he has no cause to love Odysseus or any of the Argive lords. Nor did he seek us out to beguile us with this story. He had to be brought before us in tethers from the place where he was hiding. And let my cousin Aeneas think what he will – we Trojans know well enough that the Dardanians wanted no part in this war and came to our aid only when Achilles flushed them out. If they don't wish to share in our celebrations, so be it. Let them go home. As for my sister, she is weak in the head and sees only darkness in the world. But this is our hour of triumph, Trojans. Let the Argives learn that we are stronger than they thought. One last effort brings the horse inside our city, and then Divine Athena will smile on Troy for ever.' He turned his head and looked up at the parapet. 'Am I not right, father?'

King Priam said, 'My son speaks truly. Divine Athena has denied the Argives the victory they sought and we must honour her.' But he was saddened to find that even in their hour of triumph his people were disunited. Turning to Aeneas, he said, 'You Dardanians have fought bravely at our side. Will you not share in this victory with us?'

'My father is old,' Aeneas answered, 'and neither he nor I see much cause for celebration in a war that was neither won nor lost, and where a great price has been paid in suffering. We will be glad enough to go back to our mountains and leave Troy to triumph as it pleases.'

'As you wish.' Priam turned abruptly away and looked down on his son from the parapet. Lacking the nobility of Hector and the glamour of Paris, Deiphobus had never been a favourite among his many sons, but a strong fate had given it to him to lead the Trojans through to the end of this bitter war and Priam was not about to deny him his hour of glory now. 'Break down the rampart of the Scaean Gate,' he commanded. 'Bring Athena's horse into the citadel.'

The sound of this debate had travelled through the ears and nostrils of the horse, which had been hollowed out to allow a flow of air inside its stuffy chamber. Twenty three Argive warriors strapped to the wooden benches in there had listened to the exchanges with bated breath as they sat in the gloom, wearing nothing but breech-clouts, wondering whether at any moment the Trojans might set fire to the woodwork or bring it crashing to the ground.

Next to Odysseus, on the bench immediately above the hidden trap door, sat Epeius, a plump Phocian, who for many years had held the sinecure of water-bearer to the House of Atreus. His true trade was that of a master craftsman, and it was he who had designed the horse and supervised its construction. If he had not, like all the other men around him, emptied his bowels before climbing inside the horse he had built, he would have been fouling his breeches with terror right now. Epeius had begged to be left out of the invasion force, but practice had revealed that only he could work the clever hinges he had devised to lock the trap door in place and conceal it from view: so he had been forced, at sword-point, to go along. As the last man to enter the belly of the horse, he would be the first out, and the thought frightened him so much that there had been times during the course of the day when Odysseus had clapped a hand across his mouth to silence his whimpers.

Amazingly, however, things were going well. Odysseus and Menelaus had exchanged a grim smile of relief when Sinon turned up just in time to prevent what they were beginning to dread would be a disastrous end to the mission. And chancy though the strategy of double-bluff had been, Odysseus had taken particular satisfaction in the way Laocoon, Antenor and Aeneas had manoeuvred Deiphobus into taking the decision they wanted simply by telling the truth.

Now they could hear the sound of Aeneas and his Dardanians leaving the city, and when the long file had passed and the ramp was clear again, they heard shouting and the din of hammers and crowbars as the Trojans worked to demolish the gate which had kept the Argives at bay for ten long years. The noise gave the men inside the horse some respite from their own protracted silence. They could stretch cramped limbs and take a sip or two at the ration of water they were allowed, knowing that it could only be a question of time before the horse was on the move again.

Around an hour later they heard a warning shout followed by a sudden collapse of masonry as the stone lintel over the gate came down. A cloud of lime-dust blew in through the ears and nostrils, whitening the faces of Neoptolemus and Acamas who sat nearest to the head. Moments later came the sound of men clambering over the neck and cruppers of the horse as more ropes were slung round it. They heard the screech of pulleys and the creak of a winch. Someone counted out the heaves by threes, and slowly, with the rollers groaning beneath the platform, the horse began to slide, jerk by jerk, up the gradient of the ramp.

Only the buckled leather straps that held them tightly in place kept the warriors from being jolted off the benches when the belly of the horse collided with the wall as it passed through the gateway. Then they were stuck in that narrow space, scarcely breathing for a time, as men debated how best to widen the gap through the barbican. But having struggled this far to get his trophy into the city, Deiphobus no longer seemed to care how much damage was done to the walls. More masonry tumbled and was cleared away. With some difficulty a jammed roller was freed. Then the horse was through into Troy.

Night had fallen by the time King Priam completed the rites of dedication to Athena outside her temple in the citadel of Ilium.

Apart from the voice of the king and that of Theano, the wife of Antenor, who was priestess to Athena, the ritual had been performed in reverential silence as the exhausted Trojans meditated on the long years of a war in which they had suffered so much. There had been a lowing from the sacrificial animals and a baby cried somewhere, but otherwise the densely packed crowd gathered around the horse made barely a sound.

Meanwhile, it was pitch-black inside the horse's belly. Forbidden speech, and no longer able to encourage one another with nods and smiles, each man was locked alone with his discomfort and trepidation. Then the sound of music struck up and the crowd were singing the hymn of praise to Athena. Odysseus mouthed the words to himself, reflecting on the number of times the Argive host had sung this very same hymn to the grey-eyed goddess who watches over the people when they go out to war, presides over the shouts of battle and the destruction of cities, and then watches over those who return.

The Trojans raised their voices in the final chords – 'Farewell, goddess, grant us good fortune and happiness; in another song we will remember you' – oblivious that they had worked hard and long all day merely to bring death into their city. And then the night became a time of celebration. The solemn strains of the hymn gave way to wilder music. Cheering and loud applause echoed from the walls of the citadel. Men clambered across the horse's back to hang garlands where the ropes had strained. Children jumped and played around its hooves.

Confined inside the hot darkness of their den, the Argives could hear feet stamping in the dance outside. The smell of cooked fish and roasting meat mingled with that of their own sweat until their stomachs quivered at the thought of the food and wine being consumed out there. After years of fear and want the whole city, from princes and priests to prostitutes and slaves, was letting its hair down in a banquet of excess. All the long effort of struggle and hardship was behind them now. Peace had come home and prosperity would soon follow. In the meantime, men, women and children were going to eat, drink, dance, sing, kiss, embrace and make frantic love till they dropped from sheer exhaustion.

For hour after hour the noise of revelry rang loud around the squares. Then, gradually, the laughter grew quieter and people began to wander home or fall asleep in a stupor where they lay.

Inside the horse the air grew tense with anticipation, but a drunken gang of men were still carousing across the far side of the square from where the horse stood. They were singing a bawdy rant that had been popular among the Trojan host for the scurrilous insults it heaped on each of the Argive leaders, verse by verse. Odysseus, Menelaus, Diomedes and Idomeneus had never heard the words so clearly as they did that night. They sat chafing grimly in the belly of the horse.

And then they grew tenser still as they became aware of someone climbing onto the platform beneath them and they caught the sound of a woman's voice.

'Have you come to carry me home?' she whispered. 'Isn't that why you're here – to carry me away again?' And for a moment each of the men thought that the question had been put to him; then they realized that the woman was drunk and that she was talking to the horse. 'There was a day,' she was saying, 'when all the great princes of Argos swore on the limbs of a horse that they would protect and honour me. But look at me now. Look what's become of me. It's no wonder they don't care what happens to me any more – my gentle Menelaus, my clever friend Odysseus, Diomedes who used to sigh with love for me in the old days – they're all sailing home now, and they've left us here, you and me, in this dreary city. So now there's only you to carry me away.'

Each of the princes of Argos inside the horse had felt his heart jump to his throat, and Menelaus had been so disturbed by the first sound of Helen's voice that Diomedes and Idomeneus, who were sitting at either side of him, had to restrain him from leaping up. Only moments later, at the sound of his name on Helen's lips, Diomedes himself had almost lost control. Now all of them jumped again as a voice called across the square. 'Helen, where are you? What are you doing over there?' And they recognized the voice of Deiphobus. 'Come on. Let's go back. It's late.'

A coarse burst of laughter came from the drunks who had been singing across the square.

'Sleep if you want to,' said Helen.

'Come on, we're going home.'

'I want to stay here with the horse.'

One of the men across the square called out, 'Deiphobus'll give you a livelier ride, darling!' And the others laughed loudly before making off into the night. Then there came a sound of scuffling close outside the horse, and Helen's voice saying, 'Leave me alone. I don't want to go. I want to stay here.' But Deiphobus dragged her away. And then, inside the horse, there was only silence.

Almost another hour passed before they heard the voice of Antenor directly beneath them. 'It's time,' he said. 'The city's quiet. You can come out.'

Odysseus ordered Epeius to open the trap door while the men loosened the straps and began to unpack their weapons and armour. Epeius was still so frightened that his fingers were trembling and it took some time for him to work the lock and hinges. But finally the trap swung open and a gust of night air blew into that stuffy cabin as Epeius dropped the rope-ladder from its cleats. Pushed from the back by Odysseus, he climbed down to stand shaking inside Troy.

Swinging swiftly down after him, Odysseus took Antenor firmly by the hand, and turned to look out across the plain where a beacon lit by Sinon blazed through the darkness from the top of Achilles' funeral mound. Reassured that Agamemnon's fleet must now be on its way back from Tenedos, Odysseus smiled at Antenor again, and began buckling on his armour. 'You remembered to paint the sign of the horse on your doors?' Grave-faced in the moonlight, Antenor nodded. 'Then stay inside with your family,' Odysseus said. 'By this time tomorrow you'll be king in Troy.'

One by one the others descended from the horse, stretched their cramped limbs and took great gulps of fresh air. Odysseus put a finger to his lips and gestured towards the drunks who were lying asleep around the square. Then he drew another finger across his throat. Neoptolemus and three other men hurried to despatch them, while Idomeneus led another party down towards the Scaean Gate. They found that the Trojans had done a makeshift job of closing the gate against the broken bastions, but the sentinels had drunk as much as everybody else and were fast asleep.

It was a sleep from which they never woke. Within minutes, the gate stood open, waiting for the onrush of the Argive host when it disembarked from the ships and raced across the plain. The late summer moon breasted the dark cloud that had briefly covered it. The palaces, temples and streets of the doomed city gleamed beneath its radiance.

In the experience of mortal men there can be few things more terrible than the sacking of a city. All that splendour of stone and marble so laboriously raised, the carved pediments, the free-standing statuary, the airy halls, the sacred precincts, the delicately frescoed panels, the tessellated floors, the arcades, pools and foun-tains – all that vision, skill and invention reduced, in the course of a night, to objects of no more account than the grace and dignity of the women who will be raped, the wisdom and courage of the men who will fall to the sword, or the innocence of a child's head dashed against a wall.

Yet it is so much easier to take a brutal delight in tearing beauty down than in the painstaking work of building it up – in destroying what others have made rather than in creating some-thing marvellous of one's own – that it's surprising, I suppose, that cities do not fall more often.

But once the sacking begins, a surge of evil is released that leaves men dazed and disbelieving afterwards.

★   ★   ★

Beneath an ancient laurel tree in the courtyard of King Priam's palace stood the altar of Zeus. It was there that Hecuba gathered her daughters for sanctuary when they were woken by the din of the invading army and the shouts and screams in the streets below the palace. Frail as he was, Priam wanted to bring his spear with him, ready to hold the Argives off, but Hecuba held on to him, wailing that it was madness for a feeble old man to join the fight. So they were standing together beneath the tree, trembling at the terrifying noises rising from the city, when Neoptolemus strode into the courtyard wearing his father's golden armour and followed by a band of Myrmidons.

Still only half-dressed, one of Priam's younger sons, Capys, hurried to his parents' defence and was immediately cut down under Hecuba's horrified gaze. Shouting with impotent rage, Priam bent to pick up his son's spear but was overwhelmed before he could throw it. He stood panting in the grip of two Myrmidons, and when he glanced up he was amazed to see how young was the warrior in golden armour who looked back at him with distaste, as if he was some kind of monster in a show. King Priam was wearing only his night-robe. His legs were thin and white in the light from the moon. Ashamed to be seen so, he lowered his eyes and saw the blood leaking in a thick pool from the body of his son. Capys lay so awkwardly where he had fallen that it seemed to Priam that some dislocation of reality must have taken place and this was all an aberration of his failing mind. But he could hear the women wailing around him, and his wife stood proudly at his side, dignified as ever, even though the shift she wore was thin and her heart was shaking with mortal terror.

Nothing happened for a moment. The old king began to think that the armoured boy was in awe of the captives he had taken and uncertain what to do with them. He took heart from it and was considering ways of asserting sixty years of regal authority when he saw the youth make a downward signal with the point of his drawn sword. Not a word was uttered but the Myrmidons understood. Hecuba put a hand to her mouth, gasping, as the two men forced her husband to his knees and pushed his white head forward. Then, nimble as a dancer, Neoptolemus took three quick steps towards him, raised the sword that had belonged to Achilles, brought it swiftly down on the exposed neck, and struck off his head.

The screaming women around the decapitated body were quickly bound and taken to join the other captives who were being held in the square beside the wooden horse. But Cassandra and Andromache were not among them.

Cassandra had not slept at all that night. She had lain on her bed in a frenzy of hallucinations as the pressure of prophetic insight built inside her mind. So when the Argives burst through into the city with a tremendous roar that shook the Trojans from their sleep, she heard the noise almost with a kind of relief. The nightmare vision of blood and smoke that had haunted her inner world for so long was at last released from confinement inside her brain. It brought with it the knowledge that she was not mad after all, merely gifted with a terrible power that had almost made her so.

Strangely then, her first thought was not for her safety but to give thanks.

Not even stopping to pull a robe around the shift she wore, Cassandra ran through the corridors of the palace till she came out into an empty courtyard and passed through a rear door used only by the priests into the temple of Athena. Outside in the square where stood the wooden horse, she could hear men shouting above the wailing of women and children, but here inside the temple an air of sacred peace prevailed. Cassandra prostrated herself before the Palladium, the ancient wooden image of Athena which was imbued with the power of the goddess and carried inside its mystery the secret soul of Troy.

For that very reason the Argives had long desired to capture the idol and its seizure stood high among their priorities when the city was stormed. So Cassandra had been praying to the goddess for only a few moments when the door of the temple crashed open, and a band of heavily armed warriors strode into its tranquil space. Chief among them was a Locrian captain called Aias, a small, fleet-footed man who had won a reputation as one of the most skilful wielders of the spear in the Achaian army. Knowing that whoever seized the Palladium could expect a handsome reward, he had led his company straight to the temple expecting to find no one there. But here he was, looking down into the defiant eyes of a rather beautiful, sallow-skinned young woman wearing only a thin shift, who had leapt to her feet before him with a mane of black hair tousled about her face. Aias had no idea who she was, nor did he care.

'This place is sacred to Athena,' Cassandra cried. 'Your uncleansed presence here is a sacrilege. Beware her anger.'

Aias laughed in her face. 'Athena fights on our side, little lady,' he said, and reached out to tear open her shift. Coming awake to the peril of her situation, Cassandra scrambled away from him and ran back towards the Palladium.

The Locrians closed in round her.

'You first, Aias,' one of them said. 'You can take the fire out of her.'

Aias walked towards her, gesturing with the upraised fingers of both hands for her to come closer. Cassandra turned her head and spat into his face.

Scowling, Aias wiped her spittle from his beard. Cassandra turned her back on him, wrapped her bare arms tightly about the wooden idol, gripped her eyes shut and began to utter a wild chant of prayers and imprecations. Aias looked back at his men, laughed, then reached out and lifted up her shift.

Half naked now, Cassandra was still hanging on to the Palladium with both arms when Agamemnon burst into the temple with his bodyguard and saw Aias trying to mount her from behind. 'What in Hades' name is going on here?' he bellowed. 'Do you mean to bring the vengeance of the goddess down on us?' He strode forward, pulled Aias off the girl and kicked out at him as he was trying to pull his breeches up from round his knees. The kick knocked him flying backwards among the Locrians who turned and scattered out of the temple.

Agamemnon stared at the young woman's bare white flesh for a moment, and then put a hand to her chin to turn her face towards him. The eyes that looked up at him were filled with hate.

'Who are you?' he demanded.

'Cassandra,' she hissed.

'King Priam's daughter!'

'Priestess to the god.'

Agamemnon smiled at the bayed fury in that hectic young face. Then he turned to Talthybius who stood at his side. 'This one is mine. See her conducted safely to the square.'

Having given orders for the careful dismantling of the Palladium, he left the temple to rejoin the sacking of the city, but when he stepped back out into the streets of the citadel, he cursed at the smell of burning that blew towards him. Thick smoke was rising from one of the crowded, lower areas of Troy where the textile factories were situated. Climbing the plinth of a marble statue to get a better view, Agamemnon saw flames already beginning to lick through the roof of a warehouse. He jumped back down from the plinth shouting that if that blaze wasn't brought under control, half the city would be burning before they had the chance to plunder it. Then he strode about the square, bellowing out orders and cursing men who were too rapt in a frenzy of killing to hear what he said.

Having left a guard over Priam's decapitated body, Neoptolemus led his Myrmidons through the violent din of the streets in search of the house that had once belonged to Hector. He found Andromache waiting there, comforting her terrified serving-women, with her young son Astyanax standing at her side.

One of the women screamed as the Myrmidons came in and threw herself at her mistress's feet, where she knelt in a panic-stricken welter of tears. 'Hush, Clymene,' Andromache said, leaning to put a hand to the woman's head. But her eyes were on the smallish warrior who was wearing a golden breastplate that she recognized – a breastplate that looked a little too big for him. He lifted off his helmet, wiped the sweat from his brow with the back of a bloody hand, and smiled at her.

Andromache was appalled at how young he was.

Like someone appraising a property he might buy, Neoptolemus looked round at the rich furnishings of the apartment, the costly drapes, and the exquisite paintings of woodland feasting and dancing on the walls.

'I see that the noble Hector lived in fine style,' he said. At the light, almost friendly sound of his voice, the hysterical serving-woman fell silent.

When no answer came, Neoptolemus stared at Andromache. 'Do you recognize this armour, madam?'

Too proud to show her fear, Andromache merely nodded.

'It belonged to my father,' he said. 'So you will understand why I claim you as my rightful prize. You will be kept under guard here till the division of the spoils.'

'What of my women?' Andromache asked.

Neoptolemus shrugged. 'They may remain here with you. My Myrmidons will see that no harm comes to them.' He smiled at the grateful whimpers of relief elicited by this casual gesture of reprieve.

Amazed by such courteous treatment, Andromache's voice was shaking a little as she said, 'I see that the son of Achilles is as noble as his father was.'

Neoptolemus acknowledged the compliment with a nod. He half-turned away as if to leave, and then swung his head to look back at her again.

'However, there is the small matter of your son.'

At once Andromache put her arm around the scrawny young shoulders of Astyanax, where he stood beside her wearing only his silken nightgown over his breeches. 'Astyanax is only a boy,' she said. 'He is younger even than yourself.'

Immediately she saw the fatal error of that addition.

Neoptolemus said, 'Let me take a look at him.'

Six years old and shaking in his skin, but defiantly conscious that he was among the men who had killed his father, Astyanax said, 'You can see me well enough.'

'So I can.' Neoptolemus smiled. 'And I see what I expected.'

'A little boy,' gasped Andromache hopelessly. 'Only a little boy.'

'But as you see from my own presence, madam, little boys grow into warriors who come looking for vengeance on those who kill their fathers.' Neoptolemus smiled down at the child. 'That's what you would like, isn't it, Astyanax?'

'If I had a sword I would show you.'

'Of course you would. But you don't have a sword and I won't have it said that Neoptolemus cut down an unarmed child.' Smiling, he reached out a hand. 'Come with me.' When Andromache reached out a protective arm across her son, Neoptolemus grabbed the boy by the lobe of his ear and pulled him away.

'Where are you taking him?' Andromache cried.

'Only to point out my father's tomb.'

The Myrmidons advanced to restrain her as she tried to prevent Neoptolemus from leading Astyanax towards a balcony that looked out of the room across the citadel of Ilium. The drapes were blowing in the night breeze, and a hideous din of wailing rose from the women in the square as they watched lovers, husbands, brothers and sons dragged out of the places where they were hiding to be tormented and slaughtered by the jeering Argives.

For an instant Andromache saw the hair of the two boys illuminated by the ruddy glare that was now colouring the night sky. In another, kinder world they might have been brothers as Neoptolemus pointed with his left hand over the walls towards the funeral mound where Sinon's signal-fire still blazed.

'Do you see that mound over there?' he said. 'That's where my father lies.'

Then, with his right hand, he tugged down on the child's ear, bent him over, lifted him up, and hurled him head first from the balcony.

Long before all this – before Astyanax died, before Andromache, Cassandra and Hecuba were driven like cattle into the square, before King Priam's ancient head was severed from his body, Menelaus had entered the city with only a single thought in mind. Knowing what that thought must be, Agamemnon had ordered Odysseus to keep close company with his brother once they climbed down from the horse. So while the drunkards sleeping in the square were murdered, and the Scaean Gate was secured, Menelaus and Odysseus made their way through the still silent streets of the citadel looking for the mansion that Paris had built for Helen and which was now the residence of Deiphobus. A small detachment of Spartan warriors followed at their heels.

Antenor had given them instructions and the house was not difficult to find. But, as had been arranged, they waited outside the gate to the courtyard for a time until the message came that Diomedes and his men had managed to secure all entrances to the large warehouse in which Memnon's Ethiopians were garrisoned. They would be locked in there until Troy was looted of its treasures, and then the building would be burned down round them along with the rest of the city.

While they waited, Odysseus shinned his way up onto a parapet from where he could look out to sea. In the shifting moonlight he could just make out the shades of Agamemnon's ships heading for the strand. The tiled roofs of the city stretched below him and there was hardly a sound to be heard. They had been lucky. Not even a dog had barked.

The message came. Everything was in place. Menelaus pushed at the gate expecting to find it locked. Smoothly it swung open.

The mansion rivalled Priam's palace in splendour, standing on three floors, with views from its balconies towards the mountains of Ida in the south, and northwards to the sea. The night air of the courtyard was fragrant with jasmine and lilies and the scent of flowering trees. The door to the house stood ajar.

As soon as they entered, they saw the sleeping bodies of stewards and serving-women limply sprawled about the couches and floors as though an advance guard of marauders had already despatched them. Knowing that the main force would not yet be ashore and that it was too soon to risk an alarm, Odysseus signalled that everyone they found should be killed. So the warriors moved swiftly through the house, checking each chamber, slitting throats as they went.

Moving cautiously along this trail of blood, Menelaus came at last to what was clearly the door of the master bedroom. Quietly he ordered his followers to search the remaining rooms and then hesitated outside that delicately panelled door for a moment with only Odysseus at his side. The two men looked at one another. It seemed to both that the other was breathing noisily. Both trembled a little with an almost sacrilegious sense of transgression.

Menelaus turned the golden handle and pushed open the door.

Moonlight blew in on the night breeze through the gauzy drapes over the window casement. The great bed stood at the far end of the room across a highly polished floor. An oil-lamp had been left burning on a tripod near the bed, and by its glow they could make out the huge, amorous figures of Ares and Aphrodite embracing on the great tapestry that stretched along the wall above the bed. The smell of incense hung heavy on the air.

Deiphobus lay stark naked on his back with his mouth open and the breath wheezing in his throat. Across the wide bed, Helen slept with her knees tightly drawn up beneath the crumpled sheet. Her hair, still as glossy and black as Menelaus remembered it, lay splayed across the pillow, but her face was hidden from him.

Drawing in his breath, he stepped closer to the bed.

Out of an impulse of delicacy, Odysseus remained by the door, but he pulled it quietly shut behind him and stood with a drawn sword in his hand, watching as Menelaus walked round to the side of the bed where Helen slept. He saw him take off the helmet that masked his face and place it quietly on the floor. When he straightened again, Menelaus leaned over the sleeping woman, put a hand to her shoulder and shook it gently two or three times. Helen stirred.

Odysseus heard a sharply drawn gasp of her breath. Then she would have felt the pressure from the point of the short sword that Menelaus held at her neck as he clapped his other hand across her mouth.

Apart from the hoarse judder of Deiphobus' snores, the room was utterly still.

Like figures frozen in a tableau from some moral allegory, the betrayed husband and the delinquent wife stared into each other's eyes for the first time in more than ten years, and only when he felt sure that she would make no sound did Menelaus remove his hand. Straightening himself, he moved round to the other side of the bed, pointing at her with an outstretched index-finger to keep her fixed in the place where she lay huddled in the sheet, wide-eyed, watching him.

Menelaus picked up a wine-stained napkin from beside the silver mixing-bowl on a bedside table. Uttering a small derisive snort, he pushed it firmly into the wheezing gape of Deiphobus' open mouth and closed his hand across it. Deiphobus spluttered awake to find his breathing impaired and a big, armoured man holding him down by his face and shoulder. In the same moment Menelaus lifted a knee and pressed it firmly down into his groin. Light flared inside Deiphobus's head.

When he was quite sure that the man was wide awake and knew exactly what was happening, Menelaus whispered, 'Do you know who I am?'

The dark head nodded beneath the weight of his hand. In the glow of the lamp, the eyes were bright with terror.

'You have something of mine,' Menelaus said. 'It's time it was paid for.'

Then he shifted his weight, lifted his sword and, holding the hilt as though it were a dagger, he thrust the blade deep into the man's naked stomach. Three times he twisted it there before wrenching the blade out again.

Astonished by pain, Deiphobus lifted both hands to grip the wrist that still held the napkin in his mouth. His eyes widened at the sudden eruption of blood from his wound. His feet began to kick as if in a vain effort to get away.

For a long time Menelaus held him down until the eyeballs swivelled upwards and he could no longer hear the breath in his nose. With a sigh of disgust Menelaus freed his gripped wrist. The napkin fell from Deiphobus's mouth. A hot gush of blood came after it.

Menelaus looked down. Frustrated that the thing was over so quickly, he snarled and bared his teeth. He got up from the bed, stopped, turned back, and then, as though remembering some offence he had been given by its touch, he picked up Deiphobus' lax left arm by the hand and began to hack at the wrist with the edge of his sword. Arterial blood spurted across the bed. At the third hack the hand came free. Menelaus studied the grotesque fact of it − a severed hand, still warm, and fringed like some curious marine creature, gripped inside his own. Then he flung the thing across the room.

Still unsatisfied, he brought his sword-blade sharply down across the man's face and heard the cheek bone crack. Gasping, as if in pain from the effort, he stared down at what he had done, wiped his mouth on the back of his wrist, and stood swaying in the gloom.

Spattered with the blood of the corpse lying next to her, Helen was whimpering into her hands like a child. As Menelaus looked across at her, she clutched the sheet up to her mouth.

All three living people in the room are startled then by a sudden roaring in the night. It is the sound of the Argive host breaking through into the sleeping city. Soon the whole of Troy will be loud with screams and shouting that will echo down through all the halls of time. But inside this chamber there is only dreadful silence as Menelaus looms above the woman who has broken his heart and his spirit, for since the day that Helen left him he has been unable to make love to any other woman.

Black stains are smudged around her eyes. And those eyes themselves — eyes the colour of the sea at noon, whose deeps had claimed him time and time again in the days when Helen gazed on him with a tenderness of which he had never believed himself quite worthy — those eyes are vivid with terror now.

This is the woman he has loved with all his heart. Once he had tried to do everything in his power to make her happy. And his heart winces to think of how she deserted him while his back was turned, to give herself to Paris in this bed. And worse, to think of Deiphobus mauling and fingering her. To smell the sweet stink of sex and wine and incense in this room.

His knuckles tauten at the hilt of his sword. This is what he has desired for a long time now. To trap her in this shameful bed and make her pay in blood for every insult he has taken, for every friend who has died because of what she has done, for every wretched tear he has shed alone for her.

From where he stands watching by the door, Odysseus hears Menelaus utter a small moan as he lifts his sword. He sees the reflection of the lamplight shine across the raised blade. He hears the sigh of Helen's breath as she gazes in mute appeal from the region far beyond all words to which fear has banished her. And then something happens — something so obvious and clear that its simplicity is equalled only by its beauty and its power. As though at last consenting to the sacrifice, Helen draws down the sheet still clutched at her mouth, so that first her neck and throat, and then her shoulders and the soft hollows at her collarbones, and finally her breasts, are bared.

Menelaus stands over her. Time passes. Outside, in the lower city, fire has begun to spread from house to house, adding to the terror and confusion of the night; and closer, among the stately squares and gardens of the citadel, the streets are loud with screams. Like the swift extinguishing of so many stars, darkness is falling on mind after mind out there. And though it has scarcely begun, it seems there can never be an end to this.

Yet eventually, as Odysseus looks on, Menelaus lowers the hand that holds his sword. The sword itself slips to the floor and, moments later, with the air of a man who has struggled too long with his fate and cannot now see what more he could do, Menelaus sits down on the bed beside his wife and quietly begins to weep.

The Phantasm

These things happened a long time ago and the men and women whose destinies were shaped by the war at Troy have long since relinquished their mortal form and entered the immortal realm of story. Even we who remember them as they once were cannot now have long to live. And with the passage of time our memories fade, and what is memory itself but an act of the imagination?

Others, therefore, will tell these things differently, and if some say one thing and some another, then is that not also true of yesterday's quarrel or a tavern brawl? For though there are bards who believe that Divine Apollo, with his eye for order and harmony, is the proper deity of our art, I am with those who know that Hermes too is always somewhere nearby, playing his subtle tricks with us, making the shadows dance.

So these stories will live and grow and change as long as there are bards to tell them, and anyone who claims to own the truth about the war at Troy is the mere fool of his own vanity. Yet my charity has been stretched at times by some of the more fanciful tales that have reached my ears, and strangest among them is the one that would have us believe that Helen never went to Troy at all.

I heard this story from an Egyptian trader who claimed that it is widely told around the Salt Pans of Canopus at the mouth of the Nile where Paris and Helen landed during their voyage across the eastern sea to Troy. According to this story, two of Paris's servants jumped ship while *they harboured there and sought refuge in a temple where runaway slaves are allowed to claim sanctuary. From that place of safety they spread reports that Paris had forcibly abducted Helen. When the accusation was brought before King Proteus at Memphis he ordered that Paris be placed under arrest. After lengthy questioning, Paris was deported from Egypt, his stolen treasure was confiscated, and Helen was detained in Memphis until Menelaus should come to take her home to Sparta.*

My first response was to dismiss this story as preposterous. Of course Helen had been in Troy. Odysseus had seen her there. Moreover Telemachus had visited Sparta after the war and found her reunited with Menelaus. He had heard their stories from their own lips. What kind of factitious nonsense was this?

But the Egyptian had an explanation for the disparity between my version of events and his. He insisted that the true Helen remained in Memphis for the duration of the war, while the beautiful thing that accompanied Paris to Troy was a mere phantasm – an idea of Helen that was so powerful in the minds of men that they gladly confused it with reality.

And the Egyptian insisted on the truth of his account with such conviction that all my protests were to no avail. His facts and mine simply did not agree, and even though both of us could not be right there was nothing to be done about it. Yet the more I think about these things the more I have come to wonder whether there was not, after all, a measure of poetic truth in the Egyptian's story.

For it seems to me quite possible that the wild young girl who grew up to become Queen of Sparta and was then swept off by Paris to Troy was an altogether different creature from the one who lived inside his rapturous imagination. Paris dreamed of Helen long before he met her. It was the dream he loved. And if that dream was so passionate that he could not wake from it until it was too late, then the Helen he took to Troy was indeed a phantasm. And if that were so, then no one could have known it more clearly than Helen herself.

Nor does it end there, for surely it is always a phantasm that draws us into war – whether it is a dream of power or wealth or glory, or the fear that our fellow men are alien and hostile creatures who mean to do us harm? And surely all the bitter causes of the war at Troy must have come to seem mere phantasms to those who sat weeping in the ashes of the city? And even to those who returned as victors from the war only to find that their ordeals had scarcely yet begun?

But those are other stories — stories which, out of loyalty to Odysseus and in the hope that my share in truth will survive the passage of time, I Phemius, bard of Ithaca, shall one day come to tell. For in the mortal realm only stories are stronger than death, and the god I serve requires this further work of me.

Glossary of Characters

DEITIES

Aphrodite	Goddess of many aspects, mostly associated with Love and Beauty
Apollo	God with many aspects, including Prophecy, Healing, Pestilence and the Arts
Ares	God of War, twin brother of Eris
Artemis	Virgin Goddess of the Wild
Athena	Goddess with many aspects, including Wisdom, Power and Protection
Boreas	God of the North Wind
Eris	Goddess of Strife and Discord, twin sister to Ares
Eros	God of Love, son of Aphrodite
Ganymedes	Cup-bearer to Zeus
Hephaestus	God of fire and craftsmanship
Hera	Goddess Queen of Olympus, wife of Zeus, presides over marriage
Hermes	God with many aspects, including eloquence, imagination, invention. A slippery fellow
Isis	Egyptian goddess
Nereus	Sea-god

Osiris	Egyptian god
Poseidon	God with many aspects, ruler of the Sea, Earthquakes and Horses
Zephyrus	God of the West Wind
Zeus	King of Olympus, ruler of the gods

MORTALS

Acamas	Argive warrior
Acastus	King of Iolcus
Achilles	son of Peleus and Thetis, leader of the Myrmidons, father of Pyrrhos
Actor	King of the Myrmidons, father-in-law of Peleus, father of Eurytion and Polymela
Adrestos	Trojan warrior
Aeacus	King of Aegina, father of Peleus and Telamon
Aegisthus	son of Thyestes, cousin to Agamemnon and Menelaus
Aeneas	Prince of the Dardanians
Aethra	mother of Theseus, once Queen of Troizen, now bondswoman to Helen
Agamemnon	son of Atreus of Mycenae, High King of Argos
Agelaus	foster-father of Paris, herdsman
Aias	Locrian captain
Ajax	son of Telamon, cousin of Achilles
Alexander	another name for Paris, son of Priam
Anchises	King of the Dardanians
Andromache	wife of Hector
Antenor	counsellor to Priam
Anticlea	mother of Odysseus, wife of Laertes
Antilochus	son of Nestor
Antiphus	son of Priam
Antheus	son of Antenor and Theano
Automedon	charioteer to Achilles and Patroclus

Briseis	Dardanian maiden captured by Achilles
Cadmus	founder of Thebes and husband of Harmony
Calchas	Trojan priest of Apollo who defects to the Argives
Capys	son of Priam
Catreus	grandfather of Agamemnon and Menelaus
Cassandra	daughter of Priam
Cebren	healing priest of Apollo at Sminthe
Cheiron	King of the Centaurs
Chryseis	daughter of Apollo's priest in Thebe, captive of Agamemnon
Cilla	sister of Priam
Cinyras	King of Cyprus
Clymene	Andromache's serving woman
Clytaemnestra	daughter of Tyndareus & Leda, wife of Agamemnon
Cretheis	wife of King Acastus
Cycnus	Trojan hero
Danae	mother of Perseus
Dardanians	people of the Idaean mountains (Dardania), a kingdom of Troy
Deidameia	daughter of King Lycomedes, mother of Pyrrhos by Achilles
Deiphobus	son of Priam
Deucalion	King of Crete, father of Idomeneus
Diomedes	Lord of Tiryns, Argive hero
Diotima	wise woman on Ithaca
Dromeus	Cretan legate
Electra	daughter of Agamemnon & Clytaemnestra
Epeius	Phocian craftsman, designer of the Wooden Horse
Euhippe	Centaur healer & midwife

Europa	mother of King Minos
Eurytion	son of King Actor of the Myrmidons
Eteoneus	chief minister of Sparta
Harmony	wife of Cadmus
Harpale	Dolopian priestess and companion of Thetis
Hector	eldest son of Priam
Helen	daughter of Tyndareus/Zeus and Leda. Queen of Sparta, wife of Menelaus.
Heracles	Greek hero
Hermione	daughter of Menelaus and Helen
Hesione	daughter of Laomedon, sister of Priam
Hippolyta	Amazon queen and beloved companion of Theseus
Hippolytos	son of Theseus and Hyppolyta
Icarius	brother of Tyndareus, father of Penelope
Idaeus	Trojan herald
Idomeneus	son of Deucalion, King of Crete
Iphighenaia	daughter of Agamemnon & Clytaemnestra
Iolaus	charioteer to Heracles
Isus	bastard son of Priam
Jason	Greek hero
Laertes	Lord of Ithaca, father of Odysseus
Laocoon	Trojan priest of Apollo, son of Antenor
Laomedon	King of Troy, father of Priam
Leda	wife of Tyndareus, mother of Clytaemnestra and Helen
Lycaon	son of Priam
Lycomedes	King of Skyros
Machaon	head surgeon in the Argive camp
Memnon	Trojan ally, leader of the Ethiopians

Menestheus	King of Athens
Menelaus	King of Sparta, husband of Helen
Menoetius	bastard son of King Actor, father of Patroclus
Nauplius	King of Euboea, father of Palamedes
Neoptolemus	son of Achilles, also known as Pyrrhos
Nereids	fifty daughters of the sea-god Nereus
Nestor	King of Pylos
Oenone	nymph of Apollo's shrine at Sminthe, daughter of Cebren
Odysseus	Lord of Ithaca
Orestes	son of Agamemnon and Clytaemnestra
Palamedes	Prince of Euboea
Pandarus	Trojan archer
Paris	son of Priam, also known as Alexander
Patroclus	son of Menoetius, beloved friend of Achilles
Peleus	son of King Aeacus, father of Achilles
Penelope	daughter of Icarius, cousin to Helen and Clytaemnestra and wife of Odysseus
Penthesileia	Queen of the Amazons
Pirithous	King of the Lapiths, friend of Theseus
Phaedra	wife of Theseus
Phemius	bard of Ithaca
Phereclus	Trojan shipbuilder
Philoctetes	Aeolian archer
Phocus	son of King Aeacus, half-brother to Peleus and Telamon
Phoenix	Myrmidon warrior
Phylo	handmaid to Helen
Podarces	son of Laomedon, also known as Priam
Polydamna	wise woman to Helen
Polydorus	son of Priam
Polymela	daughter of King Actor, first wife of Peleus

Polyxena	daughter of Priam
Priam	son of Laomedon, King of Troy, also known as Podarces
Prylis	Lapith farrier
Pyrrhos	son of Achilles and leader of the Myrmidons. Also known as Neoptolemus
Sarpedon	Lycian soldier, ally of Troy
Sinon	cousin to Odysseus
Talthybius	Argive herald
Tantalus	King of Elis, first husband of Clytaemnestra
Telemachus	son of Odysseus and Penelope
Telamon	son of King Aeacus, brother to Peleus and King of Salamis. Father to Ajax
Telephus	King of the Mysians and bastard son of Heracles, ally of Troy
Terpis	father of Phemius the Ithacan bard
Teucer	stepbrother to Ajax
Theano	high priestess of Athena in Troy, wife of Antenor
Thersander	friend of Diomedes and commander of the Boeotians
Thersites	Argive soldier and kinsman of Diomedes
Theseus	hero, King of Athens, conqueror of Crete
Thetis	daughter of Cheiron, second wife of Peleus and mother of Achilles
Thyestes	brother to Atreus of Mycenae, uncle to Agamemnon and Menelaus. Father of Aegisthus
Thymoetes	son of Priam
Tithonus	King at Susa, half-brother of Priam
Tyndareus	King of Sparta, father of Clytaemnestra and Helen, husband of Leda
Typhaon	Dragon

Acknowledgements

The guidance of Robert Graves' classic work of reference, *The Greek Myths, is* evident everywhere throughout this book, and I would have been lost without his patient and imaginative scholarship. Though I have tried to remain faithful to the broad outlines of the stories as Graves records them, I have not hesitated to license my own, often anachronistic, imagination wherever I felt it necessary. Having no Greek, I was also heavily dependent on the majestic verse translations of Homer's *Iliad* made by Richmond Lattimore and Robert Fagles, and on the lively prose version composed by E.V. Rieu. Jules Cashford's fine English versions of the Homeric Hymns were also an invaluable pointer to the power and beauty of the culture behind these myths. I found Michael Wood's *In Search of the Trojan War* to be an engagingly readable guide to the archaeology of Troy and Mycenae, and Mary Renault's marvellous novels *The King Must Die* and *The Bull from the Sea* were a constantly challenging inspiration.

More personally, I wish to acknowledge the help and encouragement given to me by my editor Jane Johnson, by my agent Pat Kavanagh, and by my family and friends, particularly Elspeth Harris, Stephen Russell and James Simpson. Also I owe a big round of thanks to the Happy Hour crowd at the Milk Street

Brewery for keeping my spirits up and my wits sharp. The deepest debt, however, is to my wife Phoebe Clare for bearing with me and for asking more of the book and its author than either would have found on their own.